Two rich
devastati
Sheikhs den
and men thi
get wha

The DESERT PRINCES' *Brides*

Susan Stephens was a professional singer who now loves nothing more than reading and writing romance. She lives in cosy chaos in a converted blacksmith's cottage in Cheshire surrounded by cats, dogs, guinea pigs, children and a very understanding husband. She loves playing the piano and singing, as well as riding and cooking and gardening and travel. When she isn't writing she's usually daydreaming about her next hero!

Susan Mallery is the bestselling and award-winning author of over fifty books. She makes her home in the Los Angeles area with her handsome prince of a husband and two adorable-but-not-bright cats. Feel free to contact her via her website at www.susanmallery.com

The DESERT PRINCES' Brides

The Sheikh's Captive Bride
SUSAN STEPHENS

The Sheikh & the Princess Bride
SUSAN MALLERY

All the characters in this book have no existence outside the imagination of the author, and have no relation whatsoever to anyone bearing the same name or names. They are not even distantly inspired by any individual known or unknown to the author, and all the incidents are pure invention.

Harlequin Mills & Boon Limited, Eton House, 18-24 Paradise Road, Richmond, Surrey TW9 1SR

ISBN: 978 0 263 86751 0

009-0109

Printed and bound in Spain by Litografia Rosés S.A., Barcelona

The Sheikh's Captive Bride

SUSAN STEPHENS

For Kate

PROLOGUE

THE royal council chamber in the Golden Palace of Abadan was drenched in light as Sheikh Kahlil ben Saeed Al-Sharif indicated his wish to move the meeting on.

'Highness—'

Kahlil's dark gaze switched to the face of his most trusted advisor, Abdul Hassan.

'You have reached a decision regarding your new palace, Majesty?'

Kahlil saw anticipation flare behind the eyes of every man seated with him around the council table. Even amongst such an unimaginably wealthy group the rivalry was intense. Prestigious contracts always held an opportunity for someone. But his decision would disappoint them.

'I shall not be building my new palace in Abadan.' Kahlil allowed the murmurs of disappointment to settle. 'I have identified a village in Europe—and an appropriate residence.' His thoughts flew to the village of Westbury, and the Hall—which he intended to buy. Though there was a problem, small, but irritating none the less, he remembered, thinking of Lucy Benson.

When he'd settled upon Westbury, in amongst the pile of documents sent to help him make his choice he had seen a local magazine that contained the photograph of a young woman. She had a look in her eyes that drew his attention. The caption said Lucy Benson was an interior designer, and, lately, a property developer. And she had bought Westbury Hall, the very property he intended to own. Interior decorator to property developer was a quite a leap. Could she make it?

Kahlil's mind drifted towards golden hair tumbling in exuberant waves around a heart-shaped face, and a simple summer dress clinging to voluptuous curves that made him despise the fashion to be thin. Her lips appeared red without artifice, and were parted sufficiently to reveal pearl-white teeth: teeth he could easily imagine nipping his flesh in the throes of passion. Picturing them naked together—Lucy Benson's soft body yielding beneath his hard-muscled frame—called for every bit of his control.

But the camera had captured more than her likeness, Kahlil remembered. Her character was betrayed by the stubborn tilt of her chin, and the look of sheer determination in her midnight-blue eyes. As son of the ruling Sheikh, he had every material possession a man could desire, but he came from a warrior race, a passionate land; challenge was in his blood. And she was an independent woman who would fight him every inch of the way. He could hardly wait. Taming Lucy Benson would be an interesting bonus on top of wresting the Hall from her grasp.

'The village of Westbury is well situated,' he said, turning his attention to the council again. 'It is close to the sea, so we can bring the yacht in, and only a short drive from the airport for the jet. It will be a novelty,' he added, with a closing gesture of his hand.

Everyone understood this, and the tension around the table lifted. For men who had everything, novelty was the most valuable currency of all.

'Westbury is a good choice, Majesty.'

Abdul Hassan spoke for the council, and Kahlil inclined his head in gracious acknowledgement of his approval.

'The village is prosperous and full of character,' Abdul Hassan continued, 'though some areas are in need of improvement.'

'Not all areas,' Kahlil murmured, thinking of Lucy Benson.

'Indeed, Majesty,' Abdul Rachman agreed, dipping his head respectfully. 'How may we assist you further in this matter?'

'Make arrangements for a visit to Westbury,' Kahlil instructed. 'I'm going to make a thorough evaluation of the project for myself.'

CHAPTER ONE

SHE was alone again at last. Linking her hands behind her head, Lucy Benson stared at the ceiling and gave vent to her frustration with a desperate, angry sound. Losing Westbury Hall was awful; facing her creditors was worse. Letting everyone down at the last minute was the hardest thing she had ever had to do. Her plans to renovate the grand old house where she had grown up had collapsed for want of just a little more money. The builders had found some serious and costly structural faults, and then, quite suddenly, the bank had pulled out.

From housekeeper's daughter to owner and developer had been a bit ambitious, Lucy knew, but for a few short months it had seemed achievable. She had risked everything to restore the Hall to its former glory, so that it could become a living tribute to the kindly old lady who had lived there. But she had failed Aunt Grace, Lucy thought as she took a last look around. And that hurt most of all.

She blinked back tears. She couldn't cry, not with sunlight streaming optimistically through the domed stained glass cupola—rain would have been more appropriate. Some of the opposing plans had included knocking the old Hall down. But she couldn't allow the elegant building to be supplanted by a featureless block of modern flats, she just couldn't—

'Excuse me.'

Lucy whirled on her heels, her heart thundering wildly. She had thought she was alone. The male voice was deep and slightly accented, and it took her a moment to see where it was coming from. But then she saw the man standing half cloaked in shadows by the front door. He was tall, and dark, and casually dressed—like most of the other creditors. This was not an occasion for dressing to impress, she thought dryly.

'I didn't mean to frighten you.'

Lucy wasn't convinced. There was something about the man that suggested he was accustomed to using his stature to best advantage; he was far too confident. 'I thought everyone had gone,' she said coolly.

'Am I too late?'

'No, of course not. Come in, and I'll tell you what I told the others.'

'The others?'

'Creditors,' Lucy said, retracing her steps across the black and white marble tiles. 'Please, sit down,' she added, opening the door to her improvised meeting room. There were some hard-backed chairs in the echoing dining room, and she had set up a decorator's table for people to gather around. He followed her into the room. 'Lucy Benson,' Lucy said, turning to extend her hand in formal greeting.

'Kahl,' he said, enclosing her hand in a fist that seemed to contain an electric charge.

Lucy snatched it free. 'Won't you sit down?' she said again, pointing to a chair at the far end of the table. She would feel a lot safer once he was seated.

'After you,' he said, drawing out a chair for her to sit on.

Lucy felt alert, and uneasy. All the other creditors had been up in arms, expressing their anger freely and paying no account to the fact that she was a woman. That was better. It was a language she understood. This man was too cool. He frightened her more than the others with their impassioned outbursts. Apart from confidence, he oozed sex appeal as the others had oozed sweat at the thought of losing money.

Dark flashing eyes smouldered like black coals in a face

with features too harsh to be conventionally handsome. He made her think of a warrior, a man of action—yet he had the type of tan she associated with the super-rich. Lucy frowned. So who was he? Apart from being one of the most incredible-looking individuals she had ever seen. Was he Turkish? Armenian? Spanish? She couldn't place the accent.

As the man folded his impressive frame into a chair across the table from her she judged him to be about thirty-five: dark-haired, dark-skinned, dark-eyed—and very expensively dressed. She had a keen eye for fashion, as well as for architecture. Jeans could be budget or designer, and his were the best, like the simple black top he was wearing.

As he levelled a stare on her face Lucy drew breath, forcing herself to hold his gaze. Without focusing on it, she was aware of his mouth. It was full and sensuous, with a cruel twist, matching the look in his eyes. After some heated discussion the rest of the creditors had believed her when she'd pledged to repay them. She sensed this man was different—harder, more cynical.

He shifted position, clearly uncomfortable on the narrow seat. Men just didn't come built like this—not in her world, anyhow. Even his casual clothes failed to conceal thighs made of iron, and shoulders wide enough to carry an ox.

Lucy dropped her gaze, conscious she was staring at him. And then her glance strayed to his hands. They were extremely powerful, but it didn't look as though he earned his living by them. As he reached back to fold his arms behind his head she saw his belly was flat— She had to stop this, Lucy told herself firmly. He was just one more aggrieved creditor. She owed it to him to spell out her position.

As if sensing she was ready, he tipped his head, inviting her to begin. Unlike the others, he had brought nothing with him, Lucy noticed, not even a pen to take notes. 'Well, Mr—'

'Kahl. Just call me Kahl,' he interrupted.

His dark eyes were tilted up at the corners, and his jet-black eyebrows swept up too. Like a Tartar's, she thought, wondering if he came from the steppes of Russia. Could he ride a horse as they did? A quiver ran through her as she pictured his powerful thighs wrapped around the sides of some wild stallion, or a woman—

'You have a proposition for me?'

Lucy felt herself reddening, as if he had read her mind. She rallied fast. 'I intend to pay everyone off fully—everything I owe you will be repaid,' she underlined when he appeared unmoved. Something in his stare was starting to get to her. 'Do you find this amusing?'

'Far from it,' he murmured, gesturing with his hand that she should continue.

Lucy bridled at the autocratic manner, but her sense of honour insisted she fulfil her obligations in full—even to this man. As he fingered his jaw she saw that it was shaded blue-black, even so early in the day. There was something so rampantly male about him that it made every feminine bone in her body rebel. It was a sensation she was determined to resist.

'So, you're with the architects?' she guessed, with nothing more to go on than a pair of strong, smooth hands.

'I heard that your impressive plans to renovate Westbury Hall had fallen through,' he replied.

She loved his voice. She couldn't help it. It was so foreign, so exotic— This was ridiculous! The look in his eyes was warning enough to keep her thoughts in check.

'I'm really sorry, but I've been forced to cancel all the contracts,' she said bluntly, judging the direct approach to be best. Dragging her briefcase towards her, Lucy fished inside. 'I should have yours here…'

'I doubt it.'

'I've prepared a schedule,' she said, frowning as she surfaced without any missing contract. 'You should look at this,' she said, holding out another document. 'It explains how I will pay everyone back for the services they have already provided. You can keep this copy.'

'I'll study it later,' he said, folding the pages neatly.

Lucy watched as he half stood to tuck the papers away in the back pocket of his jeans—and her gaze lingered. 'I'm sorry,' she said, with a helpless gesture when he turned and caught her staring. 'It's all I can offer you for now.'

He shrugged as he sat down again, and Lucy wondered if he was convinced by her little speech. 'That's it,' she said, when he showed no sign of moving. Did he expect something more? Lucy's heart began to thunder. 'Did you have to come far?' she said, in a voice that sounded higher than usual. When he didn't answer, she added, 'Have you been travelling long?'

'Half a day.'

'Half a day! I'm really sorry.' And she was—mortified. 'Can I offer you a drink or something?'

He shrugged. 'It's almost lunchtime.'

'Of course. Something more? We could go for a sandwich, perhaps?'

'The village pub is closed for renovation.'

Damn. She had forgotten about that. He *was* observant.

'I am hungry,' he admitted, easing back in his chair without breaking eye contact.

She was backed into a corner, Lucy realised. And now she was going to do something that was probably crazy. 'Why don't you come back to my place and I'll make you a sandwich?'

He stood at once, pushing his chair back, coming around the table to hold Lucy's chair for her.

She was definitely crazy—no doubt about it!

The man followed her into the low-ceilinged farmhouse kitchen, ducking to avoid the beams.

'The farmer must have been a lot shorter than you,' Lucy said, acting casually in spite of the frisson of awareness tracking down her back.

'So it seems.'

She felt him staring at her while she pretended to study the inside of the refrigerator as if she had no idea what was inside. 'Cheese? Pickle?'

'Whatever you have,' the exotic voice husked obligingly.

'Beer? Coffee?'

'Coffee would be great—or water.'

Yes. Water, of course. It was hot for early May.

The air seemed charged with unusual energy—but it was his energy, she realised, feeling the tiny hairs on the back of her neck stand to attention. 'You'd better sit down,' she suggested, turning around. 'Before you hit your head.'

'Thank you,' he said, moving to pull out the bench at the kitchen table.

And then it struck her forcibly. She didn't even know who he was! And here he was in her home. She had never done anything like this before—and was damn sure she would never risk anything like it again! But it wasn't every day her dreams hit the dust. Her emotions were in chaos, Lucy realised, quickly making excuses for herself.

'Aren't you going to have something to eat or drink?' he said.

'I'm not hungry,' she said, handing him a plate.

'If you won't eat, how can I?'

'Look. I don't mean to be rude—' Lucy wiped a hand across her forehead distractedly '—but exactly which company do you represent? You never said.'

'Why don't you sit down?' he suggested evenly.

'So?' Lucy prompted, perching on a stool well away from him at the breakfast bar. 'Which company did you say you worked for?'

'I didn't.' Leaning back comfortably in his seat, Kahl

looked at her. 'Do you invite many men you don't know into your home?'

'You haven't answered my question.'

'And you haven't answered mine,' he pointed out.

'Not many—I mean none.' Why was she making excuses to him? Lucy wondered, biting her lip.

'It's not safe.'

'I can assure you I don't make a habit of it. But—'

'But?' he cut in, spearing a glance at her.

'Today's different.'

He let that pass. 'You want to know which company I represent?' he said, pushing the plate away.

'Yes, I do.' He was right: this was dangerous. She didn't know a thing about him.

'I represent myself.'

'I see…'

'I doubt it.'

The atmosphere was electric and his confidence unsettling. It was as if he had planned this all along. 'I'll make coffee,' she offered, keen to put some distance between them.

'Don't bother—cold water will do.'

'It won't take a minute.'

He shrugged.

'Sugar? Milk?'

He said no to both.

She passed him the mug, and when their fingers touched Lucy gasped. It was as if a lightning bolt had shot up her arm.

'Did you scald yourself?' he asked with concern.

'No, I'm fine.'

'Sit?' he suggested, pulling out a chair for her.

She would sit—because she wasn't going to let him get to her—not in her own home, her own kitchen.

The kitchen table was narrow and his legs were long; they

almost touched her own. And then they did—shins, feet, ankles—colliding, tangling briefly. When she tried to pull away he hooked one of his legs around hers, and held her fast.

She might have cried out softly as her heart leapt into her throat; she certainly couldn't breathe. Lucy looked at him wide-eyed, and for one insane moment she thought she would fight him off, rain her fists down on his chest. But that soon passed. The contact between them was so intimate, so enticing. She knew she was lost.

'Still feeling safe?' he murmured.

Lucy dragged in an unsteady breath. 'Yes,' she said, lying through her teeth as she held his gaze. She knew he could overpower her in an instant. But he wouldn't. She was sure. Not unless she wanted him to.

The silence was so intense that for a few seconds she heard nothing but the sound of her own heart hammering in her head. And then gradually she became aware of another sound, rapid and noisy. When she realised it was the raised pitch of her own breathing her cheeks flamed red.

The man's expression was inscrutable. He was waiting for something—but for what? Was she supposed to make the first move? Lucy wondered. He was temptation on a plate. Ridiculously attractive, and with the X-factor that told her he knew just how to please a woman. But it was the look in his eyes that swung it for her. It held the promise of forgetfulness, of oblivion. She could leave all the heart-break and disappointment behind for a few hours. They were consenting adults. He offered escape, and that was just what she needed.

The chance to make love—have sex—with a complete stranger was absurdly appealing. It was uncharted territory for Lucy. She had always thought of sex as something between two people who knew each other well, who trusted each other, felt safe.

But she was consumed by arousal. The decision was out of her hands; her senses were taking the lead. Every inch of her body was tuned to his frequency. The merest change in his eyes brought her to a fresh level of awareness, and just a tug at one corner of his mouth was enough to make her want to kiss away its harshness and feel him melt beneath her touch. It was appetite, pure and simple. Even words were redundant. They were communicating now on another, very basic level.

Taking hold of her wrist, Kahl brought her to a standing position in front of him. His touch shimmered through her and he dragged her close, so she felt the whole length of his body in intimate contact with her own. It was too late to regret the fact that she was only wearing a lightweight summer dress, with a scrap or two of lace beneath it—too late to regret the fact that where this man called Kahl was concerned she had no will-power at all.

He was more athletically built than any man she had known before. He was big, gloriously big, and his strength was deliciously contained—like a tightly wound spring. He smelt divine, he felt warm and hard, and as he teased her lips apart Lucy felt her legs grow weak. She could feel his heart beating strongly in his chest as it pressed against her breasts, and her own thundering against him. It was all new sensation, all heights of pleasure she hadn't known existed; it was like getting to know someone starting at the pinnacle and working back. He was as hard as marble, but far more fluid—

She gave a low cry of surprise when he swung her up without warning. Setting her on the table-edge, he lowered her back as he moved between her legs. Then, pushing up her summer skirt, he reached for her underwear, unbuttoning his fly at the same time…Lucy felt the silky pass of something warm and smooth, and then a second pass, before he gave her the tip, catching it just inside her until she cried out and urged him on. When he took the prompt her breath shot out of her lungs in surprise at the size of him, and he waited until she was ready again.

Then the pleasure began. It was beyond anything Lucy had known. He swept the plate and mug aside, and lifted her legs to lock them around his waist. Now he could plunge deeper still, until rhythmical cries of delight left her lips. Each time he dealt her another long, firm stroke Lucy's fingers bit mercilessly into buttocks of steel, until finally her mind shut down completely and only sensation remained.

Drunk with ecstasy, at one point she called out, and he stopped.

'No!' Lucy ground out desperately, realising he must have taken her cry for reluctance. 'Don't stop. Don't ever stop—' And she laughed softly, happily, gratefully when he started to move again.

He brought her skilfully to the place she had wanted to be, tipping her over the edge into oblivion, so that for a few trance-like moments she found all the relief, all the escape she needed. But the sensation was so intense she almost passed out in his arms.

'Are you all right?'

He was breathing the words in her ear, Lucy realised, and holding her full weight in his arms. She buried her head self-consciously into his chest, so he couldn't see her face or hear her struggling attempts to catch her breath. Now it was over, and the exquisite tremors were subsiding, she really couldn't believe what they had just done.

'I said, are you all right?' he said again, softly. And, cupping her chin with one hand, he brought her head up so she had no alternative but to look him straight in the eyes.

'I'm fine,' Lucy said, swallowing hard. But she felt naked, as if his eyes had the power to strip her defences away. And his eyes were not black, but darkest sienna, she saw, with flecks of molten copper round his pupil—incredible, astonishing.

'Don't look away,' he insisted, bringing her round to face him again. 'Bed?' he suggested, one eyebrow arching slightly. 'You do have one?' he murmured, when Lucy remained silent.

'Yes, of course,' she said, straightening her clothes self-consciously. 'You must be tired.'

'Far from it,' Kahl assured her, one corner of his mouth tugging up in the beginnings of a smile. 'I'm only just getting started.'

Linking his arms around her waist, he pulled her close again, nuzzling his crotch into the swell of her hips.

'Well, in that case…' Lucy felt hunger flare inside her. She hadn't had enough of him, not nearly enough.

Taking him by the hand, she moved towards the hallway. But playing the vamp didn't come naturally to her, and she hesitated by the door.

'Just say if you want me to leave,' Kahl murmured, drawing her into his arms, 'and I'll go.'

'No,' Lucy said quickly, softly. 'I don't want that.'

'Then, if you're sure...' he said, slamming into her senses with one of his slow-burning smiles.

'I'm sure,' she said, raising her face for his kiss.

There was a moment of hazy contentment on waking, then full-blown horror and distress. She was alone! Of course she was alone, Lucy told herself, staring round the bedroom. What the hell had she expected? A one-night stand—admittedly the most memorable one-night stand in history—did not a relationship make.

Dragging up the bedclothes to cover herself, she buried her head in the pillow, conscious that every inch of her was still throbbing from the attentions of a most accomplished lover. There would never be anyone like Kahl in her life again, that much was sure. No one could be that unselfish in the delivery of pleasure, no one so tender when they held her in their arms. And now he was gone.

Lucy swallowed hard, tears stinging the back of her throat, knowing she only had herself to blame. No one had forced her to sleep with him. She had gone into it with her eyes wide open, giving herself yet one more disaster to recover from.

Getting out of bed, Lucy headed for the bathroom. A long, hot shower was a start—not much of a start, but the rest of her life would not go away.

And then she saw the flowers sitting on her dressing table in a glass tumbler. He must have cut them fresh from her garden, she realised, before he left: early roses, her favourite Lochinvar, blush-pink, fat, and lightly fragranced.

Touching the cool, dew-damp petals with her fingertips, she felt a shiver of apprehension run down her spine.

CHAPTER TWO

RAGS to riches? Not exactly, Lucy thought as she lolled back in the plush leather seat. But she was getting there. Since winning the design competition her life had certainly undergone a meteoric change. She had repaid her creditors, and was slowly building up her business again.

It was good to know that hard work and determination paid off occasionally, she thought, glancing round at her fellow travellers. Several passengers in the first-class cabin smiled back and raised their glasses. Buoyed up by complimentary champagne, Lucy radiated happiness and optimism.

Normally she was quite frightened of flying, and travelled by other means wherever she could. But the chance to fly first class with Air Abadan had been irresistible, and she hadn't been allowed to feel one flutter of unease since the smiling attendant had welcomed her on board.

It hardly seemed possible that seat belts were already being checked for landing. And, having left England in icy February, neither could she believe the announcement that it was a balmy twenty-five degrees in the desert kingdom of Abadan.

Abadan. Just the name of the country was enough to spark Lucy's imagination. Which was just as well, since the first prize in the competition was a lucrative contract to carry out the refurbishment of a receiving room at the Golden Palace. She had put everything she had into her entry, knowing it was a once-in-a-lifetime opportunity. The brief had been demanding, as quite a bit of restoration was needed before superficial decorative work could begin. Fortunately, sourcing the type of craftsmen who could restore the golden filigree that gave the Golden Palace its name was just the type of challenge she liked.

Winning was fantastic, but preparing the project had given her a second chance, and that was even more important. Even the lingering anger she had still felt over the bank letting her down had faded away as she'd been drawn deeper into her work. Interestingly enough, the sale of Westbury Hall had realised far more than she had anticipated, allowing her to clear her debts and make some provision for the future. But as far as business was concerned she was determined to concentrate on what she knew best, and that was interior design.

At the awards ceremony, at a swanky London hotel, Lucy remembered the Abadanese ambassador announcing that she had won because she'd gone the extra mile for his client. According to him, she had uncovered facts that even the ruling family was not aware of. It had made her smile at the time, and she smiled now, draining her glass.

The 'ruling family' was the one element she had found impossible to research in any detail. The Sheikh and his son remained shadowy figures. For security reasons, she guessed. Sensible, really. She didn't expect to meet up with them. And she wasn't unduly concerned. The design brief she had been given was quite specific, and she had already embellished it with her own suggestions. Passing ideas to and fro by e-mail was an easy matter. And everything she had submitted so far had been met with a positive response. She didn't anticipate any difficulties.

'Which is just as well, my darling,' she crooned, double-checking the safety harness on the travel cot by her side as the plane came in to land, 'since you're going to be celebrating your first birthday in Abadan.'

* * *

It wasn't every day she got to stay in a palace, Lucy thought, reining in her excitement as she tried to take everything in amid the overload of visual information. She had hardly believed it when the Sheikh's representative, a smartly dressed middle-aged woman, had explained almost apologetically that she was being housed in one of the older parts of the palace.

The palace! Lucy had been expecting to stay in a nearby hotel. But the palace accommodation deemed suitable for her had a nursery attached…

'Oh, yes, everything is more than satisfactory. Thank you,' Lucy said, hardly able to believe where she was. And if this was shabby, as the woman seemed to imply, she couldn't wait to see smart!

The older woman looked relieved. 'And Leila will take care of your son,' she said, turning to introduce a young girl who was standing in the background.

Lucy felt instantly reassured. Leila wore the casual uniform of a Barton nanny. The chinos and white polo shirt with the distinctive 'B' embroidered on the breast pocket marked her out as a top professional in her field. Originally Lucy had planned to leave Edward at home with his grandmother, but an unseasonal bout of influenza had put paid to that idea. The officials she had been speaking to at the palace had quickly reassured her. Edward would be well looked after in Abadan, they said. 'What's the problem? Bring him with you.'

The prospect of missing her child's first birthday had been terrible, but miraculously fate had conspired to keep them together. So now she could enjoy Edward's birthday and begin to secure his future, with the money she expected to earn from the contract.

'What do you think of Abadan so far?' Edward's newly appointed nanny asked, reclaiming her attention.

'Fantastic,' Lucy admitted. 'The scenery on the drive from the airport to the palace was amazing—rolling sand dunes stretching away to the horizon, and then,' she said, her face animated as she remembered, 'when the sun dropped lower, there were camels marching in procession along the hilltops, inky-black silhouettes against a dazzling vermilion sky.'

'You do like it.' Leila laughed. 'Can I take him?' She smiled at Edward.

Lucy hesitated only a moment, then, seeing Edward's reaction, she said, 'Of course. It looks like you've made a friend of him already, Leila.'

Lucy relaxed. If Edward was happy she knew everything would go smoothly. It was beginning to look as if his first birthday was going to be every bit as memorable as she had always hoped it would be.

Padding barefoot around her spacious quarters in her pyjamas with Edward soon after dawn, Lucy felt happier than she could remember for a long time. And, despite a restless night, she was on good form, too, she realised, hugging her wriggling bundle a little closer.

Edward constantly exclaimed and pointed as they explored the opulent interior together. Even the incredible height of the ceilings inside their suite of rooms was a revelation to him, and he was growing increasingly hard to carry as he leaned back in Lucy's arms to marvel at them.

Blowing her hair out of her face, Lucy laughed out loud with sheer happiness. She felt a growing conviction that this trip to Abadan marked a new start in life for both of them. The prestige that came with winning the competition meant her professional future was more assured, which in turn meant things would be better for Edward. And everything she did was for him.

Her life was one big balancing act, but—touch wood—it was going well, and she wouldn't have it any other way. She knew she mustn't get complacent. She couldn't risk anything going wrong later that morning in her first meeting. But there was little chance of that. She had been up half the night, pacing the room, as she went over everything in her mind.

And she wasn't the only early riser, Lucy remembered, dropping a kiss on the top of Edward's head. At one point something had drawn her to a window overlooking the interior courtyard. But by the time she'd leaned out there had been just a shadow disappearing through one of the arched doors facing her apartment.

She glanced out of the window at the same archway now, remembering that shortly afterwards the whole palace had sprung to life—temperatures later in the day would be less conducive to activity, she supposed. Then, thinking of the shadow again, she shivered involuntarily.

Edward's baby prattle stopped immediately, and he turned his face up to look at her.

'It's all right, my darling,' Lucy crooned, turning his attention to a pair of vases taller than she was, to make him laugh again.

The shadow, Lucy reassured herself, had doubtless been one of the servants who had left his bed ahead of the rest…*his*? His bed? She thought about it for a moment. The shadow had been long, and the impression she'd gained when she caught a glimpse of it had been of a man—a large man—one of the palace guards, perhaps?

'Miss Benson?'

Lucy turned, smiling, as Leila hurried towards her across the vast marble-tiled floor. It took a few words of reassurance before Leila would be convinced she wasn't late, and that Edward's early start to the day was due entirely to Lucy's excitement.

It was fun arranging Edward's day together. When her meeting with the palace officials was over, Lucy was determined they should do something about a birthday tea for him the next day. But as they discussed the particulars she became increasingly conscious of time slipping away—and she wasn't even showered or dressed yet.

'Don't worry,' Leila said, 'I'll start making enquiries while you are in your meeting—' She stopped talking as Edward claimed their attention.

'He wants to go to the window for some fresh air,' Lucy guessed. 'Try and get him outside to play while it's cool, if you can. He's got far too much energy to be cooped up in here all day.'

'I will,' Leila promised.

Lucy was halfway across the room when Leila called her back.

'Come and see this,' she insisted, beckoning to Lucy. 'Quickly.'

'What is it?' Lucy said, hurrying to join Leila and Edward by the open window. She was struck by Edward's unusual stillness as he stared down from his grandstand position in Leila's arms.

Following Edward's lead, Lucy gazed down into the courtyard. A group of men in flowing robes were striding across it at speed. She felt a thrill of excitement. There was something so majestic in their carriage, so romantic. It really brought home to her the fact that she was a guest in a great desert kingdom. The men looked nothing short of magnificent, with their white *gutrahs* held in place by *agals* of black and gold, and the man spearheading the group was particularly striking. He was clearly the leader in every respect. She smiled to see a shorter man scurrying along at his elbow, trying to keep up as he mouthed notes into a small black Dictaphone.

'That's Prince Kahlil ben Saeed Al-Sharif—the ruling Sheikh's son,' Leila explained, seeing Lucy's interest. 'He practically rules Abadan now. His father is retiring more and more from public life. They say Sheikh Kahlil will take over full responsibility for the country very soon.'

'What else do they say?' Lucy murmured as the men disappeared through an archway.

'They say Abadan is going to be catapulted into the twenty-first century, thanks to Sheikh Kahlil,' Leila confided. 'He's already hugely successful in the international business world. And he's gorgeous—'

'I'd better get ready for my meeting,' Lucy cut in diplomatically. She had to remain professional. However tempting it might be, she knew she couldn't afford to be drawn into palace gossip.

CHAPTER THREE

COOLLY yet smartly dressed, in a long-sleeved tunic and wide-legged pants in cream linen, Lucy knew she was as ready for the meeting as she would ever be. And she had no excuse to get flustered; she didn't even have to carry her own design portfolio. She was being spoiled, she realised as the young man in Western dress who had come to escort her to the meeting lifted it out of her hands. Better not get used to this, she mused wryly, following him down an echoing corridor.

Lucy's heart was thundering as her companion opened the door of the vaulted council chamber. Silence fell as she entered, then a wave of sound rolled over her as everyone rose from their seats at once. Head held high, she walked towards a lozenge-shaped table she judged to be about thirty feet in length, around which men in the flowing robes of Arabia were standing—*waiting for her…*

Lucy's throat dried. Her earlier optimism appeared premature. Her confidence was evaporating now she was faced with the reality of the scale, opulence, and importance that was attached to the project. It was an awesome responsibility.

Fortunately, before doubt really set in, the young man accompanying her placed her portfolio on the table and pulled out a chair for her. Pinning what she hoped was a professional expression to her face, she sat down. At this signal everyone else sat too. Then an older man to her left leaned across.

'His Majesty apologises,' he murmured. 'He will be a little late. But if you would care to give a brief outline to his council in the meantime, he will join the meeting as soon as he can.'

Lucy dipped her head in polite acknowledgement of this news.

She would have preferred to get the meet-and-greet part of things over with right away. But now she had to begin, knowing that at any moment the ruler of Abadan or his son might interrupt. It couldn't be helped. She would just have to get on with it regardless.

She had just completed her formal introduction to the presentation when the double doors suddenly parted with some ceremony. Unaccountably, she started to shake with nerves. All the men seated at the table with her rose at once, and turned in the direction of the entrance. This was ridiculous, Lucy told herself, drawing a few deep, steadying breaths. She hadn't felt anything quite like it since—

'His Majesty.'

Lucy remained standing sideways on to the door as an unseen courtier announced the Sheikh's arrival in English. Out of consideration for her, no doubt, she presumed. And then curiosity got the better of her, and she turned.

The striking individual who strode into the room supported by a phalanx of following attendants was too young to be the ruling Sheikh. This must be his son, Lucy guessed, and, remembering the figure in the courtyard, she felt her heart begin to race. He had such incredible presence. She felt as if she was looking at someone on a screen, from a distance. It was like looking at Hollywood's best ever stab at an Arabian prince—except that the man coming towards her was the real thing, and she knew instinctively that there was absolutely nothing contrived about him.

The sun streaming in from glass panels above the entrance doors was preventing her from seeing him properly. But she didn't need to see the man clearly to sense the aura of power he carried with him. And it was a forbidding power. He would have to be a hard man, Lucy reminded herself. Sheikh Kahlil of Abadan was a prince of the desert, a warrior through and through. He would have to be the type of individual to inspire confidence and fear in equal measure to win the respect of his people.

He covered the distance between them in a few strides, black robes billowing around him as he walked. The plain black *gutrah* on his head, captured by a gold *agal*, masked what little of his face the blinding sunlight allowed her to see.

'Miss Benson,' he murmured coolly, extending his hand Western-style in greeting.

He was much taller than she had imagined. Standing so close, he eclipsed the rest of the room. They might have been alone. Automatically Lucy grasped his hand.

As they touched, a tremor struck that jolted through every inch of her. She drew a fast breath as it pulsed through every fibre, every muscle, every nerve-ending—

'Majesty,' she managed to murmur, pulling her hand away as if he had burned her. She kept her head lowered, more to avoid the harsh, assessing stare than as a gesture of respect.

'Gentlemen,' she heard him say politely, 'please be seated. Don't let me throw you off stride—please continue,' he added to Lucy with an elegant gesture.

But there was something extra in his voice now, undetectable to those around them, but menacingly apparent to Lucy. For a moment she couldn't speak. A tornado had been let loose inside her. Her mind was in freefall, her heartbeat suspended. She gasped involuntarily, noisily, once, then became aware of the interest she was generating around the table, and swiftly gathered her wits.

'Yes, yes, of course,' she said hastily.

'Water for Miss Benson,' Sheikh Kahlil said, leaning back ever so slightly in his seat to direct the servants.

It couldn't possibly be, Lucy told herself desperately. She gratefully took the glass of water someone handed to her. Could the Kahl she knew have an identical twin. A *doppelgänger* in Abadan he knew nothing about? She took a few sips, and then made herself look up and smile reassuringly round the table. She had heard it said that everyone had a double somewhere in the world, and had always thought it nonsense. But perhaps, just this once, it was true?

'Yes, thank you. I'm ready to continue now.' Lucy was amazed by the steadiness of her voice. Under the circumstances it was nothing short of a miracle! But her thoughts swung wildly back and forth like a pendulum. Was Sheikh Kahlil Kahl? In her heart, Lucy already knew the answer. The man sitting just inches away from her, calmly arranging the folds of his robe, was Edward's father! And he didn't even know he had a son.

Suddenly Lucy was overwhelmed by fear. What might a man as powerful as Sheikh Kahlil do when he discovered he had a son? She had brought Edward into danger—

'Miss Benson? Would you care to continue?'

The Sheikh's tone was neutral, but it unnerved her. He had recognised her too, she was certain of it. How much time would she have before someone told him she was not alone…that she had her baby son with her?

Feeling his scrutiny, Lucy refocused quickly. 'Yes, of course. Forgive me, gentlemen…the heat...'

The heat! Air-conditioning in the palace didn't allow for a moment's discomfort. She would have to do better than that. But Lucy felt as if she was tumbling down a deep black hole. Her heart was thundering out of control, and her mind was paralysed with anxiety. Somehow she had to continue, and get through this—for Edward's sake, if not for her own. Once the meeting was over and she was in the privacy of her own room she would have space to think—to work out how she could get away from Abadan with Edward.

Now she knew the true identity of the man she thought of as Kahl, she would seek legal advice. Of course Edward should know who his father was. And she would tell him when the time was right… Lucy glanced around as if seeing everything again for the first time. How could she ever compete with this? How could she deny her son such a heritage? The thought chilled her, but she was careful not to arouse suspicion, and focused all her attention on the meeting.

How she got through the rest of the morning, Lucy had no idea. On the few occasions that Kahlil addressed her directly he confined his questions to the project. But his keenness of mind alarmed her. She realised she hadn't taken his intellect into account at their first meeting—she had been too distracted by his other qualities. But now she saw that no detail was too small to escape his attention, and as he probed the minutiae of her plans her fears began to grow.

Nothing *ever* slipped through his guard, Kahlil raged inwardly. But he had entrusted the competition and all it entailed to one of his advisors. This meeting had been arranged so that he could congratulate the winner, and meet them in person, and it signalled his first real involvement in a project intended to bring Abadan to the notice of the world. He was determined that his heirs would one day inherit a country at the forefront of exclusive holiday destinations, and the PR resulting from the design competition, together with the opening of the Golden Palace to the public, was crucial to that plan.

And then this had come about. *How?* Kahlil wondered grimly. He had asked for The Best, and they had brought him Lucy Benson! But she could hardly have been expected to make the connection on paper, he supposed, snapping a suspicious glance at Lucy. Twenty-one months ago he had told her his name was Kahl, nothing more.

They had enjoyed each other. That should have been an

end of it. He wasn't in the habit of inviting trouble into his life.

The competition had been set up to maximise publicity and to encourage entries from a broad range of entrants—not just the usual celebrity designers. His aim had been to discover new talent. Well, that had certainly worked, Kahlil reflected grimly. Lucy Benson had hit the ground running, winning this prestigious design contract less than a couple of years after setting up again in business, by his reckoning.

The competition had been supposed to find a new face for him to launch, with photographs of the winner flashed around the world, raising the profile of Abadan at the same time. But he had been thinking of attracting the best designers when he'd set it up, not women with questionable morals—though, as that went, Lucy Benson was still the best, Kahlil conceded, feeling his senses flare. Within minutes of their first meeting he had taken her on her kitchen table. There had been something so potent between them even he hadn't been able to resist the temptation. She had made him lose control to the point where he'd mated with her like a ravening beast, with no thought for the consequences! But it would never happen again.

He had nothing to reproach himself for, Kahlil reflected, turning the events of almost two years ago over in his mind. They had both been consenting adults. And he had made the break nice and clean, leaving before she woke—no regrets, no recriminations—better for both of them that way.

Kahlil's anger at finding himself in such an embarrassing position simmered dangerously close to the surface as he chaired the meeting. In spite of his best endeavours, his underlying thoughts remained stubbornly fixed on Lucy Benson. Was it coincidence or contrivance that had brought her to Abadan? He had been present when her dreams were shattered. Every detail of that day had to be etched on her mind. Had she somehow managed to discover his true identity after their brief and passionate encounter? It hardly seemed likely, but history proved how cunning women could be when a kingdom and a fortune were at stake. He would have to be on his guard, and wait to see what new surprises she might spring on him. Maybe she was innocent, maybe not; only time would tell.

Lucy had never been more relieved to wind up a meeting. It had gone well. No one, not even Kahlil, could fault the meticulous way in which she had prepared her submission for approval. As the room emptied, she kept her head down and concentrated on collecting up all her drawings and samples. Finally only Kahlil and the young man who had escorted her to the meeting remained.

'You may go,' Kahlil said, turning to his young aide. 'I will assist Miss Benson.'

Lucy's swift intake of breath sounded loud in the vaulted chamber, but by the time she lifted her head to protest the young aide was a distant figure, moving swiftly towards the door.

'That's all right, I can manage,' she said calmly, straightening up to confront Kahlil. Standing in silence just a few feet away from her, he was a menacing sight.

'I wish to speak to you,' he said.

He kept his voice low, but it was authoritarian and chilling. There was no 'wish' about it, Lucy thought immediately. Here in Abadan Kahlil's wish was a command. And she dared not challenge him just yet. 'Of course,' she said quietly.

'We will take lunch together—'

He made it sound about as appealing as sitting down to eat with a wounded tiger.

'—in the city,' he informed her.

Lucy felt some relief. Anywhere away from the palace, away from Edward, would do. 'OK,' she agreed, meeting

Kahlil's gaze. But her heart was banging in her chest, and her mind was a whirlwind of thoughts, all clashing together so that she couldn't make sense of anything other than the need to keep Kahlil away from Edward until she could get them both safely out of Abadan.

Kahlil's dark gaze never left her face for an instant, almost as if he could probe her guilty thoughts. But Lucy reckoned if she could confine their discussion to work over lunch she might just get away with it and buy some time. The Golden Palace was so vast it was unlikely their paths would ever cross again.

No wonder he'd left before she woke on that occasion, Lucy reflected angrily. As far as Sheikh Kahlil was concerned she'd provided a few hours' distraction. He was the heir to a kingdom. Pleasurable time spent in bed with a woman was hardly a world-shattering event for him. It was certainly not a good enough reason for him to stay and play happy families with her the next day, Lucy reflected cynically, angry that her body insisted on behaving as if Kahlil was the answer to her dreams—nightmare, more like, she warned herself, pinning a cool, professional smile back on her face.

'I'll just take my things back to my room and then I'll meet you—'

'Leave everything here. It will all be collected and delivered to your rooms—I trust everything is to your satisfaction?' he said.

'Extremely pleasant,' Lucy said. The last thing she wanted was for him to decide to check up on her accommodation for himself. 'Shouldn't I get changed for lunch?' she asked, looking for an excuse to return to Edward. She longed for the sanctuary of the nursery. Dining with the devil was not her recreation of choice.

'You are perfect as you are.'

Lucy's heart sank. She couldn't risk raising Kahlil's suspicions. She had no option but to go with him.

The words had rushed out before he could stop himself, Kahlil thought impatiently. But it was true, unfortunately; as a women and a bedmate Lucy Benson *was* perfect.

Maybe this surprise reunion wasn't so annoying after all. His lips began to curve in sardonic appreciation of the situation. The photographs that had been taken during the meeting, of him presenting a prestigious design prize to exciting new talent Miss Lucy Benson, would be flashed around the world—but no one would guess at their earlier involvement. Life moved in mysterious circles—but she was here; he might as well make use of her.

CHAPTER FOUR

SUSPENDED two hundred metres above the Gulf of Abadan, the restaurant Kahlil had chosen for lunch was exceptional in every way: opulent, hushed, clearly very expensive, and full of what Lucy immediately classed as 'beautiful people'.

The clientele certainly wasn't composed of run-of-the-mill couples, she noticed, looking around, and she wondered if that explained why Kahlil had chosen here, rather than the palace, for their meeting. Separate booths, high-backed, with velvet padded seats in crimson, allowed a degree of privacy that for some reason Lucy found alarming. Their lunchtime companions were men in flowing robes accompanied by young and beautiful companions wearing the latest fashions and fabulous jewellery.

'What kind of place is this?' she said. 'I thought we were having a working lunch.'

'Discreet,' Kahlil said crisply. The *maître d'* escorted him straight towards one of the best tables, overlooking the Gulf.

A place to take your mistress! The thought leapt into Lucy's head like an unwelcome thorn. This wasn't a business meeting, it was a negotiation, she thought angrily. Kahlil remembered everything about their first encounter, and wanted to cut a deal before they returned to the palace.

There was considerable interest as they crossed the room together, with Kahlil well ahead of her, and Lucy's face flamed red as she realised what he was subjecting her to. Tilting her chin a little higher, she smiled faintly and pinned a look of confidence to her face. The first chance she got she was out of here! She would never allow Edward to see his mother humiliated in such a way.

With a polite word of thanks, Lucy accepted the seat the *maître d'* drew out for her. Then she noticed the bodyguards stationed at all the exits: discreet men in Western dress with jackets designed to conceal a holster. A shiver ran down her spine, reminding her that her escape would amount to treason. Whisking the son of the heir to the throne of Abadan out of the country without his father's knowledge or approval would be madness—but what alternative did she have? Losing her son just wasn't an option.

Sheikh Kahlil ben Saeed Al-Sharif was Edward's father! Lucy's stomach clenched with apprehension as she stole a look at the man seated across the table from her.

Kahlil was a forbidding figure in his flowing black Arab garb. He was unmistakably a prince, a warrior prince—she amended, seeing the discreet and reverent glances he was attracting. Everyone deferred to him. It was as if the pitch of the voices around them had been turned down a couple of notches. And even the waiters seemed to be handling the china and glass carefully so that they made less clatter.

Lucy shook her head faintly as the *maître d'* approached to discuss the menu with him. It hardly seemed possible that Sheikh Kahlil—for suddenly she could think of him no other way than as a sheikh—was the same casually dressed man she had given herself to so eagerly, hoping for oblivion, for a few hours of relief… She must have been mad! She was mad, Lucy thought anxiously. Did she really think she was going to be able to hide the fact that she had a baby from him? Her thoughts travelled back to the nursery, to Edward. Maybe it would be safer for him if she just folded and gave in.

Lucy glanced at some of the other young women in the room. Most were smiling happily at their wealthy and powerful companions, and quite a few were laughing—but this wasn't the life for her. Lucy knew that for a fact. She was who she was, and had to take the consequences. She could only hope that one day Edward would understand.

Lucy took little part in ordering the food. On every point where it was possible to compromise she intended to do so. If it pleased Sheikh Kahlil to order for her, so be it. But she would not compromise her honour, her career, or Edward's happiness—in reverse order, Lucy determined, levelling a steady stare on his face.

'So, Lucy,' he began easily, 'this is a pleasant surprise.'

Not, Lucy thought, reading the sub-text behind his hard gaze.

'It's been a long time. Almost two years; a lot must have happened in that time.'

She had been dreading this moment, the moment when he finally acknowledged their first encounter. But now it had come, and she had survived it. She relaxed a little, and gave a fairly comprehensive run-down of her professional life, but nothing more. She would not succumb, at least outwardly, to the glint of knowledge in his dark eyes that told her Sheikh Kahlil was remembering every moment of their first X-rated encounter, and was now prompting her to do the same.

As if she could forget, Lucy thought, toying with the food, glad that the constant supply of new dishes filled any awkward gaps in their conversation.

'Won't you have some pudding, or coffee?' he said, when at last the meal was over.

'No, thank you,' Lucy said, folding her napkin. She had exhausted every topic of conversation in the safety zone. All she wanted now was to return to the palace—to Edward—and make plans to get home safely with him before Sheikh Kahlil learned the truth about her son and tried to stop her.

'I'll take you back.'

He stood, and instantly an entourage seemed to materialise from nowhere and surrounded them. As he waved them away, Lucy's heart thundered a warning. His suggestion was far too intimate for comfort. They had arrived at the restaurant in a chauffeur-driven limousine. What did he have in mind now?

He was devastatingly attractive, Lucy conceded as she got up from the table. It would be the easiest thing in the world to fall into bed with him. Sheikh Kahlil terrified her and attracted her in equal measure, and that was a potent mix. Just the thought of being the one woman who could tame him, who could melt his icy heart, would have been an irresistible challenge to anyone. But that was a foolish daydream, and, however many notches he had on his Arabian bedpost, she had no intention of adding one more.

'Thank you. I'll get straight to work when we get back,' she lied, thinking of Edward.

Did Lucy Benson really imagine she was fooling him? Kahlil mused as he led the way out of the restaurant. Her prim manner was something new, admittedly, but he would soon strip that away.

At the door, one of his bodyguards handed him the keys to another car: something black, and very fast, and just big enough for two. He was in a hurry to get back to the palace now. He had waited long enough. Lucy Benson had had the audacity to avoid his questions, and he wanted to know why. What had she been up to over the past months? How many lovers had she enjoyed in that time?

Before quitting the restaurant Kahlil shut his eyes for a moment to compose himself. The fact that he still wanted Lucy was an inconvenience, but not one he intended to tolerate for very much longer. She had aroused his suspicions. There was something different about her, something he couldn't quite pin down. She was far more composed, and more confident than he remembered. She must have found contentment. *With a man?* The stab of jealousy took him by surprise as he swept through the door ahead of her. He couldn't remember such a thing happening before.

Having taken a few steps, Kahlil realised suddenly that he was alone. Lucy was still standing on the other side of the door. Impatiently he went back, meaning to chivvy her along, but the moment he reached her she sailed past—even finding time to grant *him* a gracious nod on the way!

However attractive Kahlil ben Saeed Al-Sharif might be, she would never allow him to humiliate her, Lucy thought, determined to start as she meant to go on.

She sat in silence as he gunned the engine of his custom-built Maserati into life, and guessed that here, in his own country, Kahlil bowed to nothing and no one. But as far as Lucy was concerned the common courtesies of life still applied. She *was* frightened—for herself, and for Edward most of all—but that was no reason to cave in and allow Kahlil to walk roughshod over her. Any sign of weakness would only harm them both in the long run. She would have to play a waiting game—act cautiously until an opportunity to escape presented itself.

It had been a huge shock to discover the father of her son in Abadan, and an even greater shock to realise the position he held. But she had to get over it fast. There was no time to dwell on the odds stacked against her. She had to look for the positives… But Sheikh Kahlil was not your run-of-the-mill adversary. He was the supreme challenge: the one man in the world she couldn't have; the one man in the world any woman in her right mind would want. And she did. Stealing a glance at him, Lucy found herself shuddering with something she longed to be cold, or apprehension—anything but desire.

The sexual tension between them was incredible, Kahlil reflected, and all the more so because they were confined in the body of the low-slung sports car. The air between them positively crackled with energy—energy that would have to find expression somehow. Maybe he would have pudding brought to his apartment, a platter of sweet pancakes, perhaps, and then he would feed her. And when she was accustomed once more to accepting pleasure at his hands he would take her to bed. Even the most fractious of his racehorses had learned to trust him, and Lucy Benson would do the same.

There was much similarity between the woman sitting next to him and the thoroughbreds in his stable. Both were proud, and edgy, and both could be soothed and persuaded to give of their best if sufficient patience was employed. And Lucy Benson was lucky; even after her insolence at the restaurant, he would grant her the rest of the day—by which time, like the best of his Arabian steeds, she would be begging him for a good workout.

When they arrived back at the palace, a member of Kahlil's council was waiting for him at the grand entrance.

'We will meet later,' Kahlil said to Lucy after a few hushed words with the man, 'to finish our meal and to talk further.'

Lucy's heart thumped ominously. Her fate wasn't settled, it was simply put on hold. But at least it gave her chance to go to Edward. 'When shall I see you?' she said, wanting to be prepared, and well away from Edward.

'In one hour,' Kahlil informed her. 'Someone will escort you to my rooms, and my chef will prepare some delicious dessert for us.'

It was a relief to know he wouldn't come to collect her, but it was also like sand running too fast through an hourglass, Lucy thought, managing a smile. Anyone might tell Kahlil she had brought a child with her. She could only trust he had more important things on his mind than palace gossip. But time was running out.

Edward was asleep when she returned to the nursery. 'No,

let him sleep,' she said to Leila. 'It can't do him any harm. He will still be suffering from jet lag, I expect.'

'We want him bright and breezy for his birthday tomorrow,' Leila agreed, looking down fondly at Edward's sleeping form.

'Yes,' Lucy agreed, feeling her throat tighten. 'But I'd better get back now—to finish my meeting with the Sheikh.'

'Don't worry about us,' Leila said, looking with concern at Lucy's tense face. 'We'll be fine. Just you relax—enjoy your meeting.'

If only, Lucy thought as she hurried out of the room.

It was easy to understand how she had succumbed so easily to Kahlil, Lucy realised as she watched him fork up the last delicious scraps of pancake for her. And perhaps he wasn't as bad as she thought. The harsh contours of his face seemed so much softer in the candlelight.

Even though it was still only late afternoon, they might have been in a luxurious pavilion at twilight, for he had instructed the servants to draw the silk blinds, and light dozens of candles for them. It was a fairytale setting.

The ceiling was tented with exquisite fabric in a rich ruby-red, and the windows behind the delicately printed blinds were tinted, to protect the room's occupants from the harsh midday sun. Kahlil had chosen well. If some form of compact was possible between them, this was the perfect setting. And sooner or later he would have to know about Edward. She wanted to trust him. It would be wonderful if she could.

She risked a small smile as she leaned across to take a second mouthful of the warm pudding from his fork. It was dripping with orange-flavoured sauce. She laughed, embarrassed, reaching for her napkin, but he was too quick for her.

'It's running down your chin,' he pointed out softly.

'I'm sorry.'

'Don't be.'

Before Lucy knew what he was doing, Kahlil had captured the drop of sauce at the corner of her mouth with his fingertip. 'It was careless of me to feed you that last mouthful so clumsily. I'm surprised you don't reprimand me.'

As their gazes locked, Lucy felt a bolt of sensation rip through her at the thought of chastising Sheikh Kahlil of Abadan. He had tapped unerringly into one of her most seductive fantasies.

'It is my responsibility,' he continued softly, 'to make sure that when I feed you everything goes in your mouth…'

Lucy swallowed hard as he put his now sauce-coated fingertip into his mouth and sucked it clean.

'Coffee?' he murmured, holding her stare.

There was no mistaking the real question in his eyes—and it had no connection with coffee. Lucy sucked in a few steadying breaths, but it did no good. Her heart was beating out of control. *He still wanted her.* He couldn't have made it more obvious. They could simply pick up where they had left off…

Madness! She couldn't think of it! She mustn't think of it, Lucy thought, angry with herself as she remembered that her first concern was to get Edward safely away from Abadan. Only then could she seek professional advice regarding his legal position.

'Coffee,' she said firmly.

'Why are you so shy now?' Kahlil asked, turning back to her after giving his instructions to the servants and then dismissing them. 'Isn't it a little late for modesty? Or is there someone else in your life?'

'There's no one,' Lucy confessed.

'No one?' Kahlil repeated, raising one ebony brow in wry amusement. 'Then what is the matter, Lucy? Why are you so reluctant to tell me anything about your private life?'

Lucy's knuckles went white as her hands balled into fists at her side. 'I have to get back—'

'Do you want to?'

Her hesitation was a beat too long. As Kahlil reached for her hand Lucy felt herself grow weak—not at the strength of him, as his power closed around her, but at the tantalising delicacy of his touch. He drew her onward by silken threads of desire, slowly, gently, like one of his most diffident mares. And as his hold on her increased, she melted. He felt so strong, so warm, and so uncannily familiar. It was as if they had never been apart, she realised, breathing faster. And then they were on their feet, facing each other, and she was longing for him to kiss her, for him to take her in his arms so that once again she could forget—

Forget! She could forget nothing, Lucy realised, coming to with a jolt. This wasn't a matter of her pride, or even her hopes and dreams—this was Edward's future, his security, his happiness. He belonged with her. She couldn't, wouldn't, do anything, *anything* to put that at risk. 'I have to go.'

Kahlil reached out and teased a few strands of her hair.

'I mean it, Kahlil,' she said, closing her eyes against the look in his eyes and the sensuous curl of his mouth.

'I won't stop you,' he said, knowing she wanted to stay. And he wanted her to stay. But he sensed that she was wound up like a spring. Another question without an answer, he reflected, staring keenly down at her.

Did he care? Kahlil almost laughed out loud. The hard man of Abadan discovering he had a heart? This was dangerous territory where a woman was concerned, and not a place he cared to visit. 'You are free to go,' he said coolly, standing back from her.

Lucy guessed that anything other than a direct command from Kahlil could never have resulted in someone leaving his presence so abruptly. She had to be cautious. 'I'm sure you have things to do too,' she said pleasantly.

I'll walk you back to your apartment—'

'No!' The sharp exclamation escaped her lips before she could stop it.

'No?' Kahlil queried, his voice turning cold.

His eyes were instantly alert, the formidable mind instantly in gear, Lucy saw with a shiver of apprehension. 'Kahlil, please,' she said, struggling to come up with some excuse. 'I would like to check my plans one last time. There are things I have to be sure of before our next meeting,' she improvised desperately.

'Business can wait,' Kahlil informed her. 'I set the meetings, and therefore I can delay them if I wish. If you need more time, you only have to ask.'

She had to tell him, Lucy realised. He would find out sooner or later. Better she told him than anyone else. 'I have to go back now,' she explained, hearing her voice hoarse with apprehension, 'because I'm not alone—'

'Not alone?' he cut across her harshly. 'What are you talking about?'

'I have a child with me,' Lucy said, and then, bracing herself, she added, 'My son.'

'Your son!' Now it was Kahlil's turn to be completely thrown.

For a moment there was absolute silence. Lucy was frightened when Kahlil refused to look at her, but just stared over her head. She could feel his shock—and, when his shock began subsiding, his mounting suspicion.

This was the price he must pay for trusting her—and for delegating the competition to one of his advisors, Kahlil raged inwardly. Must he oversee everything personally? Clearly, yes! he concluded, raking Lucy with a look. A son! She had never said anything about a child. What type of woman was she?

Suddenly he couldn't wait to get away from her. He needed time to think, to rationalise his feelings, to decide on his next move. 'Go to him, then,' he ordered harshly. 'Go to your son!'

'His name is Edward,' Lucy said quietly as every ounce of her maternal defence mechanism sprang into action. It was terrible to hear Edward spoken about with such anger—and by Kahlil. 'My son's name is Edward,' she said again clearly.

She saw she had Kahlil's full attention now. His eyes were narrowed with distrust. But was it the fact that she had a son alone, or was it her forthrightness? She doubted anyone had ever interrupted Kahlil in his life before. But then perhaps he had never encountered a mother in defence of her child.

Snapping his gaze away from her, Kahlil tried to come to terms with Lucy's startling revelation. As a general rule, he actively encouraged expats working in Abadan to bring their families with them. A happy worker was a good worker, and nothing led to discontent more quickly than homesickness, or the longing for those you loved. The same applied to Lucy. If she had a child, then of course she should have brought him with her. What he took issue with was the manner in which she had kept the information from him. What else was she hiding?

'There is a good play scheme here in the palace, for children of my staff,' he said, turning to her, 'as well as a school…'

Lucy didn't hear any more. Had she joined his staff? Was that how he saw her? Perhaps there was a vacancy for a mistress—

She must keep her head if she was ever to return home safely with Edward. She waited until she was sufficiently composed to say, 'Edward's a little too young for a play scheme, but thank you.'

The words hung in the air between them like an accusation.

'How old is the child?

Kahlil's words plunged like a dagger into Lucy's heart. She couldn't bring herself to answer his question. 'Will you let me go to him?' she said instead, softly.

'Go,' Kahlil said, gesturing impatiently towards the doors.

Kahlil watched her fumbling with the heavy gold handles, not bothering to wait for the servants to open the doors in her haste to get away from him. He did nothing to help, just stood in silence. He would do nothing to aid her path to damnation. He didn't need to. She was doing very well on her own.

It was already dusk by the time Lucy returned to her own rooms at the palace. She was weak with relief after fleeing from Kahlil, and seeing how happily Edward had settled in to his new surroundings almost made her believe that things might be all right after all.

'He woke up soon after you left,' Leila told her, 'but he's been absolutely fine.'

'There are so many new distractions, I'm not surprised,' Lucy murmured, seeking reassurance in Edward's comforting warmth as she lifted him into her arms. But she couldn't compete with this, she realised, looking around. More things had been brought out for him to play with: chalkboards, paints, a wooden train set, toy cars, and even a rocking horse that he was struggling to push Leila away from now that he had mastered the way to ride it.

'I'm afraid he's quite determined to ride it on his own,' Leila explained, 'without me holding on to him. You must be keen on riding,' she added, when Lucy came to take her place in the firing line.

'Yes, I am,' Lucy murmured distractedly, helping Edward to settle back onto the saddle again.

'Or perhaps he takes after his father,' Leila commented, smiling. Then, seeing the look on Lucy's face, she quickly said, 'I'm sorry—I mean—'

'It doesn't matter,' Lucy broke in, reassuring the younger woman with a smile. 'You're probably right, as it happens.'

Leila's comment brought home to her the fact that she didn't know anything about Edward's father. The thought frightened her. But it did seem likely that Kahlil would ride as well as he did everything else. He was built for sport, for action—

Lucy refocused, seeing Leila was still watching her. 'Where did all these things come from?' she said, hoping to deflect the young girl's curiosity.

Leila's eyes widened. 'Apparently this was Sheikh Kahlil's nursery when he was a child,' she confided. 'The servants told me that lots of things had been kept in storage.'

Sheikh Kahlil—*my lover! Edward's father!* Even the way Leila spoke his name with such awe brought the perils of her situation home to Lucy.

'Everyone in the palace has been so kind,' Leila carried on happily, oblivious to the turmoil spinning around Lucy's head. 'The older servants told me that it was good to have a baby around the palace again—Are you all right?' she said, breaking off.

'Yes, I'm fine, thank you. I'm absolutely fine,' Lucy said, managing a thin smile. She was anything but. She was recognising that this was Edward's rightful heritage—all this attention, all this luxury, this was the privileged lifestyle she was denying her son. How could she not tell Edward about Abadan? He must learn about his second country. How could she let him grow to maturity never knowing the truth—that Sheikh Kahlil, the heir to the kingdom of Abadan, was his father?

But if she told Kahlil they had a son together, he would think she had some ulterior motive. Why else would she have kept the news of their child from him for so long? Being so rich and powerful meant Kahlil must harbour suspicions about everyone. How would he feel about a woman who turned up with a young child, claiming he was his son? And what if Kahlil took it into his head to send her away and keep Edward with him in Abadan?

In spite of Edward's protests, Lucy swept her son off the rocking horse and hugged him close. There was not going to be an easy answer, an easy solution. She would just have to get them both out of Abadan somehow, and seek legal advice when she got back.

'You must hear this.'

Lucy turned as Leila distracted her.

'We were recording some tunes,' Leila explained, 'so the children in the playgroup could sing ''Happy Birthday'' to Edward at his tea party tomorrow. Edward grabbed the microphone—'

As Leila turned on the machine Lucy had to admit the improvement in the clarity of his few words was marked. He had even tried to speak a word or two in Abadanese. But she was used to changes coming thick and fast now. She could hardly keep up with them. He had been able to take a few steps for some time, as long as something or someone supported him. And Kahlil had missed everything.

Guilt speared through Lucy as she thought of it. And then there was something far worse. She felt Kahlil enter the room. She didn't even need to turn around to know he was there. An icy hand slithered down her spine. Edward was staring unblinking at the door. And then Kahlil must have made some signal she could not see, for, without uttering a word, Leila hurried past her out of the room.

'Kahlil!' Lucy's grip on Edward tightened as she turned around to face him.

'Strange,' he said, coming closer. 'I imagined an older child. Now, why did I think that?'

Lucy's throat dried. She wasn't sure if an answer was expected of her. And when Kahlil was cloaked in formal Arabian robes, as he was now, she found the sight of him utterly terrifying. They gave him such grandeur, as well as an untouchable quality that made him seem like a stranger. And in many ways he was. Dressed head to foot in black, unrelieved apart from the gold *agal* that held his headdress in place, he was certainly a formidable figure, with his dark complexion and harsh, unyielding face. But, far from being terrified, Lucy noticed that Edward was transfixed, and didn't flinch or hide his face as the tall, robed figure bore down on them.

Instinctively Lucy took a step backwards, but the moment Kahlil was in reach Edward shot out a hand, and to her surprise Kahlil allowed him to wrap his chubby fist around one of his long, tanned fingers.

'I am very pleased to meet you, Edward,' Kahlil politely, letting the boy hang on to him.

Lucy's heart was hammering as she watched her son's reaction to his father. His eyes wore the same determined expression as Kahlil's. And, just like Kahlil, his unblinking expression seemed incapable of showing fear.

'I was just going to give him a bath,' Lucy said, starting to turn away.

'Not so fast,' Kahlil said, catching hold of her arm. 'How old is this child?'

'Edward…Edward is almost one. Tomorrow is his birthday,' Lucy said, tilting her chin to stare Kahlil in the eyes.

'Is he mine?'

She had not anticipated a question half so blunt. As Lucy tensed she felt Edward tense too.

'I asked you, is he my child?'

Kahlil delivered the words in a merciless staccato sequence, not loud enough to alarm Edward, but chilling to Lucy. The evidence was there in front of his eyes, how could she deny it? There was no mistaking the fact that Kahlil was Edward's father; the likeness between them was uncanny.

'Do we have to do this in front of him?' she said. Edward was finding the whole situation fascinating, but Lucy knew there were too many raw emotions in the air, and she wanted to protect him at all costs from the anger that could erupt at any second between Kahlil and herself.

A variety of emotions charged across Kahlil's face: tension, enchantment with Edward, then suspicion, and finally fury. 'Why didn't you tell me?'

'Please, Kahlil—'

But he strode away from her and tugged on a silken rope to call the servants.

Leila must have been hovering outside, Lucy realised, waiting for just such a summons. The young girl hesitated on the threshold, and then came hurrying forwards.

'You called for me?' she said, bobbing respectfully to Kahlil.

'Yes. Will you take Edward for his bath now, please?' Kahlil asked, dipping his head to indicate that she should remove the child from Lucy's arms.

'Of course,' Leila whispered, with another bow.

'And then leave us alone,' Kahlil instructed. 'Miss Benson will come to collect her son when we have finished our meeting.'

Lucy's blood ran cold as she passed a reluctant Edward over to the nanny. Kahlil made the exchange to come between them sound so innocent and clear-cut.

'Go with her now,' Kahlil said directly to Edward, 'and I will come to see you later.'

Lucy felt a rush of resentment at the way Kahlil had cut her out. She wanted Edward to protest, to kick up a fuss; he did neither. He simply locked gazes with his father and quietened immediately.

'I'll look after him. Don't worry,' Leila assured her, as if sensing Lucy's unease.

But there was an acute sense of threat hovering around Lucy that couldn't be appeased by Leila's reassurances. It was almost as if Edward was going for good, She battled the apprehension raging inside her, but it was all she could do to watch Leila carry Edward across the room without going after them. She had no reason to doubt the nanny, or think the young girl might run off with him. But the dangerous undercurrents in the nursery made Lucy doubt her ability to control anything in Abadan.

Her best course of action was to confront the situation calmly, and find out how Kahlil intended to proceed before doing anything.

As the door clicked shut behind Leila and Edward the room seemed ominously quiet. The quiet before the storm, Lucy thought, mentally preparing herself.

Kahlil's voice split the silence like a blade. 'Why have you brought the child here?'

Lucy stared at up him, holding her ground. 'You know why. I'm working here—I have a contract—'

'Have you come to Abadan to extort money out of me?'

'I have come here to do a job, and that is all,' she said. 'The only money I expect to be paid in Abadan is the money that is owing to me.'

'Well, you won't be getting that yet,' Kahlil said stonily. 'You haven't completed the contract. And you may never complete it.'

Was he threatening her? Trying to drive her away? Lucy's face darkened. 'I can't believe you would be so unprofessional.'

'And I can't believe you would bring the child here—a pawn in your sordid game.'

'Edward isn't a pawn in anyone's game,' Lucy said, incensed that Kahlil might think her capable of such a thing.

'He came with me because I'm a single mother, and that's what single mothers do. When their support system falls down, they adapt, they find a way to carry on—'

Kahlil's sound of contempt was meant to wound her, and it did.

'Think what you like of me,' Lucy told him coldly, 'but don't you dare bring Edward into this.'

Kahlil's gaze hardened. No one ever countermanded Sheikh Kahlil of Abadan, or gave him instructions. Lucy saw that at once.

'Can you prove he's mine?'

Lucy went cold, and for a moment she couldn't think what to say. In that instant she saw herself through Kahlil's eyes. It was obvious what kind of woman he thought she was, and every protective instinct she possessed reared up in defence of her son. 'Prove he's yours?' she said with disdain. 'Why on earth should I want to?'

Kahlil gave a short, ugly laugh. 'I would have thought that was obvious.'

'Not to me, I'm afraid,' Lucy said. 'I can give Edward everything he will ever need. I don't need you.'

'Oh, really?' Kahlil observed softly. 'That's not what you said to me once.'

The sharp reminder of their one night of passion sent a clear message. He thought she was an opportunist who seized the moment when it suited her. And in some ways he was right. She had been vulnerable then—at her lowest ebb. And in those few ecstatic hours, yes, she had needed him.

'What do you hope to gain from this?'

'Nothing,' Lucy assured him. 'And that's a low thing to say, Kahlil. It's not worthy, even of you. I don't want anything—how many times do I have to tell you that? As far as I'm concerned you can cancel my contract—'

'And allow you to leave Abadan with the job half finished and a child who might be my son?'

'It's good to see you've got your priorities straight,' Lucy said tensely. 'The contract first, your son second!'

'My son?' Kahlil repeated softly.

The blood drained out of Lucy's face. His presence of mind at the critical moment had allowed him to uncover the truth. 'I won't stay here,' she whispered.

'You'll do whatever I tell you to do.'

'I'll call the Embassy—'

'Call away,' Kahlil invited, glancing down at a telephone on the table. 'It will do you no good. A simple paternity test will establish whether or not I am Edward's father. And if the test proves positive no embassy on earth will dare to come between me and my son.'

'But you don't even know him,' Lucy said. 'You don't know Edward at all!'

'We have made a very good start,' Kahlil observed coolly. 'I see no reason why we cannot grow even closer—'

'But I'm his mother,' Lucy interjected. 'You can't take him away from me.'

'This is my country,' Kahlil said calmly, 'and here in Abadan my word is law. My people support me in everything I do. They trust me. If they hear that I have a son they will be overjoyed, and he will never be allowed to leave the country—unless, of course, I agree to it.'

He wanted Lucy to be hurt as he had been hurt, Kahlil realised, hearing himself land blow after verbal blow. But he had been staggered by the child's likeness to him. Edward was a true Saeed Al-Sharif. With or without the test, he knew his firstborn was in the palace now. It was a life-changing moment. Edward would one day inherit the throne of Abadan.

Lucy Benson had denied him the chance to know his son. How could such a betrayal go unpunished? She had denied him a whole year of Edward's life…a whole year when he hadn't even known of his son's existence. He would never forgive her for that.

'So, what are you saying?' Lucy demanded.

'If Edward proves to be my son he will stay in Abadan, with or without you.'

'No!' she said, shaking her head in disbelief. 'If you cared for Edward at all, you wouldn't say such a thing.'

'If Edward is my son I should have the chance to care for him as much as you!'

Their voices were raised, and anger crackled in the air as they confronted each other head-on. Neither one of them heard the door open.

'Oh, I'm sorry,' Leila said, hovering on the threshold. 'I forgot something for Edward.'

Hearing their son's name, both Kahlil and Lucy turned around at the same moment.

As they stared at him, Edward frowned, and then quite suddenly erupted into noisy, heart-wrenching sobs.

CHAPTER FIVE

LUCY woke herself up the next morning thrashing about on the bed. For one brief moment she was totally elated, knowing it was Edward's birthday, but then she remembered the previous day's events. They came pouring into her waking mind, leaving no room for happy thoughts, crushing her beneath the fear of what Kahlil might do.

She was in danger, Lucy realised, and, worse, she had put Edward in danger. When he had begun to cry the previous evening she had felt the same fierce and protective instinct she always experienced where any threat to him was concerned. But this time she had seen something similar in Kahlil's face. They had both hurried across to comfort him, but for the first time ever Edward had turned away from her, burrowing his face into Leila's chest instead. Wheeling on his heels, Kahlil had left them as silently as he had arrived. But the look in his eyes would stay with her for ever. It frightened her. Instead of this being one of the happiest days of her life, as she had always imagined it would be, she had never felt more alone, or more vulnerable.

Lucy swung out of bed, knowing the tap at the door heralded the arrival of a breakfast tray. Under other circumstances it might have been a welcome distraction, but with a few short words of thanks Lucy waved it away. The last thing she felt like was eating. She had settled Edward into the adjoining nursery at bedtime, staying with him until he was asleep, and she wanted to be the first to greet him on this, his special day.

She had left the door between their rooms slightly ajar, fearing the worst, without knowing what the worst might be. At one point she had even contemplated bringing Edward into her own bed, to be sure of him, but he had been sleeping so soundly she hadn't liked to wake him. Now she could hear him crowing with delight, as he always did when the sun shone brightly. And the sun always shone in Abadan, Lucy realised tensely as she hurried across the room.

Reaching the nursery, Lucy swept Edward into her arms, taking pleasure and comfort from his innocent baby scent. Just holding him close and feeling his warmth seemed to renew her strength and determination. She turned to cross to the windows and draw back the heavy curtains properly, then made a small sound of shock when she saw Kahlil standing in the shadows by the door, arms folded, watching her.

'Good morning, Lucy.'

She stood frozen, immobile, aware that at the sound of his father's voice Edward's level of excitement had increased. And now he was reaching out, leaning across, making it difficult for her to hold him.

'Shall I take him?'

Before she could reply Edward was taken from her arms, and she watched as Kahlil lifted him high above his head. She saw identical dark brown eyes lock and laugh together, and the identical sweep of thick black lashes cast shadows over olive skin. They were a pair, father and son, interchangeable, their faces so similar that Edward might have been Kahlil at a younger age. The realisation chilled Lucy as she watched them. And the look in Kahlil's eyes chilled her even more. As far as he was concerned she was a nothing, a nobody—just someone standing on the sidelines watching as Kahlil ben Saeed Al-Sharif laid claim to his son.

There was no time to lose, Lucy realised as Edward ran the tip of one finger curiously down the folds of Kahlil's flowing black headdress. She had to take Edward away from Abadan. But it would be difficult and dangerous.

Dressed for riding, in a tight fitting black polo shirt, dun-coloured breeches and boots, Kahlil looked every bit the desert prince, the warrior prince, and Lucy's stomach clenched with apprehension as he stared at her. Tilting her chin at a defiant angle, she stared right back. In spite of the way her body insisted on responding to him, she would not weaken—not where her son was concerned. Kahlil might think every woman could be bent to his will, but he was about to learn that, in her case at least, they could not.

Escape from Abadan—the thought chilled her to the marrow. But what alternative did she have? She had to make plans before matters were taken out of her hands entirely. Whatever the risks, she would not lose Edward.

She would not lose her son.

Leila's arrival, and the routine she automatically put into action, left Kahlil and Lucy with little to do other than stand tensely as the young nanny swept Edward off for his morning bath. Lucy was relieved when Kahlil left the room then, without a word or a backward glance. There was no reason for him to stay now, and with Edward gone, and a business meeting later that morning, Lucy left for her own quarters.

Calling in one last time, to say goodbye to Edward before her meeting, Lucy found the nursery alive with activity. Edward was dressed in Arab dress and sitting happily on his play mat. He looked so different. And yet there was nothing wrong with Leila dressing him in the local costume, Lucy told herself; it was cooler for him.

Edward was so happily engaged with the presents in front of him that, once again, he barely noticed her. Normally she wouldn't have taken it to heart, but today was different. This was Kahlil's doing, Lucy realised indignantly. He had made a point of coming back to the nursery before her and showering Edward with far too many gifts. She would not have

Edward growing up spoiled and arrogant like his father, careless of other people's feelings. Resentment reared up inside her, but she forced it down quickly when Leila came towards her across the room. None of this was the young girl's fault.

'I'll save this until after the meeting,' Lucy said, placing her own carefully wrapped parcel on the table. 'Please don't let Edward open it until I come back.'

But Edward was far too preoccupied with a box containing a toy Lamborghini to even notice he had yet another package to open.

'Of course I won't,' Leila said, glancing at her charge. 'Sheikh Kahlil came by,' she added, 'with lots of presents.'

'So I see,' Lucy said dryly. 'Don't worry, you've done nothing wrong,' she said, seeing the concern on Leila's face. 'Edward's going to have a great birthday. Everyone has been so kind.' But poor Leila looked more dubious than ever. 'Well, at least Edward's happy, and that's all that matters,' Lucy said firmly, moving away to escape the younger woman's scrutiny.

Picking her son up, she hid her face in his baby warmth for a few moments. 'And now there's a party to organise,' she said brightly, pulling back. 'What is it, Leila?' she added, turning when she heard the nanny's muted exclamation. 'What's wrong?'

'I'm really sorry, but—'

'Go on,' Lucy prompted.

'When Sheikh Kahlil came back to the nursery he was accompanied by one of his aides. He left instructions that you weren't to concern yourself with the party. He said he would make all the arrangements for Edward's birthday.'

'Did he indeed?' Lucy murmured tensely.

'It will be fantastic,' Leila said reassuringly.

'I'm sure it will be,' Lucy said, releasing Edward onto his mat again. 'I'll make sure of it.'

Lucy saw the look of concern that settled on Leila's face, but she was determined to have some input into Edward's first birthday party. Kahlil had no official part to play in Edward's life—not yet.

She gazed around at the piles of expensive gifts. Kahlil must have rung the nearest toy shop and had everything appropriate to Edward's age delivered to the palace. He was already sure Edward was his son! But proof would be needed, Lucy realised, feeling a stab of fear. 'Did anyone touch Edward while I was away?'

'No, of course not,' Leila said. 'Except—'

'Yes?' Lucy pressed tensely.

'Sheikh Kahlil played with him, of course, and lifted him up.'

Leila's innocent account was very frightening to Lucy. 'And Edward was OK with that?'

'Of course,' Leila said promptly. 'Edward loves Sheikh Kahlil.' Seeing Lucy's expression, she amended quickly, 'What I mean is, Sheikh Kahlil makes him laugh.'

Lucy forced a smile onto her face. 'But no one else touched him? You're sure?' The possibility of a DNA test being carried out without her permission was niggling at her mind.

'No, of course not,' Leila said adamantly. 'You know I wouldn't let anyone near Edward—apart from the Sheikh.' But she still looked very worried as she held Lucy's stare.

Leila was wondering what on earth she had got herself into, Lucy realised. 'I don't mean to criticise you,' she said quickly. 'It's just that we're in a strange country, and I have to be sure in my mind that Edward is safe.'

'I understand, and I won't ever leave him alone.'

'I believe you,' Lucy assured the young nanny gently. 'And maybe I'm being too hasty about that party. The Sheikh's people will surely know where to get everything we need.'

'Absolutely,' Leila agreed, brightening. 'They're even talking about having a funfair for all the children at the palace.'

'That would be fantastic,' Lucy agreed. She felt a little better knowing that Edward's birthday provided an excuse for a general celebration where everyone would have fun.

'Shall I take Edward, so that you can prepare for your meeting?' Leila suggested.

'I'm ready now—but what I'd really like is a few minutes alone with him—if you don't mind?'

'Of course I don't mind,' Leila said, touching her arm lightly.

The kindly gesture brought tears rushing to Lucy's eyes. She blinked them away quickly, before Leila saw. But she sensed the young girl already knew there was something very wrong.

Lucy was glad of the meeting, to discuss the design project in depth. It was a complete change of pace, and one she badly needed.

Everything went smoothly in the Council Chamber, where Kahlil behaved as if there was nothing between them other than business. He even made it possible for her to go through the agenda quickly, as if he too was in a rush to get away. And when the meeting drew to a close he left the room before she even had time to tidy up her papers.

She felt the tension starting to drain out of her the moment the door closed behind him. She was in good time to help prepare for the birthday celebrations. All she had to do was change into something more suitable for a children's party.

Lucy stood amazed at the top of a sweeping flight of marble steps overlooking the palace garden. A huge part of the grounds had been transformed into a fairground, with stalls and a skittle alley, and even a full-sized carousel, all shielded from the sun by giant-sized marquees. Clowns walked about on stilts, distributing flags and streamers to the crowds of children with their parents and teachers, and hurdy-gurdy music blasted out from several speakers. Where money was no object, anything was possible, she realised.

She had changed into jeans, sneakers and a blue gingham shirt, ready for action. Just as well, since many of the rides were suitable for Edward. At the moment he was sitting patiently in his buggy, by her side, but she knew his apparent contentment was misleading and wouldn't last long.

The marquees were air-conditioned, Lucy discovered when she wheeled Edward inside the largest tent.

'Sheikh Kahlil thinks of everything,' Leila commented.

'Yes, he does,' Lucy said—though whether that was a good thing… 'I hardly know where to start first,' she murmured, looking around.

'How about the carousel?'

Lucy jumped with shock at the sound of Kahlil's voice. She had been so sure he would not be there. At the meeting earlier he had given her the impression that he had somewhere important to go; a children's party was the last thing she had imagined. He was casually dressed in jeans, and a shirt rolled up to the elbows—just like the first time they'd met. It was a painful reminder. Gazing up, transfixed, Lucy found she could hardly breathe, barely speak.

'Well?' Kahlil said.

'Well, what?' Lucy queried distractedly. And then she realised he wasn't speaking to her at all, but to Edward. And Edward was holding out his arms, waiting for Kahlil to lift him up.

Dipping down to sweep his son out of the pushchair, Kahlil lifted him high in the air. Lucy saw his mouth settle in a look of supreme pride and satisfaction, and then, settling him on his shoulders, he walked off.

Sheikh or no sheikh, bodyguards or whatever else might stand in her way, Lucy wasn't going to let Kahlil get away with that. Pushing through the crowds, she had almost caught up with him when security men stepped in front of her, barring her way.

'Let her pass.' Kahlil's voice was low, but commanding, and they backed off immediately.

'You can't do this, Kahlil,' Lucy said tensely. 'You can't just take Edward away from me without a word of explanation.'

Glancing up to reassure himself that Edward was too busy watching the painted horses to notice the tension, Kahlil speared a look at her. 'And you can't stop me getting to know this boy any longer—a boy who is probably my son.'

'Don't you think you're getting a little ahead of yourself?'

'Am I? There is only one way to resolve this beyond doubt,' he said, settling Edward in front of him on one of the carousel ponies.

'And what is that?' Lucy said tensely, glad that Edward was too excited to notice the high-octane discussion being carried out in murmurs above his head.

'We will have a DNA test carried out.'

'No!' Lucy had known it would come to this. But she'd wanted it to happen away from Abadan, where she might have some control over the repercussions. 'Don't spoil his birthday—please, Kahlil,' she begged. 'Please, just drop it for today.'

Fleetingly, Kahlil looked as if he might consider her appeal, and Lucy's hopes soared. She didn't want to deny Kahlil the right to know his son, or keep Edward from his father. She just wanted a little more time. But then the raucous music started up again and she was left alone, while Kahlil and Edward began moving slowly away from her.

* * *

He had forgotten that it was possible to have so much innocent fun, Kahlil thought wryly as the carousel came to a halt at the end of the ride. It was a relaxation for him to be just one of many adults taking their small children for a ride on the gaudy machine. He felt elated. He had felt nothing quite like it before.

He gritted his jaw, seeing Lucy was still standing where they had left her. There was no question in his mind about Edward; they were uncannily alike. He glanced around, wondering if anyone else had noticed. But his bond with the child went deeper than appearance, Kahlil reflected, getting ready to dismount; there was real chemistry between them. And their character was identical, he noticed with amusement, when Edward refused to get down from his perch.

'Perhaps later,' he consoled the determined child. 'Your mother is waiting for you now.'

Seeing Lucy's face, Kahlil felt something close to pity. She looked so fearful, so tense and anxious. He brushed the emotion aside, remembering that she had kept him from a child he was increasingly sure now was his son. Fate had stepped in for him; fate had brought them together in spite of her deception. He had nothing to thank Lucy Benson for. Still…

'Edward will not be touched without your consent,' he told her. 'But a DNA test will be necessary. Accept it.'

Lowering Edward to the ground, Kahlil supported him as he took a few bold steps towards his pushchair. 'Soon you'll be walking by yourself,' he commented, hunkering down so his face was on a level with Edward's.

White-faced, Lucy moved between them, and secured Edward back in the stroller herself.

Let her have this victory, Kahlil told himself, waving his bodyguards away. Lucy's breach of etiquette meant that men who remained otherwise invisible, mingling with the crowds, instantly surrounded him. They were always alert for danger, but he would not allow them to restrain Lucy now, or at any other time. Whatever she had done to deceive him, she was still the mother of his son.

The mother of his son! Kahlil felt as if his heart would burst with pride. Edward: his son. He ran the child's name over in his mind, loving the sound of it. Lucy might not have admitted as much as yet, but she would not be allowed to leave Abadan until he had formally established the truth of Edward's parentage.

CHAPTER SIX

THIS would be her third full day in Abadan, and instead of improving things for Edward she had thrown his future into confusion, Lucy reflected, tossing restlessly on the bed.

And now it was time to get up, she saw, checking the clock on the bedside table.

She groaned as she swung her legs over the side of the bed, and stayed slumped with her head almost touching her knees, her long golden hair tickling her calves. She had checked on Edward so many times during the night she felt as if she hadn't slept at all. The belief that Kahlil would never snatch him from her was no consolation. She couldn't escape the thought that one day Edward would choose Abadan, and Kahlil, over her, and it frightened her.

Sensibly, the only thing she could do was get him away from Kahlil and out of the country as fast as possible. Once she was home she could arrange with a lawyer to see that Edward shared his time between them—but even that wouldn't be right, Lucy thought, lifting her head to stare blindly into the future. Even that would not be enough for a man like Sheikh Kahlil ben Saeed Al-Sharif of Abadan.

She had to get away. It was all that was left to her now. She knew what she had to do, but she had to find the right opportunity to put her plan into action.

Hurrying into the nursery, Lucy smiled down at her son, waiting impatiently, arms raised, to be freed from his cot. If they remained in Abadan it meant complying with every restriction Kahlil cared to throw at them—and she was never going to let that happen.

'Never, my darling,' she assured Edward, swinging him into the air.

There was deep tension inside the robing room of the Sheikh of Abadan.

'Leave us,' Kahlil's father commanded his courtiers imperiously.

Age might have imposed certain restrictions upon him, most onerous of which was the indignity of the stout ebony stick he was now forced to use, but Kahlil thrilled to hear his father's voice still firm and as commanding as ever. He watched the bowing courtiers back out of the opulent chamber, and waited until the door had closed behind them before turning to speak to the ruler of Abadan.

'I wanted to be the one to tell you before any gossip reached your ears,' he said, after explaining about Edward.

'If you have the slightest suspicion regarding the child's parentage he must be brought here at once,' his father said, his black eyes sharp as a hawk's above his aquiline nose. 'For his own safety, Kahlil, if nothing else. If this should get out—'

'I am confident that no one else knows about this as yet.'

'As yet,' his father observed. 'You say the likeness between you is uncanny? In your heart I believe you already know the truth.'

'I cannot be certain—'

'Until the test is done,' his father pointed out.

'You must allow me to handle this,' Kahlil said firmly. 'Lucy would never agree to a test being carried out here in Abadan. She does not trust us.'

'I take it you are referring to the mother?' The old Sheikh shook his head, seeing the irony of the situation. But he also saw his son's unbending will clearly reflected in his eyes.

And there was more—enough to arouse his suspicion that emotion was involved. Emotion clouded judgement. He would act on his son's behalf if he had to. 'There is something about this situation you are not telling me,' he observed shrewdly.

'There is nothing more,' Kahlil said dismissively.

But some internal pain as real as any wound flickered behind Kahlil's eyes, and his father knew at once what he must do.

Back in his own rooms, before meeting later that morning with Lucy, Kahlil sat with his chin on his hand, staring fiercely into the future. He had the look about him of a man who truly believed he could bend it to his will.

Adopting Edward as his heir would not be a simple matter, as his father seemed to imagine. The ruling Sheikh had lived through an age when women could be swept up and cast down again as required—though Kahlil had to smile, remembering his own mother. She had not been swept up, or cast down. If anything, his father had been the one to lose his heart, as well as his stubborn adherence to tradition, when they met.

And now there was Lucy Benson. She was hardly doormat material either. She was the very antithesis of a willing woman—in all ways but one, Kahlil remembered, feeling his senses stir. She was headstrong, unpredictable, and outrageously provocative. But did he want a woman who gave herself to a man within the first minutes of their meeting? Not to sit beside him on the throne of Abadan one day, that was for sure. Lucy Benson was not good wife material, and certainly inconceivable as consort to the eventual ruler of Abadan—but there was nothing to stop him taking her as his mistress.

A pact, Kahlil concluded finally, standing and stretching to his full height so that his shadow cast a menacing shade across the wall. There would have to be an accommodation between them. Edward would stay in Abadan, while the best minds in the land would examine the law to see if his son could be named as his legitimate heir without marriage to his mother. In the fullness of time he would select someone more suited to sit beside him on the throne.

Kahlil's lips turned down at the thought. He knew it couldn't be one of the relentlessly acquiescent women whom his father paraded before him in the hopes that eventually he might bite. They were all glassy-eyed at the thought of his power and wealth. Not one of them had been able to tempt him beyond the bedroom. As far as he was concerned they were despicable creatures—toys to be used and discarded, as they would have used him.

His expression darkened as he strode towards the door. He had better things to think about. Edward and Lucy had been placed under a discreet protection programme from the first moment his suspicions had been roused. That would have to be stepped up now, but the child would stay with his mother for the time being.

This meeting had been the best so far, Lucy thought with relief as she hurried back to the nursery. Whether she felt so good because without Kahlil there had been no tension, or whether it was just the fact that things were going so well, either way her confidence was high. For the first time she really believed she could handle the situation—

Lucy's breath caught in her throat as she reached the end of the corridor. She could feel the change even before her eyes had registered anything. Instinctively she began to run, but someone leapt out of the shadows and barred her way.

With a yelp of fright, she stopped abruptly. A tall man in dark clothes loomed over her—and he was carrying what looked like a gun.

'Edward!'

The guttural scream leapt from Lucy's throat as she tried

to shoulder past him. But the man, having caught hold of her, wouldn't let go.

'The Sheikh of Abadan,' Lucy panted, almost beside herself with fright. 'I demand to see the Sheikh!' Whether or not it was something in her voice that shook him, she had no idea, but he released her. And then she saw Leila, peering anxiously round the partially open nursery door. 'Leila, thank God! Where's Edward?'

'He's in here,' Leila said quickly, drawing her inside. 'Edward is safe.'

Lucy slammed the door behind her, leaning against it as she fought to catch her breath, and saw Edward safe inside his playpen, playing unconcerned. Shutting her eyes, she gave a soft cry of relief. 'Who ordered this?' she said, hurrying over to him.

'Sheikh Kahlil,' Leila said unhappily.

Lucy's mouth formed a firm white line. 'And where is Sheikh Kahlil now?'

'I don't know,' the girl admitted.

'Then we must ask his guard,' Lucy declared fiercely. Swinging the door open again, she called him in.

She rounded on the man the moment he entered the room, demanding fiercely, 'Sheikh Kahlil? Where is he? You'd better tell me.'

But the man only shook his head and shrugged his shoulders.

'I have a few words of Abadanese. Do you mind if I try?' Leila offered.

'No, please—go right ahead,' Lucy urged.

After a few minutes had passed Leila was able to tell her that Kahlil had gone to his stud farm as soon as he was satisfied that additional security was in place at the nursery.

The noose was tightening, Lucy realised. Soon everyone would know about Edward. Even without a parentage test Kahlil wasn't taking any chances, and the people around him weren't fools. It made the need for her to get away from Abadan with Edward all the more pressing. But before she could formulate a plan she had to know exactly what she was up against.

'I must speak to someone about this,' she said, careful not to arouse Leila's suspicions. 'I have to explain that this level of security is unnecessary. Perhaps as Sheikh Kahlil isn't available to talk to me I might have an audience with his father? Can you ask the guard about it?' she said to Leila.

Leila was already shaking her head. 'He's not like his son.' She frowned. 'He comes from a different age, a different world—I don't even know if he would agree to see you.'

'Please—do this for me,' Lucy insisted. 'This is outrageous,' she pointed out, flaring a look at the armed guard. 'I have to speak to someone—it must be possible!'

Lucy took time choosing what she would wear for her audience with the ruling Sheikh of Abadan. Despite her bravado she could hardly believe he had agreed to see her. She had rehearsed what she would say, and how she would say it, over and over, to make sure there would be no hesitation on her part—and no mistakes. She should get it right; she'd had enough time to practise her lines, she thought, glancing at her wristwatch for the umpteenth time. She had been kept waiting in the antechamber to Kahlil's father's rooms for hours. It was now early evening.

'Miss Benson?'

Lucy looked up to see the Sheikh's aide-de-camp had returned at last. He was beckoning to her from an open doorway.

'Thank you,' Lucy said, getting to her feet and quickly walking past him before he had a chance to change his mind. Perhaps she had been kept waiting in order to take the wind of righteous indignation out of her sails before the interview. Well, if that was so, it hadn't worked.

Kahlil's father was seated on a chair at the far end of the ornately decorated room. Sitting stiffly upright, he was as gnarled as the branches of the olive trees in the courtyard outside her bedroom window, and must be at least eighty, she guessed, as she bowed low in front of him in deference to his age.

'Come closer, so that I can see you in the light,' he instructed.

She saw now that his chair was more of a carved and gilded throne, made comfortable by a mound of velvet cushions. There was a fringed canopy of rich purple velvet above his head, and he looked every bit the old warrior king of Abadan.

Compromise was the way forward, not confrontation, Lucy decided. She could not take on the whole of Abadan and its ruler. She had to play by Abadanese rules—at least while she was in the country. And despite his reputation, and his fierce appearance, there was something courteous about the old gentleman that demanded she respond in kind.

She took a step forward so that she was standing directly beneath a surprisingly old-fashioned standard lamp positioned to one side of him. It cast a soft pool of light on the ruby-red rug beneath her feet, and was completed by a faded fabric shade in a colour that might once have been peach. It looked as if it must have come from some Western department store specialising in luxury goods many years before, and was certainly incongruous in such an exotic setting.

'I see you are interested in my lamp,' the elderly Sheikh commented benignly, his voice firm, if a little hoarse.

He missed nothing, Lucy realised. She would have to proceed with great caution.

'My wife was from the West—why, Miss Benson, you look surprised.'

'No,' Lucy fudged, laughing tensely, though of course she

was. But by the time she had absorbed that piece of information she felt a little calmer because she knew he was trying to make her feel at ease.

'You *are* surprised,' Kahlil's father said with a high-pitched cackle of delight. 'My son has failed to tell you that he straddles the divide between East and West?'

Now was not the right time to admit she knew as little about Kahlil as he knew about her, Lucy realised, making a non-committal sound.

'Won't you be seated?' his father invited, pointing to a similar mound of cushions, minus the throne, facing his own.

Had the ruling Sheikh not told her about Kahlil's heritage, Lucy would have been amazed by this suggestion that she should sit in his presence. 'Thank you,' she said. She sat, trying to judge the right moment to put her case. But Kahlil's father forestalled her.

'And how is my grandson this morning? I am eager to see him.'

Lucy was so taken aback she couldn't summon up a single word in reply.

'You must be pleased that I acknowledge Edward,' the Sheikh of Abadan continued. 'Now you know about Kahlil's heritage, you will understand how I am able to accept a child of Kahlil's who dilutes the Abadanese bloodline.'

Lucy felt like a brood mare, but she was equally sure the elderly Sheikh had not meant to offend her. 'If I may speak—I beg your pardon, Majesty,' she said quickly, 'I did not mean to interrupt you, but I'm sure you can understand my concern for my son.'

'Indeed,' he agreed, inclining his head graciously. 'And, equally, I am sure you can understand *my* concern for my grandson.'

'Aren't you being a little premature?' Lucy parried.

'Are you trying to tell me Edward is not Kahlil's son?'

Lucy reddened beneath the hawk-like stare.

When she remained silent, the elderly Sheikh said, 'You do not have to say anything Miss Benson; I already know the truth.'

'How can you?' Lucy said tensely.

'Quite simply,' he said. 'DNA tests have been carried out—'

'How dare he?'

'Who are you talking about, Miss Benson?'

'Kahlil, of course,' Lucy said angrily, springing to her feet.

'I can see you are upset, but, please, do sit down again.'

'Upset?' Lucy said her lips white with anger. 'That doesn't even begin to cover it! This amounts to an assault on my son as far as I am concerned. I am Edward's mother; nothing should have been done without my consent.'

'I disagree,' the Sheikh told her. 'The responsibility for Edward's welfare has been taken out of your hands—on my command,' he added imperiously, when Lucy started to protest.

Now she could only stare at the elderly man, nonplussed. The Sheikh of Abadan made it sound as if she should be relieved, even grateful to him for relieving her of such a burden! But it was Edward they were talking about—her son Edward!

'As eventual heir to the throne of Abadan,' he continued evenly, 'only we can hope to give Edward all the security and the education he needs before he assumes the mantle of power.'

'No! You cannot take my son away from me. I will not allow it!'

'You have no alternative, Miss Benson. It is a *fait accompli.*'

'You had no right to carry out tests without my permission—'

'This is my country. I will do whatever I consider necessary to protect the boy I have just learned is second in line to my throne.'

Edward, heir to the throne of Abadan! It struck Lucy so forcibly her throat dried. 'You can't—'

'Oh, but I can,' the Sheikh of Abadan told her. 'Here, my word is law.'

'Your word, and that of your son,' Lucy said bitterly.

'Correct, Miss Benson—or may I call you Lucy?'

'I think it better that we confine ourselves to a formal style of address,' Lucy said coldly, knowing that the next time they met was likely to be in court. The DNA testing might be a *fait accompli*, and Kahlil's right to claim Edward as his son something she was forced to accept, but she would not be compromised where her son was concerned, nor allow either of them to be patronised by anyone. 'If no one knows that Edward is Kahlil's son, surely he's not at risk,' she reasoned out loud. 'I will keep him safe.' She turned her burning gaze on the Sheikh. 'Let me have my son back. Let me go home with Edward.'

'I'm afraid it's not as clear cut as that,' he told her patiently. 'Please sit down again.' He waited until she did as he asked. 'Even walls have ears. Palace gossip flourishes. There are no secrets here. Even I would find it impossible to keep this type of information quiet for long.'

'Then let us go—somewhere far away, where Edward will be safe.'

'My son has rights too,' Kahlil's father pointed out. 'Would you deny Edward the chance to know his father? Would you deny your son the right to claim his birthright?'

Silence hung heavily between them as Lucy came to terms with the situation. 'If I went home and left Edward here,' she said at last, in a voice that had lost its bite, 'could you promise to keep him safe?'

'I could,' the elderly Sheikh confirmed in a kinder tone.

'Edward would have the best of everything—everything that money can buy. I promise you that. And of course, as mother of the royal child, you would receive an extremely handsome pension—'

'What?' Lucy exclaimed, springing up again. 'Do you think you can buy me? Forgive me if I misunderstood you,' she said tensely, 'but did you just offer me money in return for my son?'

'Now, now—you mustn't look at it that way—'

'And just how am I supposed to look at it?'

'It is normal in such circumstances,' the Sheikh said calmly, as if there was nothing wrong with his offer at all.

Perhaps it was a regular occurrence in Abadan…perhaps it was a regular occurrence where Kahlil was concerned, Lucy thought. In her distressed state, she would have believed anything possible…or perhaps it was time to put Kahlil out of her mind once and for all, she realised bitterly. That was the safest course of action for Edward, and for her.

'As I see it,' she said, gathering the last vestiges of her strength and determination together, 'the best thing that can happen is that I take Edward home with me to a place where he can live a normal life.'

The Sheikh didn't answer her for a few moments, and then he said, almost as if he had some sympathy for her plight, 'Regrettably, Edward will never be able to live what you think of as a normal life, Miss Benson. He is a royal child. You can never take that away from him. From now on Edward must be taught to handle the weight of responsibility that accompanies privilege.'

'He's one year old!'

'Even so...' The Sheikh of Abadan held out both hands, palm up, in an expression of finality.

Lucy remained silent as all the implications for Edward sank in. From being a happy, carefree little boy, he had been transformed into someone who would require some form of protection for the rest of his life. Could she provide that for him? She doubted it. She needed support in order to do it properly. There was only one person in the world who could offer her that support, and that was Kahlil. Who hadn't even bothered to come back to the palace now that he had secured the gates to her gilded cage! Stick a guard on the door and walk away. That was as far as accepting responsibility for his son went for Kahlil.

The thought of abandoning Edward to that sort of parenting was out of the question. They stayed together. That much she was determined upon. If she could just get them both back home in safety, to be under the protection of her own country's security services…

It was like a madness building inside her; now Lucy could think of nothing else at all—nothing but escape.

CHAPTER SEVEN

'YOU are summoned to a meeting by Sheikh Kahlil ben Saeed Al-Sharif of Abadan.'

'I see. At what time?' Lucy asked the courtier politely. Inwardly she was seething at the nature of the formal summons, but it was hardly the man's fault.

'In one hour,' he said, bowing his way out of the room.

She had been called into Kahlil's presence like a member of his staff, Lucy mused angrily as the door closed; so much for all that empty talk of how she was the mother of the royal child. She was nothing as far as Kahlil and his father were concerned—nothing but an embarrassing encumbrance.

She had sat up half the night after her meeting with Kahlil's father, waiting for Kahlil to return to the palace. And she was still smarting now from the knowledge that someone had sneaked into the nursery to take Edward's hairbrush away. A single hair, she had since learned, was all it took to prove parentage.

She would never have denied Kahlil the chance to know his son. She had just never expected to see the man she'd known as Kahl again. And never in her wildest dreams had she anticipated finding him here in Abadan, heir to the throne of one of the world's richest countries.

Kahlil might be a sheikh, and all-powerful in his own land, but that did not weaken her resolve. She would agree to equal parenting rights, but based on the laws of her own country, not Abadan. To achieve this she had get Edward back home, whatever it took.

Lucy's lips whitened as she thought of the many difficulties she would have to overcome in order to escape. She only had to think of the armed guards on the nursery door to know she was taking a huge risk. But remembering the Sheikh of Abadan's outrageous offer of money in exchange for Edward strengthened her determination. He might be a fine old man, and beloved by his people, but he had no idea how a mother felt in defence of her child. Wherever she went, Edward went too. And she would keep him safe, with or without the help of his royal relatives.

Similar situations must have arisen before, Lucy told herself. There would be ways of dealing with the problem, and people who could advise her once she got back home. But first she had to prepare herself for the meeting with Kahlil. She would deal with business, and then finalise her escape plan. There would never be a better time. Kahlil and his father were convinced she could be bent to their will, manipulated, bought off, sent packing—they were complacent, and now was the time to strike.

And strike she would, Lucy thought fiercely, putting the final touches to her make-up.

Kahlil paced the floor of his royal apartment, hands linked behind his back, in a state of brilliantly controlled fury. His father was like a tiger that could never be tamed. He was forced to admire his pluck, his unquestioned courage, and his determination to rule as if he was still that same warrior king of half a century ago, but there was no question that he had overreached himself this time.

From the moment Kahlil had discovered Edward's DNA had been tested by removing his soft-bristled baby brush from the nursery he had been in a state of simmering fury. It hadn't eased his anger to know that Edward had never been touched. He had given his word to Lucy that nothing would be done without her consent. And his word was his bond. But his father had ridden roughshod over that promise, ordering the test to be carried out regardless of anyone's wishes but his own.

It was indefensible. Edward was a small child, unable to protect himself. His parents should have been consulted—*he* should have been consulted, Kahlil amended swiftly, for he now knew for sure that he was Edward's father.

He turned abruptly as the door opened and Lucy came in. She walked forward, braving a stare that would have stopped many a man in their tracks. But she could not be put off so easily, Kahlil reflected. She finally drew to a halt close enough for him to catch the scent of jasmine. He had to admit she looked beautiful—exquisite. He had never seen her looking so feminine, or so desirable. A muscle worked in his jaw as he wished momentarily that things could have been different between them. But she was white-faced and drawn as taut as a bowstring. This was not a time to be softening towards her.

'Thank you for coming—' he began courteously, but she held up one hand and cut him off.

'Don't even try to explain away the armed guard who steps in front of me every time I try to see my son,' she said crisply. 'And don't waste your time trying to find some excuse for violating Edward's rights. No wonder you avoid seeing me. I'd be apprehensive if I were you—in fact, I'd be scared.'

'Scared?' Kahlil queried icily. He wanted to drag her to him and force her to apologise, but somehow he controlled the impulse. 'I don't know the meaning of that word.' To his utter astonishment, he was forced to catch hold of her striking arm. 'Would you hit me?' he demanded incredulously. 'Would you dare to raise your hand to me?'

Lucy rested still for a moment, panting. She knew she couldn't escape. She knew she had gone too far. 'You don't frighten me, Kahlil.'

'Then you're very foolish.' He turned away from her with

an angry sound, ashamed of rising to the provocation, but knowing he must concede that his father had overstepped the mark. 'There is no excuse for what has happened,' he said, tugging Lucy a little closer for emphasis. 'The only explanation I can give is that Edward's safety is paramount.'

'You promised me,' Lucy said tensely. 'You promised nothing would be done as far as Edward is concerned without my consent.'

She saw Kahlil's gaze sharpen. Could he feel the change in her body as he held her to him? Even while she railed at him Lucy knew she was losing control. Kahlil was the enemy, and yet still she wanted him. It didn't make sense; nothing made sense, Lucy raged inwardly, wrenching out of his grasp. She took a few rapid steps away, rubbing her arms as if he had hurt her. But he had used barely enough force to keep her still. She was just so wretchedly confused.

'The tests were carried out without my knowledge or consent. My father gave the order while I was out of the palace. The people responsible received no contradictory directions from myself—how could they,' Kahlil reasoned, 'when I wasn't there to consult? And therefore they went ahead without my knowledge—'

'I am Edward's mother!' Lucy cut in angrily. 'Why didn't someone come to ask me how I felt about it?'

'Here in Abadan, my father's word is law. And forgive me, Lucy,' Kahlil added, a flash of humour momentarily brightening his gaze, 'but it would never have occurred to my father's servants to consult you, a mere woman.'

'A mere woman,' Lucy repeated, staring up at him coldly. 'I trust you don't feel the same way?' She wondered why his slow smile should make her feel even more anxious and suspicious.

'My father's servants are all from his era. I can assure you they hold very different views to the Abadanese men of today.'

His voice vibrated through her like a soft, harmonious chord: a chord she was determined not to hear. 'And I suppose you consider yourself to be in the latter camp?' Lucy said derisively, but she felt Kahlil's warm breath on her neck bringing all the tiny hairs to attention.

'I do,' he agreed softly.

Lucy broke eye contact fast.

'A single hair from Edward's hairbrush was all that was required,' Kahlil said to reassure her. 'It hardly constitutes an assault.'

'Even so—'

'Enough of that,' he said impatiently, breaking away. 'I asked you to come here so that we could discuss the future of our son. But if you're not interested in hearing what I have to say—'

'Of course I'm interested.'

'Very well. Then why don't we sit down like two civilised people and discuss this calmly?' And then they could continue on smoothly to the subject of Lucy's terms for becoming his mistress, Kahlil mused with satisfaction.

Lucy barely rested on the edge of a hard-backed chair. 'Well?' she prompted. 'What is it you wish to say to me? Though, be warned, I'm in no mood for compromise after the way my trust has been abused.'

'We both want the best for Edward,' Kahlil pointed out. He had imposed a compromise upon his father. Lucy would stay in Abadan. In return she would be allowed to keep Edward. If she refused, Edward would stay without her. The simple solutions were always the best. His people would demand nothing less.

But there was no reason for unpleasantness. He had already determined a way by which she could not only be persuaded to stay, but would do so willingly. And he wanted her to stay, Kahlil knew, feeling his senses quicken at the sight of Lucy's upturned face. Even animated by fury and suspicion she was irresistible. She was consumed by passion, and it had brought a flush to her pale cheeks a flush he would have preferred to impose some other way. He wanted her. He wanted Lucy Benson to stay in Abadan. He wanted her to be his mistress, and to share his bed, but for now...

'Your work has been well received,' he said, skilfully redirecting the conversation. 'There is talk of you doing more.'

'How can you bear to discuss that now?'

'You will be forced to stay here a little longer.'

'Forced?' Lucy repeated tensely. 'I will not be forced to do anything. I will take the return flight I have booked, and return to Abadan as my work here demands. I have other commitments back home.'

'You will not leave until you have finished here,' Kahlil countered. 'You will not forget your commitment to Abadan.'

'Forget?' Lucy said incredulously. 'How can I forget anything about Abadan? How can I forget the fact that I have a son whose father is Sheikh of Abadan? A son who, even now, is behind locked doors with an armed guard standing outside?'

'For his own protection,' Kahlil reminded her.

'And you really think that's the way I want him to live?'

'It is merely a precaution.'

'To protect him from whom?' Lucy said, her voice rising when Kahlil didn't reply. 'No, don't tell me. I already know. There is no danger to the royal family here in Abadan. This country is as stable as it could be. *"The people prosper under the benign reign of the Saeed al-Sharif family,"*' she said, quoting directly from one of the many articles she had read.

'Well done,' Kahlil murmured sardonically.

'I did my homework before I came here, Kahlil,' Lucy

said. 'So please don't try to fob me off with excuses. The only possible danger to Edward would come from outsiders. And as far as you and your father are concerned I am the only outsider in the palace. I can only conclude that you think you're protecting Edward from me!'

She was approaching hysteria, Lucy realised, stopping herself when she heard the panic in her voice. Her cheeks were burning with emotion, and she knew she had already said far too much. Her desperation might put thoughts into Kahlil's head—he might guess she was thinking about escape.

'You're wrong,' he said coldly. 'The fact that I have a son did come as a shock. And the implications for any son of mine are immense. Let me finish,' he insisted, when Lucy started to interrupt. 'As for my father, his reaction was typical of his generation. Things were very different in his day. He was as shocked as I was to learn he has a grandson. The guards make him feel comfortable—'

'Comfortable?' Lucy shook her head in amazement, wondering how anyone could find armed guards comforting.

'He is only trying to protect Edward. It's his way of showing he accepts him into the family.'

Ice ran through Lucy at the implications of that. She felt as if she was hanging on to Edward by her fingertips whilst a whole army of Saeed Al-Sharifs pulled him the other way.

'We both want the best for Edward,' Kahlil said, reclaiming her attention.

It was ironic. They were going to discuss Edward's future, the one thing that joined them, and yet she had never felt greater distance between them. 'Yes,' Lucy agreed tensely, 'we do.'

Deftly arranging his robes, Kahlil sat stiffly facing her. 'You shall have complete freedom while you are in Abadan.'

'Freedom?' Lucy repeated faintly. All her life she had

taken her freedom for granted. She realised now how precious it was.

'You will, of course, have a bodyguard with you at all times.'

'Ah,' she murmured, feeling as if a trap was closing around her.

'You must be patient,' Kahlil said, reading at least some of her thoughts. 'You must trust me.'

'Trust you?' Lucy repeated softly, flaring a wounded glance into his eyes. Had he forgotten what had happened between them on the first occasion they'd met? Had he forgotten how he'd left her—how he had disappeared out of her life without a trace?

'Of course,' he said impatiently, frowning a little.

'But I have airline tickets to take us home.'

'This is Edward's home,' Kahlil pointed out.

Once the official announcement was broadcast over the Abadanese airwaves the die would be cast, he reflected, watching Lucy closely. Then she would have to be far more open to any suggestions he made. His people would never countenance a child so close to the throne of Abadan leaving them to live in another country.

'*You* may leave whenever you wish,' he said smoothly.

Lucy stifled a gasp. Kahlil's meaning couldn't have been driven home with a sharper knife. She could go if she liked, but Edward would stay behind. She meant nothing to him, Lucy realised as she searched Kahlil's face. Having provided him with an heir, like one of his brood mares, she was now surplus to requirements.

What she saw was a cold, hard man. As far as Sheikh Kahlil ben Saeed Al-Sharif was concerned, with or without her, the path to claiming his son was clear. She had to get Edward away—she had to get them both away, as fast as she could.

'If you have pressing business to attend to back home,'

Kahlil continued levelly, as if they were discussing nothing more than that, 'you are of course free to leave Abadan the moment your contract here is completed.'

'With Edward?' Lucy tried one last time.

Kahlil remained silent.

'I will never leave Abadan without my son.'

'Then you will never leave Abadan.'

His words were like individual hammer blows, each one crushing her hope. But she had to stay strong—she had to stay strong for Edward.

'I'm sure we can find plenty to keep you happy here,' Kahlil observed.

Lucy was beyond speech, beyond argument. She could see Kahlil was growing restless as he laid out his master plan for her captivity. After all, she mused bitterly, it was only the small matter of her liberty and that of their son Edward under discussion—why should Sheikh Kahlil waste too much time over it?

And then Kahlil stood, and Lucy knew there was nothing left for either of them to say. The talking was over; only desperate action was left to her now.

'There may even be another contract for you,' he murmured pensively.

Still business! Did he think of nothing else? 'Don't trouble to invent work to keep me here, Kahlil. I don't need your charity.'

He made a light, surprised sound. 'I was talking about paid employment.'

Remembering a tender lover, as well as agonising over where that lover had gone, were no help to her now, Lucy told herself firmly. That man had vanished, leaving Sheikh Kahlil of Abadan in his place. And she would need money very soon if she was to escape. She had brought very little cash with her—not anticipating any of this. In this instance she couldn't afford to be proud.

'Perhaps an advance in cash on the work I have already completed?'

'In cash?'

'That would be great—'

'Where would you spend it? You can have everything you and Edward need charged to my account.'

Bought and paid for? Lucy thought angrily. No chance! But she clamped her mouth shut, determined not to say anything that would harm her cause. It was far better to let Kahlil think she was content with her lot, and with the arrangements he had made for her. She decided to ignore his personal offer to finance her, and keep to the safer option of what was properly owed to her.

'Perhaps part of what I'm owed could be paid into my account back home, and I could receive part in cash here,' she said casually, to deflect his suspicion. 'I would like to do some shopping—for Edward and for myself. It would be good for both of us to leave the confines of the palace, and I'd like to see the town.'

'Very well,' Kahlil agreed. 'That doesn't sound unreasonable.'

She must feel the palace was oppressive, Kahlil conceded, and if she did, chances were his son did too. The Golden Palace was his home; he loved it. But he could see that for Lucy it held quite different associations. It was time for him to show he could be merciful. He would ease the restrictions a little in order for her to see Edward's future home in a different light.

'There is a shopping mall in town, a short drive away. I could take you.'

Lucy's heart sank, and her throat was so dry she had to force out the words. 'I couldn't trouble you—'

'It would be no trouble,' Kahlil assured her. He thought at once of introducing Edward to the brash delights of the luxury mall: to ice cream sundaes and toy shops, and children's entertainers who were employed to keep youngsters happy during opening hours.

'No, really—a bodyguard would be fine,' Lucy said, hoping her acceptance of the security measures he'd had put in place would be enough to convince him.

Kahlil made a swift mental reality check. A trip into town for a member of the ruling family was no picnic. Ideally, he should give notice. Extra security would be needed for crowd control; barriers would need to be erected. There would be dignitaries he should meet, walkabouts to perform—none of which would be very much fun for Edward. 'Very well,' he agreed reluctantly. 'I will arrange for one of my personal bodyguards to accompany you. But first let me give you some money—'

'No!' Lucy exclaimed without thinking, seeing him reach for his wallet. 'Absolutely not.'

'You agreed to an advance on your wages,' Kahlil reminded her.

Who could tell how much money she might need? Lucy reflected grimly. And not for shopping. 'OK,' she said, 'an advance which I will pay back.' And she would, however long it took, and from wherever she eventually had to send the cheque.

'Well, I'm glad that's settled,' Kahlil said, moving towards the door. 'The shops are open until late in the evening. Be ready to leave in an hour.'

Oh, I will, Lucy told herself tensely.

Kahlil saw her to the door, as distanced from her now as if she was indeed an employee, Lucy thought, as she gave him the barest of acknowledgements before leaving—enough for politeness, enough to allay his suspicions. But once he had closed the door behind her and she was alone in the corridor her mind ran with the opportunity Kahlil had unwittingly handed to her. Now she had both the means and the opportunity to escape.

Fisting her hands in triumph, she exclaimed fiercely, 'Yes!'

Butter wouldn't melt in her mouth—or that was what everyone would think, Lucy concluded with relief as she caught sight of her face in one of the many palace mirrors. Dressed casually, plainly, so as not to attract attention, she was pushing Edward in his stroller down the long corridor leading to the grand entrance.

If the attending servants only knew what she had planned, but fortunately, their mind-reading skills were not as highly developed as those of their master, or they would have stopped her by now. Even so, her heart was thundering so loudly in her ears it muffled everything else. The thought of what she was about to do was terrifying.

Stealing a glance over her shoulder, she took in the crop-haired older man Kahlil had insisted must accompany her. He was a trusted member of the palace security team, and looked sharp. But that couldn't be helped. She would have to try and find a way to outfox him.

She had to get out of Abadan. It was her only hope. She had to negotiate with the ruling family from a position of strength. She had no alternative but to carry out her plan, regardless of the hurdles Kahlil put in her way.

As the bodyguard loaded the stroller into the back of a Range Rover Vogue, Lucy double-checked the fastenings on Edward's car seat, so that it would appear natural for her to just slip in beside him on the back seat. That way she could take careful note of every landmark they passed without drawing attention to herself.

Her passport was safely stowed away in her shoulder bag. Now all she needed was the opportunity to take over the four-wheel drive. Then she intended to make for the

Embassy and seek sanctuary there with Edward until a flight home was arranged for her.

There were still a few loose ends to tie up on her existing design contract at the palace, Lucy remembered, chewing her knuckles with anxiety, but that couldn't be helped. Edward's future happiness was at stake, and their liberty. Nothing mattered compared to that. She would shoulder whatever consequences arose from the breach of contract in a safer environment…repay any money, do whatever it took.

Trying to calm herself, Lucy remembered she was supposed to be watching the road signs as they drew closer to the centre of the town; she had already missed quite a few. Sidelining her other concerns, she made herself concentrate on the direction they were taking. She spotted the flag marking the Embassy and relaxed a little. It shouldn't be too hard to find again, even if it was dark by the time they left the shopping mall. There were plenty of road lights, and the town centre was clearly marked.

The shopping mall in Abadan was fantastic, and after an hour or so Lucy knew she had never spent money so freely. But beneath the fun of watching Edward clap his hands with delight was the worrying undercurrent of their impending flight. The professional bodyguard wouldn't leave their side for a moment, and right now she had no idea how she was going to get away.

On their way back to the car park she was ready to try anything. And a risky idea had occurred to her. The buggy was loaded with brightly coloured parcels that Edward had refused to relinquish. She should have insisted that he allow them to be taken away and delivered to the palace, but now his stubbornness, so like his father's, played right into her hands. There was enough shopping to keep the bodyguard busy loading the four-wheel drive for quite a few minutes.

'Shall we go back to the palace instead?' she said to him

pleasantly, when he asked her if she would like to have a coffee before leaving. Clearly Kahlil had instructed him to make sure that her every whim was accommodated. And it would be, Lucy determined. But not in the way that Kahlil intended. If he thought he could tame her with a bit of therapeutic shopping, he was wrong.

'If you're ready,' her shadow said politely, as he offered to take some of the bags from her.

Don't try to make a break too soon, Lucy warned herself as she thanked the man for his assistance. Edward was still hanging on to a couple of packages, and she hooked the rest onto the handles of the stroller. Everything hinged on keeping her head.

Fortunately Edward was asleep by the time they reached the off-roader. Waiting until the bodyguard had opened the rear door for her to climb in, Lucy took Edward carefully from the stroller to avoid waking him, and fastened him securely into the baby seat.

'I'll fire up the air-conditioning,' the bodyguard offered, knowing the heat might be uncomfortable once they left the precincts of the shopping centre.

'Would you?' Lucy said, hardly able to believe her luck. She felt a moment's guilt, because the man was so helpful, but, remembering the bigger picture, she hardened her heart. Closing Edward's door, Lucy watched the man climb into the driver's seat and start the engine. When he climbed out again to load the remaining parcels she waited for her chance as he pushed the door to. 'Do you need any help?' she asked, moving a step closer.

'No, I'm doing fine,' he said. 'You get in—this won't take a minute.'

'Oh, no,' Lucy exclaimed. 'I've dropped something—over by the door. Look—can you see it?'

'No problem. I'll get it for you,' he offered, turning back.

Lucy was in the driver's seat the moment his back was

turned. The boot was still open, but that couldn't be helped. Slipping the engine into gear, she stamped her foot down on the accelerator, and with a squeal of rubber on tarmac they were on their way, lurching over the kerb and barely missing the bodyguard as he wheeled around, realising a beat too late that he had been duped.

Peering through the windscreen as the Range Rover careered out of the car park and joined the main road, she made an abrupt U-turn across the double carriageway, bumping over the grass verge before heading at speed towards the outskirts of town, where she had first spotted the diplomatic quarter.

She had bargained on reaching the Embassy before Kahlil's guards could give chase, and certainly long before the police closed the roads. But she would have to stop somewhere soon to close the boot, Lucy realised, glancing anxiously through the mirror. She was already drawing attention, driving at speed with the back of the vehicle wide open. People were hitting their horns and gesticulating to warn her.

She looked back anxiously at Edward, and saw with relief that he was sleeping. Missing all the fun! Except that this wasn't fun, Lucy thought, forced to brake hard when her flight was abruptly aborted by a traffic snarl-up. She fought to control the Range Rover on the busy freeway as it skidded sideways, and was thrown back when it finally slammed to a halt on the hard shoulder. Gasping for breath, she wheeled round to check on Edward. He was still sleeping. And she could secure the back now.

Taking her chances, Lucy climbed out and quickly closed it up, oblivious to the shouts and horns of other motorists blasting in her ears. Running to the driver's door, she swung herself inside and cut back into the traffic while she was still slamming the door shut. It took her a few moments to calm down again, by which time she realised she had missed the turning. And now it was dark, and headlights were coming at her constantly. It was totally disorientating—and Kahlil had to know what had happened by now. Time was running out!

'Damn!' Lucy exclaimed softly, swerving off the busy dual carriageway by the first exit that came along. If she could work her way back into town, perhaps she could pick up the right road again.

But where was she now? she wondered, gazing around. She didn't have a clue. There were no streetlights to help her. She looked to left and to right, trying to make a decision. She wanted to head back the way she had come, but by the time she had looped her way off the main road it was impossible to tell which direction she was going in, and because she was in a dip the city lights had completely disappeared.

Totally disorientated, she carried on driving round the roundabout, looking for road signs, looking for anything that might help her. But there was nothing. And two of the exits off the roundabout were blocked by roadworks. That narrowed her choice down to two minor roads, neither of which were lit, or even surfaced properly. She would have to choose one of them, Lucy realised, and trust that it led back into town, or at the very least back onto the dual carriageway.

What option did she have? Lucy wondered anxiously. She would have to stay on the back roads for now, and trust to her sense of direction.

CHAPTER EIGHT

Now she was on higher ground Lucy could see the lights of the city in the distance. If she kept them in front of her, she knew nothing could go wrong. But there were enormous potholes on the unmade road and she was making painfully slow progress. And then the clouds shifted, allowing the moon to light her way. She saw that the track had narrowed, and there were no turning places if anything came towards her.

After a wide, sweeping curve in the road, the dirt and gravel changed to sand, and a rock face blanked off the passenger window, blocking her view of the reassuring lights in the distance. Reversing back seemed the right thing to do, but when she stopped and looked out of her own window she saw a sheer drop outside the driver's door. She couldn't risk it. Not with Edward in the back. She had to press on. She slowed the vehicle to a crawl. Frequent checks showed she was going downhill, and the track was widening out again too. Surely it couldn't be much longer before she could turn around.

Kahlil's rage was like a whirlwind, sweeping all before it. His anger was the silent ferocious kind that kicked everyone's brain into gear in an instant. The helicopters were already scrambled; roadblocks were set up. He had taken no more than five minutes to change into desert gear and grab the equipment he might need, and then the Hummer was waiting for him in the courtyard, engine running, the bodyguard who had accompanied Lucy and Edward sitting in the passenger seat. He would debrief him once they got on the road.

He should flay him alive, Kahlil thought, leaping into the driver's seat and slamming the door before the servants could get to it, but he had to admit to a grudging admiration for the man. It had taken some courage to return to the palace without either one of his charges. And he was just as guilty of underestimating Lucy Benson himself, Kahlil reflected as he pulled out of the palace gates. He had underestimated her and made the mistake of trusting her.

'The tracking device is working, I take it?' he said, dipping his head to look up at the night sky to assess the weather.

All the royal vehicles were fitted with tracking devices—something he could only be grateful Lucy couldn't know about. As long as it was functioning, and the weather was kind, it would be easy to find her.

'It is functioning, Majesty,' the bodyguard confirmed, still professional and calm in spite of his blunder. 'But the weather reports are bad.'

'Then we shall just have to hope we get to them before the sand blows up,' Kahlil murmured, not liking what he was seeing out of the windscreen.

As they approached the shopping mall he said abruptly, 'Did you see which way they went?'

'She crossed the dual carriageway and headed towards the roundabout—'

'Where the roadworks are being carried out?' Kahlil demanded, and before the man could answer he added grimly, 'Two of the roads are closed. I only hope she isn't heading for the desert.'

Silence hung heavy between the two men as the implications sank in. The bodyguard began calling up his colleagues on the radio as Kahlil concentrated on driving, his glance flicking edgily from the road to the screen of the satellite system positioned in front of them. Inwardly, he was raging. She had dared to abscond from the palace with his son, the eventual heir to the throne of Abadan—no punishment was great enough for that.

But any thoughts of retribution would have to wait, Kahlil realised as he noticed the way the clouds were scudding across the moon. The imperative now was to find Lucy and Edward before it was too late.

'Which way?' he said, thinking out loud as he slammed to a halt at the roundabout.

'I'm sorry—'

'Sorry?' he said abruptly, turning to the man at his side. 'It's a bit late for that.'

'The news I have just received, Majesty,' the man explained, brandishing the receiver in his hand, 'Miss Benson *is* heading for the desert.'

Kahlil swore eloquently. 'Can we still track her?'

'For the moment. But a sandstorm is blowing up.'

'Which road did she take?'

'Towards the border.'

'Alert the border patrols. Have them converge on the vehicle. The helicopters will have to return to base because of the weather, but we can follow them by road.'

A wave of anxiety washed over Kahlil as the bodyguard busied himself with the radio again. A sandstorm could stop the vehicle dead in its tracks and cover it in minutes. The terrain, already short on landmarks, could be transformed beyond recognition in the same amount of time. Even the most sophisticated satellite communication would prove useless if the Range Rover and everyone in it was buried beneath metres of sand.

Every muscle in his body clenched tight at the thought. She didn't know it yet, but Lucy and Edward were in very real danger. The desert was merciless, even to those who knew it intimately as he did. But to foreigners, a young woman with a child, probably with no water to sustain them through the heat of the day, and no blankets to warm them during the long desert night, it was nothing short of a disaster.

He guessed Lucy was already disorientated and frightened. He could only hope she had enough sense to find some high ground and park up before the forces of nature took over and hid the vehicle from sight—maybe for good.

The initial adrenalin rush that had accompanied Lucy's break for freedom had long since subsided. The weather had changed so rapidly, and with no warning whatsoever. One minute she had been driving along on a bright, clear night, with the moon as well as a good peppering of stars to light her way, and the next she was in a total blackout.

Remembering the precipice that had crept up on her earlier, she kept her speed as slow as possible. She had managed to turn the vehicle around, but she could not find the same track she had taken to come down into the valley. The city lights were gone, and the wind was growing stronger every minute. The Range Rover rocked alarmingly every time it was caught by one of the savage blasts, and sand covered the windscreen because the wipers had given up. And now she noticed there was very little fuel left in the tank. But at least they were on the move—they would surely encounter some form of civilisation soon…

As the steering wheel bucked in her hand Lucy let out a short scream, and when they juddered to a halt she realised they had a flat tyre. There was no way she could risk trying to change it on shifting sand, with the wind threatening to turn the vehicle over at any minute. Swinging round, she checked on Edward, and saw with relief that he was still sleeping. But they had no lights, no fuel, and her phone was dead too, she realised, flinging it aside with frustration. Now all she could do was switch off the engine and wait for the storm to subside.

Kahlil swore when the satellite screen went blank. 'Let's press on.'

'But where, Majesty? Which way?'

'We've chosen a trail; we'll stay on it. The road forked after its descent into the valley—she may not have noticed if she tried to turn around. We'll keep to the left, take our chances.' And just hope I've got it right, he thought grimly.

The wind was screaming as it whipped the sand into heavy curtains of dust and grit, and Kahlil knew that even he, with his encyclopaedic knowledge of the desert, might get it wrong.

'Did you get through to the border patrols before we lost the signal?'

When the man confirmed that he had, Kahlil acknowledged the information with a curt dip of his chin. But he didn't relax at all. Even using a pincer movement, this only gave them two slim chances to find one precious grain of sand in the desert.

It was like being in a riverbed in full flood, Lucy thought. She had never noticed how like water sand could be. The sand she knew was harmless, and inactive, but this sand, blowing before the wind, was deadly. It ran in gullies, filling every nook and cranny, and rose in waves to flood the larger indentations in the land.

She risked opening the window to lean out, and got a mouthful as well as her eyes full of sand for her trouble. And now it was already well over the wheel hubs, creeping rapidly up the sides of the vehicle. Even if she could have changed the flat tyre there was no way they were going anywhere now. But there were still rock formations, standing proud of the sand, and if the worst came to the worst, she would take Edward and escape through the back window. She would climb up as high as she could, and wait there for the wind to die down.

Slamming back in her seat, Lucy shut her eyes tight and forced back tears of sheer terror. How could she take a baby outside the vehicle in this? But what would happen to them both if she stayed where she was?

After a few minutes of bitter reflection, during which she blamed herself for everything, something around her changed. Holding her breath, she listened. It hardly seemed possible. She opened her eyes, and then opened the window and leaned out. As fast as it had blown up, the sandstorm was dying down again.

The moon was like a giant spotlight, pooling light around the vehicle as the clouds of dust subsided. But there was still no sign of a road. Even the rocks she had hoped to climb up to escape the river of sand had completely disappeared in the few minutes she had looked away from them. The land outside the vehicle was a moonscape, a featureless blank, Lucy saw, her relief swiftly turning to despair. How could anyone hope to find them now?

She started shivering with terror, and with cold too. But there were travel rugs in the back, as well as a bottle of water she had picked up in the shopping mall, along with some of Edward's favourite food. At least she had enough for a picnic when he woke up.

She hadn't known silence could be so absolute, Lucy realised as she tucked a rug around Edward. Backing out of the door, she stood very still, staring around in wonder. The sky was quite clear, and looked like a piece of black velvet studded with diamonds. But there were no city lights to offer any comfort, and no roads to help her get her bearings. There was no sign of habitation at all. And her phone still refused to work.

At least Edward was warm, and they had some provisions and water to keep them going. They would be found. She had to believe that.

Kahlil exclaimed viciously beneath his breath. The border patrols had reported picking up a weak signal from Lucy's vehicle, but it had died again. Slamming his fists down on the steering wheel with frustration, he threw the gears into reverse.

'She's obviously in a dip,' he said. 'We'll retrace our steps—this time down at the lowest point.'

'But Majesty,' the bodyguard protested, knowing his primary task was to protect the heir to the throne, and only after that his son, 'the surface will be treacherous.'

'All the more reason to hurry, then,' Kahlil told him curtly, swinging the wheel around. 'You concentrate on trying to restore the satellite link.'

'Yes, sire,' the man agreed reluctantly.

Lucy was wishing a different set of circumstances had brought her to the desert. It was so beautiful. She might have been alone on the planet with Edward. Stars like so many friendly eyes seemed to be keeping watch over them until rescue came.

Now she was going crazy, Lucy thought, pulling her rug a little tighter around her shoulders as she climbed into the back seat next to Edward. There was nothing at all romantic about their situation. The valley through which she had been driving had disappeared, and they had very nearly been buried alive. Clinging to Edward for comfort, she rested her face next to his and tried not to wake him with her shaking...

She had been dozing, Lucy realised, jerking awake. How long until dawn? She leaned over to peer out of the window. There was a faint lilac shadow above the horizon that filled her with hope. And then she noticed something else. At first she thought she was hallucinating, or maybe it was just wishful thinking. She checked to see that it wasn't moonlight refracting off the sand coating the glass. But the pinpricks of light didn't stay still. As she narrowed her eyes to try and make them out, they seemed to be dancing up and down. It was headlights! Coming their way! Vehicles being driven at such speed they were bouncing over the sand dunes. Any minute now they would be found!

Rescued! Lucy gave a sharp cry of relief, then as quickly as it had come, her elation died. It could be anyone—bandits or thieves—and she had no way of protecting Edward. She stared out again. The vehicles were closing in fast.

Quickly releasing the buckles on the baby seat, she hauled the half-sleeping child onto her knee. Wrapping him completely in the travel rug, she pushed open the door with her foot and went to climb out. But the trucks had already drawn up in formation around her. There was no escape, Lucy realised, shrinking back inside the Range Rover. And now she saw they were army vehicles. But whose army?

Her fear communicated itself silently to the warm little bundle on her knee. Edward might be small, but he was strong, and it took all her strength to stop him staring out of the window.

'Please—please don't,' she begged, drawing him down below the sill. In trying to protect him she had brought him into worse danger than ever, Lucy realised, covering his head with her arm as she cautiously looked out. Their doors were locked. She'd already checked that. But men were starting to exit the army trucks—men in uniform, with guns at their sides. They could easily shoot out the locks—or worse. And the moon was brighter than ever, acting like a searchlight for the soldiers.

There was not a chance that she could get out with Edward, and even if there was where would she go? Beyond the circle of moonlight the desert was completely black. She couldn't risk it, Lucy realised, clutching Edward to her as the soldiers formed a tight ring around them.

Their appearance was terrifying. Dressed all in black, with baggy trousers and tunics secured by broad leather belts holding a sheath for curving scimitars, just their glittering eyes showed beneath the black *howlis* they wore wound around their heads—and each pair of eyes was trained on her!

She heard one of the men issue instructions, in Arabic, and then he pointed away from the Range Rover. She turned to look through the back window to see what he was showing the other men. Racing up from the rear, another vehicle, headlights flashing, was approaching at speed.

And then everything seemed to happen at once. The leader of the men approached the side of the car where Lucy was crouching with Edward, hammered on the window and with imperative gestures demanded she get out.

Stricken with panic, and only aware of the gun at his side, she fumbled with the door handle, finally managing to free the catch. But as the door swung open, she shrank back, clutching Edward tight—too tight. With a yowl of protest he broke away, and before Lucy knew what was happening the man had leaned in and snatched him from her.

With a cry she launched herself after them. But, stumbling on the treacherous sandy ground, she made achingly slow progress as she chased after them in shoes meant for town. The wind was still gusting in spiteful little eddies, and she had sand everywhere—in her eyes, her mouth, and her ears. Finally the man stopped, and Edward was within her reach! But as she lunged forward to take him back someone stepped in her way.

'Kahlil!' Lucy sobbed.

'Allah be praised—you are safe!' he cried hoarsely, seizing Edward.

But Edward was fully awake now and did not recognise

the man in front of him—the fearsome figure with a black *howlis* wrapped around his head and only his glittering eyes on show. 'Mumma!' he screamed in panic, reaching for Lucy.

For a moment Lucy hung back, certain that prison or worse was to be her fate. Kahlil had not even acknowledged her presence.

He turned and looked down at her, his eyes black and hard. 'You had better hold your son,' he said coldly, 'and then follow me.'

CHAPTER NINE

LUCY had never seen such contained fury. It was all the more alarming because Kahlil didn't need to raise his voice to have the most hardened desert soldiers back away as he strode through them. He opened the door of his vehicle and helped her to climb in. Lucy seized some comfort where she could, in the warmth of Edward's chubby arms pinned around her neck, and the texture and touch of his soft face pressed hard against her own.

She sat in silence, holding Edward, waiting for Kahlil, who was issuing orders to his men. One by one the trucks turned away, heading towards the silvery light threading across the horizon. Then, whirling on his heels, Kahlil strode back, swung in to the driver's seat and slammed the door shut.

'There is no baby seat,' he said, without sparing her a glance. 'I have never had need for one. I take it you can keep my son safe on your knee during the journey?'

'I see no reason why not,' Lucy said quietly. 'I have kept him safe this far—without your assistance or anyone else's.'

They drove in tense silence for quite a while. Lucy had no idea where they were heading, and didn't much care, as long as when they arrived she could keep Edward with her. Glancing across at Kahlil, she saw that his anger had not lessened at all.

'Do you know what you've done?' he said, taking his cue from her glance. 'You could have been killed—and Edward too! What were you thinking of?'

'I had to get away. I couldn't stay locked up with my son like a prisoner in the Golden Palace.'

'He's my son too—'

'Yes, he's our son,' Lucy said. 'But, more than that, Edward is his own person. We should both respect that.'

'Don't you dare talk to me about respect,' Kahlil warned tensely, 'when you've shown me none.' Ripping off his desert headdress, he tossed it angrily behind his seat. And, seeing him properly for the first time, Edward exclaimed with pleasure and reached out.

Kahlil's face softened immediately, and without taking his attention from the road he took Edward's hand in a gentle grasp and brought it to his lips. 'Quite an adventure, little man,' he murmured. 'Where the hell were you going with him?' he said under his breath, shooting a glance at Lucy. 'What on earth did you think you were doing, heading out into the desert without proper supplies, in the middle of the night?'

'It was early evening when we set off, and I had no intention of going into the desert. A road was closed. I became disorientated—' Lucy stopped. Why should she have to defend herself? Suddenly she felt very tired. She couldn't summon the spirit to engage in the type of debate Kahlil was after on the rights and wrongs of the situation. All she was concerned with now was that Edward was no longer in danger. She wanted nothing more than to hold him, let go of the fear in her mind for a few hours, and sleep.

'You might never have been found.'

Kahlil's voice jerked her back to full attention again,

'I should have realised you could not be trusted.'

'That's a terrible thing to say. Hurt me if you must, but remember that it was you who put me in a position where I felt like a prisoner—where I thought you were going to take Edward...' It was no good, Lucy realised, seeing Kahlil's face was unresponsive, still hardened against her.

'If it had been left up to you I would never have known Edward existed,' he said coldly.

'How dare you judge me?' Lucy exclaimed. 'You were the one who slept with me and then left like a thief in the night. You didn't even have the decency to reveal your true identity, let alone leave your telephone number.'

Kahlil controlled his desire to snap back. He knew what Lucy said about that night was true. And he could not remain immune to how desperately low and weary she was. It brought home to him how terrified she must have been. Yes, she had been foolish, and reckless, and had set herself against him, but it gave him no pleasure to browbeat her more when she was so clearly at her lowest ebb.

His emotions were in turmoil, Kahlil realised tensely. He was relieved she was safe, but angry that he cared. She had stolen his son from him in every way that a woman could steal a child away. If he were only in his right mind he would never be able to forgive her. Seeing the state she was in, and the even sorrier state to which his angry words had reduced her, gave him no satisfaction. But he should throw every reprimand he could at her. She had put herself as well as the child in mortal danger. She must learn to respect the desert as he did.

Glancing across, he saw Lucy was swaying in her seat. She was ashen-faced, totally spent. The most basic human instinct he possessed demanded he take care of her. 'There's water and food in the back—just reach across,' he said curtly.

'Thank you,' she murmured. And he couldn't help noticing how she saw to Edward's needs before her own, or how her hands trembled as she struggled with the water container.

'Where are you taking us?' Lucy said, feeling a little more composed once she had nibbled the fruit and cheese Kahlil insisted she eat. The moon had slipped behind a cloud again, and without fixed points of reference she couldn't imagine how he knew where he was going.

'We're going to my hunting lodge,' he said. 'It's closer than the palace.'

Lucy was relieved they were speaking again, but she was still badly shaken after the ordeal, and Kahlil's cold manner left her in no doubt as to his feelings on her flight from the palace. 'Will it take long?' she said, keen to keep the tenuous line of communication between them open.

'It won't take long now we are out of the *wadi*—the dried-up riverbed,' he explained. 'All the loose sand collects there and has been slowing our progress.'

'I see.'

'We will be quiet now. My son must sleep.'

His son! Kahlil made her feel like a stranger, an onlooker in Edward's life, whereas he was the one who had stepped in to make things right. But she had no one to blame but herself. As far as Kahlil was concerned, with her flight from the palace she had forfeited the right to care for Edward. And in Abadan Kahlil's word was law. Like his father's. The chance of taking Edward out of the country now, Lucy accepted grimly, was absolutely nil.

She didn't realise that she had fallen into an exhausted slumber until she woke when the vehicle slowed to a crawl. Instantly awake, she looked around. Her first sight of Khalil's hunting lodge came as a complete shock. She had been expecting something along the lines of the Golden Palace, something towering and vast, monumentally impressive. But in a blinding flash of understanding she knew that the Golden Palace was a show, and what she was looking at now reflected the other, and perhaps the true side of Kahlil's family coin.

Nothing must have changed in a thousand years—two thousand years, Lucy guessed, gazing around in wonder. The sky, like an arc over their heads, was silver-grey and pink, with dashes of tangerine where the sun was just starting to creep over the horizon. But dozens of torches still burned brightly around the encampment, illuminating tented pavilions grouped around a limpid oasis. It was a magical scene, like something she might have dreamed of. But there was a feeling of impermanence about it, as if like all the other desert landmarks the camp might shift and change, and even disappear entirely within the space of a few short minutes.

When Edward murmured in his sleep Lucy turned her attention to him, dropping a kiss on his smooth brow, feeling a rush of relief that he was safe. It had been a very long night for them both, she reflected sleepily.

Kahlil brought the vehicle to a halt outside one of the grand tents. There was a guard in Arab dress waiting for them, accompanied by two women. They all bowed low as Kahlil swung out of the driver's seat.

And then the guard was at Lucy's side of the vehicle, reaching in and lifting Edward out before she realised what was happening. She barely had time to voice a protest, and was forced to watch as Kahlil received his sleeping child into his arms and kissed his face.

Closing his eyes for a moment, Kahlil raised his face to the sky in thankfulness, and at that moment Edward woke. Instead of bursting into tears, as Lucy had fully expected, he smiled up at Kahlil with complete confidence. And then he even tried to grab hold of the guard's beard as his father took him away.

A stab of anguish pierced Lucy's heart as she hurried after them. She could see how happy father and son were to be reunited. And Kahlil was so tender with Edward she couldn't help but feel threatened. To her surprise, Kahlil stopped and, waving the servants away, waited for her to catch up.

'Just a word,' he said, dipping his head to speak to her discreetly. 'We have a chance here to discuss all the implications of our situation before it becomes general knowledge.'

'*It* is called Edward,' Lucy said, bridling at the authoritative tone. 'And do we always have to argue like this in front of him?'

'Maybe if things had been different—'

'Maybe if you'd allowed them to be, Kahlil—or is it Kahl?' Lucy shot back angrily.

'Do you think I've forgotten?' Kahlil asked her in a low, impassioned voice. 'And do you think I've forgotten a single detail I've learned about Edward since I discovered he was my son?'

'He's my son too!' Lucy retorted in a furious whisper. 'He doesn't even know you!'

'Haven't you done enough damage? Kahlil demanded, catching hold of Lucy's arm to bring her alongside him as he took off towards the entrance of the nearest pavilion. 'Don't try and put me in the wrong, Lucy. It was you who put Edward's life in danger with this foolhardy expedition—and you who tried to deny me my son!'

His staccato accusations rained down on her like bullets. Lucy accepted that everything Kahlil said was true, but there would have been no need for subterfuge had he remained with her long enough for them to exchange personal details twenty-one months ago. And no need for her flight from the palace if she had not been isolated there with an imagination that filled in every blank with dread.

They were both to blame. But all that mattered now, Lucy realised, gazing at their son, who was watching them both intently, was that Edward was safe. She smiled at him reassuringly, and Edward smiled back. But as Kahlil led them into the pavilion it was his shoulder into which Edward nestled his head.

Setting Edward down on a bank of cushions, Kahlil lowered the heavy curtain across the entrance to keep out the wind and sand. As he turned up the flame on an old oil lamp Lucy noticed the brazier glowing brightly in one corner. The tent was really cosy, she realised with surprise. The chill of the desert night seemed far away here. But still the modern world intruded, when Kahlil spoke into his mobile phone.

Once again his expression was hard and fierce. She guessed the call was to confirm the stand-down of his troops now that she had been found. But when the call ended and he turned to look at Edward she saw his face change completely. Now he was warm, and wry, and full of humour, and he made Edward laugh. Then he glanced her way and he changed again; his eyes were cold and steady, as if he was warning her to expect nothing from him in the way of forgiveness.

Kahlil would fight for his son. Lucy was more certain of that than ever. And when Edward was old enough to understand he would fight for the right to see his father. She was on the outside already, just where Kahlil wanted her.

The same guard who had greeted them on arrival slipped through the curtain and made a swift bow of obeisance to Kahlil. The two men smiled, and even Lucy smiled when she saw Edward reaching up as if he wanted to tug the soldier's beard again. She didn't need to know the language to hear the pride in Kahlil's voice. She guessed the guard must have praised Edward's courage, and she was proud of her son too, but ice trickled through her veins as she watched him interacting with his father. It seemed to her that Edward was already part of another world…

'I am sending Edward to sleep in one of the women's tents,' Kahlil said, turning to her at last, 'so that he can get some rest. They will see to him,' he insisted, when Lucy began to protest. 'And you can see him as soon as he wakes up. We will bathe now, and then we will talk.'

Kahlil had assumed control of the whole situation—of her

life, Lucy realised. Normally she would have stood her ground, but right now she was exhausted, both mentally and physically. And how could she subject Edward to any more conflict between his parents?

'The minute he wakes up, they'll call me?' she said, looking for reassurance in that staggeringly handsome face made of stone.

'They'll call you,' Kahlil said.

There was already a new slant to Edward's life, Lucy realised as he went willingly with the guard. Sitting confidently on the man's shoulders, he gave her a wave, and she gave him a wave back, and a smile. But she couldn't help feeling Kahlil had set a new regime in place for Edward: one that was harsh and demanding, perfectly suited to a fledgling desert prince.

She flared a look of anguish at Kahlil. How could he know anything about Edward's needs? Their son was still a baby.

'What's that in Edward's hand?' she said, stepping forward with alarm just as the heavy curtain was about to fall back into place.

'My gauntlet,' Kahlil said without concern.

'Of course—you hunt with falcons,' she murmured, realising Edward must have found it amongst the cushions.

And when he was old enough Sheikh Kahlil ben Saeed Al-Sharif would give his son a hawk, and teach him to ride bareback, and to shoot straight, like a true Abadanese—all the things she could never hope to teach him.

How could she deny Edward the other half of his heritage? Taking him from Abadan would deny him his birthright. When he grew up he would blame her for the loss. And when that happened she would lose him for ever. She had to search for a compromise. It had to be possible. Yes, Kahlil could teach Edward how to be a leader of men, but she could teach him how to care.

'Your bath has been run for you,' Kahlil said, gesturing carelessly to another opening in the pavilion Lucy gathered must lead to a second room. 'I will return shortly, and then we will talk.'

Lucy resisted the impulse to salute. If the situation hadn't been so serious she might have done. She was dead on her feet, but thankfully she hadn't lost her sense of humour, she reflected ruefully. And that had saved many a captive before her. She turned at a discreet cough to see two serving women smiling as they beckoned to her from the entrance to the second room.

Was she to be prepared for the Sheikh? Lucy wondered cynically as she viewed the deep bath. The surface was completely covered with rose petals, and the scent was sublime. But the women were still waiting for her to make some response, and showed no sign of leaving her as they stood smiling with stacks of fluffy white towels balanced on their outstretched arms.

Lucy bowed and smiled, and managed a few words of Abadanese which she could see were appreciated. She was delighted at the prospect of washing off all the sand and grit she had collected during the long night, but she had no intention of bathing with an audience. Taking some towels, she thanked them again and then walked to the entrance and stood beside it, so that there could be no misunderstanding. Exchanging swift glances, they pointed to a robe in ice-blue silk and then, bowing their way out, they left.

It was a relief to know she wouldn't have to wear her grimy clothes any more, and this was ecstasy…bliss, Lucy thought, sinking a little deeper into the warm, fragrant water. And it was all the better for being so unexpected in the middle of the desert. A bath made for two—that thankfully she was enjoying by herself.

Her thoughts turned immediately to Kahlil. He had come to rescue the heir of Abadan; she knew that. But it was hard to shut out the image of his strong hands controlling the wheel as she sat next to him. And then it was a very small step to recall how those hands had also controlled her, bringing her pleasure beyond anything she could ever have imagined… But Lucy knew that was one thought-robbing indulgence she could not afford.

She sat up so abruptly the water crashed over the edge of the bath. She had a crisis on her hands; this was not the time to be diverted by fantasies that belonged to the past.

'Are you still in there?'

She tensed at the sound of Kahlil's voice, realising she was aroused, and that now she was feeling guilt and shock in equal measure. 'Just a minute,' she called out, 'I'll be right there.'

Water splashed everywhere as Lucy leapt out of the bath and grabbed the towels. She wrapped herself in them quickly, as if at any minute Kahlil might come striding in and find her pink and flushed naked body stirred by thoughts of him.

Drying herself quickly, she towelled her wet hair as best she could and contained it in a towel turban on top of her head. The silk robe felt wonderful next to her skin—but she would have to do without underwear, she realised, frowning. It couldn't be helped. Kahlil was waiting, and she wanted to get their discussion over with as quickly as possible. Bracing herself, she went out to face him.

For a moment they stared at each other from either end of the tented pavilion. Kahlil had changed too, into a black silk robe that hinted provocatively at the magnificent form beneath. His head was uncovered, his thick black hair was still damp from bathing, and there was a slight flush to his high cheekbones, as if his bath had taken the form of a rigorous workout in the limpid oasis.

Lucy felt her body respond to him, melting beneath his stare. It was as if his black glittering gaze had the power to undress her—not that it took much imagination to see her nipples erect beneath the gossamer fabric. Instinctively she raised her arms to cover her chest.

'Don't,' he murmured, continuing to stare at her.

'We have to talk,' Lucy said huskily. 'And I want to go to Edward.'

'He is being well cared for,' Kahlil assured her. 'He was still awake when I left him.'

The same flood of frustration, of resentment at Kahlil's interference must have shown clearly on her face.

'He at least enjoyed the adventure,' Kahlil said soothingly, holding out his hand to her.

Lucy stared at him like a fool. Was she supposed to take his hand now, as if they were lovers, and allow him to take her wherever he chose?

'Don't you want to see him?'

'Of course I do,' Lucy exclaimed, coming to with a start. Her bare feet made no sound as she padded rapidly across priceless rugs, hurrying towards the curtained entrance.

'Wait,' Kahlil said as she drew level with him. 'You will need to cover yourself first, and put on some sandals.'

He slipped a cotton robe over her head himself and, removing the towelling turban, replaced it with a beautifully jewelled scarf in a deeper shade of blue.

'To keep out the sand now your hair is clean again,' he murmured, anticipating her refusal. 'And now these,' he said, dipping down to retrieve a pair of simple sandals that had been left for her—nothing more than a strip of leather to fit between her toes on a cork sole. 'Now you are dressed for the desert,' he said with approval.

And this time he stood aside to let her pass, Lucy noticed with interest. When all she had anticipated was his anger he showed respect. Kahlil was really a very confusing and complex man. But as he showed her into another vast tent Lucy remembered Kahlil's heritage was part Eastern, part

Western—the perfect mix in a man, maybe, but dangerous for her, when everything hinged on keeping her wits about her for the sake of Edward's safe return home.

'Safia will take care of Edward for you,' Kahlil said. 'She speaks very good English.'

Jolted from her reverie, Lucy smiled at the older woman. Edward had fallen asleep at last, clearly exhausted by his adventures. And as she gazed down at his pink cheeks she was relieved that her worries about him had been removed for now.

'You must be exhausted too,' Kahlil observed, standing at the other side of the cot. 'Would you rather sleep before we talk?'

'I couldn't sleep,' Lucy said honestly.

'Then why don't we leave Safia and Edward here?' he suggested. 'My tent is close by.'

'Yes,' she said.

Lucy knew she wouldn't be able to rest until she had found out how Kahlil intended to proceed. Once she knew that she could decide upon her own actions. But she felt a little reassured. Kahlil seemed more reasonable here. The desert seemed to have a soothing effect on him. Maybe now they could have a balanced discussion about Edward's future…

'When the sun rises,' Kahlil murmured, pausing beside the crib to gaze down at his sleeping son, 'you will see the mountains that mark the borders of your kingdom from this window.'

Lucy felt as if she had been slapped in the face—brought round from her romantic daydreams with a blow. She had been such a fool to think Kahlil would soften. He was just as tyrannical, just as hard and uncaring as he had ever been. She had mistaken his confidence in the outcome of their discussions for compromise, his easy manner for forgiveness. But as far as Sheikh Kahlil ben Saeed Al-Sharif was concerned his son's future was already cast in stone.

CHAPTER TEN

KAHLIL had tea brought to them in his luxurious quarters. Hot and sweet for her shock, Lucy gathered, as the liquid burned her tongue.

'Patience,' Kahlil counselled, removing the small vase-like glass container from her hands. They were shaking, Lucy noticed as he poured some iced water for her from a gold pitcher studded with jewels.

'May I suggest we move outside to watch the sun rising?' Kahlil suggested when she had drained her glass.

He was behaving so pleasantly, Lucy registered dimly, but she had to be cautious. She knew her normal wariness was cancelled out by exhaustion and shock. She followed him outside like an automaton, not sure she had the strength to battle with him, only knowing that with Edward's future at stake she would.

'I do this every time I come here,' Kahlil said, turning to Lucy and leading her forward out onto the veranda of his pavilion, where a bank of silk cushions had been set for them.

Lucy breathed with astonishment as she took in everything properly for the first time. The desert was laid out before them like a gently undulating beach. It stretched away to the jagged black mountain peaks Kahlil had spoken of to Edward. The play of light on rock and sand was extraordinary. The mountains in the far distance were still shrouded in mist against the silver-pink sky, but their snowy peaks were just visible. And as they watched the fiery fingers of desert sun reaching above the horizon the mist peeled back, revealing the massive range in all its splendour.

Lucy turned to look at Kahlil, gazing out across his desert kingdom. How tall and proud he was. His black robe, caught by the wind, moulded his limbs and outlined his magnificent physique. She longed to reach him—she could only hope that maybe he would make an effort too.

'I can see why you love it so much,' she said impulsively.

Did she really understand? Kahlil wondered as he turned to look at Lucy. Could she grow to love this land as he did? He stopped himself. That was an irrelevance. Then he saw her shiver again, and, finishing the tea he had been nursing in a single gulp, he went back inside the pavilion to find something warm for her.

Lucy started as Kahlil bent over her to wrap a silky-soft hand-woven blanket around her shoulders.

'You must be exhausted to still be shivering,' he said, arranging it deftly. 'It's really quite warm now.'

His touch was electrifying. He barely brushed her with his hands, but that had no relation to the intensity of her response. 'I am a little tired,' Lucy said to explain her reaction

'Blue is definitely your shade,' he added, straightening up, 'and I like the veil…very feminine.'

Tired as she was, Lucy lowered it from her head immediately, and flung it defiantly around her shoulders like a scarf.

Her hair was dry, and shimmered around her face like a golden nimbus, and he loved to see the challenge back in her eyes. Beautiful, Kahlil mused. Too bad there were so many complications… But he would have her, whatever difficulties would have to be overcome.

Lucy coloured as Kahlil looked at her. She knew she must keep the lines of communication open between them somehow. Outright defiance was no help to her cause. She had to use subtlety, and appear more malleable. 'These colours are lovely,' she said, admiring the lovely shawl he had brought her. And the almost weightless wrap was quite useful—to hide the evidence of her arousal, so intense, still so easily provoked by Kahlil.

'Do you mind if I join you?' he said, glancing down at the cushions where she was sitting.

Sheikh Kahlil asking permission for anything had to be a first, Lucy thought with surprise. And how could she object? It was his pavilion, his cushions, his desert kingdom. 'Of course I don't mind.'

This was not what she had expected, Lucy realised as Kahlil settled beside her. She was beginning to think her act was unnecessary, he seemed so reasonable. Recriminations, blame, anger, she had been prepared for. But this sudden ease between them made her hope they could talk, settle things amicably.

Confidence heightened her awareness of Kahlil's powerful body reclining so near to her own. She hadn't anticipated sitting so close to him, but she could have predicted her reaction. She was on fire. It was as if Kahlil had simply stepped across all the divisions between them to bathe her in desire.

They sat in silence, and very gradually Lucy became aware that her muscles were unknotting. Deep down she knew she should be tense, and alert, on her guard, but she was not. She should be demanding answers, looking for strategies to curb Kahlil's will, but she couldn't—not yet, anyway. Just for a little while she wanted to believe that everything would be all right. She wanted the beauty of the desert to wash over them, to let the peace of their surroundings heal the rift between them. All right, Lucy reflected dreamily, so it might be wishful thinking, but right now, reclining on silk cushions so close to Kahlil, anything seemed possible…

'Wake up…wake up, Lucy.'

Reluctantly, Lucy opened her eyes. And then she leapt

into an upright sitting position. She had been asleep in Kahlil's arms, resting her head on his shoulder! Her flesh still burned with the touch of him—she raised her hand in astonishment to her mouth. Was it a dream? She was sure she could feel the ghost of a kiss on her parted lips.

'What time is it?' she said, surfacing fast from her drowsy state.

'Almost lunchtime,' Kahlil said. 'I didn't want to wake you.'

But he had removed the wrap from her shoulders, and, looking up, Lucy saw that an awning had been erected over their heads to keep them in the shade. Even so it was hot. 'We haven't talked yet,' she said, fanning herself. All the good done by her sleep vanished as she remembered the events that had brought them to this point.

'Not yet,' Kahlil agreed, flexing his limbs and springing up. 'It will have to wait now. Edward will be ready to eat—'

'Edward! Where is he?'

'Where we left him,' Kahlil said, looking down at her, his expression hidden in the shadow cast by the giant canopy.

Lucy relaxed. 'Of course. I don't know what I was thinking.'

'He is well looked after, I can assure you. Your clothes will have been laundered if you would like to change back into them before lunch.'

Yes, she would like to change into something more conventional, Lucy thought, realising she was still wearing the exotic but rather impractical gowns. And as for lunch—Kahlil made it sound so civilised, so normal, but nothing about the situation was normal.

'I thought we would have lunch with our son—unless you prefer not to?'

And be excluded totally? 'Of course I'd like to.'

'Good. Edward will like that.'

The ribbon of fear that had started threading its way through Lucy's optimism drew tight. Kahlil sounded so confident, so sure. It was as if he had known Edward all his life and she was the outsider.

'I want to see him now,' she insisted, her throat tightening with apprehension. 'Before lunch, before I change—' She stopped, seeing the expression in Kahlil's eyes harden.

'Did you think I would have him stolen away while you were sleeping?'

Lucy reddened, knowing she had attempted to pull off something very similar.

'Don't worry, Lucy,' Kahlil said, reading her like a book. 'I don't work that way. Whatever action I take regarding my son will be out in the open, for all men to see, all men to judge.'

The thought of Kahlil taking action against her with all the might of Abadan's legal system behind him filled Lucy with dread. And then, gripping her arms, Kahlil looked deep into her eyes so she could not mistake the purpose in his.

'You don't know me at all, do you? Edward is fine. Safia is looking after him, as I told you she would. And when you are ready to go for lunch you will see him for yourself.'

It was subtle, but still there; Kahlil was dictating when she could and could not see Edward.

Her stomach contracted with resentment and with fear. Her escape attempt had failed utterly, and in fact she had only made things worse.

Lucy's swift intake of breath as emotion overtook her drew Kahlil to her. She was so strong, and to see her brought low, and to know that he was the cause of her distress, aroused feelings in him that were new. He didn't intend to kiss her. It was the last thing on his mind. He didn't mean to frighten her either, or to threaten her, and what he saw in her eyes was fear. It made him recognise his wish to bring her under his protection.

Lucy Benson was like a madness that possessed him, Kahlil realised as he drew her close. He wanted his son more than anything in the world, but he wanted Lucy as well. One the laws of Abadan would secure for him, the other he might have to seduce into submission. But he would have them both.

Even now, even at her lowest ebb, she fought him off. But as he drank in her sweetness, and murmured soft words in his own language to soothe her, she grew calmer, until at last she melted against him and slowly turned her face up for his kiss.

Kahlil's hunger surged when he saw the desire in Lucy's eyes. He ached with the need to pleasure her, to comfort and protect her. He wanted her in his bed, awaiting the pleasure he would bring her night after night…until he tired of her.

He had been forced to amend his plan to make her his mistress. The Constitution of Abadan required Edward to be a legitimate heir: for that he would have to marry Edward's mother.

It wasn't a problem, Kahlil reflected, seeing how Lucy hungered for him. She would agree to anything he suggested. Better still, she was a successful career woman. She would see the sense in putting a time limit on their arrangement. She would be hugely flattered that he wished to elevate her above the rank of mere mistress. She had everything to gain: money, prestige, the throne of Abadan for her son, for goodness' sake. What more could any woman want? And, although marriage with a woman like Lucy Benson would normally be unthinkable, it was expedient in this case, and would certainly legitimise their son as the law required.

And love?

Kahlil made a sound of derision deep in his throat as the crazy notion struck him out of nowhere. The lure of a throne, a fortune and a title would be more than enough for Lucy. He had seen the lie lived out in many other royal households. The stamp of royalty was all it took to convince even the most cynical of women that she was in love.

But now Lucy responded to his wordless growl with a soft, deep-seated whimper of her own, and Kahlil frowned, drawing back for a moment. In that instant she had seemed too trusting, too defenceless—

Love?

This time he dismissed the notion out of hand and kissed her again, passionately, hard, relishing the way she melted against him. *Lust is not love,* he scolded his inner voice triumphantly. *And lust is something I know all about.*

But as he deepened the kiss Kahlil wanted love on every level. He was hungry for it, starving. The erotic level was what he craved most now. He needed to lose himself in the silky darkness of her body, put thinking aside. He couldn't wait to tutor her in all the seductive mysteries of the East—a day of passion to seal their bargain.

'Lunch,' Lucy told him softly when he let her go.

'A late lunch,' he growled, swinging her into his arms.

'But Edward—'

'Is being taken care of,' he reminded her, dropping a quick, reassuring kiss on her brow as he carried her across the room.

It had been so long, too long, and the sexual attraction between them was explosive, their appetites insatiable. But both were aware of the clock ticking, and the promise they had made to share one meal together as a family for their son's sake.

Lucy cried out in ecstasy as Kahlil swung her round. In one move he was inside her, before they had made it to the bed. Her silk and cotton gowns were roughly pushed up out of the way so she could wrap her legs around his waist and urge him on. She was barely aware of anything now, other than Kahlil's full and total possession of her body, and her own overpowering need to find release.

Still pleasuring her, still sinking deep within her, Kahlil managed to shrug off his robe and mount the steps leading to the raised platform where they would lie together. Lucy lay heavily against his shoulder as he worked inside her, her mouth slack, her eyes glazed from a pure overdose of pleasure, and then she groaned as he lowered her down onto the very edge of the mattress. She was already tilted at an inviting angle, and uttered a small cry of alarm when he brought both her legs over his shoulders to open her wider still.

'I would never hurt you. If you want me to stop—'

'No!' she exclaimed fiercely.

Did he think her brazen? The thought slipped in and out of Lucy's mind like a shadow. But Kahlil knew her, he understood her needs… She let out a long, shuddering gasp as he began to tease her with shallow probes. She was reduced to crying out, to begging him for release with words she could hardly believe she knew. And then he went deeper still, until he was groaning with pleasure as much as she was as they hovered in intensely pleasurable suspension over the edge of the abyss.

They both wanted the moment to last for ever, and both knew equally that it could not. Lucy struggled hard to make the exquisite feeling last, to hold back, to stop herself falling, to hold on to the blissful moments. But Kahlil refused her this last indulgence and thrust into her rhythmically, moving slowly at first, and then deeper than she had ever known or thought possible. When he picked up the pace she was finally defeated, and gave a long wail of ecstasy as she tumbled into an endless dark tunnel of pulsing sensation.

'And now lunch,' he murmured when she had quietened.

'Lunch?' she said groggily.

'Take a shower,' Kahlil said. 'My bathroom is at your disposal.'

His words now were cold, so matter-of-fact it was as if another person entirely was speaking to her. Suddenly Lucy became aware that her clothes were bunched around her neck.

'Don't you want a shower?' she said, finding her voice dry and hoarse as she hurried to straighten them. But Kahlil was already halfway across the room.

'I have another bathroom through here,' he said, turning briefly to stare at her.

Of course, Lucy thought, falling silent. She might have known Sheikh Kahlil would be prepared for every eventuality, even out here in the desert.

'And don't take too long,' he said. 'We have another appointment, if you remember?'

Remember? As if she could forget their planned lunch with Edward! Lucy made a sharp, incredulous sound, but Kahlil had already gone.

News that their Prince had arrived had spread like wildfire amongst the tribesmen of the desert, and the chance to discuss Edward's future over a quiet family lunch was an impossible dream, Lucy realised as she emerged from the women's pavilion and saw the crowds. The event she had imagined would be private had been transformed into a ceremonial occasion. Though, as such, it surely had to be one of the most spectacular of its kind. She could hardly believe how many people had assembled in the hope of seeing Kahlil.

The cruel heat of midday had eased considerably by the time Lucy carried Edward up the wooden steps to the canopied area outside the royal pavilion. The light had taken on a mellow honey colour that seemed to bring out the occasional splash of bright colour, so that what she saw in front of her resembled a scene from a film. Lucy looked around in wonder. At the silken cushions heaped where she would sit. Overhead, a richly tented ceiling of white and gold silk cast a shade over the eating area below, and there were two side walls of silk undulating lazily in the breeze. The front of the pavilion was open to the elements and to the vast sandy expanse of desert, where all the nomadic people of Abadan had gathered.

There was an incongruous mix of old and new, Lucy noticed: something she was becoming accustomed to in Abadan. The decking beneath her feet would have been just as happy in a suburban garden back home, but this decking was covered with fabulous antique rugs that sank like dense pads of velvet beneath her sandalled feet.

Safia, who had accompanied her, had thought to bring some toys for Edward, but all he wanted to play with was his father's gauntlet.

There was still no sign of Kahlil, though Lucy guessed he would be amongst his people somewhere. Searching the crowds, she was surprised to see how many trucks were parked up alongside the camels at the edge of the assembly area.

'Roads criss-cross the desert now,' Safia informed her when she saw Lucy's puzzled glance light on the car park. 'Fuel is more readily available here in Abadan than water.'

'Of course,' Lucy said, realising this must be so in an oil-rich state. With a smile at Safia, she turned, shading her eyes, and stared out across the mass of people, still searching for Kahlil. And then she saw him—in the thick of it, a head taller than all the other men. He was examining some stallions that had been brought for his approval.

As if sensing her interest, he turned to look at her, and Lucy's heart leapt as their eyes locked. Whatever he might think of her, she had never felt more proud of Kahlil in that moment, or more pleased to think he was the father of her son. He looked every bit the Prince of Abadan, but there was tenderness in his face as his gaze dropped to Edward, playing happily at her side. Then he turned back to talk to the tribesmen again, completely absorbed in whatever it was they were saying to him.

Kahlil's sincerity shone through when he was speaking to them, Lucy realised with a pang of envy. The way banter passed easily between the men and their Prince showed how much they respected each other. This was what she wanted for Edward. She wanted him to grow up respecting others, and, in turn, to earn the right to have them respect him.

Kahlil had to do a double take when he noticed Lucy had arrived. And then he had to remind himself that duty took precedence over his personal life. Or had done up to now, he thought, as his astonished gaze swept over her again. Her resemblance to the photographs in his family archive had never struck him before, but it was quite incredible. He took in her casual attire, and the way she had swept up her long blonde hair into a no-nonsense ponytail, and didn't have to move a step closer to know she hadn't thought to put on make-up—a touch of lip balm, perhaps, but nothing more.

Lucy was thankful she had chosen to dress sensibly, in the freshly laundered clothes in which she had left the palace: a simple pair of cotton trousers, and a tailored shirt rolled up to the elbows. The very last thing she wanted was to cut a frivolous figure. She was a down-to-earth working mother, and she had no intention of behaving like an impostor to please her desert prince. Kahlil would have to accept her for who she was; there could be no compromise ever where that was concerned.

Lucy tensed as, having finished his conversation, Kahlil turned to her. Resplendent in his desert robes, with soft silk trousers showing beneath, he looked every inch the future ruler of Abadan. There was purpose to his stride as he came quickly towards her. The moment Edward saw his father crossing the sand towards them he started bunny-hopping with excitement. And, in spite of both Lucy's and Safia's best efforts, he refused to quieten down.

Taking the steps two at a time, Kahlil came over and, without a word to Lucy, claimed his son, sweeping him high into the air above his head. Holding him aloft, he turned to look down on the thousands of people gathered in front of him.

The massed tribesmen raised their fists high and gave a deep-throated roar of approval that ran a chill down Lucy's spine. Edward had been claimed as one of them, she realised, feeling a confusing mixture of pride and fear. There could be no turning back now.

CHAPTER ELEVEN

THEY ate a delicious meal, sitting cross-legged on cushions beneath the shady canopy. A vast selection of delicacies was brought to them, and the feast didn't draw to a conclusion until purple shadows had started to track across the mustard-coloured sand.

Kahlil devoted most of his time to Edward—and, though Lucy was growing to enjoy watching them together because it made Edward so happy, she was becoming increasingly frustrated, sure Kahlil was deliberately evading her attempts to pin him down about the future.

'There are some people I must talk to when we have finished eating,' he said when coffee was being served. 'Edward should leave us now. It will be tedious for him to have to sit still and listen.'

'But I thought *we* were going to talk,' Lucy said, conscious that the nursemaid was already moving to take Edward back to the women's tent. She was torn, seeing how tired Edward was, but knowing she would never be ready to accept Kahlil's orders where he was concerned. Moving to go with them, Lucy was surprised when Kahlil touched her arm, stopping her.

'Edward is tired,' he said. 'The women can see to him. You can go to him later.'

'But you have things to do here,' she pointed out. 'Surely it would be better if I went with Edward?'

'We still have things to talk about, and Edward will sleep now. There is nothing more you can do for him tonight.'

'But I'd rather go with him—'

'Sit down. Please, Lucy.' Kahlil's voice dropped a tone.

Reluctant to make a scene in front of all the tribesmen, Lucy settled back onto the cushions, watching Safia take Edward into the women's tent, and noticing Kahlil was doing the same.

'Before we talk, I must greet some of the elders of the tribe,' Kahlil explained the moment Edward had disappeared from sight. 'I will share a glass of tea with them as our custom demands.'

'When will we talk?' Lucy pressed.

'As soon as this is over. If you would rather wait for me inside the pavilion—?'

'No, this is fine,' Lucy said. 'I'll stay here.' Kahlil's way of life fascinated her. This was a great opportunity to learn more about the father of her son. 'Would you like me to move back,' she offered, 'so that you can speak to the other men in private?'

'I have nothing to hide,' Kahlil said dryly, 'and neither do my kinsmen. You may stay where you are.'

Lucy's pulse quickened when his hard mouth softened in the suggestion of a smile. And he was in no hurry to look away. It was she who broke eye contact first, her heart racing as her mind flashed back to their earlier passion. She could almost believe there was something more between them than their son and sexual attraction. She wanted to believe…

Then Kahlil turned away and made a sign to one of his attendants. At his signal, the line of men waiting at the foot of the stairs began moving slowly towards them.

'What did he mean?' Lucy said, turning to Kahlil as the last of the elderly tribesmen made a deep bow towards them both. 'Who is Nurse Clemmy?' She broke off to smile at the older man as he left them to join the others. He had stared at her throughout the audience with Kahlil, exclaiming in Abadanese under his breath, and then, when he'd spoken directly to Kahlil, had repeated the name 'Nurse Clemmy' over and over as he gestured towards her, his eyes bright with excitement.

'Nurse Clemmy was my mother,' Kahlil said. 'Ahmed Mehdi Bhaya has noted the resemblance between the two of you, as have many of the people here.'

'I look like your mother?'

'You are the same type of woman,' he said, in a way that made Lucy wonder whether that was a good thing or not.

Determined, stubborn, and as spirited as my most troublesome thoroughbred, Kahlil was thinking, counting himself fortunate that Lucy could not read his thoughts. But he could see she was burning up with curiosity.

'So your mother was a nurse?'

'Yes, she was.'

There was something in Kahlil's eyes that made Lucy hesitate before pressing on. 'I don't mean to pry—if you'd rather not talk about her...'

As he turned his luminous dark eyes on her Lucy felt their power through every inch of her body.

'Of course I like to talk about her. Ask me anything you like.'

'How did she meet your father?' Lucy asked, her brow wrinkling in thought as she remembered the old standard lamp in the ruling Sheikh's quarters and his father's explanation for it…There were so many clues, and now she was wishing she had picked up on them sooner, given the older man a chance to talk about his Western wife.

'She nursed him in hospital,' Kahlil said, reclaiming her attention. 'Something of a cliché,' he admitted dryly. 'But that's where everything predictable finishes and the true love story begins.'

He had Lucy totally hooked now. She was barely aware that the servants had backed away discreetly and, with the tribesmen already heading for their trucks and their camels, they were completely alone. 'Go on,' she murmured, her gaze locked on Kahlil's face.

'She was older than my father,' he said, his face softening as he gazed into the fiery haze of the desert sunset. 'She broke every convention when he brought her back here. Not only was she an older woman, but she insisted on continuing her work during her marriage to the ruling Sheikh of Abadan—something that had never been heard of before Nurse Clemmy came along.'

'She sounds like quite a woman.'

'She was.'

'What happened?' Lucy said softly, but seeing the look in Kahlil's eyes she already dreaded his answer.

'An accident in the desert,' he said flatly. 'She was trying to save the life of a child who had fallen down a ravine.' He looked away and flinched, as if the memory caused him actual physical pain. 'She should never have been out in the desert on her own.'

Anger had begun to colour his voice, and Lucy felt a stab of guilt knowing her own reckless act had only rekindled terrible memories for him. 'I'm sorry,' she said, knowing it wasn't enough.

'I thought my father would never get over it…' Kahlil stopped and eased his shoulders in a shrug. 'Our people believe she is an angel now, looking down on them, guarding them and protecting them from harm—even arranging their marriages for them.' His lips twisted halfway between a grimace and a smile.

'She sounds like a saint.'

'A saint with her feet firmly on the ground, as well as a wicked sense of humour,' he said, lightening a little. 'She always said she needed a sense of humour to survive her name.'

'Her name?'

'Clementine Ballantine.'

'It sounds like her parents had the sense of humour,' Lucy said, smiling.

'She insisted on being called Clemmy, and took herself off to college, where she trained to become a nurse. Then she fell in love with my father and came to live here in Abadan.'

'You said she continued to work?'

'She revolutionised our medical system, and brought forward the cause of Abadanese women by several hundred years.'

So what had gone wrong? How had such a wonderful legacy been allowed to slip away? What a tragedy that no one had picked up Nurse Clemmy's torch. And now it was too late, Lucy mused, looking at Kahlil. Neither he nor his father would ever allow things to go back to the way they had been when Nurse Clemmy was alive.

They were still bitter that Nurse Clemmy had left them, she realised suddenly, softening towards Kahlil as she felt his pain. Why could life never be simple? Why was the black and white of their relationship, the reasons behind their battle for custody of Edward, growing indistinct? Why did she have to care for Kahlil so much?

'She sounds like a great woman,' Lucy said sincerely. 'I wish I could have known her.'

'She *was* a great woman,' Kahlil murmured distantly. 'Truly great.'

How they ended up in each other's arms Lucy wasn't quite sure. There was a moment when she was following Kahlil's stare out into the deepening shadows, and then another when she was kissing him as if it was the most natural thing in the world…something they both wanted, both needed equally.

'We'll talk?' Lucy whispered when he released her at last.

'Later,' Kahlil promised. Standing up, he drew her to her feet.

The moon cast a silver net across the bed, bathing Lucy's flushed face in light. She wondered if Kahlil could ever get enough of her, or she of him… They were both insatiable, she decided, running her fingertips through his thick glossy hair as he moved steadily down the bed, kissing every inch of her along the way.

He had taught her the Eastern way of making love… drawing out the pleasure until she reached another level of consciousness—one that took her far beyond her worldly concerns and into another place, where pleasure ruled and sensation was everything. She felt safe, and happy, and completely loved. Reality couldn't intrude here, she thought, sighing in anticipation of pleasure as he eased her thighs apart. Kahlil could do more with his tongue than any man could hope to achieve in a lifetime of fumbling…and his hands—

Lucy cried out as he cupped her buttocks and brought her beneath him. 'Again?' she murmured with surprise.

'I'm only just getting warmed up,' he promised, slanting her a smile before claiming her mouth again with a deep, passionate kiss.

They belonged together; they were made for each other… The words in Lucy's head were borne out by Kahlil's actions, and those actions were clearing her mind of thought so that now she could only move with him, rhythmically, deeply and steadily, putting every bit of her strength behind the thrust of her hips, the clutch of her fingers as she held on to his shoulders.

With a deep groan of satisfaction Kahlil rolled away from her when they were spent. 'You are a wildcat,' he murmured, staring at the battle wounds on his arms. But he didn't seem concerned as he reached for her and brought her close. 'I cannot get enough of you,' he murmured, and Lucy thought she detected an element of surprise in his voice as he turned to plant a tender kiss on her face. 'Soon I may not be able to live without you at all.'

He stopped when Lucy shifted position to stare at him in astonishment. 'You really care for me?'

'Of course I care for you,' he said impatiently. 'And that is why I am able to say this to you—'

'What?' Lucy whispered tenderly, brushing a lock of hair back from his face. This was the man she wanted for the father of her son; this was the man she knew she could love. 'What do you want to say to me, Kahlil?'

'I want to talk to you about getting married.'

'Getting married?' Lucy breathed in astonishment. 'But Kahlil—'

'For Edward's sake,' he broke in, staring deep into her eyes as he brought her hand to his lips. 'You cannot be my mistress, Lucy. Edward's parents must be married.'

Elation ripped through Lucy, transporting her to a place she had only dreamed of before. But when she looked into Kahlil's eyes, expecting some mirror image of her own heated emotion, she saw there was nothing. She made a small sound of uncertainty, frowning, suspended in a type of limbo. Like a feather on a breath of wind, she felt her emotions could be tossed either way.

'Edward must be legitimate if he is to inherit the throne of Abadan one day,' Kahlil explained, sitting up as practical matters took over his thoughts.

'I see…'

'So I am proposing that we get married—what do you think?'

Lucy swallowed, giving herself time to collect her thoughts. She wanted to feel as any other woman might feel at such a moment: elated, overjoyed, maybe even a little disbelieving, but absolutely sure, absolutely confident. But she was not confident. She was anything but confident. There was something Kahlil wasn't saying. He had begun with a proposal when there should have been a few words of preparation first, or a special look, a lingering touch. There had been nothing.

Lucy searched his face to be sure, but there was absolutely no emotion in Kahlil's eyes. He had made her a practical proposition, and now she was expected to answer him.

'It would only be for a short while, of course,' he said, as if he thought that would offer her some encouragement. 'I'd have a proper contract drawn up. Let's say six months?' His mouth tugged down enquiringly as he looked at her.

Six months. Enough time to establish Edward's legitimacy before admitting to the world they'd made a mistake.

'Come now, Lucy—surely you can see what a good idea it is?' he said when she still remained silent. 'I'm not asking anything of you.'

'You're…not…asking…anything…of…me?' Lucy repeated, finding it hard to breathe, feeling as if a leather strap had just been tightened around her chest. 'Is that what you think, Kahlil?'

She sprang away from him as he went to touch her, landing on the floor awkwardly and shaking him off when he lunged forward to steady her. Grabbing the sheet, feeling her nakedness like a towering shame, Lucy wrapped it tightly around her.

'And after six months?' she said, her face white with shock, her eyes glittering with disbelief. 'What then, Kahlil?'

'That's when I release you,' he said soothingly, swinging off the bed to go and comfort her.

'Get away from me!' Lucy warned, taking a step back. Snatching up his robe from a chair, she flung it at him. 'Put this on. I can't bear to look at you.'

Kahlil frowned, suddenly conscious that he too was naked. Slipping the robe over his head, he gazed down at her, all the majesty of his position safely restored. 'Before you cast any more accusations at me,' he said, 'won't you listen to what I have to say?'

'I'll listen,' Lucy said tensely, facing him. She was not going to give him the satisfaction of breaking down. She forced her breathing to steady, and straightened up so he would see she couldn't be intimidated.

'We will get married,' Kahlil began, confident of her agreement. 'Edward will be made legitimate and recognised by the Council as my heir. And then, in six months' time, I will grant you a divorce. You will be free, Lucy. Free to do as you please. You know I would never stop you seeing Edward. I understand how much you love him.'

It was too much. Lucy almost broke down. She had no idea how she managed to keep her eyeline steady and the tears safely locked behind her frozen stare. She doubted Kahlil had the slightest idea about love, let alone how much love she had for Edward. And as for the love she had for the man standing before her? That was the real tragedy, Lucy thought, listening but not hearing as Kahlil continued to put his case for a marriage of convenience. Sheikh Kahlil of Abadan had broken her heart, and nothing he could do to her now would ever cause her more pain.

'I don't want to raise any false hope,' Kahlil said encouragingly, as if he sensed Lucy's disappointment. 'You must see that you could never sit on the throne of Abadan at my side—we will have to divorce. But we will live out of the public eye, I promise you. I would never subject you to gossip, or cruel innuendo. People will hardly know what has taken place—the upheaval for you will be minimal.'

And at that point Lucy almost hit him. Anger welled from deep inside her as she faced up to him. She was good enough to bear Sheikh Kahlil's child, but not good enough to sit beside him on the throne of Abadan.

But what good would anger do? she wondered, feeling her fury quickly overtaken by despair. For Edward's sake she would do this. For Edward's sake she would marry the man she loved and then be humiliated by him after six short months, when he divorced her in front of the entire world.

Lucy looked at Kahlil as if seeing him clearly for the first time. Even now she couldn't hate him. She could only love him. And if six months was all Kahlil had to offer, then she would take six months.

'I'll go further,' Kahlil offered when Lucy remained silent. 'You can go home with Edward—as soon as you like. Breathing space,' he explained, opening his arms in an expansive gesture. 'This has been a tremendous shock for all of us. I can see you need time. You *should* have time,' he said decisively, 'and I'm going to give you all the time you need.'

Lucy couldn't prevent the small sound of contradiction escaping her throat, and was glad that Kahlil was so determined to convince her that he had come up with an acceptable plan he didn't notice. There could never be enough time to come to terms with what was happening.

'When will we go?' she heard herself say. A sense of unreality swept over her. Going home was what she wanted more than anything—wasn't it? But now the moment had come the thought of leaving Abadan filled her with dread. Then Edward swam into her mind—she would be with him—her face softened.

'That's better. I was beginning to think I would never see you smile again.'

Was she smiling? Lucy wondered. The whole episode had shocked her so much she had no control over her responses

'I know this must all seem contrived to you,' Kahlil said. 'But Edward cannot be my heir under the laws of Abadan unless and until we are married. That is a fact, and there is nothing that either of us can do about it. I take it you want Edward to inherit the throne of Abadan in due course?'

His gaze rested on her face but Lucy's mind went blank.

This wasn't the battle she had intended to fight—a clean-cut legal contest to secure custody of Edward. This had turned into something heart-rending and ghastly, something unbelievably bitter and disappointing. 'Marriage...' she murmured distractedly.

'Our relationship must be legalised, recognised here in Abadan.'

'Our *relationship*?' The word grated on her. 'Don't you mean sex?'

'Don't cheapen what we have, Lucy,' Khalil said, frowning. 'I'm just stating facts plainly. I can see you need time to think about this, but you don't need to worry, I'll get my legal team onto it straight away. And if you have any difficulty locating a lawyer to act for you I'm sure I can help—'

'No, thank you,' Lucy said, quickly reclaiming her composure. 'I'm quite capable of handling that side of things myself.'

'If you're certain?'

'I'm positive.'

'Lucy,' Kahlil said, moving closer until he could brush aside the hair that had fallen over her face. 'Come here to me.'

Inwardly spent, Lucy moved like a rag doll and Kahlil brought her back into his arms. 'Surely you can see that we both need some time apart?' he murmured.

And then he nuzzled his face against her cheek, and she felt his warmth, inhaled his special scent, and tears began to trickle unhindered down her cheeks. Was this how the Sheikh disposed of a mistress when he was tired of her? Lucy supposed she should count herself fortunate. Kahlil was offering her marriage for the sake of their son. And he didn't have to. He must love Edward very much, she realised.

'I'll go and shower and dress,' she said, wiping her eyes discreetly, 'and then we can finalise the details.'

CHAPTER TWELVE

LUCY'S cottage in Westbury on a freezing cold March morning was quite literally a world away from the sultry romance of a desert encampment. And as for the Golden Palace—that seemed nothing more than a mirage in the desert, like everything else in Abadan.

Throwing back the curtains, she stared out at the main street running through the village. The road was glittering with frost, making the desert seem further away than ever. Abadan seemed nothing more now than a fantasy kingdom that only the most inventive film director might have dreamed up.

At least Westbury Hall looked magnificent after its facelift. The work on the building was almost completed. Her own dreams might have been crushed, but she was glad someone else had taken up the challenge. Rumour said it had been turned into a luxury hotel and spa, and it did seem the most likely explanation that a leisure complex had been built. There was even a helicopter landing pad on the newly reinforced roof.

As Edward claimed her attention Lucy saw how close he was to walking unaided, and felt a flash of regret that Kahlil wouldn't be there to see his son's first steps. But Kahlil had made his choice and he had to live with it, just as she had to face the prospect of a loveless marriage.

Not loveless on her part, Lucy thought, feeling frustration sweep over her. She was in control of every other area of her life, but where Kahlil was concerned she seemed to have lost touch with reality. He had no love for her and it was time to accept that fact. Their marriage would be one of expedience only.

And thanks to Kahlil she also had silent visitors to contend with. His security forces were always around—and not just the man lodged in her guest bedroom. There were more, she noticed, parked across the road in a discreet black sedan. She could pick them out easily.

Turning away from the window to prepare Edward's breakfast, Lucy couldn't help thinking about their forthcoming marriage. It had turned her into something of a celebrity in the village, as well as the envy of her friends. Only she knew the reality of the situation. There wasn't much romance in a marriage of convenience. And with the bodyguards part of her life now she was just as much a prisoner in Westbury as she had been captive to the Sheikh in Abadan. Kahlil could control events even from half a world away, Lucy realised, making a point of smiling at Edward when she realised he was watching her.

She had to guard her feelings all the time. She was determined Edward would never suffer because of the lack of love between his parents. Nor would he ever know the humiliation she felt at being deemed an unsuitable consort for the Crown Prince of Abadan. She was good enough for a marriage of subterfuge and concealment, good enough stock to provide Kahlil with an heir, but not good enough to uphold the dignity of the throne of Abadan.

Lucy jumped with surprise as the doorbell rang, and for one crazy, exhilarating moment she felt sure it would be Kahlil at the door. Rushing to peer out of the hall window, she saw it was only the mail delivery man with a large package.

Disappointment and relief swept over her in turn as she hurried to open the door. Had she really thought Sheikh Kahlil of Abadan would simply turn up unannounced on her doorstep, like any ordinary mortal?

'What on earth's this?' Lucy exclaimed as the man carried the large carton into the narrow hallway for her.

'Beats me,' he said. 'Sign here, please. I've got three more for you in the van.'

'Three more!' Lucy knew in her heart where they must have come from.

When the man had left, she sank down on the floor beside the boxes. The only thing that stopped her breaking down was Edward. She was determined not to let him see his mother crying over what she knew would almost certainly be her wedding dress and accessories.

In the first carton Lucy discovered a fabulous jewelled veil covered in crystals and pearls. Holding it up to the light, she felt sure it must be meant for someone else because it was so beautiful. Even with the evidence of the clothes she would wear on her wedding day surrounding her, marriage to Kahlil had never seemed more unreal.

When she had opened all three boxes, and rifled through the reams of tissue paper, Lucy sat back on her haunches. Kahlil had bought her after all—and for the price of a dress and a few trinkets.

'For the photographs,' his accompanying letter assured her. 'It wouldn't do for Edward to think his parents' marriage a hastily arranged affair.'

Kahlil was right again. There was no reason why Edward should be short-changed just because his mother had made such a hash of things. And his father was arriving tomorrow, Lucy saw, reading on.

Crumpling up the page, she held it to her breast. She felt weak just thinking about Kahlil's arrival. She never knew what to expect from him, or what he was thinking. One day maybe someone would strip away his defences, get to know the real man, but it wouldn't be her, however much she longed to. She had tried and failed to get beneath his steely façade.

'Come on, young man,' she said, turning to Edward, who was already delving into the boxes and scattering clothes and shoes everywhere. 'There's nothing for you in here.'

Except for a box-load of memories for when you are older, Lucy thought as she swept her son into her arms. *And then you'll have to make of them what you will. Because I won't be able to elaborate on whatever fantasy your imagination conjures up. Nor will I be able to make palatable the fact that your parents married and then divorced within the space of a few months.*

Taking Edward into the kitchen to make them both breakfast, she carried on reading. There would be a discreet civil service at Westbury Hall, Kahlil had written. So it was to be a hotel, Lucy thought, glancing out of the kitchen window. She couldn't ignore the irony—both 'Kahl' and her ambitious plans for Westbury Hall had proved a disaster, and now she was to be married at the Hall, to Kahl!

From practically every room in her small cottage Lucy had some view of Westbury Hall. That was how the idea of renovating the magnificent old building had taken such a hold in the first place. She couldn't tear her gaze away from it now, knowing her wedding was to be held there. Hopefully the decorators would be out in time—but, knowing Kahlil's influence extended far beyond the boundaries of Abadan, she didn't doubt the new owners of the Hall would make sure everything was ready for him.

While she was warming Edward's milk Lucy spotted another van turning in through the Hall's imposing gates and felt a fierce pang of regret. She had so wanted to bring the old place back to life, but the challenge had got away from her—rather like that other challenge she had encountered at the Hall, the one that had called himself Kahl.

The rest of the day passed in a whirlwind of activity. Lucy had booked into the local beauty salon for a manicure, a facial and a massage. It might be a waste of time, but there was no reason not to look her best when Sheikh Kahlil of Abadan turned up on the doorstep.

Later, when Edward was sleeping, Lucy crept up the stairs and went into the nursery just to look down at him. He looked like a sleeping fawn, innocent and untroubled, with his baby hands curled up as if he was holding her finger—or his father's. Backing away, she hugged herself, shutting her eyes tightly for a moment. The only time she ever saw Kahlil soften was when he was with Edward, and then she saw a very different side of the desert Prince—someone who might almost have made a good family man—

'Don't be ridiculous!' Lucy muttered impatiently. It was time she stopped behaving like a romantic fool where Kahlil was concerned.

Leaving the nursery on tiptoe, Lucy left the door ajar so she could hear Edward through the night. Returning downstairs, she went into her study and closed the curtains, shutting out the cold, bleak night. All her important papers were still on top of her desk, where she had left them. The marriage contract her lawyers had asked her to sign took pride of place.

She had refused all payment for herself, and Kahlil had respected that. But she knew that everything Edward could possibly need would be provided for most generously. There would be regular trips between Abadan and Westbury, and they would spend more time in Westbury than Lucy had dared to hope. Leila was to be given the job of full-time nanny—which, in Lucy's opinion as well as Kahlil's, would provide additional stability for Edward.

Kahlil had thought of everything—except love, Lucy reflected, laying down the fountain pen she had just picked up. She didn't want to read it, couldn't quite bring herself to sign such a cold-blooded document. But as long as Kahlil loved Edward, that was all that mattered.

Lucy knew the only thing she wanted, the only thing she had a right to expect was joint custody of their son. Kahlil had already agreed to grant her that without a fight. She should be satisfied. But still she was restless without knowing why.

Beginning to shiver, she saw the fire had burned low in the grate. She was glad to have something practical to do. Adding more coal, she stirred the fire into life again with a brass poker, and then sat back on her heels. 'Very soon I will be a wife—and a princess,' she said aloud, on a note of incredulity. The word *princess* was so alien to her it filled her with apprehension. 'And then, in six months' time, or even less, I will be a free woman again,' she added firmly for reassurance.

The whole marriage machine would roll on with or without her co-operation. Kahlil's staff were making all the arrangements. 'Perfect. Saves me the trouble,' she whispered, biting back tears.

Kahlil will be here today, was Lucy's first thought on waking. She was grateful for Edward's routine. It gave her something to do other than stare out of the window every five minutes.

His letter had said he would be with them by nine o'clock. So by eight Lucy was building towers with Edward out of plastic containers on the kitchen table. The table just happened to be by a window that looked over the road.

Edward saw him first—or rather he saw the sleek black limousine that drew up outside. And then Kahlil was out of the car and striding up the path almost before it had drawn to a halt. Lucy's heart was hammering so hard in her chest it hurt. She had forgotten how tall he was, how powerful. Even in the dark, formal suit he looked so regal.

She stayed out of sight, watching as he stopped before the porch to take in the cottage with one sweeping glance.

There was just a touch of humour in his eyes, she noticed with surprise, and she flushed pink as she realised that he was remembering everything about their first encounter—but Edward was jiggling up and down in her arms, eager to greet his father.

'Just a minute, please,' Lucy said to Edward firmly, watching Kahlil turn to stare at Westbury Hall. Of course—that was where it had all begun for both of them. Her heart lurched as he turned back to the cottage and reached for the doorbell.

She remembered everything too, Lucy thought on her way to the door. Every time she walked past the gates of the Hall. And every time she felt the same thrill, the same certainty that she had done nothing wrong. She smiled at Edward as she reached the front door. 'How could it be wrong when I have you?' she whispered in his ear.

The bodyguard Kahlil insisted upon, who lived in the house alongside them, like a wraith, descended the stairs like a cannonball. Stretching one arm out in front of Lucy, he swung the door open and bowed low. Heat streamed into Lucy's veins. She was glad of Edward's comforting warmth in her arms as she stood back in the shadows with him, waiting. There was a great gust of fresh air laced with cinnamon and ginger as Kahlil stepped into the tiny hall.

'Lucy,' he said, looking down at her.

Here in the low-beamed cottage, standing in the shady hall, he seemed immense, magnificent. Sheikh Kahlil of Abadan had an immense presence, Lucy thought, steeling herself to meet his gaze. She had prepared herself for this moment. She would expect nothing and therefore could not be disappointed. That was what she had told herself. But she was disappointed. There was nothing—nothing at all between them, she realised as he swept a frantically excited Edward out of her arms.

'My son!' he exclaimed softly and emotionally, holding Edward close for a moment.

She could never have truly prepared herself for this, Lucy realised, seeing the look in Edward's eyes as he gazed into his father's face. Not for the great well of longing that opened up in her heart. But what had she been expecting? That they would both be swept into Kahlil's arms like a proper family? That she would be greeted like Kahlil's future wife, with love and tender kisses in the expectation of a lifetime of happiness together?

'Did you have a good journey?' she said, forcing the traditional courtesy through her lips.

Kahlil frowned briefly. 'I could have brought the helicopter,' he said, and there was an edge of irritation in his voice as he glanced over his shoulder through the mullioned window at Westbury Hall. 'I didn't realise they'd finished the roof.'

Lucy stared up at him in bewilderment. His comment was so far distant from her own thoughts that it took her a moment to respond. 'That would have been more convenient for you,' she said at last, not sure that he was listening.

'Shall we go in?' he said, looking beyond Lucy, deeper into the cottage.

'Yes—yes, of course,' she said, backing down the hallway in front of him. 'You've had a long trip. Won't you come into the kitchen for a coffee, tea…some breakfast?'

There was something unreal about inviting the imposing figure of Sheikh Kahlil of Abadan into her humble kitchen for coffee. But Kahl hadn't been too proud to eat and drink in her kitchen almost two years ago, Lucy remembered, watching him set Edward down on his play rug.

'You've made some changes,' Kahlil observed.

'For Edward's safety,' Lucy said. She was glad to turn her back and busy herself at the Aga with the kettle and two mugs. 'This thing gets red-hot,' she turned to explain, 'so I had a guard frame with a gate made to fit around it. But it won't be long until he learns how to open it—Edward!' she exclaimed, putting the mugs down again.

Kahlil too stood frozen to the spot as Edward took his first few faltering steps unaided. Arms outstretched, he staggered determinedly towards his father and finally, in triumph, grabbed hold of Kahlil's legs.

Lucy's hand flew to her chest and she drew a deep, steadying breath. 'I'm so glad you were here for that,' she said honestly.

'So am I,' Kahlil said, his voice hoarse with emotion as he lifted Edward into his arms.

Briefly, Lucy turned away, not wanting to begrudge either of them such a special moment. But she was tormented by the fear that every step Edward took towards his father was a step away from her.

When Edward called for her attention a flood of fresh resolve came over her and she hurried to share his excitement, not caring that when she hugged Edward she was forced hard against Kahlil. There might be nothing left between them, but this was a very special moment.

Kahlil suggested Edward should be taken for a walk in his stroller. 'Don't look so worried, Lucy. I brought a friend of yours and Edward's with me from Abadan,' he said, looking towards the door.

'Leila!' Lucy said, exclaiming with pleasure when she saw the girl. 'It's so good to see you.'

'And you,' Leila said warmly. 'Shall I take Edward now?' She came in to collect her charge.

'You do seem to have thought of everything,' Lucy admitted, turning to Kahlil, conscious that Edward was reaching out for his father, reluctant to leave him now.

'Edward loves his daddy—don't you, Edward?' Leila said fondly, piercing Lucy's heart with her innocent words. 'But we could go and feed the ducks, if you like?'

Her distraction was skilful, and Edward was easily persuaded. Lucy could already feel Kahlil's influence pushing them both this way and that, and he had only been back in their lives a few minutes.

'Do all the clothes that I had sent over for the wedding fit?' Kahlil asked, when the door had closed behind Leila and Edward.

'Perfectly,' Lucy said tensely, finding her gaze drawn against her will to his strong, tanned fingers—fingers that had measured every inch of her with such accuracy.

'Good.'

As their gazes met and held Lucy turned away, feeling awkward. She wasn't sure what Kahlil expected of her. 'I've already picked up some of my old contacts,' she said, forcing a bright conversational note into her voice. 'I should be quite busy after the wedding.'

'What do you mean?' he said sharply.

'I mean I'll start work right away…'

Kahlil swore softly in his own tongue. 'Are you mad?' he said in English, staring at Lucy in amazement.

'You always knew I would keep on working. It's written into the contract on my desk. We agreed—'

'You *shall* work,' Kahlil said, 'but not here—not in this country. I have much to occupy me in Abadan. You must be with me for much of the time, and I would not expect you to sit around all day doing nothing. My people expect—'

'*Our* people—if only for six months,' Lucy reminded him, trying to stay cool, trying to be reasonable.

'Our people,' he conceded—but grudgingly, Lucy thought. 'The people of Abadan will expect to see us together, performing certain official duties.'

Lucy's patience was wearing thin. He seemed to have everything worked out in advance. She hadn't been consulted about anything. 'Isn't that a little modern?' she interrupted, stung into a sharp retort by his manner.

'Not for me,' Kahlil said, 'and not for the people of Abadan. Why, Lucy? Don't you think you can handle it?'

'I can handle it,' Lucy said, feeling her anger mounting. She was determined not to be backed into the place Kahlil wanted her to be: the willing wife, the obedient consort, the woman without a mind of her own, the person who could be swept up and dropped at will, whenever and wherever it pleased him.

'Good, then that's settled. After the wedding tomorrow—'

'Tomorrow!'

'Is there any reason to wait?'

'In Abadan you said I needed time,' Lucy exclaimed, springing to her feet. 'You said we both did. You promised I would have all the time I needed to come to terms with this.'

'I had to bring things forward; I have responsibilities. The formalities are being arranged.'

'Everything is being arranged from the sound of it,' Lucy said tensely.

'The guests have been informed; none of them has complained,' Kahlil pointed out impatiently. 'I can't see why you should be so reluctant.'

'Oh, really?' Lucy said shaking her head. 'This is my life we're talking about, Kahlil, and I won't be controlled by you.'

'You will do whatever is necessary.'

'I will do anything for Edward,' Lucy agreed. 'But if you think for one moment you can order me around, that I will become your bond slave the moment we're married, you're mistaken. I agreed to this marriage for Edward—not for myself, and certainly not for you!'

'Nevertheless, we will be married tomorrow,' Kahlil said,

standing up to face her. 'And immediately after the wedding you and Edward will accompany me to Abadan.'

Lucy couldn't believe what she was hearing. She had been so sure there would be more time. She had been complacent—too complacent, she realised now.

'There will be a civil ceremony tomorrow, here at Westbury Hall,' Kahlil continued remorselessly. 'That is so our marriage will be recognised in your country. When we return to Abadan we will have a second ceremony—a blessing, if you like—so that my people can greet and accept my new wife.'

Unable to meet his eyes, Lucy looked at her hands and found they were shaking. 'I didn't realise… I mean, I didn't think Edward and I would be leaving for Abadan straight after the wedding.'

Kahlil moved a step towards her, as if he thought she needed some reassurance.

'Don't,' Lucy said. 'Don't touch me. I can't believe you're trying to rush me into marriage like this.'

'Rush you?' Kahlil queried coldly. 'We agreed for Edward's sake.'

'Yes, we agreed, but you said it would happen when I was ready.'

'It can't wait for ever, and the time is convenient.'

'For whom?' But Lucy knew she was wasting her breath. And she *had* agreed. She wouldn't back down. 'Very well, but I won't be manipulated again.'

'Manipulated?'

'First Westbury Hall, and now our marriage…'

'Westbury Hall?' Kahlil said, watching her carefully.

'Yes,' Lucy said, unable to subdue her suspicions any longer. 'You were up to something, weren't you?' She stopped, seeing his face, and knew she had hit a nerve. 'So I am right,' she said, wishing at once it wasn't true. 'What did you really come for that day? What were you up to?

Did you have a property developer in your pocket? Or did you tip off the consortium that bought it? Or did you simply want to steal my ideas for the renovation?'

'Your ideas were always in the public domain.'

'Westbury Hall means nothing to you,' Lucy said bitterly. 'It was just a game as far as you were concerned—one you had to win.' He couldn't deny it, she gathered, when he remained silent. 'You'll never know what Westbury Hall means to me. I loved the old lady who lived there—my parents worked for her all their lives. We loved her, and Lady Grace loved us—' Lucy stopped, hearing her voice break. 'But why do I expect you to understand? You don't know what love is, do you, Kahlil? You don't have the slightest idea. You just take charge of people's lives—that's what you're good at. You have no respect for anyone. I was just a little bonus on top of whatever deal you were making.'

'I'll go now.' Kahlil's voice was as steady as if they were two strangers parting on the best of terms. 'I'm sure you must have preparations to make for our marriage tomorrow.'

Marriage! She didn't know how he could bring himself to mention it so casually.

'I trust any business meetings you may have arranged can be postponed?' he said, pausing on his way to the door.

'Yes, of course,' Lucy managed distractedly, still in turmoil.

'Excellent,' Kahlil said, striding out without a backward glance.

She felt faint, light-headed, and quite suddenly nothing seemed real. She felt as if she had just been swept up in a whirlwind and had landed somewhere she couldn't recognise, where she didn't have the skills to survive.

Lucy steeled herself as she prepared to leave the horse-drawn carriage. Kahlil had insisted upon a carriage, even though her cottage was only a few steps from the Hall. He said she must be driven around the village so that people could see her, and so that photographs of the occasion could be taken for Edward's sake. And she had agreed. She didn't want Edward thinking his parents' marriage had been loveless when he grew older. It was far better for him to believe it had been a fairytale that had lost its way.

As one of Kahlil's men stepped forward to help her negotiate the steps Lucy lifted her head to acknowledge him. He was another of the silent men she was becoming used to—interchangeable, like chess pieces, but a lot more deadly. She already felt the subtle change in her position as he stood at her side. It wasn't human kindness that made the man reach out to steady her as she lifted her skirts and picked her way carefully—it was his bounden duty now to protect her from harm.

The harness clinked behind her as the horses stamped their feet and blew down their noses, impatient to be gone. But there was no escape for her, Lucy thought, shivering in the biting wind.

Straightening the folds of her dress, she looked up as the doors of the Hall swung open to admit her. A rush of warmth and light and sound spilled out as she started up the steps. She was glad to have the posy in her hands to cling to. She had insisted on choosing the flowers for her wedding bouquet—simple blooms from the local greenhouse: jonquil, freesia and some early tulips. She had bound them herself with some supple young strands of curving purple willow. It trailed below ribbons she had laced around her fingers.

Her hands were pale and shaking, Lucy noticed, keeping her head down to concentrate on the jewelled satin slippers on her feet. The slippers belonged in a fairytale, as did the ivory satin cape lined with soft fur she was wearing over her intricately beaded wedding dress. But this was not her fairytale. She was an impostor.

She would not turn back. She would not allow anything to stand in the way of Edward's future happiness.

Kahlil's evasion the previous day still rankled, but Lucy had found a way to cope with the farce that was her wedding day. She would enjoy the luxurious feel of cool silks and satin against her naked skin as an actress might. She would relish the scent of French perfume as the couture clothes brushed her legs just as if she had donned some lovely new costume to play a part.

And that was all she was doing, Lucy reassured herself as she stepped over the threshold of Westbury Hall. She was playing a role for Edward's sake. And she would play it well.

Raising her head proudly, she saw Kahlil, waiting for her with Edward beside him in Leila's arms. And then she became aware of many more people, most of whom she didn't know.

Some she did—friends from the village, from her schooldays, from her college, and both close and extended family. Kahlil had gone to endless trouble, Lucy registered with surprise, wondering how on earth everyone had been assembled in time.

And then there were others—dignitaries from a host of foreign countries, with ribbons, and medals, and sashes, and jewels—all waiting for her arrival! It seemed quite incredible—impossible.

Swallowing hard, Lucy tried to move forward, but her earlier confidence had deserted her and her feet seemed rooted to the spot. Then Kahlil was beside her and her frozen hand was enveloped in his. He felt so warm and steady. She allowed him to lead her forward, slowly and carefully, as if she was a precious item that might crumble if he handled her too firmly.

But as soon as he felt her strength return he released her again, and Lucy knew it would have been better if he had left her to blunder around until some dutiful member of staff brought her to him. His consideration only made her more aware that, with good cause to hate him, she was in love with him. Sheikh Kahlil of Abadan was more than just the father of her son: he was the only man she would ever love. Her world, Lucy realised with a great burst of emotion. But as far as Kahlil was concerned she was merely a convenient wife, the woman who had supplied him with a son.

Lucy kept her head throughout the ceremony, behaving impeccably, responding when required, and even smiling up at Kahlil as if she didn't have a care in the world later, when they danced together. She would have forgiven his indifference towards her in an instant, forgotten every one of her suspicions about him for just one word of tenderness—one look, or one smile, something intimate and private passing between them. But he behaved towards her like a very courteous and considerate stranger.

When he finally escorted her back to her seat at the high table, Lucy gazed around. Seeing who had assembled for their wedding drove home the fact that Kahlil was an immensely powerful figure in the world at large. And she was—

'The mother of my son,' Kahlil said, introducing Lucy to the Ambassador of Abadan.

Lucy reddened as the older man bowed low over her hand.

'It is an honour to meet you at last, Princess,' he said.

Lucy's shocked eyes flickered up to meet Kahlil's steady gaze. 'It is my pleasure to meet you, Ambassador,' she said, recovering fast. Both the fact that Kahlil had taken the trouble to introduce them and the use of her new title had taken her completely by surprise.

'I hope you will excuse me for a few moments,' Kahlil said.

Gladly, Lucy thought, as he led the Ambassador away.

She needed time to collect her thoughts, to accept that, however short their marriage would be, her life had changed for ever. She watched as people gave way at Kahlil's approach, bowing low as he walked amongst them, and felt sure she would never get used to the fact that Sheikh Kahlil of Abadan was her husband.

Left to her own devices, Lucy began to relax and enjoy the celebrations. There were interesting new people to talk to, as well as many of her close friends and family. Skirting the subject of her new husband was something she was becoming rather good at, and after a while she began to believe that she would sail through the rest of the reception. It was a chance conversation that brought the idyll to an end.

'To think the Hall is to be a private home again. And after all these years.'

'I'm sorry?' Lucy said, collecting her thoughts. The Lady Mayor of Westbury had come to sit with her, and had been chattering non-stop for almost twenty minutes. 'I beg your pardon,' Lucy said, mending her manners. 'You were trying to tell me something about the Hall?'

'You must be so proud of your husband,' the Lady Mayor said, staring across the newly renovated ballroom at Kahlil, who was chatting easily as he moved around their guests.

'I am proud,' Lucy said automatically.

'He cuts a splendid figure in his tail-coat—and I imagine he would in Arabian garb. Still, I mustn't carp, or show my disappointment—his mother was English, after all.'

'I don't mean to interrupt,' Lucy said, desperate to halt the irrepressible flow of words from the older woman as concern brought questions leaping into her mind, 'but I thought the Hall was to be a hotel?'

'So did we all, my dear—until this morning. But now we hear different. And in my case,' she added proudly, 'from your husband himself. There are so many servants,' she breathed, turning around, oblivious to Lucy's shocked reaction. 'Still, what do you expect when a sheikh chooses to make his home in our village? To think,' she added, folding her hands as if in a prayer as she closed her eyes, 'that we are to have *royalty* living amongst us.'

Lucy felt as if all the life had just drained out of her. She fixed a smile to her lips, nodding politely. Kahlil had bought the Hall for his own use! Surely the Lady Mayor was mistaken?

Lucy burned with shame as she remembered her surprise and relief when she had managed to sell the Hall for well over its market price—to a consortium of businessmen, the agent had said. Now she realised it had been Kahlil's way of paying her off. He had been behind the purchase all along, paying well over the odds—to appease his conscience? she wondered, remembering how abruptly he had left her after their one-night stand. She could just imagine his shock when he discovered she had given birth to Edward!

This marriage had been forced on him, Lucy thought, going cold as she surveyed the glittering scene. It put the gloss of respectability on his unfortunate mistake. But Sheikh Kahlil could afford it. For a man as rich as the Crown Prince of Abadan this was a bargain. For the price of a wedding he got the heir he longed for, with a wife to use while it pleased him thrown in.

'Well, I've kept you from your gorgeous husband long enough,' the Lady Mayor said, oblivious to Lucy's pain as she fluttered her chiffon handkerchief at a friend across the dance floor. 'I must let you go to him—I wish you every happiness, my dear,' she gushed, leaning over Lucy to plant a damp kiss on her cheek.

'Thank you,' Lucy said, her gaze hardening as she stared at Kahlil. Taking up her challenge, he came striding back to her, taking the direct route across the crowded dance floor. Once again Lucy noticed how a path cleared automatically in front of him.

'Lucy?'

His voice was sharp—with concern or irritation? She couldn't tell.

'Lucy, what is it? What's wrong?'

'I must speak to you,' she said, collecting the folds of her gown as she made to get up.

'Of course,' Kahlil said easily, suspecting nothing as he reached for a chair.

'Somewhere private,' Lucy stressed tensely, standing up.

'Very well,' he agreed, glancing round. 'I doubt anyone will notice that we've gone. Let me help you.'

She had no option but to take his arm—and Kahlil was probably right about no one noticing their departure, Lucy thought as they walked towards the doors. Their guests could not have been happier, or more content. It was ironic that only the bride and groom were so violently at odds with each other.

CHAPTER THIRTEEN

THE double height hall, with its sweeping staircase and minstrels' gallery, was quiet after the noise of the band and champagne-fuelled chatter.

But not quiet enough, not private enough, Lucy thought, leading the way, confident that she knew Westbury Hall better than anyone else. She drew to a halt outside one of the many doors leading off the hallway. But she didn't know which to go through now, she realised. Resting the palm of one hand against the cool, flat surface, she forced herself to accept that Westbury Hall now belonged to a stranger—and that stranger was her husband.

'Here,' Kahlil said, cupping her elbow and leading Lucy towards another door. 'We can be private in here.'

Lucy allowed him to steer her into the brightest room in the house—the room the previous owner, Lady Grace, had called her morning room. 'The room where all the problems are solved,' Lucy remembered Aunt Grace saying now. She blinked back tears, almost imagining she could hear the kindly old voice again, encouraging her to look round.

'You've kept everything the same,' she said with surprise, touching a blue silk cushion reverently.

'Those are new covers,' Kahlil admitted, 'but they are faithful copies of the originals. I thought it would be what you wanted.' He stayed by the door, watching her. 'Even before you mentioned Lady Grace Frobisher I'd heard you were very fond of her.'

But Lucy wasn't listening. 'It's all the same,' she exclaimed softly. 'Even down to the china dogs in the fireplace.' Dipping down, she stroked one smooth head.

'I was having them restored—there was a chip—but then I stopped.'

'You stopped?' she said, turning her face up to look at Kahlil.

'Some things can be spoiled by restoration,' he said. 'Sometimes their charm lies in the fact that many people have handled them, have enjoyed them over the years.'

As their eyes met and locked Lucy's were troubled. Kahlil understood so many things instinctively. And yet there were so many other matters that seemed to bypass him completely. Did he have no conscience at all? He could be sensitive, and about important things, like the keepsakes she treasured, but he withheld so much—too much. 'Why didn't you tell me about all this?' she said, straightening up to face him.

'We could hardly get married at your cottage, with a bodyguard in the spare room. I had Westbury Hall restored. I thought it a suitable venue for our wedding.'

'A suitable venue?' Lucy repeated, feeling the chance she had given him had just been wasted. 'So—' she gestured around '—all this is just for prestige? For the sake of how other people see you?'

'Not at all—'

'Tell me one thing. Were you behind the bank calling in my loan? Did you make them do that?'

Kahlil looked at her, his expression unreadable. 'It was a matter of business.'

'You deceived me, Kahlil,' she told him bitterly. 'You lied to me. You stole my dreams. And then you paid over the odds for Westbury Hall and allowed me to believe I had done a good deal—when in fact I was being paid for my services like a—'

'Don't speak that way!' Kahlil's voice cut across Lucy like a whip-crack. In an instant he had grabbed her arm in one powerful fist, and, cupping her chin with the other hand, he tilted Lucy's face until she couldn't avoid looking at him. 'Don't you even think like that,' he warned. 'You are the mother of my son. You are my wife. You have just become Princess of Abadan. Don't forget it.'

'I doubt I shall ever be allowed to forget it.' Lucy averted her face from Kahlil's blazing stare. 'Let me go, Kahlil,' she said faintly. 'Let me go now. We've got nothing more to say to each other.'

'Very well,' he agreed. 'Go to your room. I will make whatever excuses are necessary to our guests.'

With an angry sound, Lucy dragged her arm out of his clasp. But then she stopped on her flight to the door. 'I don't know which is to be my room.'

'All of them,' Kahlil said steadily.

'All of them?' Lucy said, turning to face him. 'What are you talking about?'

'I bought the Hall for my own reasons, but when I came to know you better I wanted you to have it. I did all this for you, Lucy,' Kahlil said in a bitter whisper. 'I thought it would make you happy. Don't worry,' he added, backing away when she reached towards him. 'I will have one of the servants show you to a suitable bedroom. You need have no fear. I won't trouble you tonight.'

The flight to Abadan was tense and lonely for Lucy. She was sitting in the main body of the aircraft, whilst Leila had taken Edward to sleep in a private suite at the rear

Putting down the glossy magazine she had been pretending interest in for the past hour, Lucy gazed across at Kahlil and his ministers, clustered around a meeting table at the other side of the cabin. Things had gone from bad to worse since their wedding. She couldn't believe Kahlil had cheated her out of Westbury Hall, or that he'd meant to give the Hall back to her as a wedding present. Never in her wildest dreams could she have conceived of a gift on such a scale.

In her world wedding presents were toasters, or crystal glasses.

And now he was oblivious to her presence. Perhaps it was better that way. She would go and see if Edward was awake—

'Edward is sleeping; let him rest,' Kahlil said, without troubling to look at her. 'I will have lunch served here for us in a few moments.'

His uncanny knack of anticipating her intentions sent a frisson of alarm through Lucy. 'How do you know?'

'How do I know?' Kahlil repeated, turning a stare on her face.

'How do you know that Edward is still sleeping?'

Now she saw the monitor on the table in front of him. When he turned it towards her she realised the camera was trained on Edward's sleeping form. Next to Edward she could see Leila, sitting on an easy-chair, sewing a button onto a romper suit.

Security even on the royal jet, Lucy thought tensely, taking her seat again. And then she reddened, remembering the furious row she'd had with Kahlil that morning about security. She hadn't slept for one moment during her wedding night, and the last thing she had been expecting was that Kahlil would join her in the breakfast room.

She had started out wanting to apologise, to provoke a discussion at least. But Kahlil had rebuffed her. He'd preferred to eat in silence. Venting her frustration, she had complained about the high levels of security surrounding Edward, saying she feared they would intimidate him as he grew older and more aware.

'My son will not be intimidated by anything,' Kahlil had told her, stabbing a piece of omelette with his fork. 'It's time to grow up, Lucy,' he'd snapped then, throwing down his cutlery as he stared at her. 'Privilege has its price.'

Standing up, he'd thrust his chair back so violently it had made an angry, grinding noise on the wooden floor.

And then Leila had walked in, and Lucy had asked her to take Edward into the nursery for his breakfast rather than subject him to his parents' bickering. But Kahlil had walked out soon after that, brushing off her attempts to thank him for his wonderful gift. It was too late for thanks, he'd informed her coldly. And now Lucy felt as if she had never deserved to own the Hall in the first place…

Glancing down at the gold band on the third finger of her left hand, she saw how shiny it was—shiny and new and undamaged. Unlike her relationship with her husband of just a few hours. She had spent most of the flight working out how many contracts she would have to win to pay Kahlil back—for she *would* pay him back. She had made that promise to herself this morning. The gift of Westbury Hall was far too great. And after their non-existent wedding night she felt more determined than ever not to be in his debt.

She looked away as Kahlil flashed a glance at her. He looked unusually strained. She suspected the long celibate night had got to him every bit as much as it had got to her. If there was one thing that always went right between them it was sex. But there could have been so much more than that—if only Kahlil hadn't been so proud, and she hadn't been so defensive, so blinkered...

'Lucy?'

'Yes?' Lucy looked up as Kahlil moved to sit across from her.

'Is something wrong? I heard you sigh.'

'Nothing,' Lucy said quickly, dismissively. 'It was nothing. I was just daydreaming.'

'Then it is time you came to grips with reality,' he observed dryly, making a signal to the flight attendant.

Kahlil's concern was nothing more than the concern of a responsible employer for a member of staff, Lucy thought as she listened to him giving instructions to the flight attendant for lunch in the same low tone. And perhaps she could learn something from him; perhaps the six-month marriage would pass more easily if they learned to act politely but unemotionally towards each other.

'My wife and I will take lunch here,' he was saying. 'Everyone else will eat in the second compartment.'

The man bowed and went about his duties, leaving them alone. And then Lucy saw the Council members gathering up their papers as they prepared to move to another section of the plane.

'To us,' Kahlil murmured sardonically, raising a glass of chilled champagne.

Holding his gaze, Lucy took a sip. 'To us,' she repeated mechanically.

Putting his glass down on the table again, Kahlil looked at her. 'I have just finished dealing with a whole raft of problems, both large and small, troubling my employees. Would it help if I added yours to the mix?'

'No, it would not help,' Lucy said tensely. She was almost ready to accept the situation, but she wasn't in the mood for his irony. 'And as far as I am aware,' she added, 'I am no longer one of your employees. I am your wife.'

'Really?' Kahlil said, tilting his head to look at her. 'Not yet, you're not.'

Lucy gasped at his bluntness, and in the same instant felt the familiar tug of desire.

'And does your contract at the Golden Palace mean nothing to you?'

The contract! Lucy realised she hadn't even given it a thought…and there had been one or two minor complications that meant it might take longer than six months. 'Kahlil, we need to talk,' she said, putting down her glass.

'Yes, we do,' he agreed, crossing one lean denim-clad leg

easily over the other and keeping his dark, watchful eyes trained on her face.

'You know I have always intended to finish my work at the Golden Palace.' With no effort at all, Kahlil had put her on the defensive again. But he gave a small nod of his head, encouraging her to continue. 'And I will complete the contract,' she said. 'But I want neither your money nor your pity.'

'Who said you could have either?'

His eyes were narrowed, his firm, sensuous mouth curved in a cynical smile. He was playing her like a mouse, Lucy suspected. 'I just don't need a replay of Westbury Hall.'

'Explain,' Kahlil said, opening his hands.

'I want to complete my contract on the Golden Palace without your interference. The recovery of my business, the payment of my debts—everything I thought I had achieved through my own efforts—was only made possible because of you, because of your over-generous payment for Westbury Hall.'

'You built up your business before we met a second time,' he argued. 'I think you underestimate yourself.'

'I don't think so.'

And as for the Hall—I paid what I thought it was worth.'

'And now you're giving it to me?'

'Yes.'

Lucy realised she had never felt so bad about anything. But was the Hall a gift or a pay-off, a bribe for six months' good behaviour? Her thoughts started flying in all directions.

'Was buying the Hall at an inflated price your way of paying me off?'

'Be under no illusion, Lucy. I have never had to pay for sex in my life.'

She believed him, and for a moment all she was aware of was Kahlil's eyes searching her own.

'Is that it?' he said, breaking eye contact at last. 'Or is there anything else you'd like to ask me?'

Or any insults she'd like to fling at him? he seemed to imply. But what more could she say? He had deceived her over Westbury Hall, and she had made no attempt to track down Edward's father. They were both in the wrong. Neither of them could deny what they had done.

The tension between them lifted a little when the flight attendant returned with a platter of salad. Lucy knew she could either fight with Kahlil for six months, or she could try and reach some sort of accommodation with him. But in order to reach a compromise she had to state her terms clearly.

'While we are married I will continue to work—'

'You'll certainly finish your contract,' he said dryly, looking up from his fork at her through a fringe of black lashes.

'Of course I will.'

'And as for Westbury Hall—don't talk about overpayment as if it is a crime. I may have behaved clumsily, but I was pleased to pay over the odds in order to ensure you did not suffer any more financial embarrassment. I wanted you to have the chance to get back on your feet—although you surpassed even my optimistic hopes for you by winning the design competition. No one was more surprised than me to see you in Abadan with a baby in tow.'

'Our baby.'

'Our baby,' he granted. 'My son.'

'Our son.'

Lucy gasped as Kahlil took hold of her upper arms in strong hands, and drew her to her feet in front of him.

'It is time to stop playing games, Lucy,' he said tensely. 'You're my wife now.'

Desire flared between them, but Lucy was still haunted by the memory of a man called Kahl: a man who had taken his fill and then taken his leave without a single word of explanation. She was determined to hold on to her self-control.

'So you get it all?' she said coolly, meeting Kahlil's gaze.

'Yes, I do,' he agreed. 'I get my son, I get Westbury Hall, and I get a wife—quite a haul, don't you think?'

His arrogance was breathtaking. Who did Kahlil think he was? A pirate? A buccaneer who seized everything in his path that pleased him? 'You haven't got me yet,' Lucy said with defiance, but the look in Kahlil's eyes had changed subtly in a way that made her want to melt against him.

'And you haven't received your wedding present yet,' he whispered, holding her so she couldn't get away.

'You gave me Westbury Hall—I don't want anything else.'

'You don't want anything else?' he repeated harshly. 'Forgive me if I disagree, but I think you do.'

Propelling her in front of him, Kahlil steered Lucy in the direction of his private quarters on board the royal jet.

CHAPTER FOURTEEN

THERE was a bed, a desk, and a sofa in Kahlil's spacious private cabin.

'Why have you brought me here?' Lucy said, wishing there was some alternative to staring him in the face. But he had her pinned against the door, with one arm resting at the side of her head, and was quite happy to let the moment hang.

The electricity between them was incredible, and Lucy suspected Kahlil enjoyed watching her suffer. It pleased him to look at her this way, watching her cheeks grow red with desire and her eyes darken with passion. She wanted him. She ached for him. Her whole body was on fire. She wished life could be simple! If it was Edward's happily married parents would on their way back with him now to a glowing future in Abadan. Instead of which—

'Why do you think we are here?' Kahlil's thoughts cut into hers like a knife. And then, before she could reply, he said, 'I've given you everything you asked for. Isn't it time you gave me something in return?'

Lucy went cold. All her passion subsided. She was his wife, and she had agreed to six months of married life to establish Edward's legitimacy. That was the price she had agreed to pay. But she had assumed it would be a marriage in name only, followed by a pain-free divorce. However much she wanted Kahlil, sex could never be something she made available on demand.

But she had misjudged him again, Lucy realised, as with one final assessing look Kahlil pulled away from her and walked across to the slim desk against the wall, where several documents were awaiting his attention in a pile.

'Come here,' he said, selecting one of them. 'You need to sign this.'

Lucy went to join him and, forced to lean over his shoulder, read the introduction. It was the contract she had never signed.

'You don't think a lot of me, do you, Lucy?' Kahlil said, swinging round to look at her.

On the contrary, Lucy thought. Her husband was an awe-inspiring individual by any measure. She would have been proud to acknowledge him as the father of her son without all the accoutrements of immense wealth, let alone the title he bore. Kahlil was exactly the type of man she would have chosen to father Edward. It was she who could never be a suitable wife for the future ruling Sheikh of Abadan.

'Pen?' he prompted. 'You should have signed this before the wedding and saved yourself a lot of unnecessary grief. I expect you haven't even read it through.'

Lucy couldn't meet his gaze.

'Just as I thought,' Kahlil said. 'You chose not to read it. You chose to think the worst of me.'

'A marriage contract seems so cold-blooded,' Lucy said honestly.

'Not in our case, surely? Did you expect romance?' he said when she didn't answer. 'Read it now,' he said, pulling out a chair for her to sit on.

Almost at once Lucy realised that the contract was weighted heavily in her favour. Her freedom from a loveless marriage was guaranteed after six months. She could even leave Kahlil sooner than that, should she choose to do so.

'No strings—no commitment,' he said, handing her a fountain pen.

The way Kahlil wanted it, she thought. 'Couldn't I have signed this out there?' she said, indicating the main cabin.

'Even my ministers do not know of our arrangement,' Kahlil said. 'It would undermine Edward's position if gossip spread.'

That made sense, Lucy conceded, signing the document. 'Thank you,' she said, returning the pen to Kahlil.

'You should feel reassured now,' he said, going to the door to open it for her.

She had been wrong about him all along, and now it was too late to make things right, Lucy realised. Her glance brushed the bed. The covers were pristine, untouched—and likely to remain that way for ever as far as she was concerned. Kahlil had given her everything she'd asked for and more: shared custody of Edward, freedom to continue working and providing for her son. Additions she hadn't even asked for included her own suite of rooms at the Golden Palace, and all the honour due to a princess of Abadan for the rest of her life. And he had given her the greatest gift of all: her freedom. But instead of feeling elated she felt beaten for the first time in her life.

'There is one more thing,' Kahlil said, picking up a bunch of keys from a table by the door. 'These belong to you now.'

The keys felt heavy and cold in Lucy's hands. 'Westbury Hall?' she murmured, staring down at them.

Kahlil inclined his head in assent.

Now she really did have everything she wanted, Lucy thought. And now she understood how little comfort bricks and mortar offered in place of the man she loved. 'Have you finished with me now?' she said faintly.

'Should there be more?' Kahlil said.

'No, of course not. I'll go and see Edward now.'

'Yes,' Kahlil said, making no move to follow her as Lucy returned to the main cabin. 'Go to your son.'

Late spring in Abadan had to be one of the most beautiful times of the year, Lucy thought as she sat on a ledge by the open window in her bedroom at the palace. And the silver dawn was definitely the most beautiful time of day.

Today was her wedding day—her Arabian wedding day. And this time she had no expectations, no false hopes. Kahlil had been as good as his word, leaving her to her own devices, not intruding on her work or her time with Edward. She should be satisfied. But instead she felt completely empty.

She was just starting to pull away from the window when something drew her back again. And then she saw Kahlil, dressed in riding breeches, striding across the courtyard flanked by his ministers. Time passed, but everything remained the same, Lucy mused, watching the same intense little man scurrying along by Kahlil's side, trying to keep up with him. Kahlil seemed to have a lot of instructions for him today, she noticed. But of course it was Kahlil's wedding day too—a thought so obvious, and yet incredible. He was like a stranger to her, a stranger she was about to marry—unless she took the initiative and changed the situation…

Impulsively, Lucy raced across the room to the ante-room where her clothes were kept. 'Where the hell...?' she muttered impatiently, slamming things back on the rails as she hunted for her jeans.

The royal stables were within easy walking distance of the main palace—the way Kahlil liked it. He could always clear his mind, think things through, relax and expend any excess energy he might be harbouring with a good gallop. And it was exactly what he needed now.

He had no idea how he was going to go through with it. The civil ceremony in England had been one thing—the dignitaries, the pomp and ceremony had meant nothing to him…not in his heart, not where it really mattered. But here, here in the vast burning truth of the desert, the simple ceremony in front of his people—people who trusted him, people who expected the best of him—

'Don't worry,' he said in Abadanese, when a groom hurried out to await his orders. 'I'll saddle him myself.'

He looked with pride at his stallion, Helix. The horse was perfectly proportioned, and hard, like a spring wound up to its limit. Just as he was, Kahlil reflected, slapping the flank of the magnificent black stallion to show his affection. The mighty creature nuzzled his shirt, hunting for the mints he kept there as he slipped a bridle over the proud head.

'He's beautiful.'

'Lucy!' Kahlil murmured in astonishment. And then, when his heart-rate had steadied a little, he added with concern, 'Shouldn't you be back at the palace, preparing yourself for the wedding? Several of our top beauticians have been brought in to wait on you.'

'Am I so ugly?'

The sudden humour threw him for a moment. 'No, no, of course you're not,' he said wryly.

'So I'm just vain?' Lucy suggested, playing along with him.

Kahlil shrugged as he tightened the girth. 'I thought you would like it—I thought they might help you to relax.'

'Could I ride with you?'

'Ride with me?' he said in astonishment. He hesitated with his hand on the saddle. It was the last thing on earth he had been expecting. 'Why not?' he murmured. And then he looked down the line of open stable doors, where several inquisitive heads were leaning out, ears pricked. 'A quiet gelding, perhaps?'

'What about this beautiful boy?'

'Helix? Don't be silly.'

'Silly?' Lucy queried, head on one side. 'Why, Kahlil? Is Helix a *man's* horse?'

'Well, yes...' Kahlil stopped. H

teasing him. And he could see where it was leading. 'He's a very strong horse—hard to handle. Your physical strength—'

'Would not be equal to the task?' Lucy challenged, staring up at him steadily. 'I've seen your jockeys, Kahlil. They are all smaller than me.'

'And stronger.'

'How do you know that?'

They stared at each other head-on for a few seconds, then Kahlil spoke to the groom still hovering close by. 'Bring out Terco for me to ride.' And without another word he began to shorten the stirrups for Lucy, while the magnificent stallion snorted and raked the ground in anticipation of his morning gallop.

'Terco means *tough* in Spanish, doesn't it?' Lucy remarked, following Kahlil round. 'And *stubborn* is an alternative meaning, I believe. I think it's perfect that you should ride Terco,' she teased lightly when Kahlil had finished and turned to give her a look. 'But why does he have a Spanish name?'

'Because he is a Spanish horse,' Kahlil revealed, one corner of his mouth tugging up in the suspicion of a grin. 'My younger brother is a doctor. He lives in Spain. This horse was his wedding gift to me, and the name Terco is his idea of a joke. But you have chosen to ride my horse, Helix,' he reminded her. 'Changed your mind?'

'Certainly not.'

'Leg up?'

'Please,' Lucy said. She wasn't about to back down now. However terrifying the black stallion appeared as he struck sparks off the cobbles with his highly polished hooves, Kahlil needed to know she was equal to any challenge he might care to set.

The controlled pace they adopted to cross the immaculately clean stableyard gave no hint of the wild gallop to come. Kahlil increased speed slowly at first, as if he wanted to check out Lucy's riding ability, but once they reached the irresistible challenge of clear, flat scrubland he took off.

Determined not to be bettered, Lucy took his stallion to the limit. It was both the most terrifying and most exhilarating ride of her life. Leaning low over the horse's neck, she whispered encouragement into the horse's keenly pricked ears, and Helix didn't disappoint her. Lucy thrilled to the sound of his hooves thundering across the ground, and with his long nose stretched forward and his stride lengthening every moment he rewarded her encouragement with an easy win.

'You can certainly ride,' Kahlil admitted, when they drew level on a stretch of road and slowed the pace.

'Who couldn't ride with a horse like Helix beneath them?'

'Most people,' Kahlil told her dryly. 'But then most people wouldn't be brave enough to ride a horse like Helix in the first place.'

Praise? Lucy wondered, as Kahlil nudged Terco into a canter and took the lead.

She leaned back in the saddle as Kahlil led the way down a steep embankment, and then moved her weight forward to make it easier for the horse as he started up a steep, rocky hill. Stones skittered beneath the horses' hooves as they climbed up the narrow winding path, and then at last, when the path widened into a wide sandy arena, she saw the reason for their climb to the summit.

Far below them, spread out for miles across the desert, there were rows of neatly tethered camels and lines of trucks, and hordes of people milling about a vast, tented city.

'Our wedding guests,' Kahlil said, turning to look at her. 'Our people, Lucy.'

As the breeze lifted her hair into a curtain between them,

Lucy was glad of the moment's privacy. She was deeply moved, and intensely aware at the same time of the weight of responsibility she was about to take on. She was glad to share it with Kahlil, and saw the emotion in his gaze as he sat without speaking on Terco, lost in his own thoughts. It was certainly an awe-inspiring sight, and a huge challenge, but it was one she knew Kahlil embraced with humility and determination—just as she did.

They sat together quietly for quite a while, the two great horses at peace beneath them, as if the animals could sense the silent communion between their two riders more keenly than could Kahlil and Lucy.

It was as if they were all at one with the desert, Lucy reflected, breathing deeply on the warm, spicy air. The golden honeyed light, the chink of the horses' bridles as they lazily tossed their heads, the soft wind tugging at her hair… She gazed across at Kahlil, and at the same moment he turned too. And as they looked at each other Lucy exhaled slowly, feeling her whole body and spirit relax. She knew this stranger a little better now. It was as if something had passed between them. Not the fire of passion, the fire so fierce it had burned them both. This was something far deeper, and more lasting. She began to smile.

'We should be getting back,' Kahlil said, shortening the reins and turning Terco's head. 'Don't forget we are to be married today. We mustn't be late for our own wedding.'

'No,' Lucy agreed, taking one final look out over the desert encampment. And when she turned Helix and went to follow Kahlil down the stony path again his words were still echoing excitingly in her head: *We are to be married today…we are to be married today…we are to be married today…*

'That was quite a ride,' Kahlil called to her above the clatter of two sets of hooves rattling in tandem across the stableyard.

'It certainly was,' Lucy agreed, wiping her face on her sleeve.

'You're an accomplished horsewoman,' he added, making her glow with pleasure.

'You're not bad yourself.' In fact Kahlil was the most accomplished rider she had ever seen outside a show ring. And his stallion, Helix, had almost been too much for her—almost, but not quite. She had formed a pact with the mighty beast: he wouldn't throw her off and she would allow him to gallop flat out and keep his nose just ahead of Terco. Pride. It was just as important to every animal on the planet—both man and beast, Lucy reflected as she jumped down to the ground.

'Hey,' Kahlil exclaimed, just in time to catch her and prevent her falling to the ground when her legs gave way. 'Why didn't you wait for me to help you dismount?'

'Because I thought I was stronger than I am,' Lucy admitted, her legs still trembling violently after the exertions of the ride. But even if her limbs were letting her down, her spirit felt as if it had just had an injection of the great black stallion's energy. And this wasn't such a bad outcome, she conceded, relaxing into Kahlil's arms for a moment as the groom came to lead the horses away. 'That was a really great workout. Thank you,' she said, straightening up to face him.

'Thank you?' Kahlil said. 'There's no need for you to thank me, Lucy. These are as much your horses now as mine. And if I'd only known you rode so well we could have arranged to ride out together sooner.'

'That's just it, isn't it?' Lucy said quietly. 'We don't know anything about each other, do we, Kahlil?'

'We could learn.'

'Do you want to?'

He wasn't going to make it easy for her, Lucy realised

when Kahlil walked away from her without answering. She watched him carefully checking over the two horses for any unsuspected injuries now they were unsaddled.

'Sponge them down—they've had a good, hard run,' he said to the groom, shooting a faintly bemused glance at Lucy, as if he was still coming to terms with the fact that they might have something more in common than a son they both loved.

She could almost see him wondering what other surprises might lie in store…and she felt very much the same, Lucy realised as she turned to go.

'Wait.' Wiping his hands on his breeches, Kahlil came across to her. 'I just wanted to say—'

'Yes?' Lucy said, looking up at him.

'How much I enjoyed that,' Kahlil admitted, raking his fingers through his thick black hair as if he was unused to making such declarations.

Lucy felt as if the air was a little clearer, the sky a little bluer, and her heart was suddenly far too big for her chest. 'So did I,' she said softly, staring deep into Kahlil's eyes.

'Lucy, is it too late?'

'Too late?' she said.

'For you to stay?'

'I won't leave until the six months are up,' she promised.

'I don't mean that. I mean—' Kahlil looked away from her, back towards the stables, where the horses were leaning over the half-open doors as if they too were keen to hear what he had to say. 'Will you stay longer than six months?' he said.

It was as if he found any admission of personal need awkward and embarrassing, Lucy realised. 'Do you think I should?' she asked.

'I think you must,' Kahlil said passionately.

'I must?'

'Please,' he said, 'don't accuse me of trying to control you again.' His voice was strained, and his eyes lingered on Lucy's lips as if he couldn't wait to kiss them again.

'I won't,' she promised, her own gaze straying to Kahlil's firm and very sensuous mouth.

'I want you to stay longer than six months.'

'How long, Kahlil?' Lucy said, searching his eyes.

'I want you to stay with me—for ever. I love you, Lucy.'

'You love me?' she repeated incredulously.

'I don't want you to leave me—I couldn't bear it if you left me,' Kahlil admitted. 'There is no one I would rather have to sit beside me one day on the throne of Abadan, no one else I want to bear my children, and no one but you can be my wife.'

Lucy could never have imagined Kahlil expressing himself in such an emotional way. The man she knew was all duty to his country, all fierce control over his life… 'Then I'll stay,' she said simply. And if he changed his mind when he had thought it through she would take him on any terms. She couldn't contemplate a future without Kahlil.

'You'll stay as my wife?'

'We are married. And we're to be married again in just a few hours.'

'I know marriage to me will be hard for you,' he said. 'I know you will have to embrace many responsibilities. It's hardly fair of me to ask you—'

Raising her hand, Lucy placed one finger over Kahlil's lips, silencing him. 'You want me to stay here in Abadan and be your wife? You know I will. We will be married for the next six months, and then, if you want me to stay on...'

Taking her hand away and unfolding it to kiss her palm, Kahlil raised his eyes. 'If you will have me, Lucy Benson, I want you to be my wife for a lot longer than six months.'

When Lucy couldn't speak he kissed her.

* * *

The wedding was to be held in the early evening, as tradition demanded in Abadan. So she had the rest of the day to prepare, Lucy thought, coming back into her bedroom after her shower. Edward was being well taken care of by Leila, who'd said she should have some quiet time by herself.

Right now, quiet time was the last thing she wanted, Lucy thought, securing a towel around her damp hair as she wandered across to the window. She wanted to jump up and down and share her happiness with everyone. She wanted to lean out of the window and shout out the news that Kahlil, Sheikh of Abadan, loved her.

Fastening her robe a little more securely, she planted her hands on the stone ledge and stared out. She smiled, picturing the usual early-morning group, with Kahlil at its head and his loyal aide bustling along next to him. And then her smile faltered. Was she making too much of it? Had the ride into the hills been just a fleeting, if rather wonderful moment? There was such a history of mistrust and misunderstanding between them—was one morning enough to set things right?

She wouldn't know the answer to that until after the wedding. Kahlil was far too concerned with fine-tuning the last-minute arrangements.

Leila had said that over a thousand wedding guests were expected—and that might even be a conservative estimate, Lucy thought, remembering the tented city Kahlil had shown her. Tribesmen were arriving from every corner of his desert kingdom for the ceremony. Her heart thundered with excitement at the thought of it.

Pulling away from the window, Lucy smiled to herself as she remembered every moment of Kahlil's kiss. It had been so tender; he had never kissed her like that before. And romance was in the air. Even the sternest of his attendants were smiling and singing under their breath, and the women insisted on scattering rose petals beneath her feet every chance they got.

But perhaps it would be better not to get carried away. Maybe Kahlil was just trying to be kind to her, to thank her in his own way for her co-operation… But something had definitely sparked into life between them during their hair-raising gallop across the desert. Something that had brought them closer than words—but then again maybe she was imagining the whole thing, Lucy thought with a sigh.

'That's a heart-felt sigh. I thought our ride had exorcised all your devils—apparently I was mistaken?'

'Kahlil!' He had just showered, Lucy realised. His hair was still damp and he was dressed in a simple Arab robe, his head covered with a flowing white *gutrah* that contrasted starkly against his tan. 'I didn't expect you.'

'So I see,' he said, coming closer. 'I believe we have some unfinished business. But before we get to that...'

'Yes?' Lucy said, feeling her buoyant mood dissolve and wondering why.

'There's something I have to say to you—something I have to tell you. No,' he said firmly, softly, 'don't turn away from me, Lucy. There have been too many misunderstandings between us, and I want to set things straight before we are married—truly married. Will you give me that chance?'

'Of course,' Lucy whispered, wanting to stop up her ears for fear of what he might say.

'My initial intention was to take Westbury Hall from you without a moment's conscience or hesitation.' Kahlil brought Lucy in front of him so she couldn't escape the harsh truth he had to tell her. 'I wanted the Hall for myself, for my new palace, and only you stood in my way. I forced the bank to withdraw your loan. I did cheat you. As for the purchase of the Hall being a game for me—you were right. It did start as a game—but it ended as a love match.'

'And that first time we made love?'

'I wanted you. I didn't plan to fall in love—just as you didn't know that Edward would bring us back together again. I had to tell you the truth, Lucy, before the ceremony. Can you forgive me?'

'Can you forgive me?' she said softly. 'For keeping Edward from you?'

Kahlil's answer was to trace the outline of Lucy's face very lightly with one hand. 'I can only thank you for bringing my son to me, and for coming back into my life,' he said, staring deep into her eyes.

'Won't it cause comment if we are seen together before the wedding?' Lucy said, reading Kahlil's gaze.

'We have no such superstitions here in Abadan,' he assured her in a whisper. 'And I have dismissed the servants…no one will disturb us.'

Lucy felt her legs weaken and sensuous heat flood her veins. 'We will be married tonight in the eyes of your countrymen...'

'Must I wait?' Kahlil demanded softly.

'Can you?'

'No,' he admitted wryly.

'No control?' Lucy whispered.

'No wish to wait—because I love you, Lucy Benson.'

And then he kissed her, backing her towards the bed, stripping off her towelling robe at the same time. The towel on Lucy's head tumbled to the floor seconds later, releasing her soft blonde hair so it tumbled around her shoulders in shimmering disarray. And when she lifted her arms to try and arrange it more neatly Kahlil wouldn't let her.

'That's how I like to see you,' he murmured. Running his fingertips lightly over the inside of her uplifted arms, he moved on to the round globes of her breasts, cupping them in his hands, weighing them appreciatively, his fingers straying to tantalise her painfully engorged nipples. 'Now…shall

I let you wait until our wedding night, or would you like me to continue?'

For answer Lucy spread her fingers over his shoulders and clutched him tight, her eyes imploring as she dragged him with her to the bed.

'Oh, well,' Kahlil said, laughing under his breath at her eagerness, 'if you insist...'

'I do,' Lucy assured him, raising her eyebrows as she lay back on the silken coverlet. 'But you're rather overdressed,' she chastised him softly, smiling approval when he stripped off his clothes.

'Now I'm not,' Kahlil said, stretching his naked length out beside her, barely touching, so that Lucy began to tingle all over her body, from the top of her head to the tip of her toes.

'Kahlil, don't tease me.'

'Why not?' he demanded softly, running the tips of his fingers down between her breasts and on over the soft swell of her stomach. 'It's what I do best, after all.'

With a groan, Lucy reached for him. She'd had enough teasing, enough waiting too. He was everything she wanted—everything she needed. And it had been far, far too long.

They fit together so completely, so perfectly, the pleasure was almost unendurable. Sinking deep inside her, Kahlil moved slowly, deeply, and then, when she thought that it was everything pleasure could be, and was grateful for it, he sank even deeper, and moved from side to side, nudging, pressing, rubbing until she cried out in ecstasy and couldn't wait for him to tip her over the edge.

'Restraint,' Kahlil warned softly, starting to move again when she quietened. 'Haven't I taught you the Eastern way?'

'The Western way isn't so bad,' Lucy whispered against

his mouth. 'My quantity, your quality—a perfect blend, wouldn't you agree?'

Kahlil's answer was a groan of pleasure equal to her own as she reached down and cupped him, running the tips of her sharp fingernails very lightly across the tautly stretched flesh beneath his pulsing erection. And then he turned her quickly, unexpectedly, so that she was mounted on top of him.

'I've seen you ride,' he reminded her, stroking her buttocks with the most tantalisingly light touch. 'So, ride…'

'We're going to be late for our own wedding,' Lucy warned Kahlil very much later. Stretching out one blush pink arm, she picked up her wristwatch.

Every part of her was blush-pink, she realised with amusement, falling back onto the bed beside Kahlil. His stamina was extraordinary.

'Thank goodness tonight is our wedding night,' she said, speaking her thoughts out loud. She could hardly wait until he made love to her again.

'And thank goodness it will be a very different wedding night from our first,' Kahlil murmured, reaching up to brush an errant strand of hair off Lucy's face. 'I don't think I could stand another night of cold sheets and inertia.

'You too?' she said, smiling.

'Me too,' Kahlil admitted wryly.

'OK, so I promise you hot sheets and constant action,' Lucy said, laughing as she fell into his arms. 'But right now, Sheikh Kahlil, we have to get up.'

Kahlil made a sound of agreement deep in his throat. 'More's the pity. I must take you riding again very soon.'

'I can't wait,' Lucy said happily. 'Only...'

'Only?' Kahlil said, pulling her back so he could look into her face.

'Do you have any quiet geldings in your stable?'

Throwing his head back, Kahlil laughed. 'It's your stable too now,' he reminded Lucy. 'You choose whichever horse you want. Were you frightened this morning?' he said, frowning a little.

'Terrified,' Lucy admitted, remembering Kahlil's fiery stallion.

'Why didn't you say something?'

'What—and have you think me a coward? No, thank you.'

'I would not have thought you a coward,' Kahlil assured her. 'Your courage has never been in question.'

'So a nice quiet gelding next time?' Lucy suggested hopefully.

'Whatever you want…whatever makes you happy. Whatever your heart desires I will give you.'

'Then that's easy,' she said, growing still. 'Because all I want, Kahlil, is you.'

There was a fever in her wedding preparations this time. Lucy checked and rechecked her appearance in the mirror umpteen times. She wasn't a beauty. She couldn't do much about that. But did she look good enough? The Eastern robes were concealing, but flattering, and played to her generous curves. The colour and the fabric Kahlil had chosen for her were amazing—softest pale blue silk chiffon covered in tiny glittering bugle beads and pearls.

'Do you like it?' Leila said, smiling at Lucy while balancing an awestruck Edward on her hip.

'Like it?' Lucy murmured, allowing the ice-blue gossamer fabric to float from her fingers. 'Who wouldn't love a gown like this, Leila? It's so beautiful. I can't believe it.'

'Don't forget your sandals.'

They were sprinkled with diamonds—she wasn't likely to overlook them, Lucy thought ruefully as she slipped them on. Would she ever become accustomed to such wealth? She doubted it.

'Do you like your own outfit?' she asked with concern.

Leila was becoming increasingly important to her; she was part of the family now as far as Lucy was concerned. And even though time had been so short Lucy had taken special care in selecting something she thought Leila might enjoy wearing. She was to be an attendant at the marriage ceremony with Edward. Both had outfits in a subtle blue a little deeper than her own dress colour, and their clothes were fastened with tiny sapphire buttons and beaded with creamy freshwater pearls.

'I like this the best of all,' Leila said, fingering the locket Lucy had given to her as a wedding-day present. 'You're really very kind.'

'And so are you. I couldn't do this without you. Team Benson—remember?'

'Team ben Saeed Al-Sharif of Abadan,' Leila reminded her, and as Edward clapped his hands together with excitement they all began to laugh.

Kahlil surprised them, striding across the room resplendent in his wedding robes.

Lucy was grateful to Leila for putting Edward down for a moment and quickly swinging a silk robe over her shoulders. She wanted Kahlil to see her in her wedding dress for the first time at their marriage ceremony.

'Thank you, Leila,' Kahlil said, when the girl, sensing something exciting was about to happen between the bride and groom, swept Edward into her arms and quickly left the room.

'Kahlil?' Lucy said when the door shut had quietly behind Leila. 'I didn't expect to see you before the wedding.'

'I have something for you,' he said, bringing her hand to his lips. Kissing each of her fingertips in turn, he turned her hand to kiss her palm. And then placing two rings in her hand he closed Lucy's fingers over them.

'For you,' Kahlil said softly, when she looked at him in confusion.

Opening her hand again, Lucy stared down at the rings.

'I chose the diamond ring for you as the mother of my son. Something for you to remember me by when the six months of our marriage were over.'

Lucy stared at the fabulous jewel in awe. But the second ring was quite different, and as the realisation of who must have worn it came over her Lucy drew in an astonished breath.

'This ring is for an unconventional wife and an unconventional marriage,' Kahlil murmured.

'Is it really Nurse Clemmy's ring?' Lucy whispered, hardly able to believe what Kahlil was offering her.

'Will you wear it?' Kahlil said, gazing at her steadily. 'Will you marry me, Lucy Benson? I should warn you that the woman who wears this ring will stay with me for ever, and work alongside me for the good of our people. It is a ring for the woman of the Sheikh's heart to wear.'

'Then it is the only ring I choose to wear,' Lucy told him.

Something fundamental had changed between the two of them, Lucy realised when she joined Kahlil beneath the bridal canopy. The electricity, the immediate surge of desire was as strong as ever, but now there was more. And it filled her with fear, and with joy, and hope, and with all the butterfly flutterings in her stomach that a bride should expect to feel on her wedding day.

Closing her eyes for a moment, before she gave her hand to Kahlil, Lucy inhaled the exotic scents of the flowers around her. As well as over the canopy, the women had bound flowers in her hair. Fragrant blossoms circled the translucent blue veil that matched her eyes exactly, and they had put a garland around her neck too, over the intricately embroidered robe she knew they had taken hours beading and embroidering. She felt beautiful, and feminine.

There was such a groundswell of love from the people of Abadan for Edward and for herself—a love Lucy returned wholeheartedly. And now there was complete balance in her relationship with Kahlil. She knew their future together was assured. Opening her eyes, she found Kahlil smiling at her, and it was with total confidence that she placed her hand in his.

'You look beautiful,' he whispered as a hush fell over the assembled congregation. Then, bringing her hand to his lips, he turned it over and placed the diamond-encrusted ring on her palm.

'What—?' Lucy looked at him in confusion.

'For six months only,' he teased her softly, 'and then, if you tire of it, I'll buy you another one.'

'Kahlil...' Lucy chastened him in a low voice.

Then he placed the thin, well-worn gold band on the third finger of her marriage hand. 'But this ring,' he said softly, 'is for the wife of my heart. This ring, my darling Lucy, is for ever.'

The Sheikh & the Princess Bride

SUSAN MALLERY

To Sharon.
Because every woman deserves
a little fantasy in her life. This one's for you.

Chapter One

Prince Jefri of Bahania refused to believe he could be beaten by a woman. It was simply not possible. Yet here he sat in the cockpit of his F15, going over five hundred miles an hour and staring into the sun where he'd last seen the other plane soar out of sight.

"You'd better get moving, big guy."

The amused *female* voice came through his headset and caused him to grind his teeth.

Where was she? He turned his head, searching for a glimmer of sunlight on metal. Something. Anything that would give him a clue as to her whereabouts. He saw nothing.

Jefri had been flying since he was a teenager and in all that time, he'd never once been anything but confident. For the first time in his life, he felt a cold sweat trickle down his back. Seconds later a high-pitched warning tone sounded in the cockpit. She'd locked on to him. Had this been a real combat situation, he would be dead.

"Bang, bang," the woman said and then chuckled. "You lasted all of two minutes. Not bad for a rookie. Okay. Follow me down."

Suddenly her jet swooped in from his left. The machine turned gracefully, then moved in front of his. Even at this speed, she was close enough for him to read the call sign painted on the fuselage.

Girly Girl.

Jefri groaned. This could *not* be happening. He was a prince, a sheik, heir to untold wealth and land. He was the youngest son of the king of Bahania. He did *not* get shot out of the sky by a woman!

"I know what you're thinking," she said. "You're upset and humiliated. You men always are. Console yourself with the fact that no one's beaten me in a dogfight for six or seven years. This is war, not personal. My job is to make you better. Your job is to learn. Nothing more."

"I am aware of my responsibilities," he said curtly.

"You're going to hold a grudge, aren't you? I can already tell." She sighed. "Some guys are like that. Oh, well. It's your ulcer."

With that, her jet rotated as gracefully as a ballerina, then streaked across the sky. Jefri stared at the space where it had been just a heartbeat ago. How the hell had she done that?

He shook his head and keyed in the code for the

recently installed military air traffic control tower. After giving his number and approximate position in the desert, he requested permission to return to the base. When it was granted, he turned his plane to the correct coordinates and headed south.

Twenty minutes later, he landed and taxied his jet toward the large, newly constructed hangars. When he'd stopped the plane and opened the hatch, he heard someone call his name.

"Two minutes," Doyle Van Horn yelled from the tarmac. "That's the record so far. Good for you."

Good? Jefri gritted his teeth and climbed down the ladder. "It was a disaster."

When he reached the ground, Doyle slapped him on the shoulder. "You can't take it personally. Nobody beats Billie."

"That's what she said." Jefri stared at the blond man. "How long has she been with your firm?"

Doyle grinned. "Technically, all her life. She's my sister. Dad had her driving tanks by the time she was twelve. She soloed in a jet on her sixteenth birthday. You said you wanted to be trained by the best, and that's what we provided, Your Highness."

"Call me Jefri. I've told you, no formalities. It will be easier that way."

Doyle nodded. "Just checking. I thought you might be touchy after being shot down and all. Some guys are."

Jefri didn't doubt it. He watched as a second aircraft came in for landing. The jet moved lightly, barely raising any dust when the wheels touched down.

"I wish to meet her," he said firmly.

"I figured you would. They always do."

Jefri raised his eyebrows. "Do they?"

"Yup. No one can believe it. Things only get worse when they get a look at her."

"In what way?"

Doyle laughed and held up his hands in a gesture of surrender. "You go find out for yourself. Just one warning. You might be a prince and the guy who hired us, but Billie is off-limits. To everyone. Even you."

Jefri was not used to being given orders, but he didn't argue with Doyle. He wasn't interested in Billie Van Horn as anything but a resource. If she was the best, he wanted to learn from her. Then he would take her on again, and this time he would win.

Billie climbed out of the cockpit and tugged on the zipper of her flight suit. No matter how many times she sent the manufacturer her measurements, they always got the fit wrong. Whoever designed the stupid things seemed to forget women had parts men didn't.

She jumped the last couple of feet to the ground and removed her helmet. As she did, she saw a tall man striding toward her. She recognized the determined pace, the stubborn set of the shoulders. Oh, yeah, this would be Prince Jefri. No doubt Bahanian royalty weren't used to losing. Well, he'd better *get* used to it. She didn't plan to treat him any differently than any other client, which meant he was going to keep on hearing that tone-lock for the rest of her time here.

Men always hated being beaten by her. They couldn't seem to accept that a woman could be good in a dogfight. In her experience the men she trained fell into two camps. The first got angry and aggressive, often attempting to take out their frustrations in the air by bullying and intimidating her on the ground. The second kind ignored her. Outside of the classroom or an airplane, she simply didn't exist.

A few men—a very few—saw her as an actual person and were pleasant.

But no one she'd ever trained had bothered to see her as a woman. She supposed it was asking too much to find a man who could accept that she could whip his butt in the air and still want to go dancing on Saturday night.

Prince Jefri continued to stalk closer and she wondered which camp he would fall in. Was it too much to ask that he be one of the nice guys? Did royal sheiks get trained in manners these days? Were there—

The man in question pulled off his helmet and whipped off his sunglasses as he approached. At that exact second, Billie's brain shut down.

He was gorgeous.

No, that didn't describe it. She needed a better word to explain how beautiful he was—but in a totally masculine way. Was it his eyes—deep brown, thickly lashed and sensual? Was it the firm set of his mouth, the perfect cheekbones, the dark hair? Was it the combination of features, the determination in his expression?

Did it matter?

He only got better as he got closer. She'd seen his pictures in magazines, but those glossy images were nothing when compared with the real thing. She did her best to catch her breath and act normal but her heart beat at a speed approaching Mach 3 and showed no signs of slowing.

"Congratulations," the über-hunk said as he held out his hand. "You maneuver your jet like a pro."

He sounded gracious and not the least bit put out. Was that possible?

"I *am* a pro."

She took the offered hand automatically and nearly swooned at the sparks that arced between them. She could feel them, and yet the man gently squeezing her fingers didn't seem the least bit affected. So typical, she thought with wry amusement. Something about being in the cockpit of a jet seemed to render her genderless. Ah, well. In her next life she would be a sex kitten. In this one she was destined to be permanently single.

"How did you disappear into the sun so quickly?" he asked. "I was watching. You were there and then you were gone."

"Every jet has blind spots. The trick is to know where they are and use them to your advantage."

"But I could have turned such that the blind spot moved."

She shook her head as she pulled her hand free. "You were stiff up there. I knew you'd stay on course long enough for me to get lost in the sun. Now, if you'll excuse me..."

Billie turned and headed for the temporary barracks set up at the edge of the airport. If she'd thought she would lose the man of the hour by walking quickly, she was wrong. His long stride easily kept pace with hers, and he continued to pepper her with questions. She answered his queries automatically, all the while doing her best not to notice that he fit the "tall, dark and handsome" cliché perfectly. Pretty and a prince, and about a hundred times more interested in flying than in her.

"This is my stop," she said brightly, cutting him off in mid-pound-thrust ratio question, as they reached the flap of her semipermanent home. "We'll have plenty of time to discuss all of this during the lecture time, and in simulation."

"When will I fly against you again?" he asked.

She tugged the zipper of her flight suit down to her hips and pulled her arms free of the heavy fabric. It might be October in the desert, but it was still warm. She plucked at the T-shirt she wore underneath.

"We'll have plenty of air time," she told him. "Don't worry, I'll be killing you over and over again."

"I think not. About that last maneuver..."

The man didn't even notice she had breasts, Billie thought with a combination of humor and regret. She'd often thought she could step out of her flight suit and walk around stark naked and not one of the pilots would notice. Of course her brothers would see and probably kill her.

"I'm off duty until the morning," she said politely, wishing she could give him a gentle push back to his palace or wherever it was he lived. "I know you're anxious, what with getting your new air force up and running, but I don't work 24/7. Call me crazy."

With that she disappeared into the tent.

Jefri frowned. Had the female instructor turned her back on him and walked away? He followed her inside. "You don't understand. I need this information," he said, barely noticing the Spartan setting.

Billie glanced at him, then smiled. "You don't give up, do you?"

"No."

She opened the drawer of a dresser and pulled out several garments, then disappeared behind a screen.

"Okay, fly boy. I'll give you fifteen minutes, but then you have to let me get some rest. I flew all night to get here and my regular tent isn't set up yet. I'm stuck in regulation housing until then. No offense, but it's hot here and I want my air-conditioning. Oh, have a seat."

He glanced around for a chair and saw one in the corner. There was a small ball in the seat. As he reached for it, the ball moved, uncoiled, growled and snapped at him.

From behind the screen, he heard laughter.

"I see you found Muffin."

He eyed the ball of fur with distaste. "Muffin?"

"My baby. Be nice to the tall man, sweetie," Billie said. "He's paying the bills. Just go ahead and scratch under her chin. Oh, and tell her she's pretty. Muffin likes that."

Jefri eyed the tiny dog. All he saw was multicolored strands of hair and two mistrustful eyes. Hardly anything attractive.

"Get down," he said and pointed to the floor of the tent.

Muffin made a sound very much like a huff, turned her back on him and curled up in a ball. On the chair. He reached for her, but before he could pick her up, she growled.

"I would kill for a bath," Billie said with a sigh, and Jefri allowed himself to be distracted. "But we don't actually travel with a tub. Doyle says it's too inconvenient. Oh, sure, we can move millions of pounds of jets and computer equipment with no problem, but one lousy tub is difficult. What is it with guys? Why don't you get the whole point of a nice long soak?"

As she spoke she stepped out from behind the screen. Jefri began to answer, when his senses went on alert. For the first time since she'd climbed down from the jet he actually *looked* at her.

Girly girl didn't begin to describe things.

She was a centerfold fantasy come to life—big blond hair, big blue eyes and bigger breasts. Her sundress hugged her impressive curves before falling to midthigh. High-heeled sandals gave her a little height, but she still barely cleared his shoulder.

After giving him a smile bright enough to be listed as an energy source, she crossed to the fur ball and gathered it in her arms.

"How's my pretty girl?" she asked in a baby voice. "Did you say hello to the nice prince?"

Billie held the dog's paw in her hand and gave it a little wave. "Muffin says hi."

Prince Jefri of Bahania had never had anyone pretend to speak for an animal before. He glanced from the woman to the dog and back.

Billie grinned. "Okay, so you're not a 'talk to the animals' kind of guy. I can accept that. Doyle swears he hates her but I see him sneaking her treats every now and then."

She walked toward the tent flap and pushed it open. "I thought it would be cooler here, given the time of year. I guess not, though. It's the desert and all." Still cuddling the dog, she walked out into the sunlight. "Not to be too pushy, but your time is ticking away. Didn't you have more questions to ask me?"

Questions? Jefri followed her out, then saw the rows of fighter jets. Yes, of course. He'd had dozens of things he wanted to know, but he couldn't think of any of them. Not when the hem of her form-fitting dress drew his gaze to her perfect thighs, and the sway of her hips made his blood boil.

He was unused to such strong physical reactions. Women had always been easy for him. He saw, he wanted, he was offered. But Billie seemed oblivious to her appeal, nor did she see him as more than an eager student.

She spun around and faced him. ''What?'' she asked, her blue eyes wide with amusement. ''I know I haven't intimidated you, so out with it. What do you want to know?''

He had a thousand requests for information. How soft would her skin feel under his fingers? How would she taste when he kissed her? How low would she moan as he pleasured her over and over, because his fantasies about Billie were about making her surrender with desire?

''Why do you do this?'' he asked. ''Why do you fly?''

''Because I love it. I've always loved it.'' She grinned. ''And I'm damned good at it.''

''Yes, you are.''

Two airplane mechanics walked by. Both of them eyed Billie. They bent their heads together and exchanged words he couldn't hear. But he could imagine.

Jefri looked at the large tents, the open camp and then back at Billie. This would not do.

''You cannot stay here,'' he told her.

Her smile faded. ''Excuse me? You're throwing me out of your country?''

''No. Of course not. I'm saying you can't stay in this camp. It's not safe.''

Her good humor returned. ''I appreciate the concern, but I've been living in camps just like this since I was eleven. They're a little rough on the outside, but still plenty fun. It's sweet of you to worry, but you don't have to. I usually have three brothers and a father hanging around. This time there's only Doyle, but he's plenty burly and he'll make sure I'm well protected.'' She rubbed her cheek against the dog's shoulder. ''Too protected. Isn't that right, little Muffin girl?''

He ignored her conversation with the dog. ''You and your brother will be my guests in the palace.''

She blinked at him. ''Did you say palace?''

''Yes. There are several dozen guest rooms. You would be very comfortable there.''

''Do these rooms have bathtubs?'' Temptation thickened her voice.

''Large enough to swim in.''

She made a low noise in her throat. The sound made his blood surge.

''Gee, a real bed, walls, a roof and a sand-free life,'' she said. ''Color me there. Doyle objects, I'll have to deck him.''

''This is a complete waste of time if you ask me,'' Doyle muttered as the long, black limo drove between large wrought-iron gates. ''We've never stayed with a client before.''

Billie gazed out at the extensive and well-manicured lawns. ''We've never had a royal client before. It's a palace, okay? This is a once-in-a-lifetime opportunity. No one's forcing you to suffer through the indignities of pure luxury. Go back to our tent city by the airport if it makes you happy.''

Her brother glared at her. ''You know Dad would kill me if I wasn't around to keep an eye on you.''

"I'm twenty-seven, Doyle," she said. "At some point you're going to have to acknowledge that I'm all grown-up."

"Ain't gonna happen."

She shook her head at the familiar sentiment. It was hard enough being the baby of the family, but being the only girl made things worse.

Still, she'd gotten used to their high-handed treatment years ago and for the most part was able to ignore it. When she didn't care one way or another, she usually gave in. But not this time. Not when there was a bathtub on the line.

The car rounded a corner and Billie felt her eyes widen. "I can't believe it," she breathed as she took in the multistory pink palace sprawling in front of her.

The main building was huge—the size of a museum or a parliament building. Balconies circled every floor. There were turrets and arched windows and guards on the ground and lush gardens for as far as the eye could see.

"Not bad," Doyle said.

Billie cuffed him. "You're impressed. It's amazing. Too bad Dad and the guys can't be here to see it."

Her father was in South America attending a multinational conference and her two oldest brothers had special assignments in Iraq. Which left Doyle and her in charge of the Bahanian job. Easy work, Billie thought. She could train an air force pilot in her sleep. Flying was something she loved and one of the few things she did well.

The limo pulled to a stop and a uniformed guard

stepped forward to open the rear door. Doyle stepped out first. Billie grabbed Muffin and slid across the slick, leather seat. As she stepped out into the sunlight, her eyes took a second to adjust. During that second or two, her gaze landed on Prince Jefri and she would have sworn she saw him bathed in shimmering gold.

Neat trick, she thought as her mind whirled from the beauty of the palace and her body swooned from the beauty of the man.

"Ms. Van Horn." The prince nodded.

"Billie," she said with a smile. "As I'm going to be shooting you out of the sky on a regular basis, there's no point in being formal."

She thought the prince might have winced at her words. No doubt he thought he would get good enough to win against her. They all thought that, and they were all wrong. Which meant he would get more and more crabby as the training went along. Oh, well. It had happened before and she had survived.

The prince spoke to a uniformed young woman who nodded, then gestured toward Doyle. Her brother gave Billie a quick wink as he followed the maid into the castle. Billie stepped up for her escort and tried not to drool at the thought of the riches within.

"This way," Prince Jefri said.

She blinked at him. "Excuse me?"

"I will show you to your room."

Did royalty do that? She figured about the only thing a prince did for himself was breathe. Hadn't she read somewhere that some royals even had a special servant to put toothpaste on the toothbrush?

"You don't have to do that yourself," she said, thinking of her bath and how long she was going to soak. At least an hour. She had a good book she wanted to finish and a…

"Is this your first visit to my country?" he asked.

"Um, yes." She shifted Muffin to her other arm and trailed along beside the prince. "I wasn't part of the sales presentation when our firm bid for the training job."

They entered into a foyer the size of a small arena. The gold inlaid ceilings soared a good fifty feet above them. Mosaics of ancient battles lined the curved walls. Not exactly like the flocked wallpaper in that hotel in Bosnia.

He noticed her interest and paused in front of a mural of several fierce men on horses. "My people have always been fighters. A thousand years ago, we defended our land against the infidels."

She looked at him out of the corner of her eye. "That would be us, right?"

"Only if you are European."

"I'm a bit of everything." She looked at the elaborate chandelier and the stained glass windows. "Beautiful place."

"Thank you. The Pink Palace is a treasure for the people of Bahania."

"How many of them get to stay here on a regular basis?"

The prince surprised her by smiling. ''We hold it in trust.''

''I'm sure they're grateful.''

He started down the main hallway. Billie followed, noting they could have easily driven a tank and not come close to bumping into any walls.

''I did some research before I got here,'' she said, her high-heeled sandals clicking loudly on the tiled floor. ''Your country is not strictly Muslim.''

''No. Our people celebrate many faiths, and respect all.''

That's what all her reading had told her. While the rest of the Middle East couldn't seem to get it together, Bahania, and their neighbor El Bahar, offered religious freedom to all. The monarchies had ruled for over a thousand years with no hint of uprising. Ultimate power that didn't corrupt? Was it possible?

''So why the air force?'' she asked.

''To protect our oil fields. With so much unrest around us, we need to be able to secure our resources.''

''The oil won't last forever.''

''True, which is why even now we are diversifying our exports. Bahania will not be left behind in the world market.''

Pretty *and* smart, she thought with a little smile. Now if only he could see her as a desirable woman, her life would be complete. Her research had informed her that Prince Jefri was single, but she'd seen pictures of the women in his life. There wasn't a fighter pilot in the bunch.

They passed room after room. Some were decorated with elegant Western-style furniture while others had low sofas and cushions, more suited to a nomadic tent. There were paintings and frescos and statues and…

Muffin squirmed in her arms.

"What is it sweetie?" she asked.

The dog yipped and squirmed some more. Seconds later a large white cat strolled out of a meeting room large enough to hold the entire Congress.

Billie yelped and clutched her dog more tightly to her chest. "What is that?" she asked as she took a step back.

The prince stared at her. "A cat," he said with the obvious patience of one speaking to a mentally challenged person.

Annoyance overcame hormones and she glared at him. "I *know* it's a cat. What's it doing here?"

"My father has an affection for cats."

She eyed the fluffy white demon. "I read that but I thought more in the lines of a painting on velvet or some carvings. Are you telling me there are actual cats in the palace?"

"Dozens. Is that a problem?"

She saw the corner of the prince's mouth twitch, as if he was amused by her reaction.

"I'm not a cat person."

"They will not hurt you."

She wasn't all that sure. If there were dozens, they could gang up on her and take her down. "What about Muffin?"

"I'm sure your…dog will be safe."

She didn't like how he said ''dog'' and she didn't like the cats.

''Do you have an allergy?'' he asked.

''Not exactly.''

''Then what, exactly?''

''I had a bad experience when I was young.''

''With a small lion?''

She narrowed her gaze. Suddenly he wasn't nearly as handsome and not the least bit intelligent. ''Would you like to show me to my room?''

''More than life itself.''

Chapter Two

Jefri could tell his guest was annoyed and unhappy about the cats. While he didn't appreciate them as his father did, especially when they shed on all the furniture and covered his clothes in cat hair, they were little more than a mild inconvenience. But watching Billie Van Horn skitter around them, jump away and generally act as if she was in mortal danger every time one of them crossed her path, he wondered what possible trauma in her past could have caused such an overreaction.

At least wondering about her cat phobia gave him something to think about other than the perfection of her body. She was all lush curves and earthy appeal. Her scent—soap, something floral and a hint of the woman herself—made his blood heat. He wouldn't have minded his reaction if she'd been trying to get his attention, but she seemed to be far more concerned about protecting herself from marauding felines.

He led the way to an elevator that took them to the third floor. When the doors opened, a tabby sat in the middle of the hallway. Billie jumped which, considering her high-heeled sandals, made him worry for the state of her slender ankles.

''Were you attacked?'' he asked as she sidled around the twelve-pound feline.

''What?'' She glanced at him, her blue eyes wide with worry. ''Not me, but a close friend.'' She pressed her lips together. ''Muffin is only seven pounds. They could slice her to ribbons and serve her for breakfast.''

Jefri thought of how much time his father's cats spent sleeping. ''I doubt they are that ambitious.''

Billie's sniff told him she wasn't impressed by his logic.

As much as he wanted her in the palace, he hadn't intended his invitation to distress her.

''Would you prefer to stay at the barracks?''

She shook her head. ''We'll manage.''

''The room is just up there.''

He motioned to a door, then stepped ahead of her to open it. Billie stepped inside and her breath caught in an audible gasp. Jefri followed her gaze, taking in the large living area, the floor-to-ceiling windows offering a view of the Arabian Sea and the wide double doors that led to the sleeping quarters.

''Will you be comfortable here?'' he asked politely.

"Yes. And should I feel the need to take in boarders to supplement my income, there will be plenty of room." She grinned. "This I could get used to."

"You may consider the palace your home while you're in Bahania."

"You might want to be careful with an invitation like that. What if I never want to leave?"

Then she would be available to him whenever he wanted. Jefri turned the thought over in his mind and found it gave him pleasure. Too bad his father had done away with the harem. She would have been a wonderful addition.

"Please let any of the staff know if you have any needs," he said instead of telling her what he was really thinking.

"Sure thing. I can't imagine needing anything else, though. This room is amazing."

She bent over and set her dog on the floor. The fur ball trotted to the sofa and began sniffing at the furniture.

"Do you always travel with your pet?" Jefri asked.

"Yup. Muffin and I are a package deal. I've even taken her up flying with me."

He couldn't imagine why. "Does she enjoy it?"

"Hard to tell," Billie admitted. "She doesn't throw up, so that's something."

Wanting to talk about something other than the creature touring the room, he crossed to the French doors and pointed toward the sea.

"The balcony circles the entire palace. From the south end you can look toward Lucia-Serrat."

''I've heard of the island. It's supposed to be very beautiful.''

''Much of this area is.''

She shook her head. ''I had a mental picture of sand as far as the eye could see. But the city sprawls over a much bigger area than I would have thought. Of course when it ends, there *are* miles of sand.''

''You noticed that while you were flying today?''

She nodded. ''Not much else to do up there. The first few days of dogfighting are pretty boring what with…''

Her voice trailed off. He saw her swallow, then she glanced at him from under long lashes.

''So that was bad, right?'' she asked, sounding more resigned than contrite. ''I've just insulted a prince. Is there a punishment? Do I get sent to the dungeon?''

''Why the sudden concern?'' he asked. ''Back at the airport you told me I would never beat you.''

''Oh, you won't,'' she told him. ''But I should probably be more subtle about it all.''

''Because of the palace?''

''It does sort of put our lives in perspective. I'm a small-town girl and you're…not.''

''Indeed. I would not even qualify as a big-city girl.''

Her beautiful mouth twisted. ''You know what I mean. Maybe you could get me a brochure or some notes. Something along the lines of twenty ways not to insult royalty.''

"There is a person in charge of etiquette. Perhaps I should have him drop by."

Billie wrinkled her nose. "You're making fun of me."

"Only a little."

"Wow. You have a sense of humor. What's next on the surprise parade? Do you do your own laundry?"

"Never."

"A guy thing. My brothers don't do theirs either. But then that's fairly typical of—"

A sharp yowl cut through the conversation. He turned toward the sound but Billie was already moving across the marble flooring. Several sharp barks were followed by a yip.

"Muffin!" she cried as she plunged into a fray of fur, paws, teeth and tails.

While Jefri had no desire to rescue her pet, he felt obligated to offer assistance. He eyed Billie's bare legs and hands, then moved behind her, wrapped an arm around her waist and lifted her out of the way.

She squealed, adding to the din. He had a brief impression of curves, heat and potential before he set her down behind him.

"I'll take care of this," he said as he reached into the swirl of cats and plucked out a small growling, yelping ball of fur.

For his trouble he received several scratches, a bite from the dog and enough hair on his suit to change the color from black to gray.

"I believe this is yours." He handed the small, shaking dog to her.

She pulled the creature close and brushed her hands over its body. "Muffin! Are you hurt? Did those horrible, mean killers hurt you?"

After reassuring herself that Muffin had indeed survived, she turned her attention to him.

"I don't know what to say," she breathed, her blue eyes wide and anguished. "They could have killed her."

He examined his hand. Muffin's bite hadn't broken the skin, but several of the cats had left their mark.

"I think she would have survived the encounter."

He crossed to the main door and opened it, then shooed the cats out of the suite.

"There may still be one or two left in here," he said. "Just give them a push out the door."

She glanced around uneasily, then moved close. "How can I thank you?"

Her voice was low and intense. Had she been someone of his usual social circle, he would have assumed she was offering more than a polite acknowledgment of what he'd done. But with Billie, he wasn't so sure. Besides, as much as he wanted her in his bed, he intended to seduce her every step of the way. He had a feeling that with her, anticipation would only make the experience sweeter.

"It was no matter."

She shook her head and set Muffin on the sofa. "It was a huge deal. Those cats were so horrible." She reached for his hand and took it in hers. "You're bleeding!"

A few of the scratches seeped blood. Jefri wasn't the least bit concerned, but he didn't object when Billie dragged him into the large bathroom and ran water over his hand.

Her skin was smooth and warm against his own. She stood close enough for him to feel the heat of her body and the light brush of her breasts against his arm.

"You were very brave," she said.

"They were only cats."

"Killers by nature," she murmured as she reached for a towel.

He wiped his hands then touched his finger to her chin. "What happened that made you so afraid of cats? While I'll agree they are hunters, they are small enough that you would never be in danger of them."

She shrugged. "I don't like them."

"I gathered that. The question is why?"

Billie sighed. Her breath teased his skin and he dropped his hand to his side.

"When I was young, I desperately wanted a pet," she said. "Something of my own. But my mother was concerned about getting me one because my brothers were so wild. She doubted any pet big enough to hold its own with them would be a good animal for me. But on my seventh birthday, my brothers pitched in and got me a white mouse."

She smiled. "I know they did it because they

thought the mouse would scare me, but I wasn't frightened at all."

"You have three older brothers?" he asked.

She nodded.

He thought of the size and strength of Doyle Van Horn and knew that Billie would have to have been tough to survive in that household.

"I loved Missy," Billie said.

He raised his eyebrows. "Missy the Mouse?"

"Uh-huh. She was very sweet and tame. I taught her tricks."

"Such as?"

"She knew her name and she would stand on her back legs when I offered her food."

"That's not a trick. She was simply attempting to reach the food."

Billie's eyes narrowed. "She was *my* mouse. I get to say if it was a trick or not."

"Fair enough. So you had this mouse. I suspect there was a cat involved."

Billie nodded. She leaned against the bathroom counter. "We had this playroom. There was a latch up higher than I could reach and sometimes, if I slammed the door, it locked into place. One day Missy got out. I couldn't find her anywhere. I wanted my brothers to help me find her, but they wouldn't. I was mad, so I stomped into the playroom and slammed the door. It locked behind me."

Her voice remained firm, but he heard the edge of emotion. Why? Over the death of a mouse twenty years ago? What possible reason could she have for caring?

Billie folded her arms over her chest. "I walked to the window and looked out and that's when I saw Missy. Two of the neighbor's cats had her cornered. They were playing with her. Torturing her. I screamed for my brothers to let me out but they were in the front yard and couldn't hear me. My mom was at the grocery store. I was trapped for nearly two hours. That's about how long it took them to kill and eat her."

Jefri winced. "You didn't turn away?"

"How could I? She was my mouse." She sighed. "I remember sobbing and my mom finding me. She tried to convince me it hadn't been Missy, but how many white mice live in the wild?"

"So that is why you dislike cats?"

"Wouldn't you?"

He couldn't imagine having a mouse as a pet in the first place. "They were acting on instinct, not out of malice."

"Oh, and that makes Missy's death acceptable?"

"Of course not." Were they really talking about a mouse?

"It's hard having pets," she said as she straightened her arms and pushed off the counter. "But worth it. Now I have Muffin and I'm going to make sure nothing bad ever happens to her. No palace cat is going to be allowed to have her for dinner."

"The cats here are well fed."

"They'd better be."

Temper flashed in her eyes. Jefri wondered how they'd shifted topics so completely. Given his choice they would be talking about flying or how attractive she found him. So far they had done neither.

''I will tell the staff to keep the cats out of your rooms as much as possible,'' he said.

''Really? That would be great.'' She glanced at the tub. ''If you hadn't tempted me with such a great bathroom, I probably would have returned to the barracks. But this is pretty irresistible.''

Ah, so she could resist him, but not a bathtub. That put things in perspective.

''About your stay here,'' he said, deciding flying was the safest topic. ''You will have to be at the airport each day?''

''Yup. There's plenty of butt for me to kick in your nice blue skies.''

''I'm sure my men will enjoy learning from you,'' he told her, ignoring the assumption that she would continue to best him. He was going to make sure that didn't happen.

''Oh, they're going to learn, whether they enjoy the process or not.''

''I will put a car and driver at your disposal. Simply tell the driver where you wish to go and he will take you there.''

Her mouth parted. ''You're kidding? My own driver?''

''You may share him if you would like.''

She laughed. ''No, that's okay. As I said before, I could really get used to this.''

"I hope you'll enjoy your stay in my country."

He nodded at her and left. While there was much more to be said, this wasn't the time. Later, when he'd decided on his strategy he would talk to her about more than her work. He would discover the secrets of the beautiful woman who flew like a falcon and moved with the grace of the cats she found so distasteful. He would learn her strengths, her weaknesses and he would have her in his bed. He would also best her in the air. To be honest, he wasn't sure which he would enjoy more.

Billie finished drying her hair and stepped back to admire the effect. "Not bad," she murmured to her reflection, as she fluffed up a curl. She'd always been a big-hair kind of gal and the complete lack of humidity in Bahania meant no risk of her carefully poofed style going flat.

Nearly an hour in a massive tub had relaxed her. Now rested, redressed in a sundress and still jet-lagged from her trip the previous day she felt both tired and antsy.

"We should take a walk," she told Muffin as she moved back into the living room of the suite. "A couple of laps in this room would almost do it, huh?"

She grinned as she spoke, then turned in a circle as she admired the elegant Western-style furnishings and beautiful paintings. There was a thick oriental rug by the sofa and a dining area to the left. The view was as spectacular as any she'd ever seen from the ground.

Silent air-conditioning kept the room a comfortable seventy-six degrees.

"The good life," she said as she gathered Muffin in her arms. "Okay, what if we take a quick walk outside, then figure out what we're doing about dinner? I mean does the palace have room service? I should have asked the prince about it."

She would have, too, if he hadn't been so tall and princely while he'd showed her around the suite.

"The man is a hunk," she told her little dog as she carried her out into the corridor. "Wish he were my type."

Not that Billie had an actual type. That would require a level of involvement she'd never had.

"In my next life I'll be a guy magnet," she told herself. "They'll be tripping over each other to get to me."

But until then, it was just her and her dog.

Billie walked to the end of the corridor and took the stairs down. She had a good sense of direction and was able to find her way to the garden in under five minutes.

The lush cultivated space seemed larger at ground level. The various gardens spilled into each other, more formal English garden hedges giving way to serene pools surrounded by tropical disarray. She set Muffin down, careful to keep an eye on her so she wasn't cornered and attacked by marauding cats.

"Not bad," Billie murmured as Muffin began to sniff. "Easy to understand why it's good to be the prince."

Her sandals clicked loudly on the stone path. She wove her way between plants and bushes and trees, stopping to smell a flower or finger a leaf. She didn't know all that much about growing things. Her expertise required an engine and enough thrust and speed to break the sound barrier. Still, if one had to stay earthbound, this was the place.

She rounded a corner and saw a man sitting on a bench. He looked up as she approached, then stood.

''Good afternoon,'' he said with a smile. ''Who might you be?''

The man was tall and handsome, albeit older. Gray spread from his temples and there were lines by his dark, deep-set eyes. His well-tailored suit reminded her of a bank president or senator, not that she'd ever met either.

''Billie Van Horn,'' she said, holding out her hand.

''Ah, the military expert. I recognize the name.'' He shook hands with her, then motioned to the bench. ''You are a member of the family?''

''The only girl. A giant pain, let me tell you.'' She settled on one end of the stone bench while he took the other. ''The good news is I'm a great pilot and if my brothers ever make me too crazy I challenge them to a dogfight.'' She grinned. ''A fighter jet is a great equalizer.''

''I can imagine.''

Muffin trotted up and sniffed at the nice man's shoes.

''My dog,'' Billie said. ''Muffin. I'd heard there

were cats, but I didn't expect so many. I'm trying to keep Muffin from being the chef's special.''

''I doubt you have to worry. She looks capable of taking care of herself.''

''Not when she's outnumbered. There was already a fight in my room.''

The older man raised his eyebrows. ''You are staying at the palace?''

''Yes. Prince Jefri invited me and my brother Doyle.'' She leaned close. ''I confess I was seduced by the thought of a bathtub. Roughing it comes with the job, so how could I resist a few weeks in a palace? The place is amazing.''

''I'm glad you think so.''

A cat strolled up. Billie eyed it with distaste but her companion simply stroked its back.

''You fly jets?'' he asked. ''That is your job?''

''I do most of the in-air training. I also work with the pilots on the simulators. It's fun.''

''You are good at this?''

She grinned. ''The best. This morning I blew Prince Jefri out of the sky in less than two minutes. Not literally, of course.''

''How comforting. I am not yet ready to lose my youngest son.''

As the words sank in, Billie opened her mouth, then closed it. ''S-son?'' she repeated, hoping she'd misunderstood. ''You're his father?''

''Yes.''

She looked into the dark eyes and realized the resemblance had been staring her in the face.

"But that would make you..."

"The king."

"Oh, God."

She half rose, thought about *The King and I* and wondered if she was allowed to hold her head higher than his. Was that a real law or just humor for a musical?

"I can't..." She swallowed. "I didn't..." Giving in to the need to curl up and die, she covered her face with her hands and moaned. "How many laws have I broken?"

"No more than three or four."

She spread her fingers and peeked at the king. He didn't look angry. If the smile was anything to go by, he was amused.

She dropped her hands to her lap and straightened. "You could have told me."

"I did."

"I mean before. When I said, 'Hi, I'm Billie.' You could have said, 'Hey, I'm the king.'"

"This was more interesting. You would not have spoken so freely with me if you had known who I am."

"No kidding. So do I bow or something?"

"You do neither. I am King Hassan of Bahania." He nodded regally. "Welcome to my country."

"Thank you. It's great." She sighed. "I guess I'd better apologize for not liking cats."

"Caring for them is not required, although you aren't allowed to injure any."

"I'm okay with that, but Muffin may be another

matter.'' She glanced down at her dog and wrinkled her nose. ''She's only seven pounds, so I don't think she could do much more than cause a lot of noise.''

The king followed her gaze, then smiled. ''That is true. I will have to hope my cats are up to the challenge. If there—''

A loud howl interrupted his sentence. Billie sprang to her feet and headed toward the noise just as a black-and-white cat flew in front of her. She sidestepped to avoid stepping on the horrible creature and slid off the stone path. Her momentum didn't help her regain her balance and she felt herself falling.

Suddenly strong arms grabbed her from behind. Someone hauled her up, rescuing her from what could have been some serious pain. Billie caught her breath as she felt rock-hard muscles, incredible body heat and the thundering beat of her own heart.

Please God let her not have been rescued by the king. He was handsome and all that, but old enough that having a visceral reaction to him bordered on icky.

She turned her head and breathed a sigh of relief when she saw Jefri gazing at her from only a few inches away.

''Your dog seems to be in trouble again,'' he said as he righted her. ''She has a knack for finding it.''

Billie straightened and brushed off her dress. ''I would say with all these cats stalking her, she has little choice except to protect herself.''

Remembering the presence of the king a half sentence too late, she swallowed. ''Not that the cats aren't lovely,'' she added in a small voice.

Jefri raised his eyebrows, but didn't speak. The king looked amused. He bent over and scooped up a now calm and silent Muffin.

''So you *are* a troublemaker,'' he said, staring into her dog's little face. ''Perhaps you need to learn your place in the world.''

Billie hoped that place didn't involve a cage. ''She travels with me everywhere. She's sort of spoiled.''

''So I see.'' He set the dog down on the ground and patted her head. ''I would like you and your brother to join me for dinner tonight.'' He straightened. ''If you can bear to leave the little one in your room.''

Dinner with the king? How many times did that happen to a girl like her?

''Absolutely.'' She mentally flashed on her wardrobe. ''Formal? Informal?''

''It will just be family,'' he said.

Which didn't answer her question but made her wonder if the ever-hunky Prince Jefri would be there.

''Good. Would you like to inform your brother?''

Billie thought of Doyle's reaction to dinner with royalty. He wouldn't be amused.

''I'll let you tell him,'' she said, knowing even *her* brother wouldn't dare lose his temper with a king. ''He'll be thrilled.''

Jefri's mouth twitched, which made her wonder if he knew what she was thinking.

Not possible, she told herself. Men like him didn't

care about brains or thoughts. They wanted… She paused as she realized she didn't know what men like him wanted from women. But as she was neither a supermodel nor the heir to a champagne fortune, she was unlikely to find out anytime soon.

"Seven-thirty then," the king said.

"I'll be there." She bent over and scooped up Muffin, then headed back to her room. If she was going to dine with royalty she needed much bigger hair.

Jefri finished knotting his tie and turned to reach for his jacket. As he picked it up, he checked the fabric for cat hairs.

"Try this," his brother, Murat, said and tossed him a delinting roll.

"Thanks."

Jefri went to work on his jacket while Murat lounged on the recently dehaired sofa.

"She really has a dog?" his brother asked.

"It is more of a rat with fur." Of course Billie seemed to have an affinity for rodents, he thought remembering the tragedy of her mouse.

"And she shot you out of the sky?"

Jefri shrugged into the jacket and turned his attention on his brother. "Not literally."

"I can see that." Murat grinned. "I cannot wait to meet her."

"She is…unexpected."

"Sounds interesting."

Jefri said nothing as he stared at Murat. His brother rose, stretched, then chuckled.

"I *am* the crown prince," Murat said, as if Jefri needed reminding. "I may claim who I choose."

"You may not claim this one."

One dark eyebrow rose. "Why not?"

Jefri allowed himself a small smile. "She is mine."

"Ah. Does she know?"

"Not yet, but she will. Soon."

"Then I wish you luck, my brother."

"I will not need it."

Jefri was determined. Nothing would stand in the way of his learning all of Billie's secrets, then having her in his bed.

Chapter Three

Like most women, Billie had loved to play dress-up when she'd been younger, so the chance to actually put on finery for real was too good to pass up. Plus one of her job perks was attending the Paris Air Show every other year. Which meant after she and her brothers oohed and ahhed over the latest in aviation technology, she went shopping.

She stood now in one of her impulse purchases—a shimmering floor-length dark purple gown. The halter-style permitted her to show off curves and still wear a bra—always exciting. Combs held her hair off her face and allowed her to tease the curls up about another inch, while long tendrils cascaded down her back. Strappy silver sandals with four-inch heels made her feel like an Amazon goddess…well, a short one anyway.

"What do you think?" she asked, holding out two different earrings for Muffin to inspect. Her dog lay on the high four-poster bed. "These are more dangling, but these have more flash."

Muffin barked.

"I agree. Flash over dangle," Billie said and put on the smaller cubic zirconia earrings.

After a light spritzing of perfume, she pronounced herself as ready as she was going to be.

"I promise to bring you back something," she said. "I'm sure we'll have some kind of meat dish. I tucked a Baggie in my purse." She waved her tiny evening bag at Muffin.

The trick would be getting the bit of entrée from her plate to her handbag, but she'd done it countless times before and had almost never been caught.

"Okay. You be good. I'll see you soon."

Billie pushed the play button on the DVD player in the bedroom armoire, then headed for the door. As she stepped into the hallway of the amazing pink palace, she had the feeling that for the first time in her life, she was almost a princess.

"Way better than Halloween dress-up," she murmured as she started down a corridor.

As she paused by the elevator, waiting for it to take her to the second floor because there was no way she could do stairs in these shoes or the long dress, she heard a door close and the sound of footsteps. Seconds later Jefri walked toward her.

"Good evening," he said, looking more than a little spiffy in a black tux. So she'd guessed right then, "a family dinner'' in royal circles meant way dressier than jeans.

The soft wool fabric of Jefri's tux had the faintest shimmer to it, and Billie had an instant urge to touch. That would be bad, she told herself, trying not to swoon as she took in the rest of the package.

Most men cleaned up pretty well and looked good in a tuxedo, but those who had a head start in the looks department came out looking even better. Jefri was no exception. He'd brushed his dark hair away from his face, which emphasized his stern yet handsome features. The white shirt collar and cuffs made his skin seem darker. Billie avoided the sun whenever possible. She burned more than tanned and didn't want to be fighting the leather look when she was fifty.

Knowing how pale she was and how dark he was gave her a little shiver. She had a visual of them entwined in bed, looking like actors for an erotic movie.

''Hi,'' she said and waggled her fingers. ''You look nice.''

He reached for her free hand and raised it slightly, then kissed her knuckles. ''You are enchanting. The glories of my country pale when compared to your beauty.''

Okay, sure. It was a line and little old-fashioned, but it worked. Billie felt her knees get a little wobbly and her heart start to pound.

The elevator doors opened. Jefri put his hand on her back to urge her to enter first. His thumb and forefinger landed on bare skin. Goose bumps erupted, even as warmth poured through her.

''I see you left Muffin in your room,'' he said.

''I thought it was best. I always feel badly when I'm going to have fun without her, but she's watching a movie.''

He pushed the button for the second floor. ''Excuse me? Your dog is watching a movie?''

''Uh-huh. And I have to say that DVD collection in the armoire was fabulous. I had a hard time deciding, but in the end I put on *Legally Blonde II* because she has a real thing for Bruiser. That's the dog in the movie.''

Jefri's gaze never left her face, yet she felt him mentally drifting. He blinked.

''I do not understand,'' he told her. ''You are the same woman who can fly a fighter jet better than anyone I know.''

The doors opened and they stepped out.

''Yup. That's me.''

''Yet you put on a movie for your *dog?*''

''I don't really see how the two concepts relate.''

''Nor do I. This way.''

He escorted her down a long corridor. Soft lighting spilled from the dozens of rooms they passed. Talk about a lot of space. Taking a lap around each floor would pretty much take care of anyone's aerobic needs for the day.

''I heard your brother could not join us tonight,'' Jefri said.

''The rest of the equipment arrived and he wanted

to oversee that. If you ask me, he was in a snit about having to get dressed up for dinner. His loss. I'm sure the food will be amazing."

"I hope you find that everything pleases you."

His low voice scraped along her bare skin like a length of nubby fabric. Billie felt strange, sort of trembling and overheated and spacey. She had to get a grip. In the heels she wore, one wrong step could be fatal.

They turned left at a large pillar and entered what she supposed for them was a small, casual dining room. For her it was like being asked to eat in the roped-off parts of the British Museum.

A long table stood in the center of the room. From the number of chairs pushed up against the walls, she supposed it could be expanded to seat at least thirty, maybe more. Two antique hutches stood flanking a large tapestry depicting a young woman in an open kind of boat. Based on her dress, Billie would guess the scene was from the mid-sixteen hundreds.

Three chandeliers provided light over the table, but instead of using bulbs they twinkled with candlelight. Several sconces lined the walls, also providing illumination. A long buffet held a bucket of champagne on ice and unopened bottles of red and white wine, along with an assortment of liquors. Two men with trays of canapés hovered by the doorway, and there wasn't a cat in sight.

"This works," Billie said as she and Jefri strolled the length of the room.

"I'm glad you like it. Champagne?"

"Sure. I'm not flying until late tomorrow morning."

Jefri popped the bottle with an ease that made her feel like an extra in an old Audrey Hepburn movie, then accepted the delicate crystal glass.

"To new adventures," he said, touching his glass to hers. "And those we share them with."

She figured this wasn't the time for her usual "Bottoms up" so she smiled before taking a sip. The liquid bubbles tickled the whole way down her throat. Oh, yeah. This was the good life for sure.

A tall man Billie hadn't met entered the dining room. Based on his good looks and regal bearing she was going to take a wild guess and say he was another royal prince.

Bingo, she thought, when Jefri introduced him as "My oldest brother, Crown Prince Murat."

She had her purse in one hand and her champagne in the other. For one horrible second, Billie thought maybe she was expected to curtsey. Why hadn't she asked Jefri on the walk over? Before she could figure out what to do, Murat leaned forward and lightly kissed her cheek.

"Welcome, Ms. Van Horn. My brother complained of your great skill in the sky but he said nothing of your exceptional beauty."

She would have thought that older handsome prince set to inherit the kingdom would have had some effect on her when he'd kissed her. She'd braced herself for at least a toe curl, but there hadn't been even a flicker. Interesting. So her reaction was specifically to Jefri and not just to the whole good-looking-guy-in-the-palace thing. She would have to take that information out later and figure out what it meant.

"Most men don't enjoy being shot down by a woman," she said with a smile. "It's an ego thing. I don't take it personally."

"Billie is convinced I will not ever best her. I am going to have to prove her wrong."

Murat glanced between the two of them. "She does not look concerned, my brother. Perhaps you will have to content yourself with besting her in other ways."

The king entered the room, along with an obviously pregnant woman and what Billie took to be yet another of the handsome prince crop.

Jefri leaned close. "Perhaps my brother is right and I should seek other kinds of victories."

The combination of his words and his warm breath on her neck made her quiver.

"Come, you must meet our newest treasure," the king said, leading the couple toward them. "Billie, my son Reyhan and his beautiful wife Emma."

Billie had the whole purse/champagne thing under control this time. She'd tucked her bag under her arm so she was able to hold out her right hand to both of them.

"Welcome," Reyhan said pleasantly.

"Are you really a fighter pilot?" Emma asked.

"She is brilliant in the sky," Jefri said, answering for her.

"Amazing." Emma smiled. "I thought you would

be more…masculine. But you're lovely enough to be a pop star or an actress.''

Billie beamed. ''Aren't you sweet. I'm just a girl who likes to dress up. I tried being one of the boys for a long time and it never worked.''

''One cannot imagine why,'' Jefri murmured in her ear.

Murat returned with a scotch for his brother and a glass of what looked like sparkling water for Emma.

''What do you think of Billie?'' he asked. ''Is she not most intriguing?''

Jefri stepped between her and Murat. ''She is my guest.''

Billie felt a slight thrill. Was Jefri being possessive? Did he actually see her as something other than a means to fly better?

Another couple arrived—one of the princes accompanied by a petite, curvy blonde who squealed when she saw Billie.

''You're American. Yeah. We can hang out and talk while you're here. I'm Cleo. Hi. Do you realize that out of all four of the women who are in this family, I'm the only one who lives in the palace?'' She poked Emma's arm. ''You're constantly gone, as are Zara and Sabrina. It's really annoying.''

Cleo's escort, Prince Sadik, sighed. ''You have confused our guest and possibly frightened her.''

''Are you frightened?'' Cleo asked.

Billie laughed. ''No, just confused. What women? Who are Zara and Sabrina?''

''Perhaps we should adjourn to the table where we

can all straighten this out,'' the king said. ''Billie, you may sit next to me.''

So she found herself next to the king of Bahania, surrounded by honest to goodness princes and princesses. Billie had the fleeting thought that she wished her mother was still alive to take part in all this.

''All right, let me see if I have this right,'' she said over the soup course. ''Sabrina and Zara are princesses by birth.''

The king nodded.

''But Zara didn't know she was your daughter until about a year ago. And Cleo and Emma are Americans married to your sons.''

''That is correct.''

''Very complicated,'' she said as she discreetly moved the sliver of prosciutto she'd slipped off her appetizer plate into the Baggie.

''You will learn who belongs with whom,'' the king said kindly. ''Simply remember my sons favor American women.''

''Interesting point.''

She couldn't help glancing across the table to where Jefri sat. Did he favor American women as well? He seemed to be watching her, and while she wanted to believe it meant something, she'd been burned enough times to hold back. Ever since turning sixteen and having her first crush, she'd found herself interested in men who wanted nothing to do with her. It was like a curse.

''I have met one of your brothers,'' the king said. ''How many are there?''

"Three. I'm the only girl and the youngest."

"Sabrina could relate to that," Cleo said. "Her brothers made her life miserable. What about yours?"

"My mother always said they were a handful. She did her best to keep them in line."

"What does she think of your occupation?" Jefri asked.

"She died when I was eleven. I'm not sure she would have been thrilled with my hanging out with my brothers all the time, but she would have wanted me to be happy."

"Did your father remarry?" the king asked.

Billie shook her head. "We traveled a lot with the company. My mother had kept me home with her, but after she was gone, I went around the world, as well. It made for a very eclectic education." And nowhere to call home. But Billie had always known she would have to choose between her love of the sky and putting down roots.

Emma leaned toward her. "I would have thought someone raised by her father would have been more of a tomboy."

Billie laughed. "I tried being one for a while, but then I realized I made a lousy son, so I gave it up and surrendered to my inner girl."

"Hence the call sign?" Jefri asked.

She nodded.

He raised his glass. "To always surrendering to your inner girl."

If asked, Billie would have expected to explain that the royal family was stuffy and well, boring. But that wasn't true at all. After grilling her about her life—in the most pleasant way possible—they'd laughed and talked and teased just like any other family she'd met. Okay, the flatware had been gold, but the rest of the meal had been surprisingly normal.

Whether it was the combination of too much champagne, the strange quarters or an evening spent getting lost in Jefri's dark gaze, Billie found herself unable to sleep. Giving up, she left Muffin snoring softly and pulled on her robe, then walked into the living room where she opened the French door leading to the balcony and stepped out into the quiet of the night.

A moon hung low in the sky and sent fingers of light across the lapping sea. There were scents in the air, smells she didn't recognize but knew would forever remind her of Bahania. The air was still, faintly cool, but still pleasant.

"The good life," she said with a smile. "I doubt anything is ever going to top this."

She leaned on the balcony and stared down at the dark gardens. Slim shadows darted in and out of bushes. Cats, she thought grimly. No doubt out to kill. Why on earth would anyone think creatures like that were pet-worthy?

"What has you so concerned?" Jefri said as he came out of the darkness and moved next to her at the railing. "You are frowning."

His unexpected appearance startled her, although not enough to make her duck back inside. She had a brief thought that she was in her nightgown, but then reminded herself that she'd been a lot more uncovered in her evening gown.

"There," she said pointing toward the garden. "Cats."

He chuckled. "I will protect you from any who attempt to attack you." He glanced around. "Where is Muffin?"

"Sleeping. She needs her beauty sleep."

"Tell me she does not have one of those black sleep masks."

Billie laughed. "She doesn't."

"Good."

He leaned against the railing, his shoulder close to her own.

"Did you enjoy your evening with us?" he asked.

"Very much so." She glanced at him, taking in the dark slacks and the formal white shirt he'd unbuttoned. The tie was gone, as was the jacket, and he'd rolled his sleeves up to his elbows.

"I've never dined with royalty before," she said. "I thought I'd be more nervous but everyone made me feel very comfortable."

"I was concerned you thought there were too many questions."

"Not at all. I thought everyone was interested and genuine rather than grilling me."

"We are like other families?"

"Except for the prince thing."

"So you were impressed."

She smiled. "Not exactly."

He raised his eyebrows. "Why not?"

"Come on. How impressed could I be by wealth and a title when we both know I could blow you out of the sky in thirty-eight seconds?"

"Good point. However, I could impress you in other ways."

Oh, yeah, that was a serious possibility.

"I'm just the hired help," she said instead, and did her best to act casually. "In a few months, I'll be gone and you'll rule your own skies."

"Do you like that aspect of your job? Going from place to place?"

"Sometimes." She tucked her hair behind her ear. "I enjoy seeing the world, but sometimes I wouldn't mind having a permanent base of operations. The problem with that is I've yet to find a way to combine home and hearth with what I love to do."

"The flying."

"Exactly."

"How did you learn to fly?" he asked.

"My dad had always taken me up with him. I was handling single engine planes by the time I was ten. My mom tried to hold me back, which worked until she died. Then there was no one telling my dad no. I worked my way up to jets pretty quickly." She turned her head and smiled at him. "Having a mini air force in the family helped. What about you?"

"I have always loved flying. My father indulged me with lessons when I was twelve. I'm sure he thought it was something I would outgrow."

"But you didn't."

"You're right. The more I flew, the more I loved

it. I wanted to join an air force, but we did not have one here in Bahania and no other country would allow me to train. They did not want the responsibility of a king's son.''

''Huh. I never thought there would be discrimination against royalty.''

''You would be surprised.''

''Maybe, but don't expect any sympathy.''

''I am not.'' He turned so he faced her. ''Your life has not been traditional.''

''I know. I'm glad for what I've experienced, but it hasn't come free. I'm going to be thirty in a few years. I'd like to get married and start on the whole baby thing, but I don't actually meet the kind of guys who would be interested in me.''

He frowned. ''What are you talking about?''

''It's the whole blow up in the sky thing. Most men don't like it and compensate one of two ways. They get way too aggressive with me on the ground, or they ignore me. No one is ever just a guy.''

Although Jefri was making a good showing, she thought. If only he wasn't a real prince.

''You are not making any sense,'' he told her.

''Sense or not, what's what is. The men I work with don't see me as an available female.''

''Perhaps they are not willing to take on your brothers.''

Billie stared at him. ''Excuse me?''

''Your brothers. Doyle warned me away from you this afternoon. After our flight.''

She heard the words, but she couldn't believe them. "He what?"

"The message was extremely clear."

"I... He..." She pressed her lips together and reached for a rational, coherent thought. "That lying, cheating, scummy pinhead," she muttered.

Was it possible? Were her brothers the reason no one ever asked her out?

She thought about how possessive they were of her. Of the things they said and how they worried about her.

"This is so like them," she said, feeling her temper rise. She couldn't believe it. She'd been date-free for years. How many guys had wanted to take her out only to be headed off by one of her brothers?

"I'm going to make them pay."

"I would request that you not make them suffer too much."

"Why?"

"Because they have kept other men away from you."

"Oh, right and that's a good thing, how?"

"You are still available to me."

Billie barely had time to process the sentence, which was probably for the best because the most eloquent thing she would have come up with was "Huh?" As Jefri spoke, he drew her into his arms and pressed his mouth to hers, so whatever else she was going to say faded into a soft, soul-stealing kiss.

He claimed her with a combination of passion and tenderness. Firm lips moved against her own, discovering, heating, delighting. Her temper faded as if it had never been, while liquid desire took its place.

She sighed and melted against him, letting her body lean against his and her arms rest on his strong shoulders. He smelled of cognac and night and mystery. He drew her closer still until they touched as intimately as their mouths. One of his hands tangled in her long hair while the other roamed over her back.

Instinctively she tilted her head, to make the kissing easier. He responded by brushing his tongue against her lower lip. Anticipation raced through her and she parted for him. But instead of deepening the kiss, he moved away. He kissed her cheek, then along her jaw. When he reached the sensitive skin below her ear, he licked that spot and made her shiver. He took her earlobe in his mouth and gently grated his teeth.

Fire raced through her. Her breasts swelled as her nipples puckered into tight sensitive points of need. She felt overdressed and jumpy, as if her skin was suddenly too tight. Heat settled between her legs. She wanted to rub against him, she wanted to touch and be touched, she wanted to beg.

He returned his mouth to hers. Again she parted for him, but he kept the kiss chaste, barely touching, moving back and forth. Need filled her, unfamiliar yet welcome. The wanting grew.

At last, when she thought she was going to have to scream or maybe throw herself off the balcony, he slipped his tongue inside her mouth and circled it against hers.

Yes, she thought, giving in to the exquisite sensations that filled her. Arousal shook her, making her need so much more than this kiss. Yet she didn't want the kiss to end. She wanted him dancing with her like this for always.

But it was not to be. Eventually he drew back and she knew it was important to act with dignity and not whimper. In the faint light from her room, his eyes glowed with a need that both thrilled and frightened her.

"You are a woman of many surprises," he said as he stroked her cheek.

"The same could be said of you. Not the woman part," she added, feeling more than a little foolish. "You're a man of surprises."

"Thank you."

He brushed his thumb across her mouth. "I look forward to what tomorrow brings," he said. "Sleep well."

"Good night."

She waited until he disappeared into the darkness before stepping into her room. Sleep well? With her body on fire and her mind swirling? Between the kiss and what he'd told her about her brothers, she wasn't sure she was ever going to sleep again. Which was fine. She could spend the night planning her revenge against all the Van Horn men.

Chapter Four

Jefri arrived for his weekly meeting with his father a few minutes early. The king's office was near his own. Several guards stood on duty, while dozens of staff members raced around with folders and stacks of papers.

The king's senior assistant waved Jefri in. One of the wide double doors stood open and several people filed out.

Jefri waited until they'd left before walking inside. He found his father standing behind his desk, flipping through a calendar.

"I'm thinking of visiting Europe," the king said without looking up. "With Murat taking over most of my state duties and the other work divided between you, Sadik and Reyhan, there is little to keep me here."

Jefri grinned. ''Are you complaining you do not have enough to do?''

''I suppose I am. It is a sad state of affairs when a king is no longer needed.''

Jefri took a seat on the visitor's side of the desk. ''I think it is unlikely you will be beheaded anytime soon.''

His father sat down and smiled. ''How you comfort me.'' He leaned back in his chair. ''So our new air force is off to a positive start?''

''Of course. The Van Horn team is in place. All the instructors have arrived. Billie is in charge of them.''

The king nodded. ''A most pleasant young woman.''

Jefri could think of several words to describe Billie, but pleasant wasn't one of them. It was too bland, too lacking in style. Billie could never be accused of either.

''She assists in the pilot training, both with actual flying and in simulators. The Van Horn people have prepared an intensive eight-week program to forge our pilots into a team. When the initial instruction is finished, they will return to offer refresher courses until we get our own training in place.''

''Very impressive,'' the king said. ''I would advise you not to annoy her. I would hate to lose you because, to quote the young woman herself, she blows you out of the sky.''

Jefri smiled. ''I will not allow that to happen.''

''It sounds as if she is unbeatable.''

"Perhaps."

But he had a feeling he knew her weaknesses. Last night she had melted in his arms. Whatever her skills in the sky, on ground, she was mere woman. He planned to take advantage of that fact, pleasing them both along the way. He did not believe she could respond to him so easily in the night and then destroy him, however much in theory, during the day.

For now he only needed an edge to best her. In time, he would develop the skills to take her on his own.

"I am glad all goes well," his father said. "Now on to another matter. I have found you a bride."

Jefri almost asked "For what?" before he recalled a conversation with his father some months ago, when he had given in to parental pressure and agreed to remarry.

"Perhaps this is not the best time," he began.

"You are my son. It is your duty to produce heirs."

"I am but twenty-nine. There is still time."

"For you, perhaps," the king said. "But I do not grow younger. You asked me to find you an appropriate young woman." He pulled a sheet of paper out of a drawer. "You said she was to be docile, reasonably attractive and good with children. That is who I found."

Jefri wondered what he had been thinking when he had made that particular request. Yes, he had to marry, and an arranged match was as good as any, but now?

''I have other priorities at this moment. The air force takes much of my time.''

''Your bride will require little of you,'' the king said. ''You were specific when we spoke. You did not want this to be a love match.''

That much was true, Jefri thought. He had already played at that game and lost. Love was not for him. Better to find someone who could do the job and not manipulate his heart. Respect was far more important than love.

Without wanting to, he remembered a woman in the moonlight. The feel of a soft feminine body in his arms and a passionate response to his kiss. Billie was a temptation, but she did not meet any of his criteria save one. While it was possible she enjoyed children, he doubted anyone would ever accuse her of being docile. Worse, describing her as ''reasonably attractive'' was as much of an understatement as saying the center of the sun was mildly warm.

''I do not wish to be engaged at this time,'' Jefri said firmly.

He had no intention of marrying Billie, but that did not mean he could not enjoy her company.

''Arrangements have been made,'' his father told him.

''Then they need to be unmade.''

The king stared at him for a few seconds. Jefri braced himself for a battle of wills. While he might be victorious against his father, he had little success against the king.

At last the older man nodded. ''As you wish.''

"Thank you, Father." He glanced at his watch. "I am due at the airport shortly."

"Then you must go. Be sure to tell Billie how much I enjoyed her company last night." His father smiled. "Tell her that next time I will ask the staff to prepare a plate for her to take back to her dog. It is not necessary for her to slip food into her handbag."

So the king had noticed as well. Jefri grinned. "I look forward to passing along the message."

Billie knew that Doyle had been out until nearly four in the morning, overseeing the equipment unloading. In deference to his late bedtime, she waited until ten before entering his suite and stalking toward the bedroom.

Between the kiss and her fury at what she'd found out, she hadn't gotten much sleep herself, which meant she'd had plenty of time to work up a head of steam. A tiny part of her looked forward to exploding all over her brother.

As she'd expected he was asleep. She crossed to the windows and pulled open the drapes. As light spilled onto the bed, he stirred, then rolled onto his back.

"What the hell are you doing?" he growled. "Do you know what time I got to bed?"

"Ask me if I care," Billie said as she moved close to the side of the bed and glared down at her brother. "You are so in trouble. Don't for one second think you're going to talk your way out of this. I mean to have your head on a platter. Or maybe a stick. I haven't decided."

Doyle stretched and yawned. He looked amazingly unconcerned as he sat up and leaned against the headboard. His sleep-mussed hair fell across his forehead and stubble darkened his jaw.

"You're sure flapping your lips," he said with a complete lack of concern for her temper. "But you're not saying much."

She picked up one of his boots and tossed it at him. "Don't you dare dismiss me, you rat. How dare you run my life? You don't have the right."

He batted away the flying boot and stared at her. "You've gone over the edge."

"Not yet, but I'm really close." She picked up the other boot and was pleased to see him duck. "That's right. Be afraid. Because you have messed with something you're going to regret."

"Put that down," he said, lunging toward her.

She was careful to keep out of reach, knowing she was safe as long as Doyle couldn't grab her. Like all her brothers, he slept in the nude, so he wasn't going to be getting out of bed anytime soon. She raised the boot again and glared.

"You've been warning men away from me, telling them who knows what so they won't ask me out. How dare you? What I want to know is what gives you the right? I've been an adult for a long time. I'm capable of making my own decisions."

He winced. "You're crazy."

"Am I? I couldn't figure out why perfectly nice

guys who had been flirting with me suddenly showed no interest. I thought it was me. But it wasn't. It was you guys. And Dad. He's in on it, too, isn't he?''

''We just thought—''

''What?'' she demanded, threatening him with the boot. ''That I was too fragile to take care of myself.''

''After what happened before, we thought it was a good idea.''

Not a surprise, she told herself. ''Doyle, that was eight *years* ago. I'm not happy it happened, but didn't it occur to you that I'm over it?''

''What if some guy tries to hurt you again?''

''I'll deal with it. You can't protect me. It's wrong to try.'' She set down the boot. Figures, they'd done the wrong thing for the right reason. ''This stops right now. You get out of my personal life.''

He folded his arms over his chest. ''Or what?''

She stared at him, at the familiar square jaw and blond hair. At the powerful muscles. When she'd been little and the constant subject of their endless teasing, she always thought that when she got bigger she would be able to take them on. But she'd been wrong. They still thought of her as their baby sister. Someone who wasn't quite big enough or grown-up enough or good enough. It didn't matter that she could blow every one of them, including her father, out of sky in less than three minutes.

''If you all don't stop treating me like a child, I'm leaving the business.''

Doyle stared at her. ''You're bluffing. You love it too much to leave.''

She did love it, but she wouldn't stay somewhere she couldn't be her own person. "You know I get six job offers a month. I mean it, Doyle. I'll walk."

He swore under his breath, then held up his hands in a gesture of surrender. "Fine. I'll talk to Dad and the guys. It may take us a while to, you know, act differently."

"I'm sure you're more than up to the task."

He grumbled something under his breath, no doubt calling her names. None of her brothers had ever been especially gracious losers.

"I need to get to the airport," she said brightly. "I have simulation training this afternoon." She started to walk out of the room.

"Hey. What about the drapes," he yelled after her.

"Get up and close them yourself."

Feeling more than a little empowered, Billie walked back toward her rooms. She still had to collect Muffin before heading to the airport. In her own car with her own driver, she thought with a grin. Ah, it was good to be her right now.

She rounded a corner and nearly ran smack into Prince Jefri. All her breezy confidence drained away, leaving her feeling awkward, silly and tongue-tied.

"You appear to be very cheerful," he said as he stopped in front of her. "Is there a reason?"

Man, oh man did he look good, she thought as she took in the dark suit, pale blue shirt and striped tie. Princes had the best clothes and some really great tailoring.

"I, ah..." What was the question? Oh, yeah. "I just told my brother off."

"Did it go well?"

"Not bad. I believe he got the message."

A smile tugged at Jefri's mouth. "Did you threaten him?"

"Of course. Isn't that what sisters do?"

"I don't recall my sister threatening me much, but she spent much of the time in America. Was there blood spilt?"

"No, although I did throw his boot at him."

"Impressive."

She laughed. "He'd worked until early this morning. I think it's the only reason I got the drop on him, but I won't ever admit that to him."

"Of course not. Nor will I."

Awareness crackled between them. They'd kissed about twelve hours before and she was still experiencing aftershocks. Was Jefri? As a handsome prince was he used to kissing all sorts of women and had theirs been just one in a long line?

"What are you thinking?" he asked unexpectedly.

She felt her eyes widen. "Nothing important."

"I think it was very important." He moved closer. "Will you not tell me?"

"I just..." She cleared her throat. "It looks like another great day. Too bad we'll be doing simulations instead of flying for real."

His dark gaze settled on her face. "That was a rather poor and obvious attempt to change the subject."

"I know, but you're so well mannered, I figured you'd let me get away with it."

"Hmm, and here I had hoped you would tell me you had been busy thinking about last night." He lowered his voice. "I enjoyed our conversation and our kiss."

Holy moly. He was going to *talk* about it? She wasn't used to that, but then she wasn't much used to kisses from princes. Or men in general. Jeez, based on what she'd just found out about her brothers she should send every guy who *had* gathered the courage to ask her out an award of some kind.

"I had a nice time, too," she said primly.

He raised his eyebrows. "Nice? I see I must work on my technique."

Before she could respond, she felt something brush against her bare ankles. She looked down, then scrambled out of the way of a small calico cat.

"Those creatures are everywhere," she muttered.

Jefri bent over and picked up the cat. It wasn't much bigger than his hand and as he held it, the cat began to purr. Billie could hear the soft rumble.

"She likes you," he said.

"She's trying to lull me into a false sense of security before the attack."

He petted the cat. "I doubt she weighs more than five or six pounds. You do not appear to be in any imminent danger."

"So you say."

She watched as he scratched the feline under its

chin. It twisted around to get on its back and nearly fell off his hand.

"Careful," Jefri said, nestling the cat against his chest. "You are too trusting, I think."

"Especially around me," Billie said.

He looked at her. "You would not hurt a kitten."

"No, but I'd be happy to threaten it forcefully with words."

"But she has done you no harm."

"You keep saying *she*. It could be a boy."

"Unlikely. Calicos are generally female, much as marmalades are usually male. This one is maybe eight or nine weeks old."

The kitten rolled onto her back and splayed her paws as Jefri rubbed her tummy.

"Come now," he said. "Touch her fur. I suspect she is not nearly as horrible as you would have me believe."

Billie wrinkled her nose, but did as he requested. She touched the white fur under the cat's chin.

"Soft," she said in some surprise. She could feel the warmth of its body and the rumble from the purring.

The kitten blinked slowly, as if dozing off.

"She does seem to trust you," Billie said.

"I'm very good with females."

"Like that's a surprise."

He shifted the cat so it lay on its tummy, then handed it to her. Billie stepped back and shook her head.

"No, thanks. I'll admit she's kind of cute, but I'm

not interested. As far as I'm concerned, the entire cat population still has a lot to answer for.''

He set down the kitten and shook his head. ''You are a most difficult woman.''

''I know. It's part of my charm.''

Jefri stared down at the instrument panel. Everything was as it should be, but even doing everything correctly did not stop the high-pitched tone-lock he heard in his ears. He tore off the headset, hit the switch to kill the simulation and stepped out of the machine.

Again. She had done it again. At least in his first and second simulation he had lasted nearly three minutes. This time she had nailed him in less than forty seconds.

Annoyance grew to anger. He narrowed his gaze as he swept the room, finally locating Billie stepping out of her simulator. In her denim skirt and tight T-shirt, she looked more like a college coed than a fighter jet instructor. Long blond hair tumbled down her back. She wore impossibly high-heeled sandals. She was walking, breathing sexual desire incarnate and he was not sure if he should strangle her or push her up against the wall and have his way with her.

Wariness darkened her blue eyes. He saw a flash of something that might have been disappointment, then she squared her narrow shoulders, raised her chin and walked toward him.

He recognized her determination. She was prepared

to take him on—to endure his ill temper in the name of making him a better pilot.

"I know you're pissed off," she said as she approached. "You got too cocky in that last run and didn't think. You always have to respect your opponent because up there, the ordinance is real and you can get dead really fast."

Light spilled in from a window and illuminated her pale skin. Color stained her cheeks, but he suspected it came from her being upset rather than a cosmetic.

"You need to let go of the fact that I'm a woman," she told him, sounding delightfully earnest. "I have knowledge to share with you. That's it."

She continued to speak, expressing platitudes designed to restore a fragile male ego.

Of course, he told himself. This was her world. Every new client had pilots who resented her ability simply because she was a woman. How long had she been apologizing for being the best?

She was the most amazing woman. Bright, determined, talented. Erotically sensual.

He wanted her with every cell of his being, but even more than that, he wanted to make things all right for her.

"Meet me in an hour," he said, cutting her off in midsentence.

She blinked at him. "Excuse me?"

"Meet me in front of the Van Horn office in an hour." He glanced over her short skirt and tight T-shirt. "Bring a jacket."

"I have classes. I have other students who..."

He pressed a finger to her lips to still her words and to feel the warmth and softness of her skin.

"Please," he said. "I have something I want to show you."

Chapter Five

Billie walked to the front of the Van Horn office as Jefri had requested. She'd even brought along a jacket, although it had to be close to eighty degrees in the shade. Nothing in her previous work experience had prepared her for this kind of a situation and she was still figuring out how to deal with it when Jefri pulled up in an open Jeep and patted the passenger seat invitingly.

"I understand that you're the prince and everything," she said as she climbed inside, "but that's not important to the rest of my students. I have a responsibility to them as well as you and I can't disappear on a moment's notice just because you will it."

He grinned and drove through the airport. "Actually, you can. I promise not one of your students will complain."

"But that's because you're in charge of the air force."

"Yes."

Obviously she wasn't getting through. "You need to use your power for good, not evil."

His dark eyes crinkled at the corners. "I promise nothing evil will happen today."

"I'm not sure that's good enough."

"You will have to trust me."

Something she wasn't prepared to do. Not completely. He was the kind of man who hated being defeated by anyone and her ability to consistently cramp his winning streak was problematic. The thing was, she didn't know what to do about it. Usually she accepted the situation and moved on. But with Jefri…

If he'd been a lousy kisser none of this would have mattered. Or if he didn't make her heart beat so fast. If she didn't like him she wouldn't care that she had the potential to grind his ego into dust.

"Stop thinking," he told her. "You are here to enjoy yourself and be impressed."

"This isn't about flying, is it?" she asked. "That's kind of a bad place to try to impress me."

He smiled. "We shall see."

Maybe she could *pretend* to be impressed, she thought, as he circled behind the hangars for Bahanian Air and headed for a large, unmarked structure. If she could just act like other women, then she could coo and swoon and do all those girly things. Lord knows she had the hair products to go all gooey.

Jefri stopped by the door to the large structure.

"When you get out, I want you to cover your eyes."

She glanced at him. "Not exactly my style."

"Please. I want this to be a surprise."

And she wanted to see him smile again. "Okay."

She climbed down, then covered her eyes with one hand. He took the other and led her into the building. She immediately sensed the change from bright sunlight to dim shade.

"Do not move," he said, stepping away.

She heard footsteps, then a click, followed by an explosion of light.

"Now," he told her.

She opened her eyes and looked around. The gasp of appreciation didn't have to be faked. She meant it all the way down to her toes.

"You're kidding," she breathed as she took in a hangar full of beautiful restored old planes.

She spotted a Tiger Moth, a Fokker, even a Spitfire. Billie felt her chest getting tight as she tried to take in the wonders of Jefri's very private air museum.

"I can't believe it," she breathed. "You own these?"

"This is only part of my collection," he said as he walked toward the large airplane-sized hangar doors and pushed a button. The huge metal doors began to open.

"Several of my planes are at the Bahanian national museum. A few are taken around to air shows."

He walked over and took her hand, then led her to the Tiger Moth.

''Your headgear and goggles are there,'' he said pointing to a small table beside the plane.

Her mouth dropped open. ''We're going up in it?''

''Of course.'' He grinned. ''They are all fully functional.''

''I… You…'' Okay, so she was stunned past talking. Fine with her.

She circled the old plane and ran her hands lovingly along the fuselage.

''Amazing,'' she breathed.

''Here.''

Jefri tossed her a leather helmet and goggles. She slipped into her jacket, then the helmet. The step up presented a bit of a problem. Billie judged the distance, the skimpiness of her skirt and her high-heeled sandals. There seemed to be only one solution.

She stepped out of her shoes and grabbed them in one hand. After tucking her goggles into her jacket pocket, she reached for the handholds and pulled herself up and into the plane. She had a feeling that she'd probably flashed Jefri along the way, but she was too happy to care.

''She's fabulous,'' she called as he took the position behind hers.

''She's my favorite,'' he admitted.

Two men in gray jumpsuits walked over and pulled the blocks away from the wheels. Jefri started the engine. As the plane slowly moved forward, Billie studied the simple design of the cockpit, the minimal information provided.

But what the plane lacked in technology it made

up for in sheer flying pleasure, she thought as they moved down the runway then eased off the ground. The Tiger Moth flew at a speed close to a jet's stall level. They were airborne, yet only a few dozen feet from the ground. There was no pull of G-force, no sense of power or thrust or barely controlled power.

Instead she could feel the rush of the air as they moved higher and faster. The more they climbed, the more the temperature dropped, making her glad for her jacket. The airport got smaller and smaller below, yet the sky seemed infinitely vast above them. In a jet, she had a sense of wanting to get there quickly. In the Tiger Moth, she wasn't sure she wanted to arrive at all.

"Here. You try it," Jefri yelled from behind her.

She took the stick and felt the old plane respond to her touch. She slowed down, then sped up to get a feel for the parameters before trying a few lazy circles and a steep climb.

"Admit it," he said loudly. "You're impressed."

She laughed. "Absolutely. I want one."

"They're not that hard to come by."

Perhaps not, but she lived her life out of a suitcase. Sometimes it was difficult enough to get a room with a bathtub. Billie wasn't sure how she would drag another plane along. Still…maybe it was worth looking into.

She swooped over the city. The view was different than it had been in her jet. Now there was time to study the various buildings and notice how the blocks were so square and tidy. She saw the clear demarcation line where civilization gave way to the emptiness of the desert.

"I think I gave up on small planes too soon," she said. "I couldn't wait to go faster and faster. Now I'm not sure why."

"These were real workhorses in their time," he told her. "Planes like these were used to map the desert. It was too dangerous to do on foot."

A different time, she thought. Simpler. "I would have liked that job," she said. "Now there isn't any unknown to fly into."

Of course she still would have been a woman in a man's world. Somehow she didn't think it would have been any easier back then.

"You would have been at great risk," he said over the wind.

"In what way?"

He laughed. "We were not so civilized back then. The harem was still filled with beautiful women. Had you flown into our desert, I suspect you would have been captured and presented to my great-grandfather as a prize."

"I'm not sure how I feel about that."

"It would have been a great honor."

"To be one of the crowd? No thanks." She did a large figure eight. "Is there still a harem?"

"That part of the palace still exists, but it has been empty since my grandfather's time."

"How disappointing for you."

Jefri laughed. "I do not need to hold my women captive to keep them at my side."

Hardly a newsflash, she thought. All he would have to do was crook his finger and the ladies would come running. She liked to think that she would be different and at least try to resist, but she knew she was wrong.

''Go north,'' he said. ''About thirty miles.''

She checked the compass and turned the plane to the correct heading. Below them several roads cut through the desert. She searched for signs of nomadic tribes but saw none. No doubt they preferred to stay farther away from the city.

A few minutes later Jefri had her turn east. Up ahead she saw a small oasis and what looked like a very rudimentary runway.

''She will do the work for you,'' he said. ''Let her down easily.''

Billie dropped lower and lower, aiming the nose toward the runway. At the last minute, she pulled up slightly so the plane landed on the rear wheels first. A cloud of dust rose up as they slowed, then finally stopped.

''Welcome to my private paradise,'' he said.

She took off her goggles. ''Is it really yours?''

''I claimed it when I first flew here at age twelve. No one has disputed my ownership, so yes, it is mine.''

Must be nice, she thought as she collected her shoes and stepped out of the cockpit.

''Wait,'' Jefri said as he jumped down first.

He stood just below her and held out his arms. Ah, the hardships her career forced upon her, she thought cheerfully as she surrendered to gravity and allowed Jefri to catch her against his hard body.

He held her a fraction of a second longer than necessary, not that she minded, before assisting her with her shoes. They left their jackets, helmets and goggles in the plane and walked toward the clusters of plants and trees at the edge of the water.

"Are there underground springs?" she asked.

"Hundreds. My brother, Reyhan, has a house in the middle of the desert that sits on top of a spring. He and his wife live there now. The fabled City of Thieves is said to exist at the edge of an underground river."

Billie frowned. "I remember reading about the City of Thieves when I was doing research on your country. It is supposed to be hidden somehow. The way the buildings blend in with the land or something. One account I read said there was a medieval castle there."

"How interesting," Jefri said in a carefully neutral tone.

"Is it real? The city?"

He drew her close and brought her hand up to rest on his arm. "Bahania is a land of much beauty and many mysteries. Perhaps you should give yourself time to discover them all."

"Hardly an answer," she grumbled but without much energy. When faced with the beauty of the oasis, what did a mythical city matter?

He pointed out different types of trees and shrubs. She bent down to feel the softness of the grass that grew right to the edge of the large pond in the center of the oasis. The water lapped against the bank, as if driven by a tidal force.

"Why does it move like that?" she asked.

"The pressure of the feeding spring."

"Okay, so if the pond is being constantly fed with fresh water, why doesn't it overflow? It's not evaporating that quickly and I don't see any kind of drainage."

He smiled. "Yet another mystery to be solved. Things are more complex than they first appear."

He led her around a grove of palm trees where she saw two lounge chairs set up with a small table between. A cooler sat on the ground with a basket of fruit on top.

"You're kidding," she said with a laugh. "You planned this?"

"Down to the last detail. We'll be having lunch later."

"I know it's not in our plane, so did you have someone specially bring all this here?"

"Of course."

He spoke so casually, she thought as he led her to one of the lounge chairs. Talk about the thrill of royalty. She was lucky if she could convince one of her brothers to bring her back gum from the convenience store.

She settled down while he popped open the cooler. There were an assortment of cold sodas, juices and bottled waters. She liked that he wasn't going to drink while they still had to fly back.

When they were stretched out on their chairs and

sipping their drinks, she glanced around at the beauty and quiet of the desert.

"Did you run off here when you got in trouble as a kid?" she asked.

"Sometimes. My father learned fairly quickly that I could be kept in line with the threat of losing access to my planes."

"I know what you mean. In my house, getting grounded was meant literally."

He chuckled. "I doubt you received many lectures on your duties to the people and how when you got in trouble you were letting down a thousand years of tradition."

"Okay, I was spared that." She looked at him. "Did the king really bring up a thousand years of tradition in his lectures?"

"It was a particular favorite." Jefri shrugged. "According to him, I deeply disappointed all of our ancestors on a regular basis."

She couldn't imagine having that much history in one family. She got excited when she was able to stay in one place more than eight weeks.

"But you recovered to transgress another day," she said.

"Sometimes I did not wait that long." He smiled. "I liked to explore and I rarely followed the rules."

"Something tells me you still don't."

Instead of answering, he reached for her hand and took it in his. "Tell me what it was like when you were growing up. There was no king to make pronouncements."

"Maybe not, but my dad was used to being in charge. With three boys to deal with, he had to be firm."

Jefri rubbed his thumb across the back of her hand and made her skin tingle. "What about with you?"

"Until my mom died, she took care of disciplining me. I spent most of my time with her and we always got along. She used to say how as there were only two of us, we had to band together."

She felt his gaze on her face. "You must have found her death very difficult."

"I did. I was just about to enter the whole teenaged thing, when a girl really needs her mom. She had cancer, so there was some warning, but only a few weeks. By the time she realized she was sick, it was already too late. My folks had first started dating in high school and my mom once admitted they'd both been each other's first time. So when she got sick, my dad really freaked out."

She stared out at the horizon. "My dad traveled a lot and I thought that meant he didn't care so much about her, but I was wrong. I remember a couple of days after she'd been diagnosed and they'd told us, I went into their bedroom to talk to her. He was there, holding her. Crying. I'd never seen my dad cry. I didn't want to spy, but I couldn't seem to walk away. He begged her not to die. He told her he couldn't make it without her. I could feel their love for each other. I vowed then I would find someone to love me that much."

"Have you?" he asked.

She raised her eyebrows. ''We wouldn't be sitting here holding hands if I had.''

''An excellent point.''

Funny how she'd begun to believe she *wouldn't* find anyone to love her that much because no one seemed to be interested in her. Knowing that her brothers were scaring off potential boyfriends made her feel a little better. Although did she want someone who didn't want her enough to go up against her brothers?

Too confusing, she told herself, and not something to be resolved today.

''So when your mother died, you went on the road with your father?'' Jefri asked.

She nodded. ''He'd started taking the boys with him during the summer. Now, with no one left at home, we all went. Dad hired a tutor so we could keep up with school. I turned thirteen in South America and sixteen in the Middle East. Most girls get a sweet sixteen party—I soloed on a jet.''

''Would you rather have had the party?''

She looked at him and raised her eyebrows. ''Are you crazy? I'd *begged* my dad to let me fly jets for two years before he let me. He said I couldn't handle the technical information, so I studied physics and aerodynamics until he was forced to change his mind.''

Jefri watched the emotions move across Billie's face as she spoke. She was a beautiful woman, but it was not difficult to imagine the frightened young girl she must have been when she had lost her mother.

Frightened and alone, yet determined. What had *he* fought for when he had turned sixteen? As the youngest son of the king, he had been given nearly everything he wanted. If he recalled correctly his sixteenth birthday had involved a large party and a concert by a young female pop star.

"You survive in a very male world," he said.

She laughed. "At first it sucked me in. After my mom died I thought the only way to get along with my father was to be one of the guys. I thought that would make him respect me. Over time I finally figured out I would never be another one of his sons so I stopped trying."

"I cannot tell you how relieved I am."

She laughed. "No desire to date Doyle, huh?"

"None in the least."

"Around my nineteenth birthday, I said the hell with it. We were in France, at the air show. I spent two days getting my hair done, painting my nails and shopping. I went from combat boots to four-inch heels and I never looked back."

"What did they say?" he asked.

"No one even noticed for a while. My dad said he thought my skirts were too short and my brothers ragged on me for my big hair. I challenged them all to a simulated dogfight. It was the first time I beat them and I've been kicking their butts ever since."

"The power of a woman," he said, delighted by her victory.

"Something like that." She sipped her drink. "Don't get me wrong. I love my family. They're weird, but I think every family is. We live a very nomadic existence and that has made us appreciate the times when we are together.''

''Your father never remarried?''

''No. I wish he would. I know he loved my mom, but that's no reason for him to be alone for so long. I don't think she would have wanted it that way.'' She looked at him. ''Your father never remarried after your mother's death.''

''That's true. Theirs was a love match as well, although he'd been married before. I think he found raising four sons and a daughter took too much time. However my father takes long trips to Europe and America where I doubt he lacks for female companionship.''

''Good point. I doubt anyone is going to tell him she's not interested.''

He raised his eyebrows. ''Is that why you are with me? Because I am a prince and you do not think you can say no?''

She studied him from under lowered lashes. ''Pretty much.''

He saw the corner of her mouth quiver.

''I can see you are trying not to laugh,'' he told her.

''You're right, but if you could have seen your face when I said that. You believed me and you were deeply insulted.''

He released her hand and swung his legs to the ground. ''I can see I am going to have to teach you more respect for my lofty position.''

"I respect you, Jefri, but it's not as if I'm scared of you."

"Good to know. Are you ready for lunch?"

"Sure."

Billie's idea of al fresco dining involved take-out or a sub sandwich made under questionable circumstances with ingredients she didn't want to identify. But outdoor dining prince-style took on a whole new meaning. Not only was there a real wood table with matching chairs, a white linen tablecloth provided a perfect backdrop for elegant china and crystal.

A servant in a white jacket and black slacks materialized as they walked toward the beautifully set table. He held out Billie's chair and offered her a hand-printed menu of the various available selections. She looked over the many salads and entrées—not a sandwich in the bunch—then set down her menu and leaned toward Jefri.

"You're working very hard to impress me," she said.

"You told me that was not possible."

"I might have lied."

"Good."

He brushed her mouth with his and sent heat racing to all parts of her body.

"But remember," he said quietly. "These are only things and scenarios. They say nothing about who I am."

She knew what he meant. That he was more than a rich guy with hot and cold running servants. But he was wrong about his world not being part of who he was. Jefri wielded power as casually as most people drove a car. He commanded an impressive air force with enough firepower to destroy nearly any country on the planet and her job was to teach him to do that better.

"You're not exactly how I pictured a prince would be," she said.

"Is the impression better or worse."

"Different. But then I don't have a lot of experience in the royal world."

"Then we are even because I have little experience with delightful, sexy female flight instructors. Mine were always men. I would say it was my loss."

She smiled. "Absolutely."

He picked up her menu and handed it to her. "What would you like?"

"I'm not going to ask what's good. I'm assuming it's all fabulous."

"Of course it is. Oh, and if you're thinking of choosing something because you want to take the leftovers to Muffin, the king asked me to tell you to simply ask for a plate to be sent to your rooms. There is no need for you to slip food into your handbag."

She squeezed her eyes shut and held in a groan. "Did everyone notice I'd done that at dinner?"

"Of course."

She opened her eyes and stared at him. "I'm humiliated."

"You're charming. We were all entranced."

"I had a Baggie," she said, knowing it was a pretty

feeble explanation. ''It's not like I put meat directly into my purse or anything.''

''Of course not.''

''So you don't think it's odd?''

He smiled. ''I think it is extremely odd.''

''You're mocking me.''

''Absolutely.''

Billie's pleasure in her oasis lunch with Jefri lasted exactly twenty-five hours and forty-two minutes, right until she found herself once again flying with him. But instead of sharing a beautifully restored Tiger Moth, they were flying separate jets and she was coming around for another pass.

What she hated was how quickly she was going to kill him. If only he'd lasted four or five minutes, they could both feel better about the experience. But the specially designed timer that was part of the training program had yet to hit ninety seconds and she already had him in her sights.

For a brief flicker in time, she thought about pretending that she couldn't get him, but as the thought formed, she pushed it away. Her job was to make her students into the best pilots possible and that wasn't going to happen by letting them win. She maneuvered until she was able to get a clear shot, then pushed the button. The sharp sound of tone-lock filled her cockpit and his sharp inhale of disbelief filled her headset.

''You continue to surprise me,'' he said.

''That's why they pay me the big bucks.''

She couldn't tell what he was thinking from the

tone of his voice and she wasn't sure she wanted to know. She followed him down from the sky and landed. When she'd pulled her jet up to his, she hesitated before climbing down.

What was she going to say? How could she explain that it didn't matter to her that he didn't beat her in the sky? She still liked being around him, talking to him, flying with him, and she wouldn't object if he wanted to kiss her again.

"Sitting here is getting nothing done," she told herself and popped the canopy on her jet, then pulled off her helmet and climbed down.

As she crossed the tarmac, she saw Doyle walking toward Jefri. Something in her stomach warned her this could be trouble, so she hurried to catch up.

But she was too late and by the time she joined them she was just in time to see her brother slap Jefri on the back and hear him say, "It's gotta kill you to keep getting beaten by a girl."

"You get beaten by me all the time," she reminded her brother, wishing he could keep his mouth shut.

Doyle grinned. "Yeah, but I'm not a prince."

She wanted to scream in frustration. Instead she simply clenched her teeth and walked off. She didn't want to know what Jefri was thinking so she kept her gaze straight ahead as she made it back to the main tent. There she collected her street clothes and stepped into a restroom where she changed back into shorts and a T-shirt before stowing her gear and collecting Muffin.

"The entire situation makes me crazy," she told

her dog. "How am I supposed to win at this? I can't help being good and I don't want to change it."

She stepped out into the afternoon sun and nearly plowed into Jefri.

"What?" she demanded.

"I was looking for you."

"Okay. Fine. But here's the thing. I won't apologize for what I do well. I'm sorry if you're having ego problems."

"I do not consider my ego your responsibility."

He spoke quietly, even reasonably. That made her nervous. "I'm just doing my job," she continued. "Even though I know what they say. That I'm a ball-buster. It's not my plan to emasculate you, it just happens."

He grabbed her arms and led her around to the side of the tent, next to a stack of large crates.

"You talk too much," he said, his gaze intent on her face.

"I'm trying to explain."

"I understand perfectly. Put down that damn dog."

She was so surprised by the instruction that she did as he said. Then she was really glad when he pulled her close, wrapped his arms around her and kissed her.

The warm, insistent pressure against her lips made her cling to him. Heat flared, melting away all her concerns about him being upset or angry or anything the least bit negative.

His mouth moved slowly, as if giving her time to get used to what he was doing. If she'd been able to communicate without her mouth, she would have told him that she didn't mind the kissing at all. In fact, she really, really liked it. He could do more. Really.

Instead she placed her hands on his shoulders and let her body lean into his. She tilted her head and parted her lips in invitation.

He reacted with a sharp intake of air and a gentle sweep of his tongue against hers.

The kiss was as spectacular as it had been the first time. She felt her insides quiver, her knees shake and her thighs tremble. Heat poured through her, making her want and need with an intensity that stunned her.

One of his hands tangled in her hair, the other traced a line down her back until it settled on her rear. When he squeezed the curves, she arched forward, bringing her belly in contact with him.

Now it was her turn to gasp as she felt his arousal. He wanted her. After everything that had happened and what her brother had said, Jefri wanted her. Delight blended with desire and she nearly laughed.

He broke the kiss. "What do you find so amusing?" he asked, his breath mingling with hers.

"Just all of this."

"That I want to kiss you?"

"It is a bit of a surprise."

He cupped her chin and stared into her eyes. "Why? You're a beautiful woman. Unique, intelligent, desirable. I doubt there is a man alive who wouldn't sell his soul for one night with you."

She blinked at him. Whoa—talk about a great line. Right now she didn't even care if he meant it.

"I, um, thanks."

"You're welcome." He smiled as he rubbed his thumb against her lower lip. "I would very much like to have dinner with you tonight."

At this point in time, she would have followed him to the moon. "Okay. I mean, that would be great."

"Good. I'll pick you up at your room at seven. Is that convenient?"

As she'd planned to spend the rest of the afternoon soaking and grooming, seven sounded good.

"I'll be ready."

"We'll be going out," he said. "There are several excellent restaurants in the city. Will you allow me to choose?"

"Of course."

"Then it is a date." He dropped a brief kiss on her lips, then stepped back. "Leave the dog at home."

Chapter Six

Billie stood in front of her closet and reviewed her array of clothes. She believed in shopping, both as a sport and a way to relax, so there were plenty of outfits to choose from. She already knew she wanted something both sexy and sophisticated, with a touch of elegance thrown in. Which pretty much left out anything with feathers, rhinestones or too much beading.

She tilted her head, then straightened quickly as the curlers started to loosen. Tonight required perfect hair, which meant an hour spent in electric curlers and a double dose of hair spray.

''Everyone looks good in black,'' she murmured as she pulled out a clinging black dress with a deep vee and see-through sleeves. ''But it's so predictable.''

Maybe she should try a color. Not red. Somehow that just made her look trashy.

"Maybe blue," she said as she reached for a midnight-blue dress that had cost her nearly a month's salary in Paris.

The hand-painted bias-cut skirt fluttered just above her knees. The sleeveless bodice wasn't that low cut because the appeal lay elsewhere. From the waist up, the fabric was completely sheer. However the same hand-painted pattern that graced the hem of the skirt swirled across her breasts and the built-in bra in such a way that everything was perfectly covered. Yet there was the *promise* of being naked!

"This one," she said, carrying the dress into the bathroom. She had a perfect pair of high-heeled strappy sandals that made her ankles look as slender as swizzle sticks and some really high-end fake jewelry.

Billie had to admit her excitement about the evening was about more than just the whole "dine with a prince" thrill. Part of her was really happy that Jefri wanted to see her after his defeat earlier. That had never happened before and it gave her hope for his entire gender. While she believed her brothers had a part in warning men off, she couldn't help but think there had to be one or two willing to deal with their potential wrath unless their bruised egos had put them out of the mood.

A knock at the door made her panic. She glanced at the clock, but it was way too early for Jefri.

"Who is it?" she called from the center of the living room.

"Doyle."

She walked to the door and opened it. "Make it snappy," she said. "I'm busy."

He pushed past her into the room, then looked her over. "You don't look busy to me. You look like you're not doing much of anything. I need your help with some of the equipment."

"Not my area of expertise."

"Billie, I'm serious. The mechanics want to talk to you about one of the engines they're tuning. You know how you can tell what's wrong from the sound."

"Yes, it's a gift and one we can all take advantage of tomorrow. Now get out of here."

She pushed on her brother, but as he was about ten inches taller and oh, sixty pounds of muscle heavier, he didn't budge.

"What's your problem?" he demanded.

"I told you. I'm busy."

Doyle folded his arms over his chest and raised his eyebrows. "With what?"

She planted her hands on her hips and did her best to look stern.

"I have a date."

His expression hardened. "With whom?"

She knew he was mad whenever he started using really correct grammar. "I'm over twenty-one and you don't own me, so I don't have to say."

"I'm not leaving until you give me all the particulars."

She laughed. "Doyle, this isn't the nineteenth century. There aren't any particulars. A man asked me to dinner and I said yes. Get over it."

"You have a responsibility to this company."

"Oh, please." She rolled her eyes. "How many times have I covered for you? A thousand? I would say I'm entitled to a night off when I want it."

His gaze narrowed as he studied her. "It's that damn prince, isn't it?"

"I'm not sure you want to swear in front of his title. They might string you up for that."

He swore again. "Billie, I know you're mad about what we've all been doing."

"What? Oh, you mean running my life and warning off men behind my back?" She wanted to punch him but she knew that not only would she fail to really hurt him, she might mess up her freshly manicured nails.

"You were a pig," she told him instead. "All of you. You had no right and I deeply resent it."

"Fine. Be mad. Go out, but not with him."

"What's wrong with Jefri?"

"Nothing, except he's a damn prince."

"I actually know that."

He dropped his arms to his sides. "Billie, you're out of your league with a man like him."

She knew what he meant. That she was just the hired help and Jefri was royal.

"I'm not expecting anything more than dinner,

Doyle. You don't have to get your panties in a bunch.''

His mouth twisted. ''I don't wear panties.''

''I know, but you get my drift. You're making too much of this. It's just dinner.''

''Uh-huh. That's why you're spending five hours primping.''

''I haven't spent five hours.'' It had barely been two. ''Besides, grooming is fun.''

''You're not good at this kind of thing,'' he said. ''You don't have the practice.''

''Oh, right. And who's fault would that be? Hmmm. Yours?''

''Fine. Blame me. But at least start on someone easier. A regular guy. I could set you up with someone.''

''No, thanks. I'm not interested in who you think is right for me.''

She shuddered to imagine what kind of man Doyle would send her way. Someone bland, sexless and terrified of her brothers, most likely.

''He's completely wrong for you,'' Doyle told her.

''Maybe, but he asked me out to dinner and I said yes. I suggest you get over it.'' She walked to the door and held it open. ''I have to get dressed now.''

He walked toward the door, then paused. ''You're making a mistake, sis. He could crush you like a bug.''

As she knew he was genuinely worried, she decided not to kill him. ''I appreciate the concern, but I need to do this. Maybe I'm jumping into the deep end, but I'm a big girl. I know how to swim.''

''Swimming won't help if he's a shark.''

With that cheerful statement, Doyle walked out and she slammed the door behind him.

''Men,'' she muttered.

''The city planners wanted more than a typical high-rise skyline in the financial district,'' Jefri said as their car turned down the main boulevard. ''While the buildings are tall, there are levels with gardens and art museums.''

Billie leaned toward the window. ''Is that one hollow?''

He chuckled. ''Parts of it are. There is also an illusion of seeing through to the other side. That is part of the design.''

''They're beautiful,'' she breathed as she turned her head to take in all the gleaming, modern structures.

''In the late 1970s my father realized that Bahania would not always be able to count on our oil reserves. That in three or four generations, the wells would begin to run dry and it was necessary for him to prepare his country for that future. In concert with the king of El Bahar, our neighbor, he opened trade markets and made financial institutions welcome.''

She turned back to him and smiled. ''That's some family history.''

The sun had long set, leaving the city bathed in the glow of streetlights. The illumination barely penetrated the limo, so he couldn't see much more than her profile and a hint of her features. Still, her beauty took his breath away. Talking about the changes in the city over the past thirty or forty years might not be interesting, but he knew the information by heart and didn't have to consider his words. Were they to discuss something more personal, he had a feeling he might verbally stumble.

She stunned him. That the confident, capable woman who flew as if she'd been born to the sky could also look like a goddess seemed impossible. Yet it was true.

She shifted slightly on the leather seat and her hair caught the light. Soft curls cascaded down her back. A few tendrils teased her ears and her neck, although she'd piled most of her hair up on her head. Her dark blue eyes seemed to glow with feminine secrets. And that dress. He swallowed hard and did his best not to notice the transparent fabric and the way only a few brushstrokes of color and paint concealed her curves from view.

He would not be able to eat, he thought grimly. How on earth could he sit across from her in a public place and act as if nothing was wrong? He was Prince Jefri of Bahania, yet with Billie he was little more than a man humbled by a woman.

''What are you thinking?'' she asked. ''If you were some kind of wild animal I would swear you were stalking dinner.''

''You are not far wrong,'' he said and lightly touched her bare arm. ''You are most desirable prey.''

She shivered, but didn't look away. Long lashes shielded her eyes. Earrings glittered and dangled.

"Have I told you how beautiful you are?" he asked in an attempt to keep from claiming her right there in the car.

"You mentioned it a couple of times, but it's not a topic of conversation that's going to bore me." She smiled. "It's not the sort of thing I hear that often."

"Then the men you know are blind fools."

"You got that right." She laughed. "And I appreciate how kind you're being. I'm just part of the staff and you're going out of your way to make me feel like a princess. I know you usually date movie stars and heiresses."

Kind? She thought he was being *kind?*

Before he could tell her that he had no kindness in mind, they pulled up in front of the restaurant. Billie leaned toward his side, the curbside.

"Wow. Look at all those people. Is there something going on here?"

Jefri followed her gaze, then swore.

"What?" she asked. "Is there a problem?"

"Not one that can be fixed. I am sorry. I did not think to tell my assistant to make reservations in another name. I am sure he did not think of it either."

She was close enough that he could feel the heat of her body and inhale the sweetness of her perfume. Both were a temptation.

"I don't understand," she said, apparently oblivious of her amazing charms.

"These people are with the press."

''Really?'' She leaned past him to look at them through the window. Several had crowded around the limo. ''Who are they waiting for?''

''Us.''

She straightened and stared at him. ''What? Oh. Right. You're the prince.'' She clutched her impossibly small purse to her chest. ''I'm going to be something of a disappointment.''

He shook his head. ''Somehow I doubt that.''

Billie's lack of awareness delighted him. Not only had she been unaware of why the press were there, she seemed blind to her own appeal. So many women he took out were secretly thrilled to be photographed for tabloids.

''So what happens?'' Billie asked. ''Do you go on ahead and then I sneak in through the back?''

He stiffened. ''You are with me. We will walk in together.''

She eyed the jostling crowd. ''This really isn't my kind of thing. I hope I don't trip.''

''Would you prefer to return to the palace?''

She hesitated, then glanced down at her dress. ''I did sort of go to a lot of trouble to get all fancy. Will it be crazy inside?''

''No. The photographers won't be allowed in the restaurant. We'll be shown to a private table where we will dine just like any other patron.''

He could see her weighing the possibilities.

''You decide,'' she said. ''Let's do what you want.''

Not a possibility, he thought, as his wants and desires had very little to do with dining in a restaurant.

"The food here is excellent," he said, as he nodded at the driver. "You will enjoy it. We will even order a special entrée for Muffin."

Billie tried to focus on food and her dog as the rear door of the limo opened and Jefri stepped out. The explosion of flashbulbs caught her unaware and temporarily blinded her. She slid along the leather seat until she could step out in front of the restaurant. A second barrage of bright lights left her totally unable to see.

Someone took her hand. She knew instantly it was Jefri and she allowed him to lead her toward the restaurant. She had a sense of the crowd pressing close. People called out questions, but she couldn't discern one voice from another.

Stay calm, she told herself. Think happy thoughts. She didn't want to see herself with a "deer in the headlights" expression on the front of some supermarket tabloid.

They made their way into the restaurant with only a few more flashes in her face. Once inside, the elegant and quiet atmosphere instantly calmed her.

"Prince Jefri," the maître d' said with a smile. "Thank you for dining with us this evening. We have your table ready."

Jefri nodded for her to follow the man. She leaned close and whispered, "What? They're not going to put our names on a sheet of paper and then call out when our table is ready?"

He raised his eyebrows. ''Restaurants do that?''

She grinned. ''You need to get out more.''

He chuckled and took her hand.

Billie liked the way he laced his fingers with hers as they walked into the dining room. They wove through the well-dressed patrons seated at beautifully set tables. The smell of the food made her mouth water.

''Will this be acceptable?'' the man asked.

''It's fine—'' Jefri started before Billie interrupted with a soft shriek.

She stared at the table next to the empty one where the maître d' held out a chair.

''You're not here,'' she said, both furious and humiliated.

Doyle picked up his glass of wine in a salute. ''Hey, kid. You should try the house salad. It's really good and you know I'm not much of a salad guy.''

She couldn't believe it. Her brother? Here?

''You have no right to do this,'' she told him, careful to keep her voice low.

''Is there a problem?'' Jefri asked.

''Yes. Him.'' Billie pointed at Doyle and wished she could incinerate him with her gaze. ''He's spying on us.''

''She's right,'' Doyle said, sounding amazingly cheerful. ''I called your assistant and asked where you two were having dinner.'' He put down his wine. ''Just so you don't behead him or anything, I told him my sister had asked me to check because she has food allergies and wanted to make sure there was something she could eat.''

Fury filled her, making her mad enough to spit. ''I do *not* have food allergies.''

''I know.'' He grinned. ''I was being creative.'' He motioned to their table. ''You two should have a seat. The food here is great and the wine list is impressive.'' He winked at Jefri. ''You probably know all this, don't you? You come here a lot.''

Billie glanced from her brother's table to Jefri's. They were barely two feet apart. Doyle would hear everything she said, which was probably his point. While intellectually she understood he was trying to protect her, emotionally, she was outraged.

''We could ask them for a different table,'' Jefri said. ''Or would you prefer to leave?''

Billie thought of how the patrons would be watching them through the entire meal and how she would be aware of Doyle sitting so close.

She sighed. ''I'd rather go back to the palace.''

Doyle's gaze narrowed. ''Billie—''

She cut him off with a shake of her head. ''Stay out of it. You've already done enough.''

''You know why.''

''That doesn't excuse it. I'm all grown-up, Doyle. It's time to let go.''

An hour later Billie and Jefri sat on the floor of her suite, leaning against the sofa and looking over the leftovers brought up from the king's formal dinner the previous evening.

''Better?'' he asked as he poured her a glass of wine.

Billie stretched out her bare legs and wiggled her toes. Okay, even though the dress had been great, she was far more comfortable in shorts and a T-shirt.

''Much. Although my hair and makeup is a little overdone for the setting.''

Jefri, who had also changed into more casual clothing, looked her over. ''I would say you're exactly right.''

She grinned. ''You do have a way with words. Do princes have special classes in that sort of thing? Charming women and dealing with annoying photographers?''

''We are taught many skills. Being charming is one of them.''

''You're not all that,'' she said.

He leaned close and smiled. ''Too late. You have already admitted to being impressed.''

''Maybe.'' She grabbed a shrimp and dipped it in the sauce. ''So does the press usually follow you around?''

''Not as much as they used to. I would guess that you were the attraction tonight.''

''Hardly. Why would they care about me?''

''They would be interested in *my* latest interest.''

''Ah.'' Is that what she was? His interest? Was that like dating? She desperately wanted to know but was afraid to ask.

''When I was younger, the press trailed me everywhere,'' he said. ''My father was able to exert some control here, but when I was in Europe or America, things could be difficult. We were given peace only when we were at school.''

''Must be tough being so popular.''

''There are compensations.''

''Sure. Like access to any available female you want. Kind of makes you wish there was still a working harem in this place.''

He picked up his glass of wine. ''You exaggerate my reputation.''

''I don't think so. Are you telling me anyone has ever said no?''

She happened to be looking at him as she asked the question. For a split second something dark flashed through his eyes. Then he smiled.

''I would never tell you that,'' he said.

Interesting, she thought. Something from his past. She might have to do some checking on the Internet and find out if there had been a woman Jefri had cared about. She couldn't imagine anyone leaving him, though. Not just because he was a prince, but because he was a great guy and someone any woman would enjoy being with.

''What about you?'' he asked. ''What are your romantic secrets?''

Billie froze in the act of offering a piece of chicken to Muffin. Her Yorkie took matters into her own paws and jumped up to grab the morsel.

''Secrets?'' Billie asked, hoping she sounded casual rather than nervous and faintly foolish. ''I don't have that many.''

Jefri's dark eyes seemed to see into her soul. "You must have some. While I applaud your brother's concern, I believe it stems from more than fraternal worry. I think there is a reason he keeps such close watch on you."

"I… You can't know that."

Jefri shrugged. "We were to dine in a very public restaurant tonight yet Doyle felt it necessary to be there to watch over you. Why is he so afraid for your safety?"

She debated telling him the truth for all of eight seconds, then sighed.

"I had a couple of bad experiences when I was younger," she admitted without looking at him. "When I was nineteen, I went out with a group of pilots we were training. It was the first time one of my brothers hadn't tagged along. Everybody drank too much, except me. Even though I was above the drinking age, I hadn't developed a taste for anything really alcoholic. Even now I really only like wine, so I barely ever even get very tipsy."

He touched her bare leg. "Billie, as entertaining as I find your stories, perhaps tonight you could stay on topic."

That was easy for him to say. He didn't know what the topic was. She reminded herself that she was nearly ten years older and wiser. She'd learned to handle herself and to not put herself into those kind of situations anymore.

"Okay. Sure." She wiggled her shoulders in an effort to relax. "Well, you can imagine. Five guys, me and a lot of liquor. They got too friendly and when I tried to stop them, it didn't go well. Two of the guys dragged me back to the van and tried to...well, you know."

She felt him stiffen. Rage tightened the muscles of his face and his expression became frighteningly determined.

"They didn't rape me," she said quickly. "Doyle and Xander drove up before they'd done much more than scare the crap out of me. The guys took off and my brothers brought me back to the base."

Jefri wondered how much she did *not* say. There was more to a rape than actual penetration. Had they hurt her? Marked her? Bruised more than her body?

He looked at her delicate features, her pale skin and the trust in her blue eyes. Fury filled him until he wanted to destroy those who had dared to attack her in such a way.

He swore, even as he struggled for control. "What was done to them?" he demanded.

"My brothers pounded them into quivering bloody masses, then they were kicked out of the program."

He felt some small measure of satisfaction at that. But it was not enough. "They should have been thrown into prison."

"I know. I wanted to press charges, but we were in a foreign country and the laws were different." She shook her head. "It's okay. I'm better now."

He touched her cheek. "You should not have anything to get better from. Tell me their names. I will bring them here and visit Bahanian justice upon them.''

''Which involves what?''

''Prison. Beating. Perhaps death.'' He liked the idea of them dead.

Her eyes widened. ''Death?''

''No man has the right to defile any woman. Ever. It has been that way here for nearly three hundred years.''

''A really good reason to take up residence,'' she murmured. ''Look, I appreciate your concern. Really. It's very sweet of you to worry, but I'm okay. It was nine years ago. I'm over it.''

He heard the words but did not believe them. He read a fragility in her eyes that told him those ghosts still had the power to haunt her.

''I see now why your brothers are so protective of you,'' he said.

''It made sense at first,'' she told him. ''I was nervous and scared, but things have changed. I can take care of myself.''

Perhaps she could, but she should not have to.

Billie used her fork to scoop up some rice. ''Can we change the subject?''

''Of course. You should try the fish. It is caught locally.''

She took a bite, then offered some to Muffin. As the dog licked her fingers, Jefri deliberately turned his mind from what had happened before. As much as he wanted justice, it was not his place.

But he wanted it to be, he realized. He wanted to

have the right to defend her with all the power at his disposal. Deep instincts, born in the darkest parts of the desert, still lived within him. He wanted to protect her as much as he wanted to claim her as his own.

He watched her move, her long bare legs a temptation no man should have to bear. He ached with his need, but whatever plans he might have had for the evening had changed. He needed time to come to terms with her past and decide how it changed things. If nothing else, he would have to move more slowly with her.

He offered her bread, then watched her take a bite. How many men had there been since that disastrous night? How many lovers?

Not many, he decided. As amazing as he found her, there was still an air of innocence about her. Between her past and her brothers, he wondered how innocent she might be.

"What?" she asked, narrowing her gaze. "Tell me exactly what you're thinking."

He shrugged. "Nothing of importance."

"Why do I know you're lying? I shouldn't have told you about what happened. You're going to get completely freaked out, aren't you?"

"Freaked out?"

"You're going to start acting as if I'm made of glass or something. This is just so typically male."

"You appear to be upset, but I have no idea of the cause."

She rose to her knees and glared at him. "You're completely weirded out and you're not going to kiss me or touch me or anything, are you? I should have guessed.''

He did his best not to smile. ''Is that what you think?''

''Absolutely. You're afraid I'll act funny or think you're attacking me. Well, I won't. That was a long time ago and I'm completely over it.''

''You think you know everything about me.''

Her mouth twisted. ''You're not that hard to read.''

''Then I will have to prove you wrong on several accounts.''

Before she could respond, he pulled her to him and kissed her.

Chapter Seven

While Billie had to admit that Jefri held her as if she were something precious, she wasn't sure any part of that was about her past. Judging from the possessive way he pulled her against him and the deepness of his kiss, she thought maybe passion had a part in it, too.

As his hands stroked her back and his mouth claimed hers, she found herself wanting to relax against him and let the moment unfold. She wanted to tell him he could touch other places than just her back, and that maybe they could do more than kiss.

Her own desires excited her as much as they made her blush. Still she didn't move away or in any other way discourage him. She wanted this man more than she'd wanted anyone in a long, long time.

Jefri tilted his head and deepened the kiss. The more he touched Billie, the more he wanted her. Her curves called out to be explored and pleasured in a thousand different ways. When his fingers tangled in her long hair, he imagined her kissing his bare chest and her long hair tickling his sides. When she wrapped her arms around his neck and her breasts pressed against him, he thought about cupping those curves, then tasting the hard, tight nipples.

Desire and need made him ache. He was hard to the point of pain. Still, he did nothing more than kiss, despite the invitation in her kisses. For one thing, he could not be sure her brother wouldn't arrive to check on his sister, and when Jefri started to make love with Billie, he did not want any interruptions. For another, he wanted to test her, to be sure she had fully recovered from her experience. If there were still scars and tender spots, he wanted to respect her boundaries.

Still, she was difficult to resist when her breath caught and she bit on his lower lip.

"You are a temptation," he said, pulling back slightly and staring into her wide eyes. "Difficult to resist."

"The same could be said about you."

He smiled. "Then we will practice self-control together."

She pouted. "Do we have to?"

"For now."

"Is that a tease or a promise?"

"Which would you like it to be?"

She took his hand and put it on her breast. The full

curve burned him down to his soul. His arousal flexed in anticipation as he brushed his thumb across her nipple.

They both sucked in a breath.

Jefri reached for her as she moved toward him. He pushed away the coffee table so they could drop to the ground in a tangle of arms and legs and violent desire. She rolled onto her back and he braced himself on one elbow so he was above her. When he slipped his hand under her T-shirt, she smiled in obvious anticipation.

A loud knock at the door interrupted them.

Jefri held in a groan. "I will guess that is your brother," he said. "I had a feeling he would check on you."

"What?" She pushed into a sitting position. "You're kidding?"

There was a second knock, followed by, "Billie, it's Doyle. I wanted to check on you."

"I'm fine. Go away."

"No. Let me in."

Jefri stood and pulled Billie to her feet.

"I'll get rid of him," she said.

He shook his head. "I will see you tomorrow."

"But..."

He took her hand in his and kissed her fingers. "Soon," he promised and walked toward the French doors where he let himself out onto the balcony.

Billie watched the prince go and could have cheerfully thrown the coffee table after him. She understood *why* he left, but she didn't have to like it.

After smoothing the front of her T-shirt to make sure everything was covered, she walked to the door and jerked it open.

"What do you want?" she demanded.

Doyle lounged in the doorway. "I'm checking on you. Dinner was great. You should have stayed."

She stalked into the center of the room, crossed her arms over her chest and glared at him. "You made that impossible. Get off of me. I mean it."

He walked toward her, stopping only a couple of feet away. "I can't help worrying."

"I appreciate that, but keep your worries to yourself. I'm a big girl. I've had sex before." Okay, only once and it had been fairly uninspiring, but her brother didn't have to know that.

Doyle winced. "Jeez, Billie. Don't tell me that."

"Why not? Isn't all this about protecting my virtue? Don't you think the prince has his choice of women? Isn't it unlikely he's going to have to force himself on anyone?" Certainly not on her. She'd been more than willing. Based on just the kissing, the event would have been fairly spectacular. Talk about lousy timing.

"I'm not worried Jefri's going to attack you. But he could break your heart. You're playing way out of your league."

"I refuse to take relationship advice from a man who has never had a serious relationship in his life."

Doyle grinned. "I run too fast to let them catch me."

"I suspect there's a deeper reason but right now

I'm too tired to figure it out. So here's the thing. I'm going to keep seeing Jefri as long as both of us are interested and you can't do anything about it. And if you continue to bug me, I will make good on my threat to leave and get a job somewhere else.''

His blue eyes, the same dark shade as her own, studied her. ''You're not kidding, are you?''

''No. It's bad enough being the only girl in this family. I won't be treated like an idiot as well.''

Her brother's shoulders slumped. ''Okay. You win. No more following you on dates. I promise.''

As Doyle had never gone back on his word before, she decided to believe him.

''Good,'' she said. ''Now I don't have to kill you.''

He grinned, then his gaze slipped past her to the coffee table. ''Leftovers, huh? Anything good?''

''Didn't you just have dinner at that restaurant?''

''Sure, but I can always eat.''

''Bank left,'' Billie said into the microphone of her headset. ''Bank, then roll. That's it, that's it. I've got you now, you thick-headed mutant.''

She heard chuckling in her headset.

''I wonder how much of your intensity has to do with making your brother suffer for what happened two nights ago.''

As always, Jefri's rich voice made her tingle. ''There's a little of that,'' she admitted as she kept her gaze on the instrument panel where she watched as the four planes converged.

"Get him," she said cheerfully. "We'll do a double tone-lock. That will be very cool."

"As you wish," Jefri said.

Seconds later she heard Doyle swearing as he clicked on to their communication channel.

"You did that on purpose," he complained.

"Doyle got beaten by a girl," she said in a singsong voice.

One plane instantly disappeared from her radar. Seconds later the door to the simulator jerked open and her brother glared at her.

"Don't ever say that to me again," he told her, doing his best to look fierce.

Billie wasn't the least bit impressed. She stuck out her tongue. "Beat you in twenty-seven seconds. That's pretty pathetic."

He muttered something under his breath and stalked off. Jefri took his place in the doorway.

"Remind me not to annoy you," he said. "You do not seem to forgive and forget."

"Not where my brothers are concerned. We did very well this morning."

"I agree. I find I much prefer flying with you than against you."

She grinned. "A wise man."

"I thought we might try dinner again tonight. Are you available?"

She was more than available, she was practically at the point of begging. "I could make the time."

"Good. I have a plan to avoid the press."

"Which is?"

"We are going to another country."

That evening they flew over the desert in a private luxury jet, although neither of them were at the controls. Billie fingered her curls, hoping her hair was big enough for the significance of the event and took the glass of champagne Jefri offered.

"So this is why we're not flying ourselves," she said.

"Absolutely."

She took a sip and tried not to read too much into Jefri's smoldering looks, while ignoring the way her thighs kept going up in flames.

It was all too much, she thought as she took in the rich leather interior of the jet. Too much luxury, too much man and way too much class. He looked amazing in his tailored dark suit. After the last debacle, Billie had given up on original and had slipped into a simple, black cocktail dress. She felt she looked good, but what did she know about a prince's expectations?

"So, where are we going?" she asked more to distract herself than because she cared about the destination.

"El Bahar."

"Oh. They're not that far away."

"Agreed, but no one should bother us there."

"I've never been, but I've heard it's very beautiful. Too bad it's night, we're missing the desert."

"You can fly over it any time you would like."

''Not all of it,'' she said with a smile. ''There is some very restricted airspace out there.''

Oddly enough in the middle of nowhere. She'd noticed it the first time she'd planned her flight in to Bahania.

''What on earth are you keeping hidden in the middle of the desert?''

She expected a teasing response. Instead Jefri studied her intently. ''It is a secret.''

''What kind? Military?''

He shook his head. ''We think of it as a treasure.''

She tried to imagine what it could be. What kind of treasure could exist such that planes couldn't fly overhead?

As she sipped more champagne, she thought about her research on the area and recalled mention of a fabled city—The City of Thieves.

No. That wasn't possible. A secret city?

''Is it bigger than a bread box?'' she asked.

He smiled. ''Much.''

''If I drove there instead of trying to fly there, could I see it?''

''What would you like to see?''

''I'm not sure.''

''When you decide, we'll talk about it.''

''You're not exactly what I expected,'' she told him. ''I thought a prince would be different.''

''In what way?''

''I'm not sure.''

''I am simply a man, like many others.''

"Actually, you're not, but that's okay."

He leaned close and brushed his mouth against hers. "I am glad."

Billie wasn't surprised to find a limo waiting for them at the airport. They'd come into a private field next to the main international airport. Jefri had warned her to bring her passport, but their trip through customs was a simple walk past uniformed officials who bowed and offered greetings of welcome.

She and her royal date were whisked into the center of the brightly lit city where they stopped in front of a small restaurant.

"No cameras in sight," she said as she stepped out onto the sidewalk. "I like this much better."

"Many women enjoy being the center of attention," he said.

"Then I say they should go for it. I'm not into the whole 'center of a crowd' thing. I get nervous."

They walked inside and were quickly shown to a private table tucked into an alcove. Billie did a quick visual search of nearby tables before she took her seat.

"No paparazzi and no brother," she said. "This is my idea of a good time."

"I am glad you approve."

Jefri ordered wine, they discussed the menu, but all the while, she couldn't stop thinking about how amazing this was. She was out to dinner with a man who had flown her to another country for the meal because he was a prince and they couldn't go out to eat where he lived. Jefri was royal, as in his daddy owned a palace and everything.

''What is wrong?'' he asked when the waiter had left with their order. ''You have gone pale.''

''I think I just completely grasped who you are.''

''In what way?''

She waved her fingers. ''Let's start with something easier. Who *I* am. My father owns a successful company. We've always done well, but we're not exactly rolling in money. I grew up surrounded by planes and burly mechanics. I did my entire high school education by correspondence. I know more about going Mach 4 than ballroom dancing and in stressful social situations, I usually put my foot in my mouth.''

He leaned toward her and captured her hand. ''What is your point?''

She laughed. ''That I can't figure out what you're doing with me. I saw the magazine articles and the type of women you usually date. They're gorgeous. Movie stars and divas and daughters of really, really rich men.''

''I see. And you do not consider yourself like them?''

''I can hold my own.'' Sort of. ''It's just weird.''

''Two nights ago you accused me of being 'weirded out' about your past. You have a fondness for the word.''

She sighed. ''See. I can't even speak correctly.''

He kissed her fingers, which made her heart do the happy dance.

''You do extremely well. I am delighted to be with you and honored by your presence.''

''Jeez, do you know how to get the girls or what?''

"You doubt my sincerity."

"Not at all. I'm just trying to keep up."

"This is not a competition, and my world is not all you think it to be. I was sent away to a British boarding school when I was nine years old. At seventeen, I went to America, to college. My brother, Reyhan, had made the mistake of letting people know who he was when he first entered college, so he was followed and judged and kept in the press for the entire four years." He kissed her fingers again. "I learned from his mistake and decided to keep my identity a secret."

She could imagine the feeding frenzy as the coeds found out there was a single royal prince on campus. "Did it work?"

He nodded. "I managed to get through with only a few close friends finding out. I met women who were interested in me for myself." He smiled. "It was a most humbling experience."

"I doubt that." He was the sort of man women would want regardless of his royal status.

"When I reached twenty-one, women descended on Bahania. They wanted the opportunity to marry a prince. I am not sure what I wanted, but they were not it. Still, some played the game very well and I was fooled more than once."

"That's understandable." The combination of willing women and the natural desire to believe it was all about him could have made things very complicated.

"I married one of them," he said.

The statement was so unexpected that had she been drinking she would have spit.

"You what?"

He looked at her as he rubbed her fingers. "From what I could see, she was perfect. Beautiful, well mannered. There was some trace of European royalty in her heritage, her father controlled multinational banks. It was a match that delighted everyone involved."

Married? As in… She carefully withdrew her hand. "You're not married now, are you?"

He took her hand in his and smiled. "No. I am not married now."

"But you were?"

"Yes. We were married. The wedding was a state occasion and it only took me six months to realize my wife had a heart of stone."

Billie had done some reading about Jefri, but none of the articles had mentioned a wife. "You're divorced?"

He nodded. "She was not someone I wanted to be the mother of my children."

That sounded a little imperious but she understood his point. "Was it really hard to get over her?" she asked, liking how he kept circling her palm with his thumb. "I mean with your heart broken and all."

"My heart was not broken."

"I don't understand. You can't just turn off love."

"I did not love her."

The waiter arrived with their bottle of red wine, which gave Billie some time to work on getting over being stunned. Jefri didn't love the woman he married?

"How is that possible?" she asked when they were alone again. "She was your wife."

"Yes, and she could have been the mother of my children. There can be respect and mutual understanding, but love is not required."

"Hello? I've seen your brothers. They're wildly in love with their wives." So much so that she'd felt a twinge of envy.

"There is passion between them," he admitted. "But love? I doubt it."

"I… You…" She grabbed her wineglass. "That's just crazy. How can you marry someone you don't love?"

"A royal match has certain requirements from both parties."

"What about being swept away? What about wanting to be with someone so much you can't think of anything else?"

His eyes darkened. "That I completely agree with. Despite these trappings of civility, I am at heart, a man of the desert. My blood runs hot."

She nearly dropped her glass. They'd gone from talking to something very different in the space of a heartbeat.

"You know what I want," he said, his voice low. "Tell me what you desire. If it is for me to leave you alone, you only have to speak the words."

And if it isn't? But she already knew the answer to that. No one had ever asked her a question like that. No one had put it all on the line. She felt Jefri's barely concealed passion and it excited her. That he wanted her enough to plainly state it made her quiver.

As for her… She knew her heart's desire. The sensible side of her brain warned her that there was no happy ending in this. That if she allowed herself to care, she would only get her heart broken. She knew who and what he was as well as she knew she would never fit in his world. Worse, he was a man who had married because it was the right thing to do, and not for love. She wanted a husband who was completely devoted to her and their family.

So this wasn't going to lead to a happily ever after. Was she still willing to take what he offered?

She stared into his eyes. "All my life I've been fearless in the skies. There is no plane I won't fly, no barrier I'm not willing to break through."

But in her personal life, she'd allowed herself to be ruled by her brothers' pronouncements and maybe a little by her own fear.

"I don't want you to leave me alone," she said, her voice barely a whisper.

"Are you sure? We can call for the plane or stay the night."

She glanced around at the elegant restaurant. "Right here?"

He smiled. "I have a villa on the edge of the sea. It's beautiful and private."

She knew what she wanted. One night with him would be a memory she would always treasure.

"A villa, huh? Do you want to go now, or do you want to wait until after dinner?"

Jefri stared at her for several seconds, then raised his hand to the waiter. "We would like the check, please."

Chapter Eight

If she'd had time to picture a villa owned by a sheik, she wouldn't have been able to imagine a place as beautiful as the one on the edge of the sea. Their car dropped them off in front and Jefri used a key to let them in.

From the foyer, she could see through to the dark lapping ocean. The marble floor was the color of the inside of an oyster shell, the walls, a pale peach. Instead of overhead lights, there were candles everywhere. Candles and rose petals and the scent of promise.

''You planned this,'' she said, not sure if she should be upset or not.

''I hoped. There is a difference.''

He came up behind her and placed his hands on

her shoulders. At the same time he moved her hair aside, then leaned down and lightly kissed her neck. Instantly her skin puckered and her blood heated. She felt the desire course through her. Muscles tensed and between her legs, a faint throbbing began.

She decided she needed to keep her wits about her as long as possible. Even if that meant only for the next fifteen seconds.

"So, ah, do you bring women here often?" she asked.

He chuckled as he kissed his way to her spine. "You are my first, but not *the* first. This villa belongs to the king of El Bahar. It was built nearly five centuries ago as a home for the king's mistress."

He whispered the words in her ear, then lightly bit her earlobe.

"Because a harem isn't enough?" she asked, barely able to speak.

"This offers what the harem does not. Privacy."

Ah, yes. Something that seemed like a very good idea.

"So you called him early today and said 'Hey, Your Highness, I have this girl I'd like to impress. Mind if I use the love shack?' Or words to that effect?"

Jefri turned her in his arms so they stared at each other. "Why do you mock me?"

"Because I'm nervous. Is that against the law?"

He smiled. "Not at all, but I may have to punish you for your impertinence."

"Really? What does that involve?"

''Let me show you.''

He bent down and kissed her. In the nanosecond before their lips touched, she tensed in anticipation. Then, when he brushed his mouth against hers, she couldn't help melting against him, letting her body sag against his as he claimed her.

She parted for him, wanting him to deepen the kiss. She wrapped her arms around his neck and savored his eagerness as he pulled her hard against him.

He was strong, she thought, her mind blurring with need. Hard to her yielding. Her breasts nestled against the planes of his chest. Her stomach pillowed the hard proof of his desire. When she clamped her lips around his tongue, he pulsed against her, delighting her with the promise of feminine power.

''Are you all right?'' he asked as he broke the kiss and pressed his mouth to her jaw. ''Does any of this make you nervous?''

She shifted her hands to his face and cupped his cheeks. He straightened and looked at her.

''I'm not afraid,'' she told him as she stared into his passion-filled eyes. ''Jefri, I'm not a virgin.'' Funny how this was the second time in as many days that she'd made the announcement. Until now, it hadn't been an issue in years.

''After I'd been attacked, I really withdrew from men and dating,'' she continued. ''Then I realized I couldn't keep doing that, so I deliberately set out to get a boyfriend. We were in Australia for a few months and I met someone there. He was sweet and very gentle. Anyway, we became lovers.''

She remembered being awkward and scared and all the things Jefri feared she would be with him. She had a feeling that Andrew had been as inexperienced as she had been. They'd fumbled through making love several times before she'd left the country.

"My point is, I've done this before."

His dark gaze gave nothing away. "And since that first lover? Have there been many?"

"Um, well, not exactly. But that's not because I was afraid."

"Lack of opportunity or lack of interest?" he asked.

"A little of both."

"I see."

He spoke the words with a confidence that came from…actually she wasn't sure what, but it made her shiver in anticipation.

"Thank you for letting me know I do not have to worry about your past," he said as he took her hand and led her down a short hallway. "Still, it is my nature to take things slowly at first. I hope you will indulge me."

"Of course." After all, what did she know about the whole process? Well, the basics, of course, but she had a feeling that Jefri's lovemaking would be nothing like Andrew's.

They walked into a large bedroom. Rose petals littered the marble floor. In the corner stood a massive tub filled with rose-scented water. Steam rose toward the painted ceiling. A bed filled the center of the room. Cream-colored linens invited her to touch. A netted canopy offered the illusion of privacy. Here as in the main room of the house, candles provided flickering light.

"For your hair," Jefri said, handing her several clips.

She saw he'd taken them from a carved dresser by the door.

She twisted her long curls into a coil and pinned it up on her head. When she'd finished, he shrugged out of his jacket and left it on a chair.

"We're getting in that, aren't we?" she asked, pointing at the tub.

"If you do not mind."

"Before or, after, you know."

He smiled. "Before. You may step behind that screen and undress," he said and pointed.

She followed his gaze and saw a painted screen concealing a corner. Huh. She'd assumed he was going to be taking her clothes off. She wasn't sure if she was relieved or disappointed to be doing it herself.

Still she walked behind the screen where she found a chair and a silk robe waiting. She stepped out of her shoes, then unfastened her dress and carefully hung it up. Her bra and panties followed. When she was naked, she slipped on the robe.

The silk was cool and soft against her heated skin, but even the delicate fabric seemed to tease her tight nipples. The sensation was both pleasurable and frustrating.

When she walked out from behind the screen, she

saw Jefri also in a robe, although his was black and hers pale pink. He motioned to the tub.

She moved closer, then hesitated, not sure about getting into the deep, hot water in front of him. But he came up behind her and reached around her to unfasten her robe, not giving her a whole lot of choice.

Clenching her teeth against potential embarrassment, she shrugged out of the garment and stepped into the steaming tub. First one foot, then the other.

''You are incredible,'' he said, his voice nearly a growl.

Billie looked up only to stare at a reflection of herself. She'd been too focused on the water to notice the mirror behind the tub. She glanced over and met his passionate gaze in the glass. Then he dropped the robe and moved close.

''I must touch you,'' he breathed. ''For a moment. Please.''

She was unable to move, barely able to breathe. He put his hands on her waist, then moved one up and one down. The fingers on one hand reached her breast at the same movement fingers on the other slipped between her thighs. She was already wet, swollen and ready. The combination of touches with the visual before her made her want to swoon.

''Exquisite,'' he murmured before he kissed her neck. ''How soft you are. Your skin.'' He brushed his thumb against her tight left nipple. ''Your secrets.'' He slid fingers in deeper.

One brushed against that single point of pleasure

and she jumped. He bit her shoulder, then smiled at her in the mirror.

"I want to please you," he told her. "All of you."

Who was she to argue? she thought as he stepped back and she sank into the hot water.

She figured he would join her, but he didn't. Instead he moved behind her so when she stretched out, her head rested against his chest.

A tray sat next to the tub. He picked up the first bottle and opened it.

"What do you think?" he asked, letting her smell the orange-spicy scent.

"It's nice."

"I want more of a reaction than that." He continued to open bottles for her until a musky-floral scent got her attention.

"That one," she said.

"Good."

He poured some lotion onto his hands and rubbed his palms together. She'd expected soap but the liquid didn't lather. Instead it thickened and glistened like some kind of oil.

This entire experience was so out of her regular world, she didn't know what to think. But if this was basic prince seduction, then someone had to sign her up for at least a monthly session.

Jefri slipped his hands under the water and moved toward her breasts. When his palms cupped her curves, she realized the lotion was an oil. A slick, warm concoction that didn't dissolve in water and made her nerve endings even more sensitive than usual.

He circled around her breasts as if discovering every inch of them. Around and around, without touching her tight nipples. She squirmed and ached and shifted in the water, but still he touched only the pale flesh, leaving the tips mournfully alone.

Heat poured through her. Need built. He kissed her neck so lightly when she wanted to beg him to do more. Touch more, bite more, something. Anything!

At last he stroked her nipples and she nearly cried out in relief. He rolled them between his thumb and forefinger, sending ribbons of pleasure directly down her chest, through her stomach and between her legs. She ached there. She ached everywhere. She wanted with a desperation that nearly frightened her.

Arousal poured through her body, making her writhe. At last she couldn't stay silent.

"More," she pleaded.

"Yes. Move forward."

Then his hands were gone. She grasped the sides of the tub and slid toward the other end. At the same time she turned to look in the mirror as Jefri stood and dropped his robe.

He stood there naked and aroused. His need jutted forward proudly, making her want to part her legs and beg him to take her. Instead she waited while he stepped in behind her and sank into the tub.

The two of them fit easily. He pulled her against him so her back settled against his chest. His erection pressed against her back, which wasn't the least bit satisfying, but she found she didn't mind so much when he once again slipped a hand between her legs.

She closed her eyes as he began to touch her. He found that one perfect place at once and gently rubbed it. Her breath caught, then she couldn't breathe at all. Faster, she thought. No, slower. No, just like that.

She arched into his touch, wanting all of it. Tension filled her body. She clutched the side of the tub and let herself experience the steady build toward—

He put a hand on her breasts. One second he hadn't been touching her there and the next he was matching his movements and she lost control.

Her orgasm crashed into her with no warning. Suddenly her body convulsed into exquisite pleasure. The waves of her pleasure shuddered through her over and over until at last they slowed.

She returned to consciousness only to find the water in the tub still shifting back and forth. His hand still stroked her between her legs and she was slightly embarrassed to feel herself getting aroused again.

''You should probably, you know, stop,'' she said although she didn't push him away.

''Why?'' he asked. ''I like touching you.''

''And you're really good at it.''

''Turn around,'' he said.

She did as he requested, only to find herself straddling him. His dark gaze dropped to where her breasts floated in the water.

''You are a fantasy come to life,'' he said.

''As are you.''

He pulled her close and they kissed. His arousal

rubbed between her legs, exciting her. She wanted to shift just enough for him to slip inside, but before she could, he pushed her back.

"This was only the appetizer," he said as he stood.

He stood dripping and naked while he collected a towel for her and gently wrapped it around her. Only then did he claim one for himself. He dried every inch of her before escorting her to the bed where he had her stretch out on her back. From a carved nightstand he produced a condom, but he didn't slip it on. Instead he knelt between her ankles and gently kissed her instep.

From there he made his way to her shin, then her knee. He repeated the procedure on her other leg, but this time moving higher and higher still.

She didn't know what to think, what to say, so she decided only to feel. No one had ever done this to her before. She'd never really understood the combination of vulnerability and amazing pleasure when a man's mouth pressed an open kiss on the very heart of her.

Her breath caught as her body went up in flames. It was too much. It would never be enough. She ached, she burned, she wanted.

Words spilled out of her, but she had no idea what she said. He licked her everywhere, then settled on that one amazing place. At the same time, he slipped a finger inside of her and caressed her from underneath. The combination nearly made her faint.

This time she was determined to hold back as long as possible, or two minutes, whichever came first.

But there was no denying the sensations flooding

her body. Holding back her release was like trying to stop a tornado—foolish and potentially dangerous. She gave herself up to his mouth, his hands and when the first shudder of her orgasm claimed her, she gave in to the need to scream.

It was nearly an out-of-body experience, she thought, barely conscious as every cell in her body gave itself up to the magic of what he did to her. Even when the pleasure eased a little, he continued to move his finger in and out of her, making her come again and again, if not as intensely.

He drew away. She wanted to protest, only she couldn't speak or move. She was boneless, barely conscious. Then she felt something wonderfully hot and thick probing between her legs. She forced herself to open her eyes and watch as he entered her.

She climaxed again on the first full stroke of penetration. Echoing shudders claimed her as he filled her fully, as he breathed her name and moved in and out. Time ceased to have meaning. She clung to him, wanting him to find pleasure in her and relaxing with contentment as he stiffened and was still.

''Obviously I need to get out more,'' Billie said a few minutes later when they'd cleaned up and retreated under the covers. ''I'm not sure that many orgasms in a single event is even legal.''

''You are a powerful and sensual woman,'' Jefri told her as he brushed a kiss across her mouth. ''There is much more for you to discover.''

She appreciated him not making her feel freaky

about what had just happened. Frankly, she could probably live another four hundred years and never feel this good.

"You're pretty amazing yourself," she said. "I think a lot of what happened was because of you."

"I can prove you are wrong," he said. "You are delightfully responsive. I simply unlocked what is already there." He smiled. "Shall I show you?"

By ten the next morning Billie knew that she would probably walk funny for the next six weeks, but it had been worth it. Spending the night with Jefri had been beyond description. What made it even better was the slightly glazed look in his eyes whenever he turned in her direction.

"You have destroyed me for other women," he said as he held her close on the flight back to Bahania.

There was a sentiment she could get behind, she thought happily. "Me, too. Although not with women."

"Of course not."

She sighed with contentment and wondered if her smile was as happily foolish as it felt.

"Doyle's going to kill me," she said. "After he has his heart attack."

"Because you did not go home last night?"

"I'm not sure he'll care about that, but he'll be seriously unamused that I missed our morning classes."

"Shall I explain that it was with my express permission?" Jefri asked.

Billie giggled. "I'm not so sure that's a really good idea. After all, he's my brother and when he figures out what we've been doing, he may feel obligated to beat you up."

"He will not be successful."

"I suspect you're right. But it could create an international incident and we don't want that."

Jefri kissed the top of her head. "I have some meetings this afternoon, but I would like to see you tonight."

"Me, too."

"Dinner in your room?"

"Uh-huh." Dinner and then…

The plane landed at the private airport where another limo waited to take them back to the palace. Billie tried to get her brother on the cell phone, but he didn't answer.

"Strange," she said as she checked her battery. "I can't figure out why he's not picking up. He's not scheduled to fly. Maybe he's somewhere without cell coverage." Although she couldn't imagine where that would be.

"Once we are back at the palace, we will find him," Jefri told her.

She nodded and slipped into his embrace. He pressed his mouth to hers, deepening the kiss until she wanted to ask the driver to pull over and give them a minute.

Tonight, she promised herself. They would make love tonight.

Their limo pulled up behind another one.

"A visiting dignitary?" she asked as he reached for the door handle.

"I had not heard of one on the schedule." He stepped out, then turned to assist her.

As Billie walked toward the entrance to the palace, she heard loud voices. Was that—

"Doyle?"

She hurried toward the sound and came to a dead stop when she saw her brother apparently arguing with the king.

"This can't be good," she murmured. Had her brother seriously freaked out when she hadn't come home? "Doyle, what's going on?"

He spun toward her. "There you are. Where the hell have you been?"

Billie was aware of the crowd of people standing around, including a young woman of about seventeen or eighteen.

"I'm fine. Thanks for asking. How are you?"

Her brother glared at her. "I didn't ask you how you are."

"I know but things would be a whole lot better if you did."

Just then Jefri came up and put his arm around her. "What seems to be the problem?"

Doyle's gaze narrowed. "Why don't you ask your father there? Or her?" He pointed accusingly at the young woman.

"Who's she?" Billie asked.

Doyle's expression darkened as his eyes narrowed. "Prince Jefri's fiancée."

Chapter Nine

Jefri stared at the small group of people all looking at him, but he only cared about the accusation in Billie's gaze.

His fiancée?

''It is not true,'' he said quickly. ''I have never seen this young woman before.''

But even as he spoke the words, an awful truth formed. What had his father done?

''On the contrary,'' Doyle said, sounding furious. ''Everyone seems very sure about this.''

Jefri wanted to take Billie away and explain. More than that he wanted to turn back time so he could prevent this moment or at least prepare for it. Neither seemed possible.

''Hello, my dear,'' the king said to Billie as he took

her hand in greeting. ''Welcome back. I hope you enjoyed your time in El Bahar.''

''What?'' Billie looked stunned. ''Ah, yes. Thank you. It was great.'' Her expression said the emphasis was on the past tense. Things were great no longer. She looked at him, then at the young woman.

''I have to go,'' she said and bolted from the room.

Jefri took a step to follow her, but Doyle stepped in the way.

''Don't even think about it,'' Billie's brother said with a growl.

Jefri was not the least bit concerned about Doyle. He had to get to Billie and explain. There was only one problem—he wasn't sure what had occurred.

''Father?''

The king smiled. ''My son, this is Tahira.'' The king motioned to the young girl who hovered at the edge of the foyer.

Jefri studied her. She was young, perhaps sixteen or seventeen, and very petite. She barely came to the center of his chest and her body appeared small and childlike. Dark hair had been pulled back into a simple braid. She wore no makeup, no jewelry and only a plain dark dress that covered her to well below the knees.

Jefri nodded at the girl, a pointless gesture as she did not look up from her careful study of the floor, then turned his attention to his father. ''There has been a mistake.''

''I think not, but regardless, this is not the place to have that discussion.''

His father was right in that.

Jefri walked over to Doyle. ''I never asked for her,'' he said. ''I do not know why she is here.''

Billie's brother drew his blond eyebrows together. ''Is she or is she not your fiancée?''

There were technicalities involved in that question, Jefri realized. Without speaking to his father, he didn't know the truth. ''I am not sure.''

Doyle swore, then moved close. ''Don't think this is finished, Your Highness. I don't give a damn about who or what you are. You've hurt my sister and you're going to pay for that.''

Doyle stalked off in the direction Billie had fled.

''A most interesting young man,'' the king said and smiled at the girl. ''Come, Tahira. We will adjourn to one of the small sitting rooms.

Jefri followed his father down the main corridor, then along a smaller hallway. When they entered the aforementioned room, he carefully closed the door before turning on his father.

''What have you done?'' he demanded.

''As you requested. I have found you a bride.''

Tahira stood by the window, her narrow shoulders hunched. Aware that she listened to every word, he lowered his voice.

''We discussed this matter recently,'' Jefri said. ''I requested you unmake whatever the arrangements might be.''

''I recall. However, things had progressed too far. When Tahira turned eighteen, she was required to leave the school.''

Eighteen? Jefri glanced at the young woman. Was it possible she was that old?

The king smiled in her direction. ''Come, child. It is time to properly meet your husband-to-be.''

Tahira obediently walked to the king. When she raised her head, Jefri caught side of large brown eyes brilliant with terror. She swallowed and lowered her chin.

''Prince Jefri. I have no words to express my honor and joy at finally meeting you.''

If this was joy, he would hate to see her upset. ''Tahira…'' He hesitated. None of this was the girl's fault. ''The honor is mine,'' he said, trying not to sound grim.

''She has been in the convent school on Lucia-Serrat,'' the king said. ''Her father was my finance minister until he was killed in a car accident when she was only seven. He was a dear friend and his wish was for me to provide for his only child.''

Jefri knew enough to read between the lines. Tahira had no one. There might or might not be any money from her family, but that did not matter. The king had sent her to the convent school where she would be well educated in the social graces, cooking and child-rearing, if not in the ways of the world. He doubted she had ever seen a man his age before.

Whether his father had originally planned for her to marry one of his sons or he had thought to offer Tahira in marriage to some highly placed official, obviously, she had not been prepared to make her way in the world on her own.

''She speaks several languages,'' the king continued. ''The sisters also said you were gifted in sketching and painting. Is that not so, child?''

Tahira barely nodded. ''The sisters were kind to me and offered many compliments, Your Highness. I would not dare to say I have talent.''

''Of course not,'' Jefri murmured, wondering if there was a way out of this hell.

''She meets all your requirements,'' the king said. ''She is very pretty.''

Hard to know, what with her still staring at the floor, Jefri thought. Although her appearance was the least of it.

He had to get to Billie and explain. He had to make this right with her.

''You have arranged rooms?'' he asked his father.

''Of course. Something with a view of the gardens. I thought Tahira would find that familiar. You had beautiful gardens at the school, did you not?''

Tahira nodded.

Jefri swore silently. ''I must excuse myself,'' he told his father, then glanced at the girl. ''Welcome to Bahania,'' he said stiffly and hurried out of the room.

He made his way to the third floor and Billie's suite. As he turned the corner, he saw Doyle lounging by the door. The large man stepped into the corridor and smiled coldly.

''I figured you'd come sniffing around here,'' Doyle said angrily. ''She's not here and I'm not telling you where she is. What I will tell you is you're the lowest form of life there is. This may cost my family the contract and me my freedom, but I plan to beat the crap out of you. Prince or not, you don't have the right to act like this.''

Gone? Where could she be? Jefri thought of the possibilities and decided Billie would retreat to the airport and the Van Horn complex there.

''Are you listening to me?'' Doyle demanded.

''No,'' Jefri told him. ''But I understand your fury. I have two sisters and I would do the same for them. The problem is you are not in a position to beat the crap out of me.''

Doyle narrowed his gaze. ''You think I care that it's against the law?''

Jefri did not have time for this but he knew Doyle would not let him walk away until this was resolved.

Jefri moved close to the other man. They were about the same height and size. ''Do not let the tailored suits fool you, Doyle. I have been trained by masters. You will not get off the first punch.''

Doyle's hands curled into fists.

Jefri shook his head. ''You must believe me. I would never hurt her.''

''Too late for that. Where the hell do you get the right to take her away for the night? She's not your plaything.''

''I agree. She is an amazing woman who constantly surprises me. Now I must find her and explain.''

''There's no way she'll forgive you.''

''That information will not stop me from trying.''

Doyle flexed his fingers. ''If she's still mad when you're done, then you and I are having it out. Just so we're clear. And for what it's worth, you'd better have a hell of a good story."

Jefri nodded, then left. He raced down to the garages where he collected his Jaguar and headed for the airport. He didn't have a story at all. He only had the truth. But would it be enough?

Billie found that reaching a personal best on a video game where she saved the world from outer space-based villains didn't make her feel any better. She was a little surprised she'd done so well, what with the tears blurring her vision. There wasn't a single part of her that didn't hurt. Even her eyelashes ached. Her body felt pummeled and her heart… She didn't want to think about the damage done to that organ.

Funny how she'd tried to prepare herself for the reality of her situation with Jefri. She'd thought she'd known who and what he was. A prince. Not the kind of guy a woman like her had a chance with. She'd accepted theirs would be an affair and she'd been happy with that. But finding out he'd been engaged the entire time made her feel slimy and gross. As if she were the other woman. Which she very well was.

How could he have done that? She would never have guessed he was that kind of man. He'd struck her as honorable, which just went to show she was an idiot.

It hurt, she thought, as fresh tears spilled down her cheeks. This hurt more than anything, even that night when those guys had gone for her. They'd tried to damage her body, but Jefri had messed with her head and her heart.

She brushed her hand against her face and concentrated on the screen. More spaceships flew into view. She began to systematically fire at them, racking up points like crazy. All the explosions and sound effects from the machine provided a comforting blanket of white noise, but they didn't prevent her from hearing steady footsteps on the concrete floor.

Every muscle in her body tensed. She knew who approached even before he spoke. The need to run overwhelmed her, but she had a feeling he wasn't willing to let her grieve in peace. Instead he would want to have his say and make it right. How like a man. Just once, she would like to see one of them take responsibility instead of weaseling out of everything.

"I know what you are thinking," Jefri said when he came to a stop behind her.

"Somehow I doubt that."

She hated that she didn't have to turn to know it was him. Her heart sensed his presence.

"You are thinking that I am a lying, cheating bastard who used you to get what he wanted. You are thinking you were tricked."

She released her hands from the controls and let the aliens claim her last ship. With her eyes closed, she did her best to keep breathing.

"Pretty close," she admitted.

"Billie, you have to believe me. I did not plan for any of this to happen. Not you and what we did last night and certainly not that scene today. I would never hurt you.''

She drew in a deep breath and wiped her face before turning to face him. Her stomach flinched when she realized he was still gorgeous. Turning into scum hadn't affected his looks.

''Imagine what you could do if you tried,'' she said, doing her best to hold the tears at bay and keep her voice steady. ''With a little effort, you could do a serious number on my heart.''

He reached out to touch her, but she stepped back. ''Don't do that,'' she said.

''You are right. I apologize.''

She nodded stiffly. ''So what exactly is the purpose of this visit?''

''To explain.''

''Are you or are you not engaged?''

''The situation is more complex than that.''

''Funny, because from where I stand, it seems fairly simple. Just answer the question.''

He shoved his hands into his front pockets. ''I am Prince Jefri of Bahania.''

''I already know that, but thanks for sharing.''

His steady gaze locked on her face. ''My father expects me to produce heirs. After my disastrous first marriage, I decided that I was not the best judge of who I should claim as my wife, so I agreed to let my father arrange a match.''

Billie heard the words but had a heck of a time believing them. ''You're willing to marry someone you've never met?''

He shrugged. ‘‘At the time it seemed a simple solution to a problem I did not want to deal with.’’

‘‘We’re talking about your entire life. This is the woman you’ll grow old with. She’ll be the mother of your children.’’

‘‘Exactly.’’ His dark eyes narrowed. ‘‘I wanted the right woman to give me strong sons and daughters. My father would be able to learn about her family, her education. What she would be like as a mother.’’

Billie thought about pointing out Jefri could do the same if he would simply invest a little time.

‘‘Let me see if I get this straight. The king wanted you to marry and you told him that if it was so important, he could take care of finding you the bride himself.’’

‘‘Yes.’’

‘‘That’s insane. What if you hate her?’’

‘‘My father would ensure compatibility. The point is a few weeks ago my father mentioned he’d found me a bride. I told him I did not want any arrangements made. I assumed the matter was closed. But I was wrong.’’

Billie stared at him. ‘‘If you’re lying…’’

‘‘I give you my word. I did not know about Tahira yesterday.’’

She supposed that was something. At least he wasn’t a complete bastard. ‘‘And now?’’

He hesitated long enough to make her furious.

‘‘What?’’ she demanded. ‘‘Are you engaged or not?’’

‘‘As I said, the situation is complicated.’’

''By what?''

''Tahira herself. She was raised in a particular way.''

''What? By wolves?''

''Nuns.''

Billie took a step back. ''Are you telling me this girl is fresh from the convent?''

He nodded.

''Great. Let me guess the rest. She has no family, nowhere to go and golly, she's been trained to be the perfect princess.''

He sighed. ''Why do I know your understanding is not a good thing?''

''Because you're not always an idiot. So what exactly makes her the perfect princess?'' Billie couldn't remember anything about the girl. Just that she'd been painfully young.

''She is all I requested.''

Not sure she wanted to hear this, she still insisted, ''Give me specifics.''

''I requested a wife who was reasonably attractive with a docile temperament and a fondness for children.''

She blinked. ''What? You asked for that? This is a marriage, not eBay. You can't just place an order and then wait for the future princess to be delivered.''

''Why not?''

Billie wished she was big enough to slap him and have it hurt. Worse, she hated the sudden need to smash in his perfect face, but she couldn't seem to shake it, either. She thought briefly about her high-heeled sandal, but didn't think she was strong enough to actually pierce stupid, male flesh with the heel.

"I do not expect to love her," Jefri said as if that explained everything. "Ours would be a marriage of convenience."

"Tell me about it. A marriage in the tradition of all great misogynistic monarchies. I'm sure you'll enjoy sleeping with your reasonably attractive, docile wife and that together you'll produce reasonably attractive, docile children."

"You do not understand."

"I understand perfectly. That's not a marriage and it's sure as hell no way to live a life. If that's what you want, you're not the man I thought."

She clung to that revelation and hoped it would be enough to help her get over him. Gathering her tattered dignity, she headed for the exit.

Unfortunately Jefri wasn't going to allow her a clean getaway. Instead he followed, keeping up with her easily.

"You are angry," he said.

"Thanks for the news flash."

"In time you will understand."

She doubted that. Her fantasy was that in time he wouldn't matter to her. Not that he mattered now. Okay, they'd had some laughs and a really fabulous night, but that didn't mean anything. She hadn't fallen for him.

He reached for her arm. She spun toward him.

"Don't touch me," she said, her voice low and angry. "You no longer have the right."

"Billie, you have to be reasonable."

"I don't think so. I don't think I have to be anything I don't want to be, and certainly not because you said so."

"Please. You mean the world to me."

"Ha! Even if I believed you, I wouldn't care. If you need a woman, I suggest you go check out Miss Docile and Reasonably Attractive. I'm sure she'll welcome you with open arms."

Chapter Ten

Billie hid out at the airport for another hour, but knew she couldn't stay there forever. Not unless she planned on moving back. The option gave her pause—was she willing to give up the perfect bathroom because of a broken heart? She quickly decided that living tubless would only add to her pain, so better to be at the palace and suffering than in a tent and hating life.

Once back at the palace, she found herself unable to stay in her room, so she collected Muffin and hurried toward the garden. Maybe being outside in something so beautiful would ease her spirits.

"I didn't expect to recover in fifteen seconds," she told her dog as she set her down on the path. "But I would appreciate being able to breathe without shooting pains in my chest."

Muffin gave her a quick sympathetic look before hurrying off to check out the nearby plants and shrubs. Billie sank onto a stone bench and contemplated her options.

She could leave. Contract or no contract, she could simply walk away from the job.

As soon as the thought formed, she dismissed it. She didn't run away and she didn't quit. Which left her in the unique position of having to regularly see the man who had hurt her.

Could she do it? "Dumb question," she murmured. "Of course I can do it. The trick will be doing it well."

She probed at the open wounds to gauge their depth. How long until she recovered? How long until she was able to look back at all this and know it had been an important lesson for her to learn? If nothing else, the sex had been fabulous. She'd figured out she had the kind of body that responded really well to the right sort of touch. Maybe she should stop thinking about Jefri and start figuring out who she could find to replace him. Would taking another lover make her feel better?

She wasn't sure of the answer to the question, but the thought of another man doing what he had done made her stomach roll. Okay, so she would need a little time and distance before searching out another lover. That was fine. She had time.

Muffin trotted past on her way to another tree where a long sniffing session was in order. Billie watched her, then stiffened when she heard footsteps on the path. Her heart fluttered, then slowed when she realized they didn't belong to Jefri.

How horrible that her world had been reduced to him or not him. Funny how she hadn't known she was involved and now she had to work on getting over him.

The king rounded the corner in the path and moved toward her. Billie knew bolting wasn't an option so she braced herself for the interruption and rose to her feet.

"Please," he said as he waved her back onto her seat. "Do you mind a little company?"

"Of course not, Your Highness."

He sat next to her and took her hand. "I will admit that spending time with such a beautiful young woman brightens my day."

She did her best to smile. "While I appreciate the compliment, you're in a position of great power. Doesn't that mean you can get all the young women you want?"

He raised his eyebrows. "You are right. I had forgotten. I will see to acquiring as many as possible this very afternoon."

Her smile turned genuine. "That would make for an interesting to-do list."

"I agree. My staff would not know what had happened to me." He patted her hand, then released it. "Tell me about the training. It goes well?"

"Yes. You have excellent pilots in the program." None better than Jefri, but she wasn't going to talk about him if she could help it. "We're taking their individual strengths and honing them, while shoring up weaknesses. At the same time, we're working on making them a team. Your deserts will be well protected from the skies.''

''That is good to hear.'' The king sighed. ''Times changed. A hundred years ago could anyone have imagined having to patrol the deserts in such a fashion?''

''Probably not. But change isn't always bad.''

''I agree. We must keep up with the times, as they say. Move forward. Invest in our future.''

''Is that what Tahira is?'' she asked before she could stop herself. ''An investment in the future?''

She kept her gaze on Muffin rather than the king, but she felt the monarch study her.

''I am an old man,'' he said. ''Is it so wrong for me to want grandchildren to brighten my days?''

''Not at all. I wish you a great many.''

He patted her knee. ''Our ways are different and can be confusing, but the desires of a parent are universal. We want our children to be happy, to produce the next generation.''

''You're certainly going to get that.''

''You do not approve of Tahira.''

Billie glanced at him. ''I don't know her, but I'm sure she's a lovely young woman.''

''Then you do not understand why Jefri would enter into an arranged union.''

''I'll admit that practice is a little mind-boggling.''

''He was married before. Did he tell you?''

She nodded. ''He said she wasn't what he thought.

That she was more interested in money and position than being his wife.''

''That is correct. When Jefri learned of this, he came to me to ask for a divorce, which I granted. He was sad to see his marriage end, but not heartbroken. I realized then he had never loved her.'' The king looked into the distance. ''I have married for duty and for love, and I have learned that marrying for love is better. I tried to tell him that, but he would not listen. When it was time for him to produce heirs, he asked me to find him the proper bride.''

Billie bristled as she remembered Jefri's list. ''Docile, reasonably attractive and good with children.''

The king raised his eyebrows. ''He told you that?''

''Sometimes the prince only *looks* intelligent.''

He laughed. ''Perhaps you are correct. I waited for him to find his own bride, but he did not seem to be interested in looking, so I agreed to conduct the search myself.''

''Enter Tahira.''

''Yes. She is a good girl, raised by the sisters, instructed on how to be the right kind of wife.''

Billy couldn't help thinking of the trained animals in a circus.

''How lucky for her,'' she said, hoping the words didn't sound too sarcastic.

''You do not approve.''

''I doubt my opinion matters.''

''There are other circumstances,'' the king said. ''Her father was a close friend of mine and I promised to look after her. The school sheltered her from the world and now she has to leave.''

Billie turned to him. ''You chose the school specifically. You wanted Tahira to be innocent, raised in a manner to make her worthy of being a princess. You thought she *should* marry one of your sons.''

He nodded.

''Why not Crown Prince Murat?'' she asked in a moment of desperation.

''Tahira would not survive the rigors of being queen. She isn't strong enough.''

''Which leaves only Jefri,'' Billie said dully.

''It is a matter of honor. To break the engagement now would be to dishonor the memory of my friend and Tahira's good name.''

Of course, Billie thought. Why would anything be easy?

''Tahira could break things off,'' the king added. ''If she wanted to.''

''Right.'' Because she had so many other choices. No doubt she'd been raised expecting to marry Jefri from the time she could grasp the concept. What young woman in Tahira's place would *want* to say no?

''Still, I will not force my son into a marriage he does not want,'' the king said. ''Should Jefri come to me…''

He let the words trail away, but she had already figured out what he meant. Should Jefri go to his father and demand the engagement be broken, the king would agree. But there would be a scandal and Jefri would be seen as selfish and willful. Tahira would be dishonored and while Billie wasn't sure what went along with that, she knew it couldn't be good.

It was a lot to ask, based on one night of great sex.

"Jefri won't come to you," she said with a sureness that made the ache inside worse. "He and I…" She swallowed. "We never had a relationship. There's nothing for either of us to get over."

"As you wish, my dear."

It wasn't as she wished, but it was exactly as it was. Billie excused herself and called for Muffin. Most of the time she really liked her life, but sometimes, like now, it sucked.

Billie and Muffin walked back to their room. Billie figured she was due a long soak in the massive tub. She would use her most expensive bath salts and do her best to float away her troubles. She would stay in until she got all wrinkly, then she would put on the fluffy robe provided by the palace, curl up in bed and watch chick flicks from the DVD collection. She'd more than earned the time to lick her wounds.

But as she walked toward her door, she saw someone leaning against the wall. As her heart didn't even flicker, she knew it wasn't Jefri. Muffin gave a little bark of excitement and ran down the hallway. Her dog only ever got that happy when Doyle was around.

"What do you want?" Billie asked as she approached. "Just so you know—I'm not in the mood for a lecture."

"I wasn't planning to give one," he said as he held

her dog and fondled Muffin's ears. "I'm just checking on you."

"I'm still alive, still breathing. Is that information enough?"

One look in Doyle's blue eyes told her the answer was no. She sighed, then pushed opened the door and stood back to let him in.

"You have ten minutes," she said. "Then I want to take a bath."

Her brother set down the dog. "How bad are you hurt?" he asked.

The unexpected question, not to mention the concern in his voice, nearly did her in. Tears burned in her eyes and she had to blink them back.

"I'm fine."

"You never were much of a liar," he said, his expression grim. "Dammit, Billie, I tried to warn you."

"I'm fine," she repeated, doing her best to mean it this time. "We had a few laughs, a good time and now it's over."

Doyle narrowed his gaze. "Tell me he didn't break your heart."

She dismissed the statement with a flick of her wrist. "I didn't know him long enough for him to break anything. Come on. It was a few days. Am I happy that there's now someone else? No. But I'm not destroyed. I'll get over this and move on with my life."

She liked how the words sounded, how *she* sounded, but there was a cold place inside that told her she might not be telling the truth about any of it.

Better not to go there, she thought.

"He's a bastard," Doyle said flatly as he shoved his hands into his slacks pockets. "I should go beat the crap out of him."

"While I appreciate the sentiment, I would urge caution. There are several flaws in your plan."

"Such as?"

"Jefri isn't totally to blame. He didn't know about Tahira either."

"He sent his father looking for a wife. In my book that makes him damn guilty."

"Agreed, but he also asked him to call off the search." Billie tried to focus on the sweetness of her brother wanting to take care of her rather than the pain of Jefri's betrayal. "He was just as shocked as the rest of us."

"But you're the one who was hurt," Doyle insisted. "I should go find him right now and reduce him to mush."

"Not a good idea. Whatever the outcome, you'd probably be thrown in prison. I doubt they'd treat you very well, so I'd be forced to sell myself to the head guard just to get you food and water."

Doyle moved close and cupped her cheek. "I'm not kidding, Billie. I want him to pay."

She nodded. "I'm not kidding either. I want you to stay out of this. You're not in charge of my life."

"I told you this would happen if you got involved with him but you wouldn't listen."

She hadn't wanted to listen. She'd wanted to be

with Jefri. He'd excited her and challenged her. She'd thought…

She'd thought a lot of things, she admitted to herself. She'd wanted the fantasy—a handsome prince who adored her. Well, for twenty-four hours she'd had just that. Now it was back to the real world.

She stepped back from Doyle's touch and squared her shoulders. "I'm going to be okay with this," she said firmly. "I'm a little rattled by what happened because coming home to Jefri's fiancée seems grossly unfair, but I suppose that's the downside of dating a prince. We had a good time. I don't regret what happened and I refuse to apologize for it."

"That sounds pretty tough."

"It's the truth. You can believe it or not."

He shook his head. "This is why we've all tried to protect you. Left on your own, you get into trouble."

"It's my life, Doyle. You can't protect me forever. And while we're on the subject, let me point out at least I took a chance. When was the last time you got involved with any woman who wasn't a brainless nit? God forbid you meet a woman you can actually connect with on some level other than sex. But that would ruin it for you, wouldn't it? I don't know what you're running from or what you're afraid of, but I suggest you get yourself a little bit closer to normal before you start making accusations about me."

"You don't know what you're talking about."

"Want to bet?"

He glared at her, but she refused to back down. Doyle blinked first and turned away.

''Let me know if you change your mind about me beating him up,'' he grumbled as he walked to the door.

''I will. And I appreciate that you worry about me, even though you don't have to.''

''You're my sister,'' he said gruffly.

She smiled for the first time since learning about Tahira. ''I love you, too.''

''This phase of the training involves teamwork,'' Billie said two days later.

She stood at the front of the largest classroom in the main hangar. Several diagrams covered the dry-erase board behind her. She'd been lecturing for the better part of an hour.

No one looking at her would ever guess anything was wrong, but Jefri knew. She might sound confident and strong, but she hadn't once looked at him.

''The sky gets small pretty fast when four or five fighters are covering the same territory. While you can't predict what your enemy will do next, you should be able to sense what your team is going to do. That's why we're spending so much time on the topic. I want you to develop a sixth sense about your teammates' actions and strategies. I want each of you to be able to predict what the other will do.''

She continued talking, outlining how much time would be spent in simulations before they went out in jets.

''Crashing is so much simpler when we do it on a simulator,'' she said with a grin.

The men laughed. Billie's gaze swept around the room. For a split second, it landed on him. He sensed her instant tension before she quickly turned away.

He felt her pain, and he ached in return. He had tried to speak with her, but she avoided him. For how long? When would she allow him to explain? And if she did, what was there to say? The problem of Tahira had yet to be solved.

''All right,'' Billie said. ''Let's go try all this theory on the simulators.''

The pilots rose and followed her out of the classroom. Jefri hung back, biding his time. Even if she avoided him during the day, she still came home to the palace in the evening.

She led the first pilots through the simulation of flying together in formation. In less than three minutes he heard the sound of an explosion followed by swearing.

Billie looked up from her seat at the master control console.

''You know, this whole flying thing means we can do more than go back and forth. We can also go up and down.''

The pilot who'd messed up stepped out of the simulator and grinned sheepishly. ''I wasn't looking down.''

''Which explains why you crashed into the plane below yours. This is not a good thing. Okay, who's next?''

The team worked through the program until they had finished. Finally only Jefri was left.

He stepped toward the simulator. Billie pushed the buttons to set the controls, then stepped aside to let him enter. Before he took his seat, he glanced at her.

"How long do you plan to avoid me?" he asked, his voice low even though they were the last two people left in the simulation room.

"Indefinitely," she said. "The computer will act as the other pilots. The program is simple—don't try to get fancy."

He'd heard the lecture before. "I know what I'm doing."

"Really?" She stared at him. "I'd have to say I don't agree with that statement."

She moved back to the main controls. "Push the start button when you're ready."

He settled himself into the seat and focused on the cockpit. The detailed simulation made it seem as if he were actually flying. After familiarizing himself with what was expected, he reached for the controls, then started the program.

He immediately found himself in the middle of an attack. There were three other planes with him and one of the enemy. One of the planes on his side signaled tone-lock.

Jefri instinctively banked left. The second the sensation of movement washed over him, he knew he'd made a mistake. He wasn't alone in the skies and—

The windshield cracked and the controls shuddered in a poor imitation of a crash.

Billie jumped out of her chair and raced over to the simulator.

"What the hell are you playing at?" she demanded in obvious fury. "How dare you fly so badly? That was barely ten seconds."

He knew she was right. Unfortunately his attention was not on his job.

"This is damned expensive equipment and my time is valuable. If you're not willing to take this seriously, then get out of here and free up some time for someone who is."

Fire flashed in her eyes. Her breath came quickly. Even in anger, she was beautiful and passionate. Need flooded him. Not just to have her with him in bed, but to simply talk and touch. There were so many things he hadn't been able to find out. They'd had too little time together.

"Well?" she asked. "Do you think this is a game?"

"Not at all."

"You lasted less than ten seconds," she pointed out again. "We both know you're better than that."

"I am sorry," he told her.

He meant for more than the simulation. She pressed her lips together.

"It doesn't matter."

"Yes, it does," he said. He reached for her hand.

She pulled back. "Don't do that. You're engaged."

"Not officially."

"It's official enough for me. Besides, there's no way you could want someone like Tahira and someone like me. We couldn't be more different."

"Who said I wanted Tahira?"

She tucked her hands behind her back. "You asked for someone like her."

"Maybe I made a mistake."

Something flickered in her eyes. Hope, he wondered. But then the emotion faded.

"You're going to have to live with that mistake," she said. "It's a matter of honor."

His mouth twisted. "You have been speaking with my father."

"He didn't tell me anything I didn't already know. You made your decision long before you met me. There's nothing either of us can do about it."

"If I could change things, would you want me to?" he asked.

She stared at him for a long time. He tried to read her thoughts, but he couldn't. Her blue eyes gave nothing away. Heat flared between them, as did wanting. He refused to believe that was only on his side. Billie had to feel it, too.

"No," she said at last, then turned to walk away.

Chapter Eleven

Billie felt as if she'd joined the cast of a popular but intense daytime drama. There was intrigue, royalty, steamy sex and a bright, young ingenue with a broken heart.

''So this is sweeps week,'' she murmured as she walked toward her room in the palace. She could only hope that her life would calm down over time. She didn't think she could stand this emotional pace much longer.

Her suite door beckoned. After an afternoon of simulation training, ending with that heated discussion with Jefri, all she wanted was to be left alone for the rest of the day. No more outbursts from her brother, no meetings with the king, no sensual, smoldering close encounters with Jefri. Just peace and quiet.

She opened the suite door. ‘‘It’s me,’’ she called to let Muffin know she was home.

As usual her small dog yapped in greeting, but she didn’t bound over to see her. That was because Muffin was neatly curled up in Tahira’s lap.

Billie stared at her uninvited guest. The young woman sat on the floor by the sofa. Several fashion magazines lay scattered around her. The one she held dropped from her hands as she quickly pushed Muffin off her, then scrambled to her feet.

‘‘I’m so sorry,’’ Tahira said, panic filling her eyes. ‘‘I did not mean to intrude. I waited outside, but the maid said I should come in and then your dog was so friendly and these magazines…’’ Tahira ducked her head and twisted her fingers together in a picture of abject misery and contrition.

Billie dropped her purse on a table and kicked off her shoes. She felt both old and weary. If she’d been a drinker, this would have been the moment to indulge. Instead she found herself wishing for a really big bowl of chocolate chip ice cream.

‘‘It’s okay,’’ she said as she walked over to the club chair and sat down. Muffin instantly jumped on her lap.

‘‘I intruded,’’ Tahira said, still not looking up.

‘‘You sat on the floor and read a few magazines. That’s not exactly the same as identity theft. Really. It’s fine. Have a seat.’’

The girl sank onto the sofa. ‘‘You are very kind.’’

What Billie felt the most at the moment was crabby and out of sorts. Nothing in her world was right and most of that had been caused by the teenager sitting across from her. Hard to believe that someone so quiet and shy could be the reason, yet there it was.

Tahira's long dark hair hung nearly to her waist. The heavy weight overpowered her delicate features and petite body. Billie wasn't all that tall but next to the teenager, she was practically a giant.

Jefri's fiancée had dressed in another shapeless, ugly dress. Obviously princess preparation with the nuns hadn't included classes on being a snappy dresser. Her gaze drifted down to the magazines scattered on the floor. They were all about clothes and makeup and relationships. Not exactly favorites in diplomatic circles. Had Tahira even seen a fashion magazine before?

"What did you think of those?" Billie asked, pointing at one glossy cover.

Tahira glanced at her and smiled. "They're wonderful!" she breathed. "The clothes are so amazing and the women... I could never look like that."

"Most of us couldn't," Billie said with a laugh. "We shouldn't even try. But it's fun to get ideas about clothes and that sort of thing."

Tahira fingered her moss-green dress. "I have no fashionable clothes. Not yet. At the school we dressed modestly. The sisters didn't approve of anything else."

"You're not at the school anymore."

"I know." Tahira sighed. "This palace is so different from what I grew up with. There are so many men."

"I guess they weren't allowed at the school?"

"Not at all." Tahira looked shocked at the idea. "There were priests, of course. And one of the doctors was a man, but he was very old. I met the king a few times. He was kind enough to visit me every year or so."

Billie found it difficult to imagine such a life. "What about trips? Didn't you go anywhere on vacation?"

"No." The girl shook her head. "We traveled a little on the island, but only in groups and never in the tourist season."

Sounded like prison to her, Billie thought.

She put Muffin on the floor, then collected the magazines. "I've read all of these," she said, thrusting the stack at Tahira. "You may take them if you'd like."

"Really?" Tahira's eyes brightened. "You are very kind."

Less than you might think. Billie shrugged as she resumed her seat. "It's no big deal."

The teenager hugged the magazines close. "You fly jets."

Billie laughed. "Are you asking or telling?"

"Both, I suppose. Prince Jefri mentioned it. He said you are very talented. Your work, it sounds exciting and dangerous."

"It's all I know."

"I'm afraid to fly," Tahira said in a small voice. "The plane goes so quickly and then the ground is far away. It doesn't seem right."

"It gets easier with practice."

The girl scooted to the edge of her seat. "It's not just flying," she admitted softly. "Many things frighten me. Prince Jefri, for one. He is so tall and commanding. When he speaks I think about running and hiding behind the sofa."

Billie resisted the urge to run screaming from the room. This was not a conversation she wanted to be having. Certainly not with Jefri's fiancée. But it seemed as if the girl had no one else to help her.

"There's no need to be frightened of the man you're going to marry," Billie said with a smile. "He's not that scary. Actually, he's very nice and kind."

Tahira's mouth thinned. "I never know what to say when I'm with him. Most of the time I don't say anything. He's nothing like the sisters."

Billie grinned. "I would have to agree with that. But it's a good thing."

"Maybe." She glanced around as if making sure they were alone. "I don't think he likes me very much."

Billie bit back a groan. This wasn't fair. Why her? There were other women in the palace. Cleo, Prince Sadik's wife. Or secretaries and female staff.

"You barely know him and he barely knows you," Billie said, trying to be reasonable. "You need to spend more time together to figure out if you like each other."

Tahira looked doubtful. "I thought I would know.

I thought when I finally met Prince Jefri, my heart would beat faster and my knees would get weak.''

Billie stared at the girl. ''What exactly do you know about weak knees?''

Tahira ducked her head. ''Some of the girls had families. They went home for holidays and when they came back they brought books for the rest of us. You know, stories about falling in love.'' She glanced up and bit her lower lip. ''Do you think it was wrong of me to read them?''

''Of course not.''

''I wasn't sure and there was no one to ask. So when I met Prince Jefri I thought…'' Her voice trailed off. ''Perhaps the feelings will come later. As you say, we don't know each other.''

Billie tried to be fair. Tahira seemed like a sweet enough girl, but she was no match for a stubborn, arrogant, wonderful man like Jefri. He was going to run her in circles. Not that this was her problem.

''Give it time,'' she said.

''I will,'' Tahira promised. ''I'm doing all I can to make the prince proud of me. I've been keeping up on current events so that when I attend the state dinner at the end of the week I can speak without embarrassing him.''

''Sounds like a plan.''

The state dinner, huh? Billie had been invited and until Tahira's arrival, she'd been looking forward to attending, but now she wasn't so sure.

''I don't know what to wear,'' Tahira said, then

swallowed. ''My clothes from the convent, well, the sisters picked them out.''

Ah, so that explained the problem.

''Now you can pick out your own,'' she said, going for cheerful and wondering how she could politely ask Tahira to leave. Billie felt the beginnings of a headache at her temples.

''I know nothing of fashion or even what is appropriate. I know three languages and the correct way to address every head of state, but not what to wear at a formal dinner. If I'm wrong, Prince Jefri will be disappointed.''

Billie held in a groan. ''I'm sure there are some stores in town that...''

''Yes,'' Tahira said eagerly. ''The prince has told me to go shopping. I have an appointment tomorrow morning. I was hoping you would come with me.''

Billie wanted to say no. Even though she loved shopping nearly as much as flying there was no way she wanted to spend an entire day with Jefri's fiancée. Even if the girl was clueless.

''I'm not an expert on dressing for the palace,'' she said, trying not to feel as if she were kicking a puppy.

''But you are so beautiful. And you have such style.''

Billie knew there was going to be trouble if Tahira thought *she* was stylish. ''I think I like sparkle a little bit more than the average princess,'' she said.

''No. Your clothes are perfect.''

Billie knew she was being punished. Probably for giving in to Jefri in the first place. Maybe it would be easier to surrender to the inevitable and get it over with.

''Why not,'' she said with a sigh. ''I'll go shopping with you.''

Tahira's whole face lit up. ''Thank you so much. You are very kind. Is ten in the morning acceptable?''

''Sure.''

She would have to let Doyle know he was on his own for classes. Her brother would complain, but so what? Besides, a day spent with Tahira meant a day not spent with Jefri and right now she could use a break from his particular brand of temptation.

Billie decided to bring Muffin along for moral support. Plus her dog always loved a good shopping spree. Promptly at ten the following morning, she made her way to the main entrance of the palace where she found Tahira waiting.

The girl had traded in her ugly green dress for an ugly brown one. Her long hair had been pulled back in a plain braid and not a dot of makeup touched her skin. Billie itched to have a go at her thick eyebrows. Some plucking, a bit of eye shadow and lip gloss and the girl would be a hundred percent more attractive. She was less sure about the hair. Of course it needed cutting but in what kind of style and how long should—

''Good. You are here.''

The words, spoken in a low, male voice, made her insides quiver and her thighs tremble. Still clutching

Muffin, Billie turned and saw Jefri walking toward them.

She glanced back at Tahira. ''Your fiancé is coming with us?''

''Yes. When I told Prince Jefri about our outing, he wanted to join us.''

Her dark eyes pleaded with Billie. Whether for Billie not to leave her alone with him or for Billie not to be angry, she wasn't sure.

Jefri stopped in front of her. ''I will accompany you to the boutique.''

Billie did her best not to notice how good he looked in his tailored suit and how much she wanted to step into his embrace.

''It's shopping,'' she said, determined to ignore her reaction. ''Men hate to shop.''

''I will make an exception this one time,'' he said, his gaze never leaving her face. ''Tahira requires a complete new wardrobe, including formal wear. I will speak with the person in charge and make sure you are both well taken care of.''

Of course he would, she thought as he put a hand on the small of her back and led her out of the palace. He would take charge because that is what he did—instinctively, she would bet. He would spend the day with them, always *there* so that she would be unable to think or function.

Tahira trailed after them, obviously unaware of the undercurrents swirling around. When they reached the limo, she went first, stepping in and settling on the side bench rather than the rear one. Billie followed, with Jefri sliding in after her. Which meant the two of them were sitting next to each other.

"I love your little dog," Tahira said as the car pulled away from the palace. She leaned forward and patted Muffin. "The cats are nice, too. There are so many."

"Billie is not fond of the cats," Jefri said. "They made her nervous."

Tahira looked concerned. "They won't hurt you," she said earnestly. "Most of them are very gentle. I like how they purr when I pet them."

As the girl spoke, she looked at Billie and Muffin, but never at Jefri. Apparently she hadn't been kidding when she'd said she was afraid of him. Billie wanted to tell her not to sweat it—that while he might act all high and mighty, Jefri was simply a guy. Okay, a guy with a lot of money and an incredible history, but still, he was human.

She thought about how they'd argued and laughed and how he'd never seemed to mind that she was the better pilot. If only, she thought, then shook her head. There would be no "if onlys." Not in this situation.

The boutique stood on a wide street at the edge of a large bazaar. Tahira gazed longingly at the gaudy silver bangles and lengths of embroidered cloth, but Jefri steered her into the elegant clothing shop. Billie and Muffin followed.

The store smelled of flowers, spices and money. It was just the sort of place where Billie loved to spend an afternoon and do some serious damage on her credit card. She had a feeling that today was going to be different. With Jefri around, she would need to stay on her toes and not allow herself to slip into the shopping zone.

The owner waited just inside. Tea and coffee were offered while Jefri explained their purpose. Tahira was to be provided with a new wardrobe. Billie would offer guidance.

Billie glanced down at her high-heeled sandals, skintight jeans and red leather wrap shirt. Her style leaned toward gaudy and fun. Tahira was destined to be an actual princess. Maybe it would be better to keep her advice-giving to a minimum.

"You must allow me to thank you for your kindness in this matter," Jefri said when Tahira had been led away to the dressing rooms.

Billie set down Muffin. When she straightened, she was careful to keep her distance from Jefri. "No thanks are necessary."

She plucked a black lace blouse off a rack and winced when she saw the twelve hundred dollar price tag. Talk about pricey.

"I want you to pick out whatever you would like," he said.

She put the blouse back and drew in a deep breath. "I don't need your money. I can afford my own clothes."

"I know you can. I am trying to…"

She looked at him. "Yes? Trying to what?"

He glared at her. "You make a difficult situation impossible."

"Me? What did I do?"

''You stand there, taunting me.''

Billie glanced over her shoulder to make sure he wasn't talking to anyone else. ''I'm not taunting you.''

''You tempt me with every breath. And now, when I try to offer something insignificant and make a gesture, you throw it back in my face.''

What? Were they having separate conversations here?

''What gesture? The clothes?''

''Yes. I cannot say how I feel. I cannot offer you gifts, except like this.''

A dilemma fit for a prince, Billie thought, not sure how to react. ''Look, I'm okay with all this.'' Not really, but what else could she say? ''I don't need—''

He touched her arm. The light contact barely grazed her leather shirt, but she felt it down to her bones. The world around them seemed to disappear. There was only the moment and the man and what could have been.

''Please,'' he breathed.

''It's just clothes,'' she told him.

''Is it?''

She didn't understand the question, but in the end it was easier to simply shrug and say, ''If it means that much to you.''

''It does.''

The owner returned then. She was a tall, white-haired woman who had the elegant European bone structure.

"Tahira will begin with casual clothing. Come, child."

Tahira appeared in an elegant pantsuit. The tailored jacket emphasized modest curves, while the cut of the pants made her legs look longer.

"Very nice," Billie said with a genuine smile. "Do you like it?"

The girl hesitated, then glanced at Jefri. "What do *you* think?"

He nodded.

Tahira beamed. "Then I like it, too." She walked back to the dressing room.

Billie managed to keep from rolling her eyes. "She is far too worshipful. You must really like that."

He frowned at her. "I do not need my ego stroked by a child."

"Too bad, because that's what you signed up for. Next time you're ordering a bride, you might want to specify an age range."

His eyes narrowed. "There will be no 'next time.' Requesting an arranged marriage was madness."

Too bad he'd figured that out too late, she thought glumly.

"She's a baby," she reminded him. "You can't hurt her."

"So now you take her side?"

"Someone has to. I mean it, Jefri. You are her entire world."

He stared into her eyes. "That is not what I wanted."

"It's what you got and now you're stuck."

As was she. She glanced around on the pretense of looking for Muffin. "I need to go find my dog," she said and hurried away.

She wouldn't care, she told herself. Not about him. Not about what could have been. There was no future here. When the contract was up, she would get in her plane and fly away without once looking back. There was no alternative.

The morning crawled by. Jefri had not considered the torture of being confined with Billie in the small area of the shop and having to pretend she didn't matter. He couldn't touch her or have her close to him. He had to keep his attention on Tahira, enduring her overeager smiles and attempts to please him. The girl had no opinions of her own, no thoughts, save his. He supposed he should have enjoyed that, but he did not.

Billie kept carefully out of reach, as elusive as a beam of light. She disappeared on the pretext of looking for a certain dress, or getting another size for Tahira, or finding her dog. As Muffin had curled up on a cushion on the floor and gone to sleep, the latter excuse was the most feeble, but a part of him understood why she felt the need to pretend.

Tahira appeared in a light green dress that skimmed her knees. The silky fabric clung to her body. In her own youthful way, she was attractive, he thought, as disconnected from her as if he viewed a sculpture. She was reasonably intelligent and gentle of spirit. Her only sin was to not be the woman who haunted his dreams.

''What do *you* think?'' he asked before she could request his opinion.

Tahira blinked at him. ''But you are the prince.''

''So I have been told. You have not answered my question.''

She looked confused, as if her opinion had never been requested. Carefully, she faced the mirror and studied herself.

''The color is good,'' she said slowly. ''The length does not suit me. The hem should be an inch or two shorter or longer. Some fullness here,'' she touched her hips ''would soften the silhouette.''

''As you wish,'' he said.

She met his gaze in the mirror. ''What do you mean?''

''Have the dress altered or find another that suits you better.''

Her eyes widened. ''But you did not say what you thought.''

''I know.''

Tahira looked as out of place and frightened as a wild rabbit. She darted back to the dressing room.

''You need to pace yourself,'' Billie said as she appeared from around a rack of dresses. ''Too much freedom all at once will only terrify her.''

''So I see.''

She fingered an evening gown without looking at it. ''I'm glad you're going to be kind to her.''

''Is there another choice?''

''Of course, but I like that you don't think so.''

''You have yet to try on clothing.''

She shrugged. ''This place isn't exactly my kind of store.''

''Why do I know that is not true?'' She walked around the rack of dresses and he followed. ''There must be something that tempts you.''

When she didn't answer, he began to study the evening gowns. They were all elegant and formal, but nothing about them caught his eye until he saw a beaded dress. The various shades of blue were as beautiful as the Arabian Sea. They swirled across the fabric in a glittering pattern that dazzled the eye.

''This one,'' he said, pulling it out and handing it to her.

''No, I couldn't,'' she said automatically, even as her fingers rubbed the delicate fabric.

He took the dress off the rack and handed it her. ''Of course you could.''

She took it and held it up against her. Her blue eyes darkened to the color of sapphires. ''It's more of a princess dress, which isn't exactly me.''

He stared at her, wanting what he could not have and unable to want what he could.

''Try it on,'' he insisted.

She gave in with a little nod and disappeared into the dressing area.

Jefri sank down in one of the chairs provided. He studied the way Muffin curled up on her cushion and the fabric of the carpet. In desperation, he reached for the newspaper lying on a small table. Anything to keep from imagining what Billie was doing right that moment—how she would have to undress down to just her panties before pulling on the dress and how she would look as she stood there nearly naked.

Wanting poured through him. Need grew until it overwhelmed him. Desperation propelled him to his feet. He had the thought that he would follow her into the small dressing area and claim her as his own.

Would she resist his touch? Would she yield? He knew how she would look, the texture of her skin and the scent of her body. He knew how he could carry her away on a wave of pleasure that left her boneless with contentment. He knew his own reaction to claiming her as his own.

''Prince Jefri?''

Tahira's small voice drew him back to reality. He opened his eyes and looked at the young woman in the simple black gown. The heavy fabric overwhelmed her small frame and made her seem like a girl playing dress-up.

Before he could speak, Billie appeared next to her. The shimmering fabric hugged every curve, as if the gown had been made for her. The light reflecting on the beads made her skin glow. She was a goddess next to a mortal.

Tahira stared at her reflection in the mirror and knew the dress was all wrong. It didn't hang right and there was something about the fabric itself. But what, exactly, eluded her.

She held in a sigh of frustration. If only the sisters had spent a little bit of time helping her learn how to dress instead of insisting she learn so much about geology or physics, she would be better able to handle her new position as Jefri's fiancée. So far the prince hadn't asked her a single question about rock formations.

Billie said something to the prince and he laughed. Tahira liked the sound of his laughter, even if she couldn't think of anything funny to say. But Billie always knew exactly what to say and how to act. She was perfect.

Tahira eyed her friend and the blue dress she wore. It was stunning. Jefri moved behind them both and placed a hand on each of their shoulders. While Billie smiled, Tahira stood there, frozen, the hand a lead weight on her skin.

She told herself to relax—that this was the man she would marry. But somehow she couldn't ever picture herself and the prince being together as a couple. When he talked to her, she didn't know how to answer. When they were alone, she felt only awkward and afraid. None of that seemed like love to her.

But he had honored her with his desire to claim her as his wife and she knew she had no choice but to go through with the union.

Chapter Twelve

"Everything is so beautiful," Tahira said enthusiastically as she opened box after box of clothing. "You have been more than generous." She turned around. "I am not worthy."

Jefri stood in the center of the suite and watched concern tighten the girl's expression. He forced himself to smile.

"You are more than worthy. These clothes are necessary. The sisters have many wonderful qualities, but they did not provide you an excessive wardrobe."

Tahira flashed a smile. "I was thinking the same thing at the store. How helpful is it that I can discuss quantum mechanics when I don't know what shoes to wear with what dress?"

She raced to the rack containing her formal gowns and reached for the first garment bag.

"What shall I wear Friday, Prince Jefri?" she asked as she pulled down the zipper. "It will be my first state dinner. I want to dress correctly."

He appreciated her enthusiasm, even as it made him feel old and out of place.

"The black one?" she asked. "Not the red. That is too sophisticated, I think. There is that lovely green one…"

She continued to chatter, but he didn't listen. Instead he prowled the confines of the living room and wished he could be somewhere else.

He crossed to the French doors and stared out at the gardens below. A woman walked along a path and for a moment, he thought it was Billie. His heart jumped until he recognized his sister-in-law. No. Not Billie.

"I've never had my nails done before," Tahira was saying. "Billie mentioned my hair. That I need to get it cut. What do you think?"

He looked at the young woman standing by the pile of white and gold boxes. "Would you prefer it shorter?"

"I don't know." She fingered her long braid. "Shouldn't you decide?"

She asked the question like a child and he did not want to be her father.

"No, Tahira," he said gently. "The choice is yours."

"But…"

She looked confused, as if such freedom had not occurred to her.

"You are no longer at the school," he told her. "You are free to do as you wish with your life. You may be as you choose."

Free to walk away from him, he thought, knowing she would not.

"You mean like a career?" she asked. "But we are to be married."

"The wedding could wait a while." Forever?

"Oh." She sat down on the sofa as if the thought was too much for her. "I have no idea what I would want to do. Not flying, like Billie. The thought terrifies me." She smiled. "I have trouble imagining her in a jet. She's so feminine and pretty all the time. I love her hair. The curls are perfect and I like the way she does her makeup. I wonder why she never married."

"Perhaps she never met the right man."

"I suppose. Or maybe she doesn't need to be taken care of all the time. She's independent. I wish I could be like that."

As soon as Tahira spoke the words, she covered her mouth with her hand and stared at him. Panic made her tremble.

"Prince Jefri," she began in a hushed tone.

He stopped her with a shake of his head. "You do not need to apologize, child. There is nothing wrong in wanting to be independent."

She swallowed and dropped her hand back to her lap. "But you have honored me by wanting to marry me. I can't forget that. Not ever. I swear, I will do my best to be a good and dutiful wife. You have my word.''

Not exactly what he wanted to hear.

He crossed to the sofa and pushed aside several boxes so he could sit next to her. For the first time since meeting her, he took her hands in his.

''Tahira, you must listen to me. You have been raised believing you have only one destiny and that is to marry me. But the choice is completely yours. You are free to choose another life. Should you decide you do not want to marry me, I will understand and support your decision in any way I can. You are young and it is a difficult and permanent choice.''

Her fingers moved against him. Her skin was warm and she smelled of flowers. Yet he felt nothing. Her youthful beauty left him unmoved.

Her dark gaze settled on his face. ''You are kindness itself,'' she said fiercely. ''Your goodness only convinces me that marriage is the right choice.''

He held in a groan. ''As you wish,'' he said, releasing her and rising to his feet.

She stood as well and clasped her hands together in front of her chest. ''Prince Jefri, I will do all I can to make you happy. I will be the most dutiful wife ever. I swear.''

''Of course you will, child. I have no doubt.''

He nodded, then walked to the door. With Tahira, he would get exactly what he had asked for. That was the hell of it.

Billie figured it was a good news, bad news situation. On the plus side, she was attending her first ever formal state dinner as a special invited guest of the king. She had on a killer dress and looked fabulous. Her date looked nearly as good in a carefully tailored tuxedo. The downside was that her date was her brother Doyle and that she would have to spend the evening watching Jefri pay attention to Tahira.

She reminded herself that the option was staying in her room with Muffin and watching movies. As she figured she could deal with the emotional angst of her situation on her own time and that this evening was a once-in-a-lifetime event, she'd put on her brand-new fancy dress and prepared to dance the night away.

She and Doyle followed the sound of conversation down the long corridor on the first floor and entered the massive ballroom. Dozens of chandeliers hung from a thirty-foot ceiling and illuminated the vast space and chatting guests. An orchestra sat at one end of the room. There were small tables and chairs, several strategically placed bars and waiters circulating with food and champagne.

Doyle gave a low whistle. ''This is just the meet and greet, right? There's a dinner that follows, then dancing?''

''That's what the invitation said.''

''All right.'' He scanned the room. ''Lots of beautiful women. I think I'd like to be the king.''

Billie gave his arm a warning squeeze. ''Do your best not to embarrass me.''

''Cross my heart.'' He kissed her cheek. ''Stay away from royalty.''

"You got that right."

He grinned and sauntered off, only to be immediately claimed by a dark-haired woman in a very low-cut dress.

"The boy always seems to fall on his feet," Billie murmured as she turned in a slow circle.

She spotted a waiter with a tray of what looked like champagne glasses, but before she could flag him down, she sensed something hot and tempting trickle down her spine. She clenched her muscles in anticipation. Seconds later, she heard Jefri's voice.

"Good evening," he said, coming up behind her and offering her a full glass of bubbling champagne. "You look exceptionally beautiful."

"Thank you." She clutched the glass with both hands because the alternative was reaching for him and that wasn't allowed. Instead, she let her gaze roam over him, taking in the tuxedo, the dark and smoldering gaze.

"Where's Tahira?" she asked.

"Speaking with a friend. Someone she knew from school is here and they are catching up. And Doyle?"

Billie motioned to the crowd. "I'm sure he's either being seduced or is seducing someone even as we speak. He looks good in a tux and women always appreciate that."

Jefri took her arm and led her to the side of the room. She told herself not to go, to plant herself in one very public place and refuse to have anything to do with him, but she couldn't seem to resist. Not when he looked at her as if she were the answer to all his prayers.

''What are you thinking?'' he asked when they stopped in a shallow alcove.

''That we have to stop running into each other.''

He left his hand on her arm and began to rub his thumb against her bare skin. ''That is not what I was thinking. I want to thank you for helping Tahira with the shopping.''

''She's very nice.''

''Yes. She is all that I asked for. I could not be more miserable.''

She flinched. ''Jefri, don't. She's—''

''A child and no more interested in me than I am in her. This is a matter of circumstances. A twist of fate that must be untwisted.''

''Are you going to break off the engagement? Let her go?''

Instead of answering her, he moved close. So close that she could feel the heat of him. His body brushed against hers in a gesture that claimed as well as enticed.

''I want you,'' he breathed into her ear. ''Every moment, with every heartbeat. I think of you in my bed. Naked. I want to touch you and hold you. I want to taste you and excite you. I want you wet, aroused, screaming.''

His hand moved from her arm to her stomach where he pressed his palm against her. ''Do you remember what it was like?'' he asked softly.

She couldn't speak or move. It was all she could

do to keep standing. "Of course," she whispered. "I can't forget, but that doesn't mean anything."

"It means the world."

She met his gaze and allowed herself to get lost there. For a moment or two, she imagined the possibilities, what could have been if things were different.

"I can't," she said and stepped away from him. "You can't either."

His gaze sharpened. "I am Prince Jefri of Bahania."

"Exactly. If you were someone else, this never would have happened. Tahira would be engaged to someone else and we..." She wasn't sure what they would be, but it wouldn't be this.

"Billie, I want you."

And she wanted him. She supposed that's what it came down to. A problem with no resolution.

"I should go," she said.

"No. Do not leave the party."

She stared at her glass. "I meant the country. This would be easier if I weren't here."

"You would quit?"

"It would make our lives go more smoothly."

"Is that what you want?"

Five simple words, she thought sadly. A question she couldn't answer. Not if she told the truth. Because she didn't want to go.

She pushed past him and entered the crowd in the ballroom. Maybe if she just kept moving, she could leave all this behind and simply have a good time.

She walked around a large woman in black satin and nearly ran into a well-dressed older man.

"I'm sorry," she began before she recognized the king.

He took her hand and patted it. "Where are you off to in such a hurry?"

"Nowhere. Just walking."

"I see. Then if I'm not taking you away from anything too important, there are some people I would like you to meet."

Billie nearly stumbled in surprise. "Me? Who?"

"The French ambassador is here. A very impressive woman. And the British prime minister. You haven't met him, have you?"

Billie laughed. "Gee, I haven't. Shocking but true."

The king drew her close. "He will be charmed, my dear. Perfectly charmed."

Tahira hovered behind a large column and watched the dancing. She had survived her first formal dinner, which was more than she'd hoped for. For the past three nights she'd had nightmares about spilling, dropping or saying the wrong thing. She'd awakened sweaty and trembling, unable to get back to sleep for hours.

Now the dinner was behind her and the worst that had happened was she had bored the people sitting around her.

"Perhaps not too great a sin," she murmured to herself as she swayed in time with the music.

The king of El Bahar had been seated on her left and while he had been most kind, he had been far more interested in his lovely wife who had been seated across from him. The Spanish ambassador had been on her right. She spoke enough of the language to get by but when he'd started talking about the wines his country exported, all she'd been able to do was nod as if she knew what he was saying. She tried not to imagine the look on his face if she'd admitted she'd never had Spanish wine, or any wine until that very night.

Several different ones had been served at dinner. She'd tried them all and had been careful to only take a sip or two. She hadn't wanted to get tipsy. Not that she would know what tipsy felt like.

A flash of blue caught her eye. She smiled when she recognized Billie dancing with the crown prince.

So beautiful, Tahira thought with a sigh. Billie had piled her blond hair up on her head. Long, dangly diamond earrings fell nearly to her shoulders, while her beaded blue dress hugged all her curves.

Tahira thought of her own small breasts and boyish hips. If someone put a dress like that on her, it would simply fall to the ground.

As she watched, the crown prince said something and Billie laughed. Tahira smiled as if she shared the joke. Billie always knew the right thing to say. She'd heard plenty of laughter at that end of the table.

''I want to be more like her,'' she said fiercely, wondering if it were possible. Could a mouse be transformed into a beautiful and exotic bird?

"More like who?"

Tahira spun toward the voice and saw a man standing behind her. Her mind went blank for a second before she recognized Billie's brother Doyle.

"You frightened me," she admitted, pressing a hand to her throat.

"Sorry. I saw you hiding back here and I came to find out why you're not dancing."

Dancing? She winced at the thought. While she had taken lessons and practiced several times a week with the other girls at the school, she had found out during her one awkward dance with Prince Jefri that dancing with her friends was very different from dancing with a man.

"I have danced," she said. "Once."

"Let me guess. With your fiancé. But not with anyone else."

She shook her head. "No one has asked and I'm not sure..."

Before she could complete her thought, Doyle grabbed her hand and pulled her close.

"You're not married yet, right? So I won't be beheaded for taking you out on the floor."

His eyes were the most amazing shade of blue, she thought hazily. Like the sea by the coral reefs off the island. A deep blue that called to her and whispered secrets.

"Tahira?"

"What?"

He grinned and her heart flipped in her chest.

"You didn't answer my question."

She blinked. ''What did you want to know?''

''Are beautiful princesses-to-be allowed to dance with handsome strangers?''

She laughed, then felt herself blush. She wasn't beautiful, but he was kind to say so.

''You're not a stranger,'' she said. ''You're Billie's brother.''

''You say that as if it makes me safe.''

''It does.''

His expression darkened. ''Don't believe that for a moment, princess. I can be very dangerous.''

His words made her shiver, but with excitement rather than fear. ''I'm not a princess.''

''But you will be.''

For once she didn't want to think about that. ''In time. But for now I am simply a girl.''

''Not a woman?''

She blushed again and ducked her head.

He touched her chin. ''Sorry. I didn't mean to make you uncomfortable. Come on. Dance with me.''

Before she could answer, he pulled her into his embrace. His arms came around her and then they were moving to the music.

Tahira didn't know what to think, what to feel. No man had ever held her quite so close. Well, except for Prince Jefri. But he'd held her stiffly, while Doyle pulled her against him. They touched everywhere. One hand rested low on her back while the other claimed her fingers.

He was tall, but not too tall. She liked how strong he was and how she felt tiny by comparison.

"You're thinking too much," Doyle complained with a smile. "I can hear your brain working. Which is disappointing. You're supposed to be so swept away by my charms that you can't think of anything but me."

"How do you know I wasn't thinking of you?" she asked and was delighted when he laughed.

"Miss Tahira, no one told me you were a flirt. Did they teach you that at your convent school?"

Her? Flirting? Was it possible?

"Not at all," she admitted. "The sisters would not have approved."

He lowered his head until his lips were very close to her ear. "They don't need to know."

His breath made her shiver. Deep inside her chest, a funny little feeling began to grow.

This was nice, she thought. More than nice.

Doyle pulled her even closer. "You smell good. What's the name of your perfume?"

She looked at him. "I'm not wearing any."

In less than a heartbeat, his expression changed. Something dark flashed through his eyes.

"Don't tell me that, Princess," he said, his voice low and almost angry.

"I don't understand. What's wrong with me not wearing perfume?"

"No woman should smell that good on her own."

"Oh."

She had no idea what he was talking about. Was he angry? Talking to men was more confusing than she had ever imagined. When she was with Jefri she had to search her mind for something to say. With Doyle, she didn't worry so much, but she was still confused about the outcome.

They danced together in silence for a few minutes before he said, ''So you're really going to marry him.''

''What?''

She looked up and saw Prince Jefri dance by. She turned her head so she couldn't see him.

''Of course. He does me a great honor by requesting my hand in marriage.''

''Uh-huh. Has he?''

She glanced at Doyle. ''Has he what?''

''Proposed. You know, down on one knee, vowing to love and honor 'til death do you part.''

''Oh. No. Not like that.''

He hadn't said anything, really. One morning the sisters had come in and told her it was time to leave. So she'd packed her things and had been brought to the palace.

''The king told me,'' she said.

''That's romantic.''

''Ours is a marriage of arrangement. I had hoped, of course, that I would be offered to one of the princes, but I didn't dare dream it would really happen.''

Doyle stared at her. ''Tahira, you're not a commodity. You don't have to wait around to be offered to someone.''

''Why are you angry?''

''I'm not. I just don't understand how someone like you can sell herself so short.''

''Someone like me?''

''You're sweet and funny. Pretty as hell. It's annoying that you're so damned honored to be given to someone like him. You could have a whole lot more.''

Several things distracted her. First, Doyle's energy. He obviously cared, which surprised her and pleased her. Also, he'd sworn. She wasn't sure she'd ever heard anyone use actual swear words before. Last, but certainly not least, were his words themselves.

''He's a prince,'' she said. ''How could I do better?''

''You could marry someone you love.''

Love? ''But I *will* love him. In time.''

''How do you know?''

No one had ever asked her that before. ''I just do.''

It had always been that way. All her life she had known there was a chance she would marry one of the king's sons. To that end she had studied and prepared, always hoping. Yes, at first she and her husband would be strangers, but in time, they would fall in love.

''It's the way things are,'' she insisted.

The music slowed and Doyle led her off the floor. ''Life isn't that tidy. You're banking your whole life on something that may or may not happen. Wouldn't you rather fall in love with someone first and *then* marry him? Or maybe you don't have to get married at all. What about that? You could explore the world. Get a job. Live.''

He made it all sound possible, when she knew it wasn't. "I'm going to marry Prince Jefri."

"Why?"

"Because I have to."

As soon as the words were out, she wanted to call them back. She covered her mouth with her hands and stared at him.

"No, you don't," he said quietly.

Her eyes began to burn. "You don't understand," she said as she lowered her hand to her side.

"Actually, I do. Come. Dance with me again."

She started to move away, but then he took her hand and she found herself being led back to the floor.

Had to, want to, what did it mean? She *wanted* to marry Prince Jefri. She'd wanted it all her life.

"Stop thinking," Doyle whispered against her ear.

He pulled her closer. She let herself relax against him. Gradually her mind stilled and there was only the music and the man.

Jefri stood in the shadows and watched Tahira dance again with Doyle. They'd been together nearly an hour. He tried to find some measure of jealousy within him, but he could not. All he felt was guilt every time the girl laughed.

She never laughed around him, never smiled, barely spoke. He knew the fault lay with him. Had he tried to draw her out or tease her? Had he worked to make her smile? Of course not—he'd been too busy blaming her for not being Billie.

Speaking of which…he turned his attention from

Tahira, to the woman who occupied his mind. She danced with the British prime minister. As he watched, the older man threw back his head and laughed.

Jefri's reaction was as quick as it was powerful. He wanted to stalk across the room and rip her from the other man's arms. He wanted to insist that no one dance with her, speak with her, touch her. Only he should be allowed such privileges. Yet he could not. He was bound to another.

He looked between the two women. So different, he thought. They had nothing in common save their gender. Given the choice…

But there was no choice. Once he'd asked his father to find him a bride and his father had chosen Tahira, events had been set in motion. Events that could not be changed, regardless of his own needs and feelings. What was desire in the face of honor? He was a prince and a sheik. If his word had no value, who and what could he be?

Chapter Thirteen

"I hadn't thought I could design my own clothes," Tahira said as she laid out a length of fabric. "When Billie mentioned it, I didn't even know where to begin, but the sisters taught me to sew years ago, so I know the basics. In my trips to the bazaar, I've been able to pick up some wonderful lengths of cloth."

She smiled. "What do you think of this one?"

Jefri glanced down at the fabric draped across the coffee table. Thin lines of gold shot through the deep red material.

"It's very nice," he said, not knowing what else to tell her.

Tahira's smile faded. "You don't like it."

"I have no opinion. If you like it, then make something." He tried to sound kind and interested, even though he hadn't been listening to much of what she'd said.

"But if you don't approve." Her mouth twisted. "You think my hobby is foolish."

"Not at all." Boring, maybe, but not foolish. "Tahira, whatever delights you delights me."

"Billie said it was important for me to find some interests," she told him. "Things that would occupy my time. You're so busy with your responsibilities. Not that I'm complaining, of course. I would never complain."

"I know that, child."

Tahira would never complain, never speak out against anything he might want to do. She was obedient, soft-spoken and kind. In the past month since the ball and his realization that he had no choice but to keep his word, Jefri had made a serious effort to get to know her. She was all he could have asked for and nothing he wanted. Worse, Billie had befriended her so every time he was with Tahira all the girl talked about, aside from clothes, design and fabric, was Billie.

"I'm glad you are settling in and finding things that bring you pleasure."

Her eyes widened and she looked away. "I'm only interested in pleasing you, Prince Jefri."

"Of course."

"Is there something else you require of me?"

"No."

She reached for another bolt of cloth and began to explain what she would use it for. While he tried to listen, his mind drifted to his flight training that morning. He'd lasted all of four minutes against Billie. When they'd met up again on the tarmac, she'd given him a quick smile of congratulation.

"You're doing great," she'd told him.

"I thought I'd get good enough to beat you," he'd admitted.

"No one gets that good."

She'd grinned then, and he laughed and for that moment in time, the world had been right. Then she'd turned away as if she didn't know him. As if they had never been lovers.

He understood her need to withdraw. The pain of wanting and not having was too great. But even though he respected her decision and agreed with it, for him, nothing had changed. He still ached when he saw her. He still dreamed about her. He could still pick her out in a crowd simply by the delicate scent of her skin. He listened to the rapid click of her high heels in the hallway and had even taken to seeking out Muffin knowing that Billie was always near her dog.

There were nights when he decided he would simply take her and disappear. He told himself they could find refuge in the desert, living out quiet, happy lives away from the real world. Except he knew he could not claim to care about her if he also sought to clip her wings. Billie had been born to fly.

Which left him trapped in circumstances that seemed intolerable.

"You will excuse me," he said, cutting Tahira off in midsentence.

She blinked in surprise. "Yes. Of course."

He walked out of her suite and headed for the business wing of the palace. He ached in a way he wouldn't have thought possible, and knew the pain would never go away. When Billie left Bahania, she would take his heart with her. Such a thing could not be allowed.

The guards outside the large carved doors nodded as he approached. Jefri stopped in front of the desk inside.

"Is my father in?" he asked the forty-something male assistant.

"Of course. I'll let him know you're here."

Jefri was announced and stepped into his father's large office.

The king of Bahania sat on an old sofa by the window. Several cats lay around the room. Two curled up on different chairs, while one had stretched out in a spot of sun on a bookcase. Jefri picked up a gray short-haired cat and set it on the ground, then brushed off the cushion and took its place.

"This is a surprise," the king said cheerfully. "I assume you have no crisis to report? The air force still flies?"

"Yes, Father. We have improved greatly. The Van Horns have done an excellent job."

"Good. They have lived up to their reputation." His father leaned back in the sofa and smiled. "What can I do for you, my son?"

Jefri drew in a deep breath. "I cannot marry Tahira, Father. I have tried. For the past month I have spent time with her, learning about her. We have taken walks, long drives, spent afternoons picnicking by the sea. She is a lovely young woman with all the qualities I requested."

The king frowned. "Then what is the problem?"

"I cannot care about her. I am in love with someone else."

His father patted the cat on his lap. "I see," he said at last. "And that young woman would be?"

"Billie."

"Ah."

Jefri couldn't tell what his father thought by his expression or the tone of his voice. Perhaps he should explain more.

"I do not believe it is within my power to make Tahira happy," he said. "She needs someone who will see her for herself, and not for what she can never be. I will do whatever I must—settle money on her, send her to college. I want her happiness more than anything."

"Have you discussed this with her?" the king asked.

"Not yet."

"What if she decides her happiness lies with you?"

"Then she is mistaken."

His father glanced at him. "She has lived in the palace for nearly six weeks. People have noticed, speculated. If you were to cast her aside now…"

"She is not being cast aside," Jefri insisted. "There has been no formal engagement."

"Tahira has considered no life except that as your wife. Promises were made. Will she not see this past month as courtship?"

Jefri stared out the window. Of course she would. How else could Tahira interpret events?

"She does not love me," he said.

"How do you know? Have you asked? Are you going to break this girl's heart and destroy her life? She is only here because you asked for her."

Jefri felt sure his father wanted to tell him something, but that he would not speak outright. So what was the clue? Something about Tahira. Did the girl love him? She could not. Surely she saw how wrong they were for each other. Or did she expect so little that an unhappy arrangement was enough?

Too many questions, he thought in frustration.

"This cannot be," he told his father.

"This must be," the king said.

Jefri rose to his feet. "I will find another way."

His father said nothing as he stalked out of the room.

The king watched his youngest son leave. When the door had closed, he smiled.

"It is safe. You can come out now."

Something moved under the wing chair. Two small brown eyes glanced around cautiously.

"He is gone," the king said, then patted the space next to him on the sofa.

Muffin jumped up and cuddled close. The king stroked her back.

"You see," he said. "Everything is going according to plan. It is just a matter of time until we have exactly what we both want."

Tahira sat in the garden, doing her best not to cry. But it seemed the harder she tried not to, the more her eyes burned.

Something was very wrong. Somehow she had displeased Prince Jefri. But what had she said or done? All she thought about was what she could do to make him happy. She listened dutifully as he talked about flying and jets, even though all the technical information made her head ache. She did her best to enjoy all their visits to museums and parks. She had asked several times and he always said he didn't mind that she was spending her free time designing clothes.

So why were things between them even more strained than they had been at the beginning? And why had he spent the past two days avoiding her?

"Beautiful women shouldn't cry."

Tahira jumped when she heard the words. She turned on the stone seat and saw Doyle walking toward her.

She hadn't seen him in nearly two weeks, and that one encounter had been a brief conversation at a family dinner. Even knowing it was wrong, she couldn't help being delighted to see him now and she hoped he would have time to talk with her.

‘‘I’m not crying,’’ she said even as she wiped away the tears that had trickled down her cheek.

Doyle sat next to her on the bench. ‘‘What could possibly make you so sad?’’ he asked.

‘‘Nothing. I’m fine.’’ Now.

She looked at his handsome face, the easy smile that always made her lips curve up in return. She wanted to get lost in his dark blue eyes and never find her way back.

‘‘So how’s my favorite princess?’’ he asked as he took her hand in his.

‘‘I’m not a princess,’’ she said, trying to tug her fingers free.

He didn’t let go.

She glanced around to make sure they were alone. She could not be seen holding hands with a man other than Prince Jefri. Not that the prince had ever tried to. When she realized they were in a secluded part of the garden, she allowed herself to relax and enjoy the warm touch of Doyle’s skin against hers.

‘‘So what’s the problem?’’ he asked as he brought her knuckles to his mouth and kissed them.

She felt the warm contact clear down to her toes. He’d kissed her hand! Just like that. While talking! As if… As if…

She couldn’t even think. No one had ever done that. Of course no one had ever kissed her anywhere before.

Why? Why had Doyle done that and why had the contact made her tingle?

‘‘W-what was the question?’’ she asked.

He grinned. ''Why are you hiding out in the garden and trying not to cry?''

''Oh. That.''

She pulled her hand free of his embrace and held in a sigh. ''Prince Jefri doesn't like me very much.''

''Huh. That doesn't sound good, what with you two practically engaged.''

She stared at him. ''What do you mean, practically?''

''Has he proposed?''

''Well, no.''

''Are you wearing a ring?''

She glanced at her left hand. ''No.''

''In my world, that means you're not completely engaged. Is it different here?''

Tahira hadn't thought of it that way. ''But there is an understanding. I was raised to marry a prince. Jefri asked for his father to arrange a match.'' Her shoulders slumped. ''I fear he is disappointed in me.''

''No way.''

''It's true. We have nothing to talk about. Things aren't very comfortable.'' She wanted to mention that the prince had never once held her hand or tried to kiss her, but she couldn't bring herself to admit that to Doyle.

''You don't have a lot of experience with the boy-girl thing,'' he told her. ''Maybe you're making things out to be worse than they are.''

She didn't think so. ''I was too sheltered,'' she said. ''I wish I were more like your sister. Billie has a career and accomplishments. She's so confident.''

''She's okay,'' Doyle said. ''Why can't you have a career if you want one?''

''Because.''

''There's an answer.''

Tahira didn't know what else to say. ''I would have to go to college.''

''So?''

''But that would never be allowed.''

''Why not?''

Two simple words. Two words with the power to alter the very fabric of her world.

Could she? Was she allowed to express preferences and make choices?

''I was raised to marry a prince,'' she repeated.

''Times change. It's a new century, kid, and you can be a whole lot more than some guy's possession if that's what you want.''

She didn't know what to think. The possibilities overwhelmed her.

''I never thought…''

''Then it's time to start thinking.'' He grinned. ''I do have to warn you, though. Once you leave the palace, it's a big, bad world out there and guys like me are going to want to eat you up for breakfast.''

She frowned. ''What?''

He leaned close. ''I'm talking about men, Princess.''

She ignored the title. ''What about them?''

''They're going to want you.''

As in… She wasn't sure as in what, but it sounded exciting. ''I don't think Prince Jefri wants me.''

''Then he's an idiot.''

She gasped. ''You can't say that about a prince.''

''Sure I can. I'll say it again. He's an idiot.''

Then, before she could think or catch her breath or figure out what was happening, Doyle leaned close and brushed his mouth against hers.

Tahira couldn't believe it. He'd kissed her! Just like that. With no warning or anything. Just a quick, fabulous, amazing touch.

''You look stunned,'' he said, sounding faintly amused.

''I am.''

''Let me guess. No one's done that before.''

''The king kisses my cheek.''

''Not the same.'' Doyle shifted closer, then cupped her chin. ''We're going to try it again. This time, close your eyes.''

''Why?''

''Because I said so.''

''Oh. All right.'' She obediently closed her eyes.

He chuckled. ''Why do I know you're going to get headstrong in a hurry?''

''I have no idea. How long do I keep my eyes closed?''

''As long as you want.''

A soft puff of breath was her only warning, then his mouth was on hers again, but this time it was much more than a brush. His lips pressed against hers in a way that made her blood heat and her fingers curl into her palms. She practically squirmed in her seat as her brain tried to process all the bits of information.

Like how softly he kissed her, yet how firm his lips were. How she could feel the heat from his body surrounding her like a blanket and how her skin felt extra sensitive.

He shifted, dropping the hand that had been cupping her chin to her waist. She felt his individual fingers and the way he squeezed her.

He drew back. "Put your hands on my shoulders."

She opened her eyes and stared at him. "We shouldn't be doing this."

"Because of the prince?"

She nodded.

"Let him get his own girl."

"I *am* his girl."

"Not until I see a ring. Now either put your hands on my shoulders and brace yourself for another kiss or run back inside like a good princess-to-be."

Tahira stared at him. The choice was very clear. The part of her telling her to run seemed to be getting more and more quiet while the part of her that wanted to keep on kissing Doyle got louder and louder.

Slowly, tentatively, she raised her arms until she could rest her hands on his shoulders. He was big and muscular and solid. She liked that. She liked a lot of things.

"What did you think about the kissing?" he asked.

She ducked her head and blushed. "It was very nice."

"Ready for more?"

She nodded.

"Ever hear of French kissing?"

Her breath stuck in her throat. Of course she had. In books. And sometimes other girls talked. About how a boy…or in Doyle's case, a man…would put his tongue… They would kiss with…

"Tahira, look at me."

She forced herself to raise her head and meet his gaze. The kindness there eased her embarrassment.

"You're a beautiful woman. I like you and I want to keep on kissing you. I'm sorry if that makes your life more complicated, but I can't get all worked up about that. What I *do* care about is making you uneasy. I don't want to rush you or make you uncomfortable."

Her heart swelled until her chest ached. He liked her! He cared about her!

"I think you should kiss me now," she said.

"Bright girl," he murmured, right before his mouth claimed hers.

Billie wandered through an unfamiliar wing of the palace. It was her day off and while she'd planned on spending it in town, an unexpected rain storm had trapped her indoors.

It wasn't that she couldn't be out in the rain—although humidity did have a way of making her hair go flat—it was that the rain made her sad, which made her want to curl up and think, which under her current circumstances, was not a good thing. So she had decided to take Muffin for a long indoor walk through the wonders of the palace.

On the fourth floor, in the back, she found what

looked like an old schoolroom, complete with a few desks and a blackboard. Dozens and dozens of books filled several low bookcases. There were shelves with toys and plenty of windows to let in light.

While Muffin investigated corners, Billie walked into a large playroom. Several airplane models hung from the ceiling.

‘‘Big mistake,’’ she whispered as she touched the plastic prop on one. She had a good idea of who had painstakingly built them, and then hung them. Of course it was silly to spend time in the palace and expect to escape from thoughts of Jefri.

Still, she kept getting blindsided by thoughts and wishes and dreams. Funny how a whole month after that single night, she still remembered everything about their time together. She still missed him and was coming to grips with the concept that she might have made the mistake of falling in love with him.

If there were—

A soft sound caught her attention. Odd notes of music. She turned in the direction of the sound and walked down the corridor. The music got louder. She pushed open a door and found herself in an old-fashioned nursery. Emma, Reyhan’s very pregnant wife, stood by a crib. She held a music box open on her hand.

‘‘Hi,’’ she said as Billie entered the room. ‘‘Exploring?’’

‘‘A little. It seemed that kind of day.’’

Emma glanced out the window. ‘‘Rain does that to me, too. Most people just want to curl up and read, but I get restless. Reyhan came in for some meetings and insisted I accompany him.''

Billie stared at the other woman's huge belly. ''When are you due?''

Emma grinned. ''In three weeks.''

''No doubt he's terrified you'll give birth while he's gone.''

''I promised I wouldn't, but did he listen?'' She closed the music box. ''Besides, I like it better at the desert palace. It's more like a house than this place.''

Billie laughed. ''You say that like it's a good thing.''

''Into the palace, huh?''

''Let's just say I love my bathroom more than I should.''

Emma nodded. ''It's very beautiful here. I'll admit that. I mean look at this nursery.''

Billie had to admit the room was amazing. There were mobiles and murals. A long changing table stood against one wall. The decors—blue and pale gray—screamed boy.

''So they really do hate women here,'' Billie said with a laugh.

''Nope. There's a fussy pink nursery next door. They certainly had the room to do both.''

''What are you having?'' Billie asked. ''Do you know?''

''I wanted to be surprised,'' Emma told her. ''Reyhan is convinced we're having a boy. Of course Sadik was sure of that as well, and Cleo had a girl.'' She touched her belly. ''At this point I don't care if it's puppies, I just want it out.''

Billie had never believed in biological clocks or pressure to start a family but at that second, she felt a distinct emptiness low in her belly.

Muffin scampered through the room, stopping long enough to sniff Emma's ankles before darting out the other door.

''She's doing well with all the cats,'' Emma said. ''When I first heard you had a small dog, I'll admit I was worried.''

''Me, too. But she gets along great with them. Sometimes she's gone for hours and I have no idea where she's been.''

''Ah. A dog with a secret life. So you're enjoying your time here, too?''

Billie nodded. ''Even without having a secret life. I love my work and the pilots in the air force are very talented.''

''I've heard you regularly beat them. Is that true?''

''Oh, yeah. They love it.''

Emma chuckled. ''Why do I doubt that? How does Jefri take it?''

Billie tried not to react to his name. ''With a lot of class. He was shocked at first, but he's gotten over it. Most guys simply can't handle it.''

Emma looked at her. ''Let me guess. Pilots are the only men you meet.''

''Of course.''

''It makes sense. If nothing else, life has a sense of

humor. So you're stuck with men who can't accept you're better than they are.''

''Much of the time.'' Although not with Jefri.

Don't think about that, she told herself. Don't think about him.

''What happens when you want to settle down?'' Emma asked.

''I don't know. For a while I thought I would have to give up my career and settle for something more traditional. But then I realized I can't stop being who I am simply to get married. I'll just have to keep looking until I find someone extraordinary enough to handle it.''

''He'll be lucky to have you.''

''Thanks.''

Emma opened her mouth, then closed it. ''Okay, my thimble-sized bladder just started complaining. Excuse me while I waddle off in search of a bathroom. But before I go, Cleo and I are getting together for tea in a couple of hours. Please join us.''

''I'd like that.''

''Good. All right. This is me waddling.''

Emma waved as she walked out of the nursery. Billie moved in the other direction, toward the girl nursery. As promised, it was a paradise of pink and lace.

Billie closed her eyes and let the pain wash over her. If only…

If only Jefri had never spoken to his father. If only Tahira had never arrived. What would have happened? She would have fallen in love with him because that seemed to be her destiny. What about him?

She wanted to believe what she read in his eyes. She wanted to know that they could have been together, always. Happy, in love.

While she was living in her fantasy, she would imagine herself as pregnant as Emma, standing in this nursery, preparing it for her daughter. A daughter with her style and Jefri's eyes. She imagined him standing behind her, pulling her against him, whispering he loved her.

A single tear trickled down her cheek.

She called for her dog and when Muffin appeared, she picked her up and gathered her close.

''We have to go get pretty,'' she said. ''We're having tea with a couple of princesses.''

She brushed away the tear and vowed to stay strong. Wishing for the moon would only give her a cramp in her neck.

Chapter Fourteen

"You do not understand," Jefri said, both angry and frustrated with his brother.

Murat lounged on the sofa and sipped his scotch. "I understand perfectly. You're engaged to Tahira but are in love with Billie."

"Stating the problem again does not solve it."

"Agreed. You already know the solution. Dump Tahira."

"I cannot."

"I agree there will be some small scandal and she may be hurt, but if you love the other woman…"

Jefri glared at Murat. "Tahira would be ruined."

"She would recover."

"When did you get to be such a bastard about women?"

"I am not. I'm suggesting you be."

Jefri saw the amusement in his brother's eyes and wanted to throw his glass across the room. "You are not helping."

"I know, but in truth, you do not want help. You want a magical solution. There isn't one. You will have to choose. A moment of unkindness to Tahira or a lifetime of unhappiness with her. Although I have to admit, should you choose honor and duty, as you have been raised to, then you will turn your back on Billie. I, for one, would be most interested in helping her get over you."

Jefri didn't remember moving. One second he was pacing the length of his brother's luxurious suite, the next he had his brother by the shirtfront.

"She is mine," he growled.

Murat raised one eyebrow. "As bad as all that? Then I do not envy your choice."

Jefri released him and straightened. "I should not have done that."

"Probably not, but as I am not yet king, I won't have you beheaded. You might want to fix yourself another drink."

Jefri looked down at the glass he'd dropped on the carpet. "She makes me insane."

"Which one?"

"Both. I don't suppose..."

Murat smoothed the front of his shirt and shook his head. "Thank you, no. I have no interest in a child like Tahira. Although she seems nice enough, she is far too young and inexperienced."

"You would want a wife who was not a virgin?"

Murat frowned. "Of course not. I meant inexperienced in life. Tahira has much to learn and I am far too impatient to want to teach her."

Jefri picked up his glass and set it on the tray, then collected another and poured a second drink.

"Your time will come. Once I am engaged, Father will turn his sights to you."

"I suspect he already has," Murat said grimly.

"And after all this time, no one has caught your eye?"

His older brother grinned. "Many have caught my eye. None has held my attention."

"What of—"

Murat cut him off with a glare. "Do not say her name."

"It's been nearly ten years."

"I do not care if it has been twelve centuries. Her name is not to be spoken."

Jefri sipped his drink, but didn't speak. So even after all this time, his brother still did not want to hear Daphne's name. Interesting.

But his amusement faded as the ramifications of his brother's reaction sank in. Ten years after the fact Murat had not recovered from the woman who left him at the altar. Sadik and Reyhan loved their wives with a devotion that was almost embarrassing. Was it a family trait? Was he destined to love only one woman for the rest of his life? And if that was true, how could he survive while married to someone else?

* * *

Funny how destroying the Bahanian air force didn't make Billie feel any better. Still, it had been a good day. Jefri had held out nearly six minutes and his improved performance made her proud.

As she walked along the concrete bunker-style corridor on her way from the training center at the airport, she calculated how much longer was left on the training contract. While company personnel stayed to work the transition, Billie was assigned to flight training and that work would be finished in about three weeks. Nineteen days, to be exact. Not that she could decide if leaving would be a good thing or a bad thing.

On the plus side was the chance to reclaim her life. She could stop thinking about Jefri every waking moment and instead figure out what she wanted to do with herself. Was she happy? Were there other things she wanted to accomplish? Since that one fateful night, he had been her sole focus and she needed that to stop. The other plus would be an eventual decrease in pain. How nice not to have a constant ache in her chest. How nice to wake up looking forward to the day instead of dreading it.

On the negative side of things was the fact that once she left Bahania, she would never see Jefri again. At least not in person. No doubt she would see pictures in various magazines and maybe even on the news. Some cable channel would probably do a special on his wedding. Billie shook her head. She would not be watching that. Tahira was a sweet enough girl, but

Billie couldn't stand the thought of her married to Jefri.

At least Doyle was off her back. In the past few weeks he'd barely bugged her about her feelings for Jefri. In fact he'd been pretty great. Which made her wonder what was up.

"Doyle would say this was a situation he couldn't win," she said aloud, then grinned, when she realized he would be right. But as her brother, he didn't have to win.

Still smiling, she turned the corner and nearly stumbled when she saw the man walking toward her.

Even in the harsh fluorescent light, he looked gorgeous. Still dressed in his flight suit and boots, striding purposefully toward her, Prince Jefri of Bahania was the epitome of male grace and power.

She came to a stop in the center of the empty corridor. There was nothing to say to him, nothing that could be resolved, yet she couldn't seem to move. Her senses went on alert, her body trembled, her brain got fuzzy. All because he was near. If they'd been outdoors, she would have expected a couple of little birds to break into song.

He slowed as he approached, finally stopping in front of her. They stared at each other, gazes locked, bodies stiff. The air seemed to crackle with electricity. She tried to figure out something to say—something significant. In the end, she went for something easy.

"You did well today."

He nodded. "I have learned much from you."

''Now you'll be able to beat the bad guys at their own game.''

''Should they attack the oil fields from the sky, we are prepared.''

He looked gaunt, she thought. As if he hadn't been eating or sleeping. She could relate to both. Falling in love and then getting her heart broken was even better than getting the flu for losing a couple of pounds.

They were alone in the stone corridor. The tunnel-like space was so quiet, she would swear she could hear both their heartbeats.

''Are you—''

''I thought—''

They spoke at the same time. She ducked her head.

''You go,'' she said.

''No. You first. Please.''

She looked at him, then wondered what she could possibly say. That she was sorry? She wasn't. Not for anything, except the obvious of his engagement. But even knowing what she knew now, she wouldn't *not* want to care. He'd touched her in a way that no man had, and that touching was about a lot more than just making love.

''I'm glad I met you,'' she whispered.

His expression tightened. ''As am I. You are an extraordinary woman.''

Neither of them stated the obvious. That if things had been different… But they weren't.

''Jefri, I—''

She couldn't say who moved first. Maybe she'd reached for him. Maybe he had taken a single step.

One second they were a good arm's length away from each other and the next they were in each other's arms, holding, pressing, kissing.

His mouth found hers, even as his arms wrapped around her body and drew her close. She went willingly, wishing she could climb inside and be a part of him forever. She wanted to feel his heat, his strength. She wanted to know all of him. Even as his mouth pressed against hers and she rediscovered the glory of kissing him, she was aware of his hard body, so different from her own.

Everything felt right, she thought as she tilted her head and parted her lips. He claimed her instantly, sweeping inside her mouth and touching her tongue with his.

He tasted as tempting as she remembered. They moved together in a dance designed to arouse and incite. She clutched his shoulders, hanging on to keep from falling. He pressed his fingers against her back, as if afraid she would bolt.

Had she been able to speak, she would have told him she never wanted to leave. That his arms would always be home. But to say the words meant breaking the kiss and that she couldn't do.

She wasn't sure how long they stood there, kissing, holding, wanting. Need built inside, but the sensation was bittersweet. Unfulfilled desire added a sharpness to her broken heart. She raised her hands to his head and tunneled her fingers through his hair.

And still they kissed—pressing, rubbing, wanting. He pulled back enough to nibble along her jaw. She sighed her pleasure as he kissed the sensitive skin on her neck. Their breathing increased until they were both nearly panting. Finally he drew back and cupped her face.

"Why do you leave me?" he asked, his voice thick with emotion.

She didn't ask how he knew she would go. She supposed there were those who would say, "Stay. See each other on the side. No one has to know." But that wasn't them.

"You have a life here and I belong somewhere else."

"The skies?" he asked.

"Pretty much."

He brushed his thumbs against her cheeks, wiping away tears she hadn't felt fall. Emotions filled his dark eyes.

"I love you, Billie," he said quietly. "With my heart and my soul. You have my heart in your possession. Treat it kindly."

She'd hoped he would admit he cared, but she'd never expected this. Tears flowed faster.

"I love you, too. More than anything." She sniffed, then stepped back and wiped her face. "This is so stupid."

"Our feelings?"

She laughed. "No. Me crying. For the first time in my life, a man is telling me he loves me and all I can do is cry."

"I am touched by your tears. You are not a woman who cries often."

That was true. "I try to save them for special occasions."

"Like this."

"I've never had an occasion like this."

She'd always thought that when she fell in love and that man loved her back, things would be happier than they were right now.

He moved close and kissed her.

"You are magic," he said. "I never expected to find someone like you. Not now."

Not while he was engaged.

His mouth twisted. He stepped back and clenched his hands into fists. "This is madness. I will go to her and tell her it is impossible. You are the one I want to be with. Not that child."

The words were exquisite torture, she thought, as the weight of the pain nearly drove her to her knees. That he would offer to do that for her.

She looked at him. More than offer, she thought. He meant it.

"You can't," she said, forcing herself to speak the truth while she still had the strength. "She loves you."

"She doesn't know what love is."

"Perhaps, but she cares as much as she can."

He dismissed her with a wave. Billie grabbed his arm.

"I've been spending time with her," she said. "You are all she speaks about. Every thought she has, everything she does is for you. She speaks about having your children, growing old with you. She talks about her duty to your country.'' She released him and ducked her head.

''I've tried to convince her otherwise,'' she admitted. ''Just little hints that she could have a different life if she wanted. A career. Freedom to travel. Meet other men.'' She squared her shoulders and forced herself to look at him. ''I'm not proud of that, but I did it.''

He pulled her close and kissed her. ''I'm sure you were kindness itself.''

''I was selfish. But the point is, Tahira was never interested. You're her world. You gave your word and we both have to respect that.''

''So the three of us are destined to unhappy lives?''

She didn't want to think of that. ''In time,'' she began.

He released her. ''In time what? I'll grow to love her? Knowing how I feel about you, do you believe I could love Tahira? Are there two women more different?''

''You have to try.''

''I see. And what about you? Will you go look for another man?''

Eventually, she thought. ''I'll have to. I want a husband and a family.''

Jefri turned away. She felt his pain because it was her own.

''I'm sorry,'' she whispered.

He shook his head. ''No. You are wise. I am the fool. I wish for what I cannot have and refuse to accept anything less.''

He turned back to her and reached into his pocket. ''I have something for you. I have been carrying it around for a long time, not sure if I should give it to you. If you would accept.''

He pulled out a wide, intricately carved gold bracelet. Different precious gems added to the pattern.

''They are very old and very rare. This one dates back to the early nine hundreds.''

She took the stunning bracelet and turned it over in her hands. ''There's no way to get it open.''

He smiled. ''That is part of the appeal. This is a version of a slave bracelet. The unlocking mechanism is hidden in the design. Some were made for the women in the harem. That way if they escaped, the bracelet marked them as a possession of the king. Others, like these, were made for the woman who possessed the king's heart. They offered protection, a free right of passage anywhere in the country. Those who aided her were rewarded.''

He reached into his pocket again and held out a tiny key dangling from a delicate gold chain. ''You see where the diamonds surround the sapphire?''

She found the spot on the bracelet and nodded.

''The key fits there. If you choose to wear the bracelet, know that you will always have a place to call home here. When you are ready, remove it.''

She knew what he meant. When she loved another, she could take off the bracelet as a symbol of letting go.

Billie traced the wide gold band. The diamonds, sapphires and rubies glinted in the harsh lighting.

There was so much history in this single piece of jewelry. So much beauty.

"This should be on display in a museum," she said.

"I would prefer you to wear it."

She held out the band and he unlocked it. She slipped her wrist inside and snapped it closed. The cool metal fit perfectly.

Jefri slipped the chain over her head and she tucked the key under her blouse.

"Know you are protected," he said. "That if you become lost, all you have to do is ask and you will be directed to me. Whatever happens, wherever you go, there will always be a safe place for you here. When I am gone, my heirs will honor the promise of the bracelet until the day you draw your last."

He spoke the words as if they were a prayer...or a vow. They filled her heart with love and made her ache.

She took his hand in hers and leaned against him. "Maybe I'm not strong enough to do this. Maybe I want us to run away together and say the hell with the rest of the world."

He touched her lips with his fingertips. "You need only speak the words."

She glanced at the bracelet, then into his face. He meant it, she thought with amazement. If she asked him to go away with her, he would. He would turn his back on everything for her. The realization humbled her.

It was all there, she thought. Just out of reach. She

only had to grab for what she wanted and it would be hers. But at what price? How many people would be hurt or disappointed? Not just Tahira. What about Jefri's family? How long would he be content to be estranged from them? He was a prince and a sheik. He could trace his lineage back over a thousand years.

"Speak the words," he repeated.

She drew in a breath for courage. "No."

Sadness darkened his eyes. "Are you sure?"

She wasn't, but she nodded because it was the right thing to do.

"Please take me back to the palace," she whispered. "I'm going to need a long bath and a lot of chocolate to get through the rest of the day."

He kissed her. "I will love you forever."

"I'll love you just as long."

They drove back to the palace in the back of a limo. Billie snuggled close, resting her head on his shoulder. She closed her eyes against the sights of the city she had come to love, knowing that her days there were dwindling. She could feel the weight of the bracelet on her wrist and wondered how long it would be before she was willing to take it off.

She had a vision of herself as a very old lady, showing up at the palace and demanding refuge. Somehow she knew that a handsome young prince would appear. He would speak gently, telling her of his father's death and how Jefri had loved her to the end. Then she would be taken to a pretty room where she would live out her last.

It all sounded romantic, she thought. But in reality,

it sucked. Besides, she wanted to spend her last days surrounded by a large, loud family, not alone in a foreign country where no one knew her.

So in time, she would have to find the courage to put her love aside and go out and make a place for herself. There were good men out there. Men who could make her happy.

Or maybe she didn't need a man. Maybe she could start adopting kids and make a family that way. She had a lot to offer—a big heart and plenty of love. She could buy a house somewhere and settle down. As long as she was near an airport.

The limo slowed. She opened her eyes and saw they'd entered the palace grounds. Several guards approached the limo and motioned for the driver to stop. The rear door jerked open.

''Oh. Prince Jefri,'' the guard said. ''My apologies. I'm under orders to search every vehicle.''

Jefri stepped out. ''What is going on?''

Billie followed him. There were dozens of guards everywhere. Up at the entrance to the palace, she saw the king talking with someone. It didn't look like a happy conversation.

''This can't be good,'' she said.

''I agree.''

Jefri took her hand and led her toward his father. As they approached, the king dismissed the other man and turned to them.

''You are here at last,'' the old man said, looking both angry and worried.

''What has happened?'' Jefri asked.

''Tahira is missing, and so is Doyle Van Horn.''

Chapter Fifteen

Jefri followed his father into a private room off the entrance. It wasn't until he saw the king glance down that he realized he and Billie were still holding hands.

"When was Tahira last seen?" he asked, not concerned with what anyone might think, including the king.

Billie touched his arm. "I don't know what's going on here, but I know Doyle won't hurt her."

"Do not be concerned. I trust your brother as well." He turned his attention back to his father. "Are you sure they are together? Did they leave a note?"

"Tahira did." The king handed over a scrap of paper. "I cannot believe she has done this. Run away. Of all the ungrateful, disloyal actions…"

The king continued to rant, but Jefri ignored him. Instead he read the few lines Tahira had scrawled.

"I can't do this," she had written. "Prince Jefri, I apologize for dishonoring you in this way, but I must escape. Please try not to hate me."

Hate her? He shook his head. Hatred would require a depth of emotion he did not possess.

"She doesn't say anything about Doyle," Billie murmured. "Maybe he's not with her."

"They are together," the king said. "She has shown a particular attachment to him. I did not mention anything because I thought it was a friendship, nothing more." He glowered. "Young women cannot be trusted."

Billie released Jefri's fingers and tucked her arm—the one with the bracelet—behind her.

"Are you saying they had a romance?" Billie asked, sounding surprised.

"I am not sure how far things have gone. If he has defiled her..."

Billie paled. Jefri touched her arm.

"Nothing has happened yet."

They watched as the king stalked to the other side of the room, picked up a phone and barked out orders for more guards to be sent into the city.

"He doesn't look happy," she whispered. "I don't want to know the punishment for defiling a future princess."

"The old laws have changed."

"Great. But what if the new laws aren't any more forgiving?" She stared at him. "Are you angry?"

"That Tahira and Doyle may have run off together? No. I want her back and safe because she is my responsibility, but I have no emotional attachment past concern for her well-being.''

''If she and Doyle did, um, well, you know, what would happen?''

He understood the question. Would there still be an engagement?

''Let us first find out what has happened,'' he said, not wanting to wish for too much. If Tahira had fallen in love with Doyle, all of Jefri's problems were solved. But he had a feeling life wasn't going to be that simple.

He urged Billie to go up to her room and promised to notify her when he had word. Then he closed the door and faced his father.

''I am furious,'' the king said.

''Yes. You appear most upset. I am surprised.''

His father glared at him. ''Why? Tahira is like a daughter to me. To think she would be so disobedient injures me greatly. Plus there is the shame she visits on our family.''

''Yes. A wayward bride is fodder for the media.'' Jefri narrowed his gaze. ''You said you have seen them together?''

''What?'' His father paced to the window and stared out. ''A few times. In the garden. I thought nothing of it.''

Jefri found that difficult to believe. ''Tahira might be eighteen chronologically, but in experience, she is still very much a child. Did you not consider that Doyle Van Horn could easily seduce her?''

"I trusted him! I allowed him to live in my palace and in return I expected him to respect his place."

"But to put temptation in his path like that."

His father turned on him. "What are you saying?"

"That you could have stopped this some time ago, and yet did not. I wonder why."

The king turned back to the window without speaking. An idea formed in Jefri's mind and he could not seem to shake it.

Was this all part of a plan on his father's part? Not Tahira's arrival—Jefri himself had set that disaster in motion—but the rest of it? Under normal circumstances the king would never allow a future bride to one of his sons to spend afternoons alone with another man, let alone enough time for them to plan an escape. Then there was his father's insistence that Jefri marry Tahira. That she would be destroyed if he broke off the engagement. Had that been a ploy to make him realize the depth of his feelings about Billie?

"You are a wily old man," Jefri said with a shake of his head.

His father stared at him. "What are you talking about?"

"You have too much time on your hands. First you played Reyhan with Emma, insisting they spend time with each other before you would grant them their divorce. You suspected they were still in love and forced them into each other's company until they could not deny what they felt."

His father smiled. "What makes you think Reyhan

was the first?'' he asked before walking out of the room.

Jefri stared after him. Had his father played a hand in Sadik's marriage to Cleo? Had he been toying with Jefri as well?

He was torn between fury at the old man's meddling and pity for Murat—the last single brother.

Two hours later a shamefaced Tahira and a pale but defiant Doyle were returned to the palace. The king chose to meet them in the royal chamber where the large throne and formally dressed guards were designed to shake the confidence of the strongest of men.

Jefri stood at his father's right hand and glared down at Doyle. Whether or not Jefri wanted to marry Tahira, she was his responsibility and he did not take the situation lightly.

''You were a guest in this house,'' Jefri told Doyle. ''You were treated with honor and expected to act in kind. Instead you have taken one of our greatest treasures for your own personal pleasures.''

Doyle frowned. ''She's not a vase or a picture. She's a woman.''

''Exactly. A special young woman with great potential. She is not yours, Doyle Van Horn. You had no right.''

Tahira choked on a breath and threw herself in front of Doyle.

''Don't hurt him. Please, Prince Jefri. I know what

I did was wrong and unforgivable, but don't hurt him.''

Doyle put his arm around her. ''Don't apologize. You did nothing wrong.''

''In that you are correct,'' Jefri said. ''You are the one charged here.''

Tahira blanched. ''No! You can't. Please. I beg you.''

Doyle stood straight and strong. ''I'm not afraid of you.''

''You should be,'' the king said sternly. ''We have kept the peace here for over a thousand years and we have done that through the use of fair laws that apply to all. No one has the right to kidnap an innocent young woman for his own debased pleasures.''

''I didn't kidnap her,'' Doyle ground out through clenched teeth. ''I was trying to help her escape.'' He looked at Jefri. ''You don't want her. You can barely stand her and you'll never love her. So why the hell are you insisting on marrying her?''

He turned to Tahira. ''You're just as bad. Tell him the truth.''

She ducked her head. ''I am here to do Prince Jefri's bidding.''

Doyle swore. ''Tahira, for once would you just say what you want? Nothing horrible will happen. I promise.''

Tears filled her eyes. ''They're going to kill you.''

''We're not that savage,'' the king said. ''But there must be a reckoning.''

Jefri had heard enough. He stepped down and took

Tahira's hand. "Come, child," he said kindly. "We will speak in private."

As he led her out of the room, he glanced back at the guards. "Hold him until I return."

He showed Tahira to a small antechamber behind the throne. There he settled her on a chair and got her a glass of water. When she had the tears under control, he pulled up a chair next to her and sat down.

"Are you all right?" he asked, careful to keep his voice calm and gentle.

She nodded, clutching the glass in both hands. "Doyle didn't hurt me. You have to believe me."

"I do. I know he didn't carry you off against your will. You wanted to go with him, didn't you?"

Her eyes widened as she nodded.

"Over the past few weeks, you have become friends."

"Yes."

Good. His father had been telling the truth about that. Now to get the rest of the information.

"Do you love him?"

She shrank back in her seat. "No, Prince Jefri. No. I would never… We haven't…"

"I believe you, but you do care for him?"

She blushed and stared at the glass. "Doyle is very kind to me. When we talk, he makes me laugh. We talk about different things. The world. There is so much I haven't seen."

"And you want to see it?"

She nodded.

"Without me?"

Her breath caught and she raised her face. "You are so wonderful. You have honored me in so many ways and I am grateful."

"Tahira, I am not interested in your gratitude. I want your happiness. I was led to believe that you desired this marriage above all things, yet I now think that is not true. Would it not be better to simply tell me what is in your heart rather than risk a life of unhappiness because you are momentarily afraid?"

"You sound like Doyle."

"Apparently he has occasions of true wisdom."

That made her smile. She sucked in a deep breath. "I do not want to be married," she said, speaking quickly as she tightened her grip on the glass.

He took it from her before she snapped it and cut herself. Relief swept through him. He thought he might drown in the sensation. His future suddenly lay before him, a bright road of promise. But he had to be sure.

"What do you want?" he asked.

"I would like to study fashion design. In Paris. That's where Doyle and I were going. We weren't running away to be together." She blushed again. "Not exactly. He was going to help me find a place to stay and look into school."

"You speak French?" he asked.

"Yes. And Italian. They make lovely shoes there."

He smiled. "So I have heard." He took her hand in his. "Tahira, you have honored me with your loyalty. I am sorry you felt you had to sneak away to achieve your heart's desire. That was never my intent.

I would very much like to help you get settled and find a school."

He would take care of her financially, as well, but there was no need to discuss that now.

"You're not angry?" she asked, sounding stunned.

"No. I am delighted." More than that, but again not a conversation they needed to have.

She flung herself at him. "Thank you, Prince Jefri. Thank you a thousand times."

"I appreciate your enthusiasm at not becoming my wife."

She giggled. "You know I don't mean it that way."

"I do."

She straightened and stared at him. "About Doyle. Please don't hurt him. He didn't do anything wrong."

"So you keep saying." He pretended to consider the matter. "I suppose you want to keep seeing him."

Tahira nodded eagerly.

"He is several years older than you," Jefri reminded her. "That could present some problems."

"I can handle them."

Her confidence made him smile. "As you wish. But your visits with Doyle will be chaperoned for the time being. Until you find your place in the world."

Tahira hugged him again. He held her briefly, knowing there was somewhere else he would rather be.

Billie paced the length of her suite, pausing every few minutes to listen for footsteps. When she finally heard them she raced to the door and jerked it open.

"What happened?" she demanded as Jefri entered the room and pulled her into his arms.

"I love you," he said as he kicked the door closed and pressed his mouth to hers.

Billie surrendered to his embrace, to the feel of his body pressing against hers.

"I love you, too," she murmured, barely able to speak as she clung to him.

He bent low and swept her up in his arms. Muffin looked up from a cushion on the sofa, yawned and went back to sleep. He laughed.

"Good. Because you are not invited." Then he walked into the bedroom and closed the door there.

"What happened?" Billie asked again as he set her on her feet and reached for the buttons on her blouse.

"Tahira wishes to study fashion design in Paris. She has no interest in marrying me and seems to have some fondness for Doyle."

He pulled the blouse open and gazed at her breasts. "You are so beautiful."

Warmth flooded her. She tugged his shirt free of his trousers. "You're not half-bad yourself. So there's no engagement?"

"Not anymore. I suspect my father knew what was going on the whole time and that he played me to get me to see how much you mattered."

"You're kidding."

"No."

He bent down and claimed her with a kiss that left her weak with longing. He stroked her body, removing clothing as he went. She did her best to help take off his, but she was continually distracted by things like his mouth on her breasts or his fingers between her legs.

He touched her and loved her until she couldn't think, couldn't breathe, couldn't do anything but feel.

Poised between her thighs, he stared into her eyes.

"Stay," he breathed. "Stay with me."

She lost herself in his dark eyes. "Of course I'll stay."

"I want you to marry me. Have my children. Be a part of me, a part of my country. I cannot survive without you."

Tears burned in her eyes. She blinked them away. "I love you, Jefri. I can't imagine being anywhere else."

"Then you'll say yes?"

"Yes. For always."

He plunged into her, claiming her with an intimate pleasure that swept her into another dimension.

Later, when they could both breathe easily, she snuggled close.

"I guess I never have to take this off now," she said, holding up her wrist and admiring the bracelet.

"You will never have to worry," he told her. "My people will love you as I do. This will be your home. The palace and the skies."

She rested her chin on his chest and looked at him. "So you're not going to get all weird and tell me I have to give up flying?"

"Of course not. You belong with the clouds. The difference is now I will join you there."

"I'll still beat you in a dogfight. Don't think marrying me is going to change that."

He laughed. "I now have a lifetime to practice. Eventually I will win."

"In your dreams."

His smile faded. "You are my dream. My fantasy. For always."

She sighed. "You're really good at this."

"I am very much in love."

"Me, too. In fact—"

A faint scratching caught her attention. "Oh, give me a sec. Muffin needs to go out. I just have to open the suite door."

Billie stood, slipped on Jefri's shirt then walked out to the living room where she let out her dog. Then she hurried back to the bedroom.

"Where were we?" she asked as she slipped back under the covers.

Jefri reached for her. "I believe we were here."

Muffin trotted down the long corridors of the palace, ignoring all the cats she passed. At the large, carved doors she waited while the guard let her in, then she hurried over to the big sofa opposite the window.

"There you are," the king said as he patted the cushion next to his. "Did you not see? I told you things would work out."

Muffin jumped up next to the king. The white cat there shifted to make room, then began to groom Muffin's face. The small dog sighed with pleasure.

''Only Murat is left,'' the king said. ''But not to worry. I have given the situation much thought and I have come up with an excellent plan. Would you like to hear it?''

* * * * *

The Wedding Planners

Join these three beautiful brides-to-be as all their wedding dreams come true!

Available
16th January 2009

These three lucky ladies have a millionaire's ring on their finger!

Available
20th February 2009

Planning perfect weddings…
finding happy endings!